BELVA PLAIN

Random Winds

FONTANA/COLLINS

First published in Great Britain in 1980
by William Collins Sons and Co Ltd
First issued in Fontana Books 1981

Made and printed in Great Britain by
William Collins Sons & Co Ltd, Glasgow

Random Winds

BELVA PLAIN has lived in New Jersey for twenty years with her husband, an ophthalmologist, and children. After graduating from Barnard College she wrote several short stories for women's magazines, later phasing herself out of writing in order to concentrate on her family.

Evergreen was her first novel after she returned to writing and *Random Winds* is her second. Both books have been bestsellers in England and America.

Available in Fontana by the same author

Evergreen

To my children,
and to the memory of my parents

PROLOGUE

DAY OF WRATH

On Adirondack lakes ice boomed and cracked. Grainy snow, melting at last, slid into the ditches along mired roads. Dr Enoch Farrell drew his watch out of his vest pocket: he had made good time. Once past the Atkinses' farm the road flattened and there were only three easy, level miles to home. He drew the buggy's curtains tighter against the sweeping rain that threatened his fine, polished bag. The best black calf it was, with brass fittings, the parting gift, along with a well-bound Gray's *Anatomy,* of Dr Hugh MacDonald, who had been his preceptor in Edinburgh. He never went anywhere without the *Anatomy,* although surely he must have memorized it by now! He never went out without his current reading either, for this hour trotting home at the end of the day was his best, perhaps his only, truly private time. And rummaging, he searched for *Bleak House*. To think that Dickens was dead these thirty years or more and now, in this first year of a new century, his work was as alive as if it had been written yesterday!

Things were heaped in the bag. Jean was always straightening it, but it never stayed that way. Opium, laudanum, stethoscope, Hop Bitters – fine stuff, good for any dozen ailments – no Dickens. He must have left it at home. Damn, he was always forgetting things! If it weren't for Jean . . . Well-matched, they were: she so practical and precise, while he – could he dare think of himself as a leaven, bringing brightness and humour to the household?

So his thoughts ran.

Left now, and across the wooden bridge where the river, which had been iced over only last week, was running fast. The little mare began to speed, and there was home with its twin chimneys, front porch and two square office-rooms. Very nice! Nicer still when the mortgage should be paid off, whenever that might be! It didn't look imminent. A man could count himself lucky to keep abreast of the daily expenses: four children with another on the way.

Enoch climbed down in the barn, unhitched Dora and led her to the stall. A couple of hens, disturbed in their straw, rose squawking. The barn cat rubbed his ankles while he covered the mare with a dry blanket. It gave a man a good feeling that even these poor, dependent creatures were safe and warm under his roof. And speaking of roofs, he ought to get that leak mended before it got much worse.

The children were half-way through supper. Alice, the baby, clattered on the high-chair tray when she saw him.

'I thought you'd be even later in this weather,' Jean said. 'Heavens, your cap's wet through! Your knickers are soaked! Sit down, while I get the stew. I've kept it hot and there are biscuits, too.'

'Ah, those'll hit the spot on a night like this.'

He washed his hands at the sink. A fine convenience it was, to have water running in the kitchen. Easy on the woman of the house and sanitary besides. He took his place at the head of the table, said grace and picked up his fork.

Jean's hands rested on the apron beneath which lay her growing baby, in its seventh month. Her pink, anxious face was flushed from the kitchen's heat. Four child-faces turned towards Enoch, mixed of his flesh and hers: her bright, almond eyes in Enoch Junior and the baby, Alice; his temper and his laughter in May; her quickness, her reserve in Susan.

'Well, anything new happen around here today?' he inquired.

'Nothing much. Oh yes, Mrs Baines came. She always manages to come when you're out.'

'What's the trouble?'

'Walter again. Sounds like the Quinsy sore throat, the way he always gets.'

'I suppose I'd better hitch up and go back over there.'

'Indeed you'll not, after the day you've had, and in this rain! Besides, they never think to pay you. It's always "next time, Doc".'

Enoch sighed. 'I know. But he tries, Jean. The man works awfully hard.'

'So do you.' She rose to put more stew on his plate and poured coffee. 'I made brown Betty for dessert.' Then she added mischievously, 'Anyway, I told her what to do for the throat.'

'You did what?'

'I told her what to do. I've heard you tell it often enough to know it by heart, haven't I? Red flannel around the throat, goose grease on the chest, soak the feet in a tub of hot water with powdered mustard and camphor ice to keep the fever from cracking his lips. Right?'

'Dad! Dad! I did elevens and twelves in the multiplication tables today and I – '

'Enoch Junior,' Jean rebuked him, 'you're interrupting. And anyway, this is grown-ups' time. You're not supposed to talk at the table.'

'Let him talk, Jean. What'd you want to tell me, son?'

'I wanted you to hear my multiplication.'

'Tell you what. You go start your homework on the parlour table, and soon's I finish my supper, I'll join you. May and Susan, you're excused, too.'

The room grew quiet. Alice sucked on her bottle and Jean dished out the pudding. A coal fell softly in the stove.

'Had a nasty business today with Hettie Simpson,' Enoch remarked. 'Did I tell you this would have been her eleventh? Just as well she miscarried, I suppose. Expect she might have bled to death if I'd been much later getting there. I packed the uterus, but I'll need to go back early in the morning. It worries me, she looked so white.'

'She can't be more than thirty, can she?'

'Thirty-two, and looks nearer fifty.'

If she lives this time, he thought grimly, it'll only happen again, unless the consumption gets her first. And Jim Simpson? Why he'll cry a bit and have another wife in a couple of months, some strapping girl of seventeen who'll start a family for him all over again. Yet you couldn't blame the man. Who would do the work and look after the children if he didn't marry in a hurry?

'You look so tired,' Jean said softly.

'I didn't know how much till I sat down, I guess.'

She peered through the window into the dismal murk, out of which the wet tin roof of the shed glistened like dull silver. 'This weather's enough to exhaust a person. Seems as if spring'll never come and it'll never stop raining.'

When they went to bed the rain was still beating mournfully, persistently, upon the roof. For a long time Enoch lay awake, listening to the ominous beat.

In the morning they were astonished that the rain had not slackened. All through that second day it never varied in its determined steady fall, neither speeding up nor slowing down, just marching evenly, like soldiers' stern and solemn feet.

And the third day.

Then came the north wind. It struck with fury and the night was loud with complaint. Water poured like a river through the gutters; the house shuddered. The rain swayed as the wind gusted and died, gusted and died. The roof was lifted from the toolshed, the torn wood screeching as it parted. From the tight house where his children were asleep, Enoch peered into the yard and saw that the chicken coop was holding. But he went back to bed with uneasy thoughts of planets rending, flung away from the sun.

Just after midnight, there was an almost imperceptible slowing of the rain. Alert ears could isolate the sound of individual drops, with a fraction of a pause between them: cessation, then a violent spurt, and another cessation. Finally came a startling stillness in which one heard, regular as a metronome, great drops plopping from the eaves and the shaken trees.

At last in the morning the sun came out with a burst of spangled light. Water stood in a pond two inches deep in the yard. Under the porch roof, soaked sparrows clustered, chirping through the daily family prayers. Jean had lit the Franklin stove, but the parlour was cold and Enoch hurried the prayers.

'The sun will soon draw all this water up,' he observed, closing the great Bible with a bang. The children wanted to know whether there would be school that day.

'Of course there will, but the road will be a mess. You'll

need your high galoshes,' Jean told them.

'I'll try to get back early enough to do something about the toolshed roof,' Enoch said. 'See if you can dry off the tools before they rust, will you?'

Jean packed the lunch boxes and tied May's scarf, fastening it down with a large safety pin on the chest. May, like her father, always lost things.

'Now, Enoch Junior, mind you don't run on ahead. It's slippery wet. I want you to help your sisters through the muddy spots so they don't fall and dirty themselves.'

'Aw,' said Enoch, 'why do I always have to?'

'Because you're a big eight-year-old boy, and your sisters are small.'

The parents watched their three march down the road, the boy obediently between his sisters. There marched the future! Yes, and the sum of the parents' pasts; such love, such hope encompassed in those chattering three, so carelessly kicking pebbles on their way to school! They watched until the children were out of sight, then smiled at each other. Jean went back into the kitchen and sat down heavily in the Boston rocker by the window to enjoy a second cup of coffee. Enoch went to the barn and hitched the horse. The storms had set him three days behind with his house calls and he would have to cover a lot of ground.

At noon, just as the children were having lunch, it began to rain again. But it was a very light rain this time. No need to send them home early, the young teacher thought as she glanced out of the window, especially since they had already missed a couple of days this week. The younger children played indoors during the lunch recess, while some of the older boys, wearing rubber mackintoshes, went outside. In any case, by two o'clock, shortly before school was dismissed for the day, the drizzle had stopped.

And at two o'clock, a mile and a half upstream, in one incredible, unexpected instant, an old earthen dam collapsed. Rumbling and crumbling, with thunderous roar and colossal surge, it burst, it fell apart. A blinding spray rose into the air, tumbled, splashed and crashed, leaving a dazzle of fine mist upon the ruins. The lake behind the dam, swollen by tons of melted ice, poured into the river. And the river slid over its banks. It plunged through the narrow valley. It gathered strength and speed. Like a merciless, violent army come to pillage, it advanced.

At two-thirty the children were dismissed from school to walk home. A quarter of a mile behind them the mighty wall of water rushed, flooding the whole valley now, flooding the houses up to the second storey, wrecking and smashing. It gained on the little flock of children as they meandered and as the seconds passed. They heard its distant rumble before they saw it. Towering doom rose high at their backs. They began to run. Horrified and screaming, they scrambled and raced. But the water raced faster.

Late in the afternoon Enoch came down from the hills and beheld catastrophe. He pulled on the reins and stared aghast. Water lay where farms and roads had been that morning. Stagnant at the edges, it was torrential in the middle, speeding in a dirty brown froth.

My God, the schoolhouse! That was the schoolhouse roof, the only red roof in the neighbourhood! A dreadful faintness almost toppled him. Then panic came. He thought he heard himself screaming at the mare. He whipped her, which he had never done before, and the mare sped.

Here the road lay on an elevated ridge from which he could look down on the water, some twenty feet below. Treetops poked up from the swirling current, strewn with terrible debris: here a dead cow, its stiff legs spread as if beseeching the sky; there, drowned chickens in a coop; an ice chest; a parlour table with a square marble top. On a flimsy branch a terrified cat clung, its mouth strained open in a wail too far away to be audible.

Enoch trembled and went cold.

His own house lay beyond the place where the river curved sharply to the east, and he saw as he approached that the water had risen over the front steps. The stable, lying on lower ground, was covered to the eaves. One of the three strong, young maples that fronted the road had been ripped up. Flung into standing water in the yard, its fibred roots protruded like torn ligaments.

He jumped down, waded thigh deep to the porch, and banged the front door open.

'Jean! Jean!'

Water had seeped into the parlour, soaking the Brussels carpet, trailing long feelers down the hall towards the kitchen. Over everything lay the foul stench of wet wool.

'Jean! Jean!'

He ran upstairs, bounding two steps at a time.

'Jean, for God's sake, answer me! Where are you? Jean!'

He went back to the porch and stood in his waterlogged boots looking wildly around, up at the sky and down. Under his tongue there was a burning and the salt taste of blood. It was so quiet! The yard was always noisy. The first things you heard were the cackle of chickens and the dog's bark. Then he realized that the chickens had been drowned and the doghouse was under water.

He climbed back into the buggy, wrenching the mare's head roughly, lashing her towards the road leading to the village centre, which lay beyond the curve of the river and the flooding.

The crazed man and the terrified horse tore down the road. So quiet, he thought again. Eerie quiet. Even the birds were still. April, and no birds.

At the church there was a crowd of buggies and wagons and people on foot. He pulled into the yard.

'Where – Do you know where – ' he began, addressing a man whose face he knew. But the man looked blank and hurried past.

People filled the narrow stairway to the basement, going down and struggling back. A fainting woman was being carried up. All about was a murmur of sound, soft crying and low talking.

Enoch pushed his way down. The taste of blood under his tongue was still salty sharp. He put his finger there and drew it out to look at it.

Against the back wall on the floor, the bodies lay in a long double row covered with sheets and blankets. A young man knelt on the floor next to a body from which the sheet had been drawn away. Enoch recognized the dead face. Madeline, he thought, Madeline Drury; he felt nothing.

Beginning at the left, he lifted the covers from the faces. Nettie Rogers. The old woman who lived with her – he'd forgotten her name. Jim Fox's boy Tom, the one who had had infantile paralysis last summer. He moved faster, hurrying down the row.

'Doc! No!' Someone caught his sleeve, pulling hard at him. 'Doc! No! Sit down! Reverend Dexter's been looking for you. He wants – '

'Damn you, leave me!' Enoch cried, wrenching his arm free. And then –

Oh God! Almighty God! His children! Enoch, Susan and May lay side by side in a row. Like dolls they lay, stiff as Christmas dolls, May in the pink scarf, the cotton-candy pink that Jean had knitted, still wound about her chest and secured with a safety pin.

My girls. My little boy. He heard a voice, a mad voice, his own, as if from far away, from another country. He sank to the floor, rocking on his knees.

'Oh my God, my girls, my little boy!'

Strong arms came at last and drew him away.

They had taken Jean and Alice to a house near the church. Reverend Dexter led Enoch there.

'Have they told you about Jean?' he asked.

'What?'

'Jean,' the parson said gently. 'The shock, you know. But the women knew what to do. They took care of her.'

'The shock?' Of course. Jean was in her seventh month. He hadn't thought – But he must think. She would need him. And he quickened his steps.

In the kitchen of a strange house Alice was sitting in a high-chair while a stout woman spooned cereal into her mouth. She seemed to spend her life in a high-chair, being fed.

'She's in there, sleeping,' the stout woman said, nodding to Enoch.

He knew the woman, as he knew everyone in the village,

but again he couldn't think of the name. He walked to the bedroom door, then turned back, hesitating.

'Did she – did she see them?' he asked.

'Not exactly,' the woman said. 'Reverend here, he wouldn't let her see.'

'I'm grateful to you for that, Reverend,' Enoch told him.

He stood looking at his wife. Her face lay in the crook of her arm. Her dark hair was loosened. He drew the blanket up softly over her shoulder. Currents of rational thought, which in this hour past had been stopped, began to flow again. So tender, a human body, a human life! Nothing more to it than a few pounds of fragile bone and soft tissue. Yes, and years of nurturing and thousands of hours of loving care. Wiped out, gone as if they had never been, like last year's leaves! And the marvellous years of youth, the dignity of adulthood and learning – all these forfeited, all these now not to be – Oh, my children! A cry caught in his throat.

'Doc?'

The man of the house – Fairbanks, yes, yes of course, that was the name – came to the door.

'Doc, have you got a minute? Me and my brother Harry was over to your place already. You know your pantry well? Well, the roof is stove in where the maple fell on it. But we was thinking, if you can buy the material, Harry and me'll fix it. Harry owes you a bill, anyway. Did you know the branch breached at Lindsey Run? It flooded out for six miles downstream.'

'Thank you,' Enoch said.

'Think nothing of it, Doc. We all want to do what we can for you. Say, it's a good thing you had your mare with you. The stable almost got drownded.'

A mare. When my children – Get out! he wanted to cry. Kind fool, get out and leave us!

'I'll go ask my wife to make some tea when your missus wakes up,' Fairbanks said.

Jean opened her eyes. 'I'm not asleep,' she whispered.

Enoch knelt on the floor, laying his face against hers, his cold, wet cheek upon her wet cheek, and stayed there like that.

'God's will,' she whispered after a long time. 'He wanted them home with Him.'

God's will that their babies should drown? Son of a minister he was, reared on the Bible, but he couldn't believe that. God the Creator, yes! And God the giver of righteous laws; but God who decrees the individual fate of every living creature on the planet and orders the death of a child? That was hogwash. Hogwash! Yet it gave her comfort.

'Yes,' he murmured, 'yes,' and with his free hand smoothed her hair.

'I love you,' she said.

I love you, she says, out of her blood and grief. She reached up her arms to draw him near, but they fell back weakly. He understood that she wanted him to kiss her, and he bent down and pressed her lips.

Then he said, 'Jean, Jean, my girl, we'll start again. We'll have to love each other so – And I'll take care of you and Alice and me. We're all that's left.'

'You're not forgetting him, the new one?'

'Him?'

'The baby, the boy. You haven't seen him?'

'But I thought – '

Mrs Fairbanks, coming in with the tea, overheard.

'You thought it was a stillbirth? No, no, Doc. Look here.'

She raised the window shade. A sad lavender light slid into the room from the quiet evening sky. On a table near the window lay a box, and in it one of the smallest babies Enoch had ever seen. Scarcely larger than a raw, young rabbit, he thought.

'I bought a new pair of arctics on sale last week. Luckily, I still had the box,' Mrs Fairbanks said.

And Jean called out, 'I want his name to be Martin!'

'Not Thomas, after your father?'

'That'll be his middle name. I want him to be called Martin.'

'Well, all right.' He looked at the child. Four pounds, if that. Nearer three and a half, he'd guess.

'Poor Jean, poor lamb,' Mrs Fairbanks whispered. 'Likely she'll be losing this one, too.'

The baby fluttered. Its toy hands moved, and under the blanket its legs jerked weakly. Then it wailed, the doll's face crumpling and reddening, the eyes opening as if in protest or alarm.

Mrs Fairbanks shook her head. 'No,' she repeated. 'He can't live. That's sure.'

Something welled up in Enoch, and he shook a furious fist at the universe.

'No!' he cried fiercely. 'No! Look at those eyes! Look at the life in those eyes! He will live, and he'll be strong, too. So help me God, he will.'

BOOK ONE

THE ASCENT

CHAPTER ONE

At the top of the long rise, Pa guided the horse towards the shade and drew in the reins. He pulled off his woollen jacket and laid it on the seat next to Martin.

'Professional dignity be darned!' he said. 'The next patient will have to look at me in my shirt-sleeves whether he likes it or not.'

The sun was ahead of the season, Ma had remarked that morning. Shadbush was still in bloom, and barn swallows were barely back from the south in time for Decoration Day.

'We'll just wait a minute here,' Pa said, 'and give the mare a rest.'

The sweating animal stamped, slapping her tail. She had been making a strange sound for the last half hour, more like a plaint than a whinny.

'Something's bothering her, Martin.'

'Black flies, do you think?'

'Don't see any, do you?' Pa climbed down to examine the mare. He pulled the harness aside and swore.

'Damn! Damn, look at this!'

The flesh along the horse's back was rubbed bloody raw in a line as long as three fingers put end to end.

'Laid open with a whip,' Martin said.

'No doubt, and left to suppurate.'

Martin nodded, feeling a twinge deep inside at sight of the wound, feeling also a certain pride at being the only boy in the fourth grade who knew the meaning of words like 'suppurate' or who, for that matter, had a father like his.

'Poor little livery stable hack!' Pa cried. 'At the mercy of every drunken lout who has the money for its hire. Reach in my bag for the salve, will you?'

The little mare quivered, her muscular back rippling and twitching.

'Now a wad of gauze, a thick one.'

When he was finished, Pa got the water bucket. The mare drank gratefully. Martin gave her an apple. Then the two stood watching, pleased with themselves, while the mare chewed, salivating in a long, thick rope.

'She's a nice little thing,' Pa said. 'Wish I had the money to buy her and give her a decent home.'

'But we've got Star, and she'll be ready to take out again as soon as her foal's a month old, won't she?'

'You're right. I daresay the man would want thirty dollars for her.' Pa sighed. 'Well, might as well start. One more call at Bechtold's and then home in time for the parade.'

They moved on again. 'Just look up there, Martin, at the side of that far mountain! You can gauge the height by the kind of trees you see. At the bottom there's oak, but oak won't grow more than twelve or thirteen hundred feet up. After that, you get balsam. Way up top there's spruce, all that bluish green stuff.' He leaned over Martin, pointing with out-thrust finger. 'Those are the oldest mountains in the United States, you know that? See how the tops are rounded? Worn away, that's why. And I'll tell you something else.' He pointed to the left. 'Down there, all that level land was once buried underwater. Can you believe that?'

'You mean the ocean was here once?'

'Yes, sir, that's just what I do mean.'

'When the ocean came, what happened to the people? Did they all drown?'

'No, no. That was millions of years before there were any people here.'

At the foot of the hill, making a wide S-curve, lay the river.

'Pa, is that the river that overflowed and drowned Enoch Junior and Susan and May?' Martin knew quite well that it was, yet he always asked.

His father answered patiently. 'That's it.'

'Then I was born, and you had me instead of Enoch Junior as your boy. Do I look like him?' To that, too, he knew the answer.

'No, he was small and sandy, like me. You're going to be

tall, I think, and of course you're darker, like your mother's family.'

'Do you like me more than you liked him?'

'The same. A man's children are the same to him, like his own ten fingers.'

They drew into the Bechtolds' yard.

'Wait out here, Martin,' Pa said.

'Can't I come in and watch?'

'I have to change a dressing. It might make you feel bad to see the cut.'

'No it won't, Pa. Honestly, it won't.'

What his father didn't know was that Martin had already seen much blood, having peered many times through the shutters of a first-floor window when he was supposed to be amusing himself outdoors. He had watched Pa set a compound fracture. (The little grey tip of bone pierces the flesh; the ether cone silences the screams.) He had seen the mangled stomach of a man gored by a bull. He had also seen his father wrestle down another man who had been beating his wife, and this last had impressed him most of all, although he had known it would be wise not to mention having seen it.

'All right then, come in.'

A scythe propped carelessly in a dark corner of the barn had sliced Jake Bechtold's leg to the bone. Pa pulled the nightshirt up. Carefully he unwound the bandage, revealing a long, blood-encrusted gash, black and criss-crossed with stitches. He studied it for a moment.

'It's doing well. Better than I expected, to tell the truth. No infection, thanks be.'

'We're grateful to you, Doc.' Mrs Bechtold wrung her clasped hands. 'You always seen us through.'

'Not every time, Mrs Bechtold,' Pa said seriously.

'Oh, that! That was in God's hands. There wasn't nothing you could've done more than you did do, Doc.'

When they got back in the buggy, Pa sat in silence for a while. And then he broke out. 'Oh, it's hard, it can be so hard! Sometimes such awful things happen, you can't put them out of your mind as long as you live!'

'What awful things, Pa?'

His father paused, as if the telling would be too difficult. Then he said, 'It was in my second year here, almost into the third. I never go to Bechtold's without living it all over again the way I did just now.'

'Was it anything you did?'

'No, it was something I didn't do. I wasn't able. Jake had the flu. While I was in the bedroom examining him, their little girl, just three years old she was, pulled a washtub full of boiling water off the stove while her mother's back was turned. We laid her on the kitchen table. I can still hear how she screamed. Once in my life I'd ordered a lobster. It was when I first came to this country and stayed those three days in New York City. A lobster is bright red when it's boiled, you know, and I remember I couldn't bring myself to eat it. The child looked like that. I thought, "I don't know what to do. I'm supposed to know and I don't." A lot of people came running in, wailing and crying. They poured cold water on the child. I didn't think to tell them not to, although really it wouldn't have made any difference what they did. The child was sure to die. Finally I found something to do. I got a scissors and began to cut her clothes off.

'Her body was one terrible blister. I couldn't even look at the face. When I pulled off the stockings, the skin came with them in long strips, like tissue paper. I took some salve out of my bag. It had gone liquid from the hot sun, so I dribbled it all over the child's body. Everybody was looking at me, just standing there watching, as if there were some magic in that jar of melted salve.

'The child lay moaning on the kitchen table all that afternoon. Someone asked, "Why not put her in a bed?" "No," I said. "Best not to lift her." We put a little pillow under her head. Her pulse was so faint, I don't think she felt anything. At least I hope not. We waited. Nobody talked. I heard the cows lowing, wanting to be milked. I'll never forget the sounds they made, they and the child's moaning. All the neighbour women came. Shortly before dusk the little girl died. I pulled the cover over her face. I still hadn't looked at it.'

Martin shivered. Pa's tales always made him feel he had been there when they happened. He had been in that kitchen with him and the dying girl; he had been on the deck with him when he sailed away from Ulster, out past the breakwater and the headlands, out to sea.

'I shouldn't be telling you this, should I?' Pa asked. 'Your mother would be angry. She'd say you're too young to know how hard life can be.'

'I'm not too young. I'm nine.'

'You're a lot older than nine in many ways.' His father's arm, which had been resting on the back of the seat, slipped to Martin's shoulders. His father's hand felt warm and firm, making a union between the two of them.

'Pa,' he said, 'I want to be a doctor.'

Pa looked at him carefully. 'Are you saying so because you think I'd like to hear it? Is that it?'

'No. I really mean it.'

'You may change your mind.'

'I won't change my mind.'

Pa had a little twist at the corner of his mouth, not a real smile, only the start of one, the way he did when he was pleased about something, or when he and Ma had some secret.

'Well, you're smart enough,' he said now.

'Alice is smarter.'

'Maybe so. But she's not going to be a doctor, that's for sure. There were a couple of women in my class at medical school, and they were pretty bright too, but if you ask me, I don't think it's decent. There's man's work and there's woman's work. Doctoring, to my way of thinking, is man's work.'

'You always say it's God's work,' Martin said shyly.

'Well, of course it is that. Take Bechtold's leg, now. It's true, we've learned a lot about sterilization; twenty years ago you'd thread a needle and stick it in your coat lapel. But even so, you can still have infection. With all our knowledge, we must remember to be humble. Never give way to pride in your skill. Another time you might not be as lucky.'

The buggy rumbled across the bridge. Martin leaned over the side, where the water was high with springtime flooding. Close to the bottom of the bridge it swirled, jewel-green, beautiful and dreadful. The power of water! Power to drown or to freeze or scald. Yet it could be so soft, closing over you on summer afternoons, all silky cool while you floated and were so gently borne.

Pa said suddenly, 'I'm going to buy this mare. He'll sell her if I offer enough.'

'You said we didn't need her and we couldn't afford her.'

'We don't and we can't. But I can't send her back to the livery stable, either.'

Martin smiled. In a way he could not have put into words, he understood that this tenderness towards the animal was connected with the sharp, cruel things they had been talking about.

They circled through Cyprus. Men were putting red, white and blue bunting around the bandstand and all the stores were closed, except for the soda fountain. Martin could anticipate delicious flavours: teaberry, chocolate and Zip's root beer. Oh, the smells and music, the feel of a holiday!

Now they were trotting down Washington Avenue, from which the side streets led to open country. These were shady streets; iron deer stood on their lawns and porches held stone urns filled with red geraniums. You wondered what lay inside the lofty houses where maids in striped aprons swept the steps and gardeners clipped the hedges.

A woman in a white dress and a light, flowered hat was coming out of a house. Two little girls, all white and lacy like her, walked beside her. They were younger than Martin. One of them looked very queer, he saw. There was something wrong with her shoulders.

Pa halted the buggy and tipped his hat.

'How are you, Mrs Meig?'

'Very well, Doctor, thank you. And you?'

'The same, thank you.'

'Is this your boy, Doctor?'

'Yes, this is my son, Martin.'

'He's going to be a handsome man.'

'Handsome is as handsome does.'

The lady laughed. Even her laugh was pretty. She had come quite close to the buggy so that you could smell her perfume. Narrow silver bracelets flashed on her wrists. Martin stared at her, then at the daughter who was just like her, except for the bracelets: the girl had a gold locket lying in the hollow of her throat. He looked at the other girl and quickly looked away; you weren't supposed to stare at a cripple.

Pa tipped his hat again and clucked to the mare. It had all taken half a minute.

'Who was that?' Martin asked.

'Mrs Meig. That's their house.'

He twisted around to look back. The house was strong and dark, built of stone. It had a curlicued iron fence and starry flowers scattered on the grass.

'Did you see all those wild flowers, Pa?'

'Those are daffodils, and they aren't growing wild, only made to look that way. It's what they call "naturalizing",' his father explained. He knew everything.

Suddenly Martin knew what was exciting him. The house looked like a castle in a book about knights! It was smaller, of course, but it was secretive like that. It made you want to know what went on inside.

'Have you ever been inside, Pa?'

'Yes, once. The parlour maid was sick and they couldn't get Dr Pierce. That's how Mrs Meig came to recognize me.' Pa grinned. 'It was a miserable, wet night, I recall, and I guess Dr Pierce didn't want to go out just for a maid.'

'What's a maid for, Pa?'

'Why, when you have a big place like that you need people to take care of it. The Meigs own the Websterware factory down by the canal where they make pots and pans, you know. I guess half the men in Cyprus work there.'

But Martin was thinking of something else. 'What was wrong with that other little girl? She looked awfully ugly.'

'Don't say that. She can't help the way she looks. She has a curvature of the spine.'

'What's that?'

'Her spine wasn't made right before she was born. You can be thankful it didn't happen to you.'

True. It would be terrible to be humpbacked like that. The kids would make fun of you in school. He shuddered.

Ma and Alice were already waiting on the porch when they drove into the yard. They had summer dresses on and white shoes. Alice wore a broad blue sash and bow.

'Don't they look pretty, standing there?' Pa asked.

'That lady was prettier than Ma. And the little girl was a whole lot prettier than Alice.'

Pa rebuked him. 'Don't ever say that, Martin, you hear me?'

'I only meant Ma and Alice haven't got big white hats like those.' It was not what he had meant, however. 'I wish they did, don't you?'

'It's not important,' his father replied.

His mother was in the mood of the holiday. She ruffled Martin's hair, grazing his cheek with the harsh skin of her fingertips.

'Hurry up, you two!' she cried gaily. 'You've ten minutes to wash and change.'

Ordinarily, passing his sister as he went into the house, Martin would have pulled open her sash. Just because she was a year and a half older, she needn't think she was queen of the roost! Now, though, some sudden tenderness kept him from spoiling Alice's careful bow. He could not have explained what it was that he saw in his mother and sister just then: something vulnerable and wanting, perhaps, although they were smiling at this moment and happy. He only felt the dim confusion of contrast: that startling glimpse, just a few seconds' worth, of a house, of a fragrant, slender woman and a flowery girl-child; then this house and these two whom he knew so dearly. Something stirred in his heart, a kind of longing, a kind of pain.

Some days are marked for recollection, days which, on the surface, are not very different from all the other thousands in the chain of years. But seeds have been sown which will lie hidden quietly until their time, until a commanding shaft of light breaks through; then all the concentrated life in the seeds will stir and rise. Perhaps it was unusual for a boy only nine years old to make a resolution and have a revelation all in one day; perhaps more unusual still for him to know, as they were happening, that he would remember them.

Yet it was so.

CHAPTER TWO

Long before sunrise Martin awoke with instant awareness that this morning was different. He was leaving home. The college years close by at Hamilton had been little more than an extension of home, but this, he knew, would be a final departure. After four years at Cornell Medical College, after four years of New York City, the life of this house would be unfamiliar and he would be someone other than he now was.

The suitcases stood near the door, black shapes in the greying dawn. When they had been fastened shut and taken away, what would be left in this old room to which he had been brought on the day of his birth? The bed, with its loopy crocheted spread, the ink-stained desk and the maple dresser on which his toilet things had been placed in parallel lines, equidistant from the edge. Like his mother, he was compelled towards neatness and precision. He could never think constructively until everything was in order, notes arranged alphabetically in the notebook and papers in their folders. A neurotic trait! But one couldn't help the way one was made.

Guilty and melancholy thoughts crossed his mind sometimes. If it had not been for the deaths of those other three, especially of the brother, he would not have been going away to become a doctor. Oh, then, what would he have become? Death and survival! One life thrives on the destruction of another! He had been thinking more often lately about those three. Perhaps it was because they lay in the graveyard not half a mile down the road, and would be lying there this morning when he passed to meet the train that was taking him away.

Pa knocked on the door and came in just as Martin swung his legs out of bed.

'You realize I haven't been in the city since I arrived on the boat from Ulster? And I wouldn't be going this year if riding down with you didn't give me a reason.' He yawned widely. 'Excuse me. Didn't sleep well last night.'

'Excited?'

'Partly, and overtired, too. I was up most of Wednesday watching old Schumann die.'

'I remember him. Alice and I used to think he looked like Santa Claus.'

'Yes. Well, it's sad that after eighty-seven years a human being can't go out without a struggle. Even morphine didn't help much.'

Martin, pulling on his sharply-creased new trousers, thought: How will it be for me when I witness my first death?

'He went through some hard times, too. For a while there during the war some folks wouldn't talk to him because he came from Germany. Said he kept the Kaiser's picture on his parlour wall, which wasn't true. Did I tell you I delivered his granddaughter's baby last week? A hard birth, a breech. Takes some doing, a breech. I remember when I had my first one. That was back in the nineties. I'd never seen the patient before. There were no X-rays then, and I remember when I reached in and realized those were the feet presenting, I was scared to death. Never been so scared in my life.'

'And?'

'And I lost the baby. The mother was all right, but – it's an awful thing to lose a life, perfectly formed! They blamed me. Two of the woman's friends deserted me after that. Went to Doc Revere, who didn't know as much as I did. Had filthy hands, black fingernails. He hadn't even heard of Semelweiss and gloves. But they thought it was my fault.'

'And was it?' That was one thing about his father: you could be straightforward with him.

'Might've been. A skilled man might've been able to turn the baby – I don't know.' Enoch shook his head. 'There's an awful lot I don't know.' He stood up. 'Let's go down for breakfast. Your mother's got pancakes and sausage.' At the door he turned back. 'Just one thing more I want to say. Martin, I envy you, born in a time when you'll learn things I couldn't dream of! The answers to dark secrets will come as clear as day. Maybe even cancer in your lifetime! Well, I'll see you downstairs.'

Martin stood still in the centre of the room. Point of departure. Yes, yes, he wanted to be a doctor! Yet he feared. What if he didn't do well? Suppose he were to discover that it had been a mistake; that after all, he wasn't fitted for it! How then would he turn back? How would he face his father and face himself?

Sunlight, moving westward now, stained the whole rug bright blue. The closet door stood open, revealing empty hangers swinging from the rod. A child-sized baseball bat lay on the floor, along with a photo of the Yankee team and a pair of old sneakers. He stood for a moment in the doorway touching these things gently with his eyes, before leaving them behind. It was like what they said about drowning: a rush of memory, a whole life up to the last minute. Did everyone, departing, feel like this? He knew they must, but also that they didn't, exactly. For each one is unique. Each one's thoughts belong to him alone, and the way he will take belongs to him alone.

CHAPTER THREE

In a copybook, between thick cardboard covers, Martin kept a diary. He liked to believe that when he was older, in more leisured hours, these pages written in the rapid hand that hardly anyone except himself could read with ease, would keep time from consuming him without a trace.

Turning his pages, then, flipping and skipping at random, the searching eye perceives the intimations and the forecasts

My first week in New York is over. Pa stayed a day and a night, long enough to see me settled in. We had a very good dinner at Luchow's. I watched him counting out the bills These years will be hard for him.

I took him to Grand Central to catch 'the cars'. (He still uses that old-fashioned expression.) I never realized until we stood there together how small he is compared with me. The only feature we have in common is the nose, a profile like the ones on Roman coins. It gives the face an ascetic look. He says our noses are the result of the Roman occupation of Britain!

I waited until the train had left and all you could see was the tail-light moving down the track. I shall miss him with his ragtag quotations, his stars and rocks and Greek mythology. There can't be anyone quite like him. Tender, feisty, absent-minded little man!

I am on my own.

This was my first day in the dissecting room I thought I would vomit and the humiliation scared me. Then I looked at my partner, Fernbach – we were assigned alphabetically to share a cadaver – and he looked sick, too So we both began to laugh, a stupid, embarrassed laugh.

I tried not to look at the face. You can make believe that the rest of the body is a machine: it has no individuality. But the face is the person.

Maybe for the first time in my life I am really aware of man as a perishable thing. I guess I've just accepted without challenge what they taught in Sunday school – all those lofty, consoling words about man's immortal soul. But the body of man can be crushed! It rots like any animal that has been run over and thrown to the side of the road. There is no dignity. All privacy is stripped away. The sphincters relax. I find a scar, a white rip across the shoulder. Was it from a childhood fall, a drunken scuffle or an accident while decently supporting a family? No matter now.

How ugly the body, on the table under the strong lights, invaded and marauded by strangers like me! Yes, and beautiful, too, as an equation or a snowflake is beautiful. Design, evolving and altering with subtle patience, for a hundred thousand years.

My floor is a league of nations. There are Napolitano, Rosenberg, Horvath, Gault and a fellow from Hong Kong, Wong Lee. His father owns a bank there. He doesn't mention it, but everybody knows it.

My best friends are going to be Tom Horvath and Perry Gault. Tom reminds me of my father. That's funny, because no two people could look less alike, Tom being six feet tall, with what they call a leonine head and a big homely face. His father's Hungarian, his mother's Irish. 'Makes me a typical American,' Tom says. He's a little bluff and opinionated, but I feel his honesty and gentleness. It is the gentleness that is most like Pa.

Perry is the brain. He's got a photographic memory for everything from anatomy to baseball scores. He's small and quick, with enough energy for any three people, a hot temper and a soft heart.

They think I'm superstitious because I have 'feelings' about the future. I feel that Perry and Tom and I are going to be involved in life together, perhaps even in great struggles. Ridiculous? Maybe!

Six months already fled. I've been trying in such free time as I have to learn something about this enormous city. I have so much to learn besides the fine print in all my fat texts. There's so much out there in the world! Went down to the

Fulton Fish Market yesterday. Shoving crowds and red faces. Piles of iridescent fish, pink and grey under a gloss of wet silver. Thought of that Flemish artist Breughel I saw at the museum one Sunday.

Then I walked over to Fifth Avenue past the library lions – there's a place where I could lose myself – and on uptown. What a treasury! Paintings in gilded frames. A model room with tall windows and a view of gardens. Pyramids of books. Photographs of Rome – umbrella pines and marble. Freud's *Interpretation of Dreams*. Was he right, or is the brain just chemistry, I wonder?

New York is a feast and I am so greedy, I want to know it all. After an hour of roaming I don't want to go back to my small room and memorize the course of the brachial artery. But I do!

My second year! I've been watching some surgery and it's very, very sobering. There are stars here: Jennings, Fox, Alben Riker. Saw a radical mastectomy on a woman about my mother's age. Quiet, resigned face. Knows she will not beat this illness. Watched Riker remove a tuberculous kidney yesterday. A master, with golden hands.

Wouldn't it be marvellous to be a surgeon? But where and how to get the training? One has to make a living. Who can afford it? I do believe, though, that the day will come when there will be more specialists than general men. Medicine is growing more and more complex. Tom disagrees. Anyway, he says he can't wait to be finished, to open an office and marry his girl, Florence. He says I'm lucky to have my father's practice to step into. He's right about that, I know.

Tom worries because at the end of my second year I still don't have a girl. The thing is, he's happy with Florence – they've been going together since high school – and thinks I ought to do the same. It's generous of him, but I don't want a girl right now. Problem is, 'nice' girls want to get married. It's understood that if you hang around with one for six or seven months, she has a right to know what you plan to do next. Even the parents get that look on their faces, either too warm and friendly or else ever so slightly cool. In either case, you know what they're worried about, that she's wasting her time. To be fair about it, I can see their point.

But I'm not wasting my time, either – what little time I have! Met a nurse up from North Carolina – Harriet, red-haired and rosy-pink. A strawberry. Looked so innocent. It took me all of twenty-five minutes to find out she isn't. Luckily, she's got an older sister with an apartment in the Village.

My time is racing so, I can't believe it! I'm three-quarters of the way towards writing 'Doctor' in front of my name. They say young people think they have all the time in the world, but it's never been like that for me. Sometimes I feel as if I'd just been born and other times I'm in a panic because I'm already twenty-four – a third of my life gone by – and I'll never do or see everything I want to do and see. I didn't know there was so much; how could you know, living in a place like Cyprus? Yet, it's true that there are people living here in the city who could be happier living in Cyprus.

I've heard Edna St Vincent Millay read poetry in the Village. I've gone to the opera – standing room, of course, but it's worth it. My God, how splendid it is! The lights and the sudden darkness; the curtain rising and the music pouring . . .

I've been reading about a man in Canada, a Dr Banting, who has discovered help for diabetes through injections of insulin. He's had astounding success. Imagine being a discoverer, a benefactor like that! How must he feel with the whole world's eyes turned on him? To be like that! Oh, not for admiration, but to *know*! To know that you know! Martin, Martin, is there an ugly streak of vanity in you? I hope not.

But I wish I didn't have this itch. I feel that if I don't do something big, discover something or develop some stupendous skill, I will have failed. They say, of course, that most beginners are romantic about themselves, that it's only naiveté and youth. I wonder.

*

The folks want me home again for the vacation. Pa says I can ride around on house calls with him and that now it will all mean a lot more to me. Two months will be too much, though. I figure on a month before I come back here and gird myself for senior year. They're reorganizing the main library and I can get a job lugging books. I need the money. Can do a lot of reading, too.

Home on vacation. A curious thing happened today. I went with Pa on a call to one of those fussy Cyprus houses with the turrets and the iron deer that I used to think so grand. The man of the house had a bad case of grippe. I waited in the library while Pa went upstairs.

It was a dreadful room with too much heavy oak furniture and, over the sofa, an awful picture of a barefoot running nymph with windblown scarves carefully arranged to cover genitals and breasts. I was staring at it when someone spoke.

'Horrible, isn't it?'

I jumped. Then I saw who it was: a tiny girl about twenty years old, a hunchback not five feet tall. Kyphotic. She had a fine head and dark curly hair.

'Sorry I scared you,' she said. 'I'm Jessie Meig.'

I told her I was the doctor's son and she wanted to know whether I was a doctor, too. I said I was going to be, this time next year.

I don't know why I'm writing all this down, except that it's been such a strange day.

'I thought you were calling on my sister,' she said. 'If you want to see her, she's in her studio across the hall.'

I told her I didn't know her sister.

Then she said, 'Well, when you do know her you'll probably fall in love with her.'

'Why on earth should I?'

'Because men always do. But nothing ever comes of it. At least, not yet. Father will keep them away until he finds someone he approves of.'

I was so dumbfounded by all this that I didn't know how to answer.

And she said, 'Anyway, Fern's not really interested in men right now. She wants to be a great painter. Besides, she's timid to start with. If I looked like her I wouldn't be timid, I can tell you that.'

'I would hardly call you timid,' I said.

She laughed. 'You're right, I'm not. For a person like me it would be fatal. I'm not afraid and I don't worry. Now take you – you're not afraid, but you are a worrier. I see it in your face.'

Perhaps she felt she had to be startling, to entertain? I don't really know. But I was beginning to be amused.

'I guess I am,' I said. 'It runs in the family. My father worries about the progress of mankind and Mother worries about the roof over our heads.'

'I suppose you're poor,' she said.

By this time nothing surprised me, so I said, Yes, we were, fairly so.

'Too bad. Country doctors work so hard for so little.'

I was actually beginning to like the bite in her speech! Most of the time people talk and don't say anything real, anything they truly mean. You could see this girl was honest and intelligent. What a foul trick nature played, attaching that bright head to such a body!

And suddenly something came flashing up from the bottom of my mind.

'Why, I remember you. We were in the buggy – that's how long ago it was – passing this house and you came out with your mother and sister. I can see you clearly.'

What a stupid, bumbling idiot I was! Because, of course, what I meant was: *I remember the hunchbacked girl*.

So I tried to cover up quickly. 'I especially remember your mother.'

'She died seven years ago.'

Then I tried to cover up some more and moved to the bookshelves. I must say, they did have a lot of great books. And I started mumbling about Sandburg's *Lincoln* and how that was one of the first things I was going to buy when I could afford it.

We talked some more about books until Pa came downstairs and we left. I'm still feeling red in the face. A strange encounter.

A week later Pa found a package on the front porch. It was for me, Sandburg's *Lincoln*, with a card from Jessie Meig! 'Anybody who wants anything as reasonable as a book shouldn't have to wait for it. So please accept this and enjoy it.'

I suppose I could have written a note of thanks, but since I almost had to pass the house on an errand in Cyprus, I thought it would be nicer to stop by with my thanks. So I went in and asked the maid for Miss Meig, but instead of seeing Jessie, I was taken to the sister. She was at work before an easel and I could see she didn't want to be disturbed, so I said I was sorry about the mistake and backed right out.

It's queer, though, how much I remember of the few seconds I stood there! The most startling face looked up at me: dark, almost olive, with extraordinary pure blue eyes. I've never seen such eyes. Her hair is curly, like Jessie's, but shorter. I thought of the way curls are carved on ancient Greek statues. She wore a white smock. There was a drop of paint on her sandals. And that's all, except that I don't understand why the picture stays so sharp in my mind.

That nonsense Jessie spoke about people falling in love with Fern?

No need to worry! I can't afford to complicate my life for a good long while yet. I shall probably never even see the girl again.

Still, I feel a sense of drama, sitting here, writing these words.

CHAPTER FOUR

The senior year flew by faster than any of the years before it. Martin really began to feel like a doctor. A subtle power came to life in him, as though he could instinctively smell out disease; could feel it pulsing under his fingers and glimmering before his eyes. He began to plan an intellectual game, even taking notes on the subway.

'A labourer, large man in a yellow windbreaker. Italian. Must have been a good-looking, powerful youth. He is eating a doublenut chocolate bar, crunching and chewing with pure pleasure. Putting on fat. In a few more years his strength will ebb. At fifty he'll be jelly and flab. Hypertensive already, I'll wager, although he doesn't know it. What does such a man do?

'A man of forty. Sombre, intelligent face. Anglo-Saxon. A green pallor. Cigarette-stained fingers. Reaches for cigarettes, observes "no smoking" sign, shoves them back into pocket. Ulcer type. A lawyer, perhaps? Underling in a large firm. Burdened with responsibilities and nightwork.'

His mind stretched. He felt himself reaching with new curiosity into far corners, to the Academy of Medicine to hear a psychiatrist lecture on hypnotism, to listen to new theories about cancer and new procedures in the operating rooms.

One man, a neurosurgeon, attracted him especially. He was a Spaniard, Jorge Maria Albeniz, trained in Barcelona, a frail, elderly man with a formal European manner. Behind his back the nursing staff spoke of him fondly as 'The Duke'. By the medical staff he was thought to be talented but odd. It was said that, if he had wanted to, he could have made a fortune. But most of his time was spent in his basement laboratory or at the clinic where he treated the sick and taught. He liked to operate only when the case was so difficult that other men were reluctant to take it.

Martin watched one day while he removed a pituitary tumour from a young woman. The tumour was too far gone for complete removal.

Albeniz spoke as he worked.

'With X-ray treatments, she may have a few more years. Her children will be that much older, nearer to being able to take care of themselves. We're buying time, that's all.' He looked up at the silent young men surrounding him. 'As you see, there is a terrible lot we still do not know how to cope with.'

This simple honesty touched Martin. Brainwork, he thought, must be the most challenging field of all. And he looked in wonder at Albeniz. How did a man get to be like that?

He began to feel a new and unfamiliar restlessness.

It followed him home on vacation. Suddenly he noticed things he hadn't seen before. His father had some absurd and ignorant opinions.

Of a man with chronic headaches he said that they ran in the family.

'I remember how his Uncle Thaddeus used to fall into rages with them. He'd be so sorry afterwards. You've got to keep spices out of the food. They thicken the blood and you get congestion in the head.'

Martin made no comment. So much for the temper headaches that might have been caused by anything from sinus to migraine to allergies, tumour or incipient psychosis. Or maybe only worry over the mortgage. Spices in the food!

He went with Pa on a house call. The family had a fat little four-year-old boy of whom the mother was proud.

'He's a bruiser, ain't he, Doc?'

'Hello, there, Dale,' Pa said. 'Yes a fine, fat boy. Anyone can see he gets plenty of your good rich cream and butter.'

'Only thing, all last winter, I don't know why I forgot to mention it to you, he complained that his arms and legs hurt. Not real bad, I could tell, because he didn't cry. It just ached him, you know.'

'Where? In the joints?'

'Knees and elbows.'

Pa waved his hands. 'Nothing. Just growing pains. He's growing too fast, that's all. I wouldn't worry about it.'

When they were outside, Martin observed, 'Don't you think you ought to consider rheumatic fever? And the child's too fat besides.'

'No, I don't and he isn't,' Pa said shortly.

Well, some sort of father-son rivalry was only to be expected! They had been singularly free of all that up until now. He certainly didn't want a rivalry to pull them apart. So again he kept still.

On the third day at the noon meal, his mother inquired about someone's baby.

'A lot better,' Pa told her. 'Dover's Powders and an enema. That does it.'

This time Martin couldn't resist. 'Pa, we don't use Dover's Powders any more.'

'What do you mean "we don't"? Why, I've been using that stuff since before you were born!'

Martin opened his mouth to retort. Then he thought: An older man must be allowed to keep 'face'. If I'm to show him anything new, I must do it carefully and in private. We'll need to work well together, and we will –

Still, a restlessness, the same that had been with him for weeks now, or for months, came over him. He could hardly sit still for the tingling in the solar plexus. The meal, with second helpings for Pa, with coffee for his mother, seemed endless.

'How about my borrowing the flivver this afternoon?' he asked. 'Thought maybe I'd run up to Cyprus on a couple of errands.'

When he had finished at the drugstore and the hardware store, he got back in the car to go home. There was, after all, no place else to go. It was a day of January thaw, with dripping icicles overhead and slush underfoot, a good day to go home, bring the restlessness under control and do some studying for midterms.

That being his intention, it was never quite clear to him how it happened that on Washington Street, heading towards home, he suddenly swung the car around and found himself, three minutes later, parked at the kerb facing two iron deer in front of a dark stone house.

There was the same shocked disturbance of equilibrium as the first time.

'Why are you staring at me?' she asked.

'Because I've never seen a face like yours.'

'It can't possibly be that unusual!'

'You must know it is. Blue eyes don't belong in such a Spanish face, such a Greek face.'

'There's no Spanish in me, or Greek either.'

He supposed she was not 'beautiful', in the accepted sense; she was tall, almost as tall as he, and her colouring was too strange. But there was something so – so *dreaming* in her soft expression, as if she were seeing things he couldn't see!

In the left hand she held her brushes like a fan. Now. choosing one, she bent to the easel and laid a stroke of red on a bird's wing: three scarlet birds sat on a wire fence against a background of snow.

'Am I interrupting your work?' he asked.

'No. This one's finished. At least, it's the best I can do with it.'

He knew almost nothing about art. Perhaps this was merely a sentimental postcard? But it was vivid and it appealed to him. So he said sincerely, 'It's a pretty piece.'

She considered it, frowning slightly. 'I can't really tell. So far, I've only imitated, you see. Look at this, for instance.'

This was a small square of canvas covered in many tones of pink, whirling from fuchsia to pearl. Looking closely, one saw that these were trees in blossom, their dark forked branches buried in the billowing pink.

'Monet. I was trying to be Monet. The water-lily thing, you know. And over there, those boats drawn up on the beach, that's Winslow Homer.'

' "M.F.M.",' he read in the corner. 'What's the "M" for?'

'Mary. My name is Mary Fern. They call me Fern at home because Mother's name was Mary. But I'd much rather be called Mary.'

'Then I'll call you Mary. I saw you once when I was about

nine years old,' he said irrelevantly.

'I know. Jessie told me . . . She says you'll be a wonderful doctor. You weren't embarrassed, the way most people are when they meet her. They never seem to know how to talk to her.'

'There shouldn't be any different way of talking to her.'

'There shouldn't be, but there is. People are sorry for her. And of course, she knows it.'

'How hard it must be for her, having to live so close to you all her life!'

Instantly Martin regretted the exclamation. But Mary answered simply.

'I know. We don't get along very well.'

'She can't be much older than you?'

'Younger. We're thirteen months apart.'

There was a stillness in the room. Airy and white as it was, with its white walls and the view of the winter day, through uncurtained windows, it had no relation at all to the rest of the cluttered house.

'I like this room,' he said. 'I feel peace here.'

'There is peace here. Most of the time. Except when I'm in one of my rebellious moods.' Mary laughed. 'I'll bring coffee. Just clear those paint pots off the table, will you, and we'll have it by the window.'

The sun struck glitter from the gilt rims of the cups and from the ring on her finger, moving round and round as she stirred the coffee. The ring was a topaz set in curiously twisted gold. Her nails had sharply marked half-moons. There was a small mole in the centre of her cheek. He had never felt such tremendous, intense awareness of another human being. It became necessary to speak naturally.

'What did you mean by your "rebellious moods"?' he asked.

For a moment she didn't answer. Then she said, 'You see – maybe it's entirely foolish, this thought of greatness in art – but how can I know unless I'm taken seriously?'

'And no one does?'

'My mother did. If she were living, I'd be in New York or somewhere studying. But Father thinks it's all "nonsense"

If I had any money of my own – '

'You'd go away?'

'Oh yes! Yes! I do so want to see somewhere else!'

And she made a free gesture with her arm. 'Haven't you ever wanted to – get beyond?'

'All my life, as far back as I can remember.'

'And have you done it?'

'In a way. My beyond is my work. Medicine.'

'Ah, then you're very lucky! I don't even know whether my work is any good! I've done nothing yet. Nothing. And I'm already twenty.'

'You're in a great hurry. I understand.'

'Do you? Do you ever feel you want to hear all the music ever written, see all the great cities, read all the books, know everything?'

He smiled. 'All that and art, too?'

'Art, too. I have to find out who I am. Because I'm surely not Monet or Winslow Homer, am I?' Then with sudden embarrassment she said, 'I'm sorry. You can't possibly be interested.'

'You're wrong.'

'Well. You did ask about my "rebellion", didn't you? It's not very savage or successful, so far. And sometimes I'm even ashamed of it.'

'Why should you be?'

'Because of Jessie. After all, I have so much. She has so little.'

He nodded. What conflict must be within these walls!

His eye fell on a watercolour framed on the wall between the windows: a girl in a swing, her curved back half-hidden by a fall of leaves.

'That's Jessie?'

'Yes. She didn't like it. But nobody sees it in here.'

'It's very good, I think.'

'It's the truth, anyway.'

'People don't always want to see the truth.'

'Oh, Jessie sees it well enough! It's Father who doesn't, or won't. She needs so much to talk to somebody about her life! What's to become of her? Father's not a person one can really *talk* to. He wants to pretend there's nothing the matter, while all the time he's so afraid.'

Martin didn't know what to answer.

'What will become of her?' Mary repeated.

'Won't she just stay here as she is?'

'Father won't live forever. And I'll do what I can for my sister, but I probably won't stay here, either.'

He felt absurd alarm. 'Suppose you were to be married?'

'I doubt I shall marry anyone from Cyprus.'

He wanted to ask, 'Why? Is there anyone? Do you – ' But that, too, would have been absurd.

When they went to the door, he told her he'd be back for a while in the summer after graduation and asked whether he might come again.

'Come. But come and see Jessie, too.'

'Do you always think of Jessie?' he asked curiously.

'Wouldn't you, if she were your sister?'

He considered, feeling the moment with acute and sudden pain: the allure of the girl, the melancholy of the house and, over all, his old familiar sense of time eluding.

'Yes,' he admitted. 'I probably would. So I shall just be a friend to both of you.'

Spring came and commencement and there he was home again. His mind was filled with Mary. He thought of all the clichés in the language. 'Head over heels.' 'First sight.' 'Chemistry,' whatever that might mean. All were expressions which he had once found unbelievable.

He was, of course, too easily moved; he knew that about himself. He was embarrassingly given to tears not easily blinked away. Only a month or two ago, for example, passing an exquisite baby in a carriage, a Della Robbia cherub with bright hair, he had stopped. The baby had given him a smile so miraculous, and he had been so touched, that the mother, seeing the absurd rise and glisten of his tears, had hurriedly wheeled the carriage away, thinking no doubt that he was some sort of madman and possibly dangerous.

Now joy pierced him through: his own, and the joy of the eyes in that dark, poetic face.

But he hardly ever saw her alone and the summer days

were vanishing. Birds flash among dense trees; fish flick into deeper water, out of sight. So their interrupted minutes fled.

Twice Martin took her to the movies. The third time, at the father's suggestion, Jessie went along. Once there was a picnic, a family affair. In the evenings the family sat together in the library, Jessie and the father playing chess.

Mr Donald Meig was a pale tan presence. He wore impeccable pongee summer suits and his pale tan hair showed the even tracks of the comb. His smile was courteous and faintly supercilious. Clearly, Martin's presence was not welcomed. It was tolerated because he was the doctor's son.

'Fancies himself an aristocrat,' Pa said.

Meig was not a money snob – for he would despise that as vulgar – but a 'family' snob. He liked to talk about 'good old stock'. As if all human stock weren't equally old! At his table he sat among a clutter of Irish silver and English porcelain, with a stuffed swordfish over the golden oak sideboard – a big fish himself in the little pond of Cyprus.

'Your mother's people were Scotch-Irish?' he inquired once of Martin, and without waiting for an answer, 'I've some of that myself. It's not the usual strain around here. Most of the Scots-Irish went to the Appalachians. There's a branch of my family there still. Went west through the Cumberland Gap to Kentucky, you know.'

Martin hadn't known. His mother's people had gone from Scotland to the north of Ireland and, after a couple of generations there on the farms and in the cloth mills, had come here shortly after the Revolution to work again on the farms. Pa, of course, was a much later arrival from the same part of the world. These simple histories were taken for granted at home; one neither concealed them nor boasted of them.

Meig concluded pridefully, 'People tend to settle near their own kind, naturally. Like the Dutch in the Hudson River Valley. We've some Dutch in our family too. No landowners, no Van Cortlandts, just small farmers, poor and hardworking.'

Well, Martin thought, everyone has his quirks. Nevertheless, he asked Mary, 'Is your father the absolute authority in everything, always?'

'I suppose you could say he is,' she told him. 'I don't want you to think he's a tyrant, though. Aunt Milly says he ought to have gotten married again, it would have been better for his disposition. Only, he's afraid to marry someone who wouldn't be good to Jessie. So you see, he's really a good father. I try to remember that.'

Martin wondered what the mother could have been like. Probably she had been like the daughters, for even Jessie had gladness, with her energetic, tossing head, her opinions and her curiosity. Meig was so profoundly different! The woman must have been suffocated in that house, he thought.

'May I ask,' Meig said to Martin, 'why you call my daughter "Mary"?'

'Because she likes the name,' he answered.

'Well, I'm sure I don't know why. She has always been called "Fern" at home.'

His mouth closed in disapproval. As if the world and all the people in it were too common, too intrusive?

And yet, sometimes, Martin had caught him looking at Mary as though he were wondering that such radiance could have come from himself.

Grape summer, dusky blue. Rose-red summer, bees in clover!

'Why are you smiling?' Martin asked.

'I was watching that bee,' Mary said. 'See how greedy it is!'

Its burrowing body was furred with gold dust, buried in the flower, in its damp and tender warmth. And Martin flushed at the parallel image which flashed into his head. He felt the tingle of heat in his neck. Could she have such thoughts too? For the first time in his experience he felt he knew too little about women.

They walked in warm rain. He had never known anyone beside himself who didn't mind being soaked in rain. Outside of someone's open window they stood hiding behind a wet syringa, listening to the Quartet from *Rigoletto* coming over the radio.

'I remember,' Martin said, 'the first time I knew that music could make you laugh or cry. There are so many different kinds! The organ in church, all waves and thunder, or the band in the town square that makes your feet dance. Then there's another, different kind. Once at Reverend Dexter's, I heard four men playing violins. I remember wishing I could hear music like that again.'

'My mother played the piano,' Mary said. 'We used to get out of bed and sit at the top of the stairs to listen. The house was different, then.'

'You really want to get away, don't you?' he asked gently.

'I think I do, Martin. And then I think: It's home, I'd miss it. I'm confused . . . What I really want, with all my heart, is to paint! To put everything down that I feel in my heart, in here! The meaning of life!'

How young! he thought, with tenderness.

'I think, if one can do that, one will never be lonely. But then, you would first have to experience life, wouldn't you, before you could paint it?'

How young, he thought again.

'I hope you don't have any ideas about that girl,' Pa said at supper one night. 'You've been spending a lot of time over there.'

'Enoch!' Ma cried.

'No, no, Jean. Martin knows I don't interfere. It's only a cautionary word or two, which he can take or leave. They're not our kind, Martin.'

'What kind are we, Pa?' Martin spoke mildly, yet there was a tension in him, not of anger or resentment, but apprehension over being told something he might not want to hear.

'Why, it's self-evident,' Pa answered promptly. 'Can you see that girl washing dishes in this kitchen? The worlds don't mix.'

Worlds. Are we then destined to stay in the one world for which we were made, like pegs in holes or keys in locks? The design cut and not to be altered? Yet, look about you, it is often so.

'I wonder how long the Meigs will go on living like that,' his father said. 'They say the plant's gradually going downhill.'

Martin was surprised. 'Websterware? The backbone of the town?'

'I've some patients who work there, and they tell me the business has been running on its own momentum for years. Meig isn't the man his father and grandfather were, you know. He's in over his head and too proud to acknowledge it.'

His sister Alice remarked, 'Rena works in the office at Webster's. She says people all know Mr Meig keeps Fern shut away here until he finds the right marriage for her. Disgusting, isn't it? As if a woman were a prize racehorse to be mated with a prize stallion.'

'Alice!' the mother cried.

Alice tittered. Ever since she had been 'going with' Fred Partridge, she had become bolder, almost smug in her new security. Soon she would enjoy the status of a married woman. Fred, who taught gym at the consolidated school, was a decent fellow, as neutral as his own eyes and hair, and totally incurious about everything. Once Alice had had yearnings. She had been serious and enthusiastic. Now her enthusiasm was visibly draining away. She was 'settling' for Fred Partridge.

Martin felt sadness for his sister, as for all eager, young and shining lives, all women who were not Mary Fern.

His mother was saying, 'I hear the crippled one is smart. Is that so, Martin?'

'Her name is Jessie,' he corrected stiffly. 'Yes, she is.'

'And is the other one really so good-looking?'

Alice cried, 'I can't imagine who told you that, Ma. She's thin and much too dark, and – '

Martin stood up, murmuring something, and fled.

In the motionless air the candles made stiff tips of yellow light. Moths struck with a fleshy thump on the screens. Conversation, on this last night before Martin's departure for the city and internship, moved around the table between Jessie, Donald Meig and an aunt and uncle from New York. Only Mary and Martin were silent.

He was ill at ease and his feet hurt. He had bought white shoes, an extravagance because they would be so seldom worn, but he couldn't have come to dinner here without them. Clothes were insurance, a kind of statement that a person 'belonged', whatever that meant. Idiotic! But that's the way it was and always had been. 'Costly thy apparel as thy purse can buy.' Shakespeare knew about people like Donald Meig. He knew everything about people.

Mary was serving a salad from the bowl which had been put before her. The gauzy, cherry-coloured sleeve had fallen away from her bare arm. She had the look of someone who had strayed by accident into that room and that house.

Jessie was laughing; she had a hearty, appealing laugh that sometimes brought tears to her eyes. It was really a pleasure to watch her! It occurred to Martin that in these few weeks he had become accustomed to her, sitting with her summer shawl gathered in stiff, concealing folds, her rapid hands moving as she talked, her bright eyes observing everything.

And recalling suddenly what she had said about her sister at that first meeting, he wondered what she might be guessing, what she knew.

A sharp ache shot through Jessie for the young man in the cheap suit and the stiff, new shoes; the earnest young man with the proud, quick face and the eyes looking so hungrily at – someone else!

Oh, if I had Fern's body what I would do! she thought. Soft, dreaming thing, she lives in fantasy. I would make sure of that young man. He's worth a dozen of any others I've seen. The way he looks at her over the top of the glass when he drinks, pretending not to!

Oh, if I had her body!

Long ago, the maids talked, two of them standing in the bathroom. 'Poor child,' they said.

I looked around for the child before I knew the child was I.

'If she had come first, they would never have had another, so it's a good thing that – '

In the mirrored door, I saw myself, naked and pink. There were Fern and Fern's friend, come to stay overnight. And I saw they were alike, and I the different one. How old was I? Four? Five?

The seamstress came to make my dresses with wide, embroidered collars. Berthas, they used to call them, and they were so pretty, ruffled or pleated for concealment. They didn't conceal. I took the hand-mirror, and twisting, I could see my back, could see how the cloth where the ruffles stopped was stretched over the sharp knife-blade of bone.

I remember those long rides in the car and the doctors' waiting rooms where Mother read *Heidi* aloud while we waited. Heidi was a brave girl and I must be brave, too. Then the doctors came in their white coats. They were kindly and tall, touching my back with cold fingers. There was much talk, and after that the long ride home.

'Tired?' Father would ask Mother, and she would answer, 'No, I'm all right.'

At the best toy stores they stopped to buy new dolls. They never knew I didn't care that much about dolls. I had rows of them, stupid-looking things with long yellow hair and patent leather shoes. I used to undress them, taking off their lace-edged panties and petticoats. Their backs were smooth and straight from their shoulders to their little round behinds. They looked like Fern.

Once at school I stood with a circle of children dancing around me. I can hear them now: they're laughing and pointing. 'Jessie is a – ' they chant, but I don't remember the word. Don't want to perhaps? I remember the teacher, with her indignant, trembling voice, coming at a run. The children flee and I walk inside with her, hand in hand.

In the playground I had been so fierce and proud, but now at her gentle comfort, I sobbed on the teacher's shoulder. She reached in the drawer and gave me her clean handkerchief. It smelled of eau de cologne. I can smell it still.

Aunt Milly wants Fern and me to go to Europe with them this winter. They'll stay at the Carlton in Nice. Me at the Carlton with Fern! Tea-dancing. Steps leading down. You stand at the top of the flight, waiting to be seated. Eyes turn up to see who you are. And I shall be standing next to Fern. No! Thank you. And thank you again.

Mary stirred uncomfortably. If only Jessie would take that

look off her face! A moment ago she was laughing and now she looks thunder-dark. Will I never grow used to her?

'Jessie's handicapped,' they told me so seriously, long years ago.

I must have been still a baby. I thought 'handicapped' meant there was something wrong with her hands, until the day I noticed her back.

'What is that? Does it hurt?'

'No,' Mother said, 'it hurts only in her mind.'

I remember thinking that, if everybody looked like Jessie, then I would be the queer one and people would stare at me.

'They don't mean to stare, they don't mean to be unkind, they're only curious. But she will have that all her life,' people said.

Yet she was always tougher than I. Peppery as she was, it was she who did the hitting.

'You must never hit her back, never,' they said. 'You're so much stronger! Suppose you were to hurt her? To break a bone? What then?'

And I could see her tumbling, shattered on the floor, like that Oriental vase which Uncle Drew had brought from China and which a maid had broken, bringing lamentation to the morning.

I hit Jessie. She struck the table edge and a great reddening lump like an egg rose on her forehead. Feet came running – Carrie, the cook, Mother, Father. I was stiff with fright. She wailed and they picked her up. Father whipped me, me, his favourite, as I knew even then. He was so proud of me! His fierce voice, his fierce face were like an ogre's.

'Don't you ever hit Jessie again! Don't you touch her! Do you hear?'

Uncle Drew took me aside. He was the only one who felt sorry for me. I stood between his knees while he sat on the sofa, his hands on my shoulders.

'You haven't hurt her, Fern. Everyone's excited, but you haven't hurt her, Fern. Remember that. It's only a bump and will go away in a day or two.'

I didn't want to go away to school. I had friends here. And I didn't want to leave my dogs! But Jessie had no friends. A small, private school would be better for her, they said.

Mother said, 'We can't send Jessie away to school and keep you here, can we?'

And Father said, 'You will meet nicer girls in boarding school, anyway.'

But the girls all came from New York or Boston or Montreal. It was the same as having no friends at all.

Now she doesn't want to go to Europe this winter. If she doesn't go, Father will want me to stay home, too. But I'm going. No matter what, I'm going.

I shall be sorry to leave Martin. I might fall in love with him if I could know him a little longer. And still in a way it seems I've always known him. Even his silence speaks to me. Is it possible that he loves me already? But he's going away tomorrow . . . But he will come back. It's only a few months, after all. Maybe, then . . . And I shall see Europe . . . all the sparkle . . . I've never been anywhere at all.

I think Jessie has fallen in love with him, though. I'm sorry if she has. I hope she hasn't. Life is very, very harsh.

'It will be such joy having you with us, Fern,' Aunt Milly was saying and then, addressing Martin, 'We've invited Fern and Jessie to go to Europe with us, did you know? We shall leave just after Labour Day and spend the winter. I do wish, Jessie, you would change your mind and come along, too.'

Jessie shook her head.

'It would do you the world of good, you know. Take you out of yourself. You really do need – '

'I really do need a new spine,' Jessie said, and laughed.

Aunt Milly blushed. 'Oh, Jessie, I only meant – '

'I know what you meant, Aunt Milly. You meant well.'

'Nice is wonderful in the winter, very mild,' Uncle Drew observed. 'You can always change your mind, Jessie. Up to the last minute.'

The voices crossed the table in a neat little fugue.

Aunt Milly said to Fern, 'You'll be seeing the great art of the world. It'll help immensely in your career, you know.'

'Career!' The father was irritated. 'Don't, please, give her more grandiose ideas than she already has. It's a pretty hobby and that's all it is.'

'Excuse me, but you're hardly a judge,' Mary said.
'And you think you can judge?'
'No, but there are other people in this world who can.'
'Was that thunder I heard, by any chance?' Uncle Drew asked, changing the subject.
Martin smiled at him, receiving a knowing, answering smile. A kindly soul! Worlds removed from the heavy-handed petty tyrant at the head of the table!
'Mary, let's go for a walk,' he proposed when they had left the table. 'And Jessie come, too.'
'I don't want to,' Jessie said.
Mr Meig frowned. 'It's going to rain any minute.'
'Rain won't hurt anyone,' Aunt Milly told him.
'We'll not go far,' Martin said.
The town was closed for the night. Houses wore shut faces; their windows were drooping eyelids. A horn blew somewhere, a forlorn, far call in the silence. They circled through dwindling streets from pavement to asphalt to dirt, and where the fields began, turned back, talking of this and that and of nothing in particular.
'So you'll be going away,' Martin said. 'I'll miss you, Mary.'
The words were unforgivably banal. He wanted to say such beautiful, extravagant things: I'm enchanted, I think of you all day. Why was he so awkward, so tongue-tied? Was it the family, the gloomy house, the gloomy father? Perhaps, in another setting more private and free, or if he were a few years further along and had something definite to give –
The smell of rain was in the air when they came to the gate. Eastward, the clouds were darkening with approaching storm, but in the west the afterglow still streaked the sky in lines of copper and rose and a yellow like the inside of a peach.
'Oh look!' Mary cried. 'It sparkles! Martin, look!'
But he was not looking at the sky. He was looking at her, standing there with her hand held to her throat and the wonder on her face. There was a pain in his heart that he couldn't have believed possible.
At the front door they stood cramped between overgrown

laurels. And quite suddenly the rain came, spattering on the leaves.

'Well,' he said. 'I guess I'd better start.'

'I'll think of you. We all will.'

He had meant only to kiss her goodbye. But when he had caught her to him, he was unable to let her go. How long he would have held her there he didn't know, but someone stirred in the vestibule as if to open the door. So she turned quickly into the house and he went clattering down the steps into the rain.

CHAPTER FIVE

This was the way of it: He was Dr Farrell, intern, responsible for lives. Agitated relatives waylaid him and the squawk-box pursued him. His irrevocable signature went on every record. Pray it wasn't written as witness to a mistake he'd made! Best not to think about that, though; just step forward and begin, the way a child learns to walk.

The emergency room stayed in motion all night. One lived on black coffee. He slept on a cot or dozed off, rather, for a few minutes until a nurse came to shake him awake again. The doors would swing open, and another stretcher come rolling through. On the wards, the ominous nights were filled with sighs. Unbearable pain was unbearable to watch. He dreaded the terminal cancer patient most of all; the breakdown of personality in even the most stalwart was terrible. He had not known that desperate people, even the very old, call out for their mothers.

At times he thought he felt the weight of the pain-filled building, ten storeys high, lying on his shoulders.

'What's different about you?' Tom asked.

'I don't know. What is?'

'You're only half here. Is there some trouble with your father or something?' Martin had often said his father worked too hard and his blood pressure was too high.

'No, no, I'm just a little tense, I guess.'

There was no one in the world whom he could trust more than this friend who was searching him now with inquiring eyes, but he couldn't, he didn't want to, talk about Mary.

If only his mind were clear again as once it had been! If only the work were all he had to think about! But he trembled inwardly: trembled at seeing the name of the Meig plant in the weekly paper, forwarded from home; trembled at seeing a patient named Fern, a fat woman with a brogue and abscessed tonsils.

He trembled when the mail came. She sent a card from Lake Champlain: *Visiting here for a few days. Love.* He read it over and over, studying the shape of the words. She wrote in backhand. He wondered what that meant, whether it said anything about her personality. Then a card came that had a picture of an ocean liner. It had been mailed from Cherbourg. He imagined her walking in the rain on a cobbled street. He ached for her. It was a definite physical ache in the chest. One could understand why the ancients had believed that the heart was the seat of the emotions.

His own emotions came close to the surface. He broke off with Harriet, in a scene that he had wanted to keep gentle but that she made angry. His desire for her, for anyone but Mary, had drained away, as if a sluice had been opened.

A tragedy took place in the hospital when one of the nurses killed herself. She had been going with Dan Ritchie, resident in orthopaedics; he had promised to marry her, then changed his mind. The horror of this shook Martin deeply. How the suffering must have cut to make a human being want to die! But he thought he could understand it.

He was thankful for being overworked. It was the only way he would get through the winter.

What he saw first on the stretcher was a young girl in a tight pink sweater and skirt. It crossed his mind that she looked like a girl who would be named 'Donna' or 'Dawn'. And on a necklace of cheap beads her name was spelled out: Donna. She had been run over in the rain. Her face was gashed and her arms, which she must have flung out to save herself, had been crushed.

Standard procedure, he thought, accustomed as he was by now to quick judgement and quick action. Neurosurgery later to save the ulnar nerves. Useless hands, otherwise. Patch the face while waiting. Sedation, of course. Local anaesthesia. He called out orders. Black silk. Fine needle.

'This won't hurt,' he said.

Never did this before. Where to find a surgeon Saturday night? Common sense. Trick is: very, very small stitches.

Careful. Careful. Suture. Tie. Knot. Cut. Again. Suture. Tie. Knot. Cut.

When he was finished, the pathetic face was criss-crossed with black silk and he was sweating. He leaned down.

'Donna? I'm all through.'

She was, mercifully, half asleep. 'Will my face be all right?'

'Yes,' he said confidently.

The mouth, large and cherry-coloured, quivered. 'Do you promise I won't be scarred?'

'I promise.'

'Will I be a cripple, Doctor?'

'Of course not,' he said. And forgive me for the lie because I really don't know.

They had cut the pink sweater off. Somebody began to cut the necklace.

'No,' Martin said. 'Don't do that.' And he pulled the clasp towards the front to unfasten the beads. They would be precious to Donna.

After she had been wheeled upstairs he kept thinking of her, and the next morning was still thinking of her. Mentally, as was his habit, he constructed her life. She lived in a walk-up and worked in the five-and-ten. For lunch she ate a tuna fish sandwich and a chocolate soda. She stood in line at the funerals of movie stars, chewing gum in wads. He felt an indescribable sadness. Some patients did that to him. What would become of her with paralysed hands?

Dr Albeniz was to operate in the forenoon. Martin arrived when it was all over and the doctors were back in the locker room.

'It was very close,' Albeniz said, replying to Martin's question. 'But I'm fairly sure she'll be all right.' He seemed surprised. 'Why, do you know the girl?'

'No. I was on duty when she came in. I sutured her face.'

'You did?' There was strong emphasis on the 'you'.

Martin felt quick dread in the pit of the stomach.

'I'm afraid I'm the culprit.'

'Culprit?' Albeniz, who was tying his shoes, glanced up. 'On the contrary, I asked because it's a superb job. By the looks of it she will have scarcely a scar.'

Martin swallowed, disbelieving. 'I guess I was just lucky then.'

'You had your nerve, knowing nothing about it!'

'Yes, sir.'

'You have good hands. Are you interested in surgery?'

'Not particularly.' He corrected himself, 'No, I'm not.'

'Well, it was a superb job,' Albeniz repeated.

Martin flushed, both with pleasure and misgiving. What had he dared to do, knowing so little? He had just been awfully lucky! Very generous, though, of Albeniz to say what he had.

A week or two later, Albeniz ran past him in a corridor. Speed was his eccentricity. It seemed that all the greats had some eccentricity or other! Jeffers wore rubbers even when the sun was shining. Albeniz never took the elevator, preferring in his haste to run up three flights of stairs. When he saw Martin he stopped.

'Would you like to know how your patient is getting on?'

'Oh, yes,' Martin said, pleased at being treated like a colleague.

'Well, for a while I had my doubts, but she will definitely have usable hands. Also a presentable face, thanks to you.'

It seemed necessary to say something polite in return. 'After what you've done for her, my suturing seems unimportant.'

'Not so. It's not very good for one's mental health to have scarred cheeks, you know.'

'But your work is vital. I've seen you work and I've been – I guess you could say I've been thrilled each time.'

Albeniz smiled. 'Well then, I give you a standing invitation to come and watch whenever you're free.'

The operating room was fitted out in porcelain and stainless steel, gleaming silver-grey. Beyond the great window, the winter sky was a darker grey. Albeniz and his resident, the anaesthesiologist, the nurses, the assistants and the sub-assistants moved quickly in an ordered pattern, their feet making no sound. It was a subaqueous ballet, a serious dance around the table on which the patient lay, his shaven head firmly clamped. The green curtain hanging on its frame separated his head from the rest of his body. A profusion of tubes was connected to various parts of that body; to someone who didn't understand them it appeared to be only a tangle of tubes. But they were the weapons of this little army which was fighting for the life of the man on the table.

The excitement was unlike anything Martin had ever felt before. He stood with the explorers, with Balboa sighting the Pacific Ocean and Magellan rounding the world.

Bare and exposed lay a human brain. Albeniz looked up from it to the X-ray, hanging directly in his line of vision. There the arteries turned and curved like grapevines or Virginia creeper. There lay the dark blot and clump of tumour. Martin's heart pounded. He tried to remember what he had learned about the brain; neurons, axons, dendrites – and could only think: There somewhere in that roughly corrugated mass, that lump made of the same stuff as stomach or liver, ran the electricity of thought. Out of it came words, music and commands to clench a fist or kiss beloved lips.

'Clamp,' said Albeniz.

His hands in their pale gloves moved inside the patient's brain, moved among those billions of neurons.

'Cautery,' he said. 'Suction.'

Five and a half hours later it was over. Albeniz looked up. His eyes, above the mask, were weary.

'I think I got it all out.'

Martin knew he probably had, but no surgeon would ever say, 'I know I have.'

He was awestruck.

A fine surgeon is an artist, thought Martin. All eyes are on him. He may be a simple, modest man like Albeniz or a bully like some others I've seen. But either way he is respected: he has a great gift. What I should wish is to be like Dr Albeniz.

What am I dreaming of?

In such limited free time as he had, Martin observed Dr Albeniz. He went to his laboratory and to his clinic. With curiosity and fascination he followed some cases through surgery and into ultimate rehabilitation – or else to post-mortem He asked questions, but not too many.

Someone asked, 'You going in for neurosurgery? That why you've been hanging around Albeniz?'

Not very likely! Who could afford to go in for graduate work? Only very special people, types who could drift through Europe from clinic to clinic, spending a half-year here and a half-year there with the great authorities of Germany or England, steeping themselves, acquiring knowledge and finally, a name. For that sort of thing you needed independent means. Certainly you needed time. Probably too you needed a mentor to foster and advise.

He was about to go off duty one afternoon when he was summoned to Dr Albeniz's laboratory. Perplexed by the summons, he went at once. The doctor was hanging up his lab coat.

'I was wondering whether you like Italian food. There's a place just a few blocks down Third Avenue.'

'I've never had any,' Martin said.

'Good! It'll be a new experience, and everybody likes Italian food, even Spaniards like myself.'

Outside on the windy street Albeniz explained, 'In case you're wondering about this occasion, it's just because I like to talk to the rising medical generation now and then.'

'It's very good of you, sir.' Martin hoped he didn't appear as awkward as he felt.

When they were seated with a clean, darned cloth and a basket of bread between them, Albeniz asked, 'Would you like me to order for you?'

'Please do.'

'All right then. Clams oreganata to begin. Pasta, of course. Salad. Do you like veal? Veal pizzaola, then. Isn't it ridiculous to eat like this without wine? A fine, dry wine with the sunshine in it? You Americans are such Puritans with your Prohibition.' He sighed, rubbing his hands to warm them and was silent a moment. He took off his glasses and rubbed the bridge of his nose.

'You know, I've been watching you watch me these last months. You find my work interesting, don't you?'

'Yes, I – ' Martin began, but Albeniz interrupted him 'Tell me why you wanted to be a doctor.'

Martin said slowly, 'It always seemed, as far back as I can remember, the most exciting thing I could imagine.'

'Yes?'

'And I was curious. It's like solving puzzles. You want to go to the next one.' He stopped, feeling the inadequacy of his explanation.

But the other man smiled. 'I'm glad you didn't say "to help humanity", or "because I love people". Some such rubbish. I hear young men say that and I don't believe them.'

Martin was silent.

'Of course you rejoice when you've done something good for another human being! And of course you feel pity when things go wrong! But if you feel too much pity, you break your heart. Or you go crazy.' He waved an admonishing finger. 'You have to be disciplined, controlled and expert, a puzzle-solver, as you just said. Then, when the mind is beautifully clear and very cool, then you can really do some good. Sometimes. You understand me?'

'I think so.'

The clams were brought. Albeniz took a mouthful, then laid the fork down. 'We know so little. Take my field. It's only for the last thirty years or so that we've dared to go very far into the brain. Neurosurgery is a new discipline and most of what we know we've learned since the war.' He paused, picked up the fork and put it down again.

'Although, taking another point of view, it's very old. Ancient, in fact. The Egyptians trephined the skull four thousand years ago, using sharpened stones.'

With a clean fork, he pressed a diagram into the tablecloth.

'You were in the war, weren't you, Doctor?'

'I worked in a British military hospital. My clinical training I had taken in Germany before the war.' Albeniz shrugged. 'Medicine knows no politics, or shouldn't. But that early work was crude. There were too many infections. We've come a good way since then.'

'I see that.'

'Did you know we're going to have a separate department starting in September? At last we'll be removed from general surgery. And high time.'

'I didn't know.'

'Well, it's just been decided. Of course, that will be only a start. What we ought to have, what I dream of, is an institute where neurosurgery and neurology could be combined. Then we could truly study the whole brain: its function, pathology, even the tie-in with what is called "mental illness", which has, I've long been convinced, a physical cause. Perhaps God knows how many physical causes.' He sighed. 'But, as I say, that's only my dream. I haven't the money or the influence to make it come true. I'm no good at medical politics. I'll just be grateful for this little new department and let it go at that.' He made a small pyramid with his fingertips. 'I'm talking too much. Tell me, what do you think about what I've just told you?'

Martin shook his head. 'I haven't any right to think. I don't know anything about it.'

'Well spoken! I like that! I detest these fellows who go on rounds and wisely nod their heads, pretending to know, when they haven't the slightest idea what it's all about. How do you like the veal?'

'Oh, great! Some change from the cafeteria!'

'I should hope so. Tell me, what are you planning to do when you finish in June?'

'Work with my father. He's got a general practice upstate.'

Dr Albeniz studied Martin. His austere face softened.

'Are you happy about it?'

No one had ever put the question like that. People assumed he was happy. You finished your internship; then you went into practice, and if you had one already waiting for you, why then, you were just very lucky indeed! So he waited a moment and then, for the first time, expressed the truth.

'No, sir, I don't think I am.'

'I see.'

'I guess I haven't wanted to admit it, even to myself.'

He turned away, looking at an amateurish painting of

Italy, candy-pink roses against a white wall and a gaudy blue sky.

'Have some more pasta. You're thin enough to afford it.'

'Thank you, but I'm not all that hungry.'

'I've upset you with my questions, haven't I?'

'A little, maybe.'

'More than a little. You know, or maybe you don't know, that I've been observing you? Ever since that time you sewed up the girl's face. It's strange that you should have come to my attention through work that's not in my field, but I knew that the hands which could do that without having been taught could do much more.'

Martin waited. He became conscious of his heartbeat.

'And then you began coming to watch me, and you came to the lab and you asked intelligent questions.'

The beat accelerated.

'You're aware, of course, that you've earned a reputation this year?'

'Well, I –'

'Come, come! Dr Fields tells me you're the best intern he's had in his service in ten years.'

'I didn't know that, sir.'

'Well, you know it now. So hear me. I'm coming to the point. In this new service that I'm to have, I can train two young men. I already have one coming from Philadelphia in the fall. I'm asking you to be the other.'

Martin looked at him dumbly.

'You understand what I'm driving at. I wouldn't have to waste words with you. I'm doing a lot of talking now, but the fact is, I don't talk much when I'm working. I'm an impatient man and I need people around me who grasp my meaning quickly. I could work with you, Martin.' He paused, then added thoughtfully, 'I want a man who will grasp the whole concept of the brain, not just a skilful surgeon-mechanic. I want someone who has curiosity. That's the key word, curiosity. What do you say?'

'Forgive me. I'm stunned.'

'Of course, it's a new idea for you! This would be another world from the one you had been planning on – sore throats, measles and cut fingers. Not that we don't need good men who're willing to do that. Men like your father. What do you think he will say to this?'

'He'll be terribly disappointed, I'm afraid.'

Sick over it. Dread sank in Martin like a stone.

'Yes, I can imagine. I've never had a son, but I can imagine your father would want you to come home. Still,' Albeniz said quietly, 'there are always some who have to break the soft family ties no matter how it hurts. In a way it's like being a soldier or a monk. I was forty before I got married. In Europe men marry later; it gives them time to develop. My wife knew she would come second to my work. Late at night, on Sundays if need be, I'm at the hospital. It is my devotion. Perhaps I express it badly, English not being my native language.'

'No, sir, you express it very well.'

'You think so? Yes, well, devotion, then. Look, I move my finger. An electrical impulse in my brain provides the energy with which I move the finger. Simple, eh? You think so? Of course you don't! What if the signal is given and the finger refuses to move? What if a finger moves when the brain doesn't want it to? These are the tantalizing mysteries. We still know nothing. Nothing. Talk of exploring the poles! Here's exploration for you!' He broke off abruptly. 'You have a girl?'

Martin flushed. 'Yes . . . No . . . I mean, there's nothing official, but – '

But her face floats over the pages of my textbooks and no matter what else I'm thinking of, part of me is always thinking of her.

Albeniz smiled. 'Well, you'll work that out. There's always a way.' He stood up. 'You will get twenty dollars a month and your keep. You will live penuriously, unless, of course, your family has money.'

'Oh no!'

'Then you will live penuriously. There are worse things. In time, you'll be rewarded for your work with some of life's comforts, but you will deserve them then, which is more than can be said for a lot of people who live in comfort. Well, I'm going back to the lab for an hour and then home.' He shook Martin's hand. 'The next time we come you'll try the spaghetti carbonara.'

Martin was half-way back to his room before he realized that Albeniz hadn't even waited for his acceptance. He had simply taken for granted that no young man could do anything other than accept. And of course, he had been right! There was such a beating and fluttering in his chest that he couldn't shut himself indoors just yet; he had to move, to walk.

He went rapidly across town. Past Fifth Avenue, where the great stores were shut for the night. Past Sixth Avenue where the last late workers were leaving the office towers. Westward and southward through shoddy streets. Blowing papers wrapped themselves around his ankles. A luncheonette released the smell of frying grease. Near Times Square a Chinese restaurant wore a garish red-and-gold faked pagoda front. The lights of a dance palace blinked in and out. 'Fifty Gorgeous Girls. Fifty.' And it was beautiful. Everything was beautiful.

After a long time, he turned back. He felt like shouting out his glory. Remembering his father, he pushed the thought away, knowing that he would handle things somehow because, as Dr Albeniz had said, there's always a way.

Then he thought of Mary. She would be home soon and he would talk to her. How foolish of him not to have told her how he felt before she left! Not that she hadn't known! He smiled to himself. Well, in another month he would put everything into words; he'd buy her a little ring; the three years wouldn't be all that long to wait. Her father – there was another problem, of course, but not insurmountable, either. Donald Meig's displeasure was hardly the end of the world!

He sat down at the desk and began a letter. He thought of asking her then and there to marry him, but the words looked either too stark or too florid and he decided he'd rather wait to speak them aloud and hear her answer. For the present he would only describe the marvel that had occurred tonight.

When he had finished he stood for a while looking out of

the window. The soft, cold air of February, faintly damp with the nearness of spring, washed over him. A light went on in the wing of private rooms across the street. An ambulance, its tyres making a small sigh on the pavement, rounded the corner. He took a long breath and spoke to his empty little room.

'I am going to be a great doctor.' It was half a declaration and half a wondering question. 'I am going to be a great doctor.'

By two o'clock in the afternoon of the following day everybody knew about Martin. He was the only intern in the programme who would be going on to specialize. It was something to talk about, to be envious of or impressed by. Tom puzzled over it.

'Oh, it's a stupendous opportunity,' he admitted. 'But I don't know, Martin, it's a depressing speciality. The patients are all strangers, people you'll never see again. And most of them die, you know they do.'

'But if we take that attitude, they always will. The idea is to keep them from dying, isn't it?'

'Well, I can't wait to get out on my own. Beats me how you can even think of another three years.'

Tom and Florence were to be married in July and he was to set up practice in Teaneck, New Jersey, with three thousand dollars borrowed from their families. The early marriage Martin could understand and envy, but not the haste to leave the hospital.

I love it here, he thought. For me it's the heart of the world.

Never before had he experienced such euphoria, such joy. Everything blossomed. He found himself singing as he moved around his room in the mornings. All the faces on the street were friendly. He wanted to walk up to people, grasp them by the buttonhole and shout at them: Isn't it a wonderful life? There's so much you can do with it! So much work, so much love – if only there were more time! Yes, it's so wonderful and there'll never be enough time for it all!

Then one day he decided to tell Tom and Perry about Mary. Their goodwill, their good wishes for him brought the usual tears to his eyes and their usual jokes about those foolish tears of his; they knew each other well!

Tom asked, 'Have you told your father yet about Albeniz?'

'No, not yet.'

'Well, what are you waiting for?'

'I'm a coward, I guess. But I'll do it when I go home next month. When Mary gets back.'

He'd had only a postcard since he had written his news. They had been moving about all over England; she would write a real letter soon. In the meantime she wanted him to know that his news was wonderful. She was happy for him and proud.

He stuck the card in the mirror above the dresser and read it over morning and night.

At last there came a thick envelope, postmarked 'London'. Cutting the lunch hour short, Martin went to his room, locked the door and sat down, enjoying his anticipation. His eyes sped over the pages –

'. . . Alex's mother has been a friend of Aunt Milly's and Uncle Drew's for years. He's a wonderful person. You would really like him! His wife died when their baby was born, a beautiful little boy, Neddie . . . The wedding will naturally be very small, but I don't mind. Jessie and Dad will come over for it, and we shall have the ceremony at Alex's house – so old, deep country and yet not far from London. You can see sheep on the hills in back of the garden . . . I know you will be surprised at the suddenness of all this. I am myself! But I am so very, very happy.'

He thought at first that she was talking about someone else who was going to be married, a friend or someone met on her travels. He read it again. Then he went to sit on the edge of the bed. He put his head in his hands and felt ill: giddy, as though he were going to vomit.

You would like him, she dared to write! Like him!

Martin groaned. For an instant he had a crazy sensation: he was imagining this, it was a nightmare and in a minute he would wake up. But no, there it was, three compact pages in her own backhand script.

Why? How? Didn't she know what he felt for her? Had she felt nothing, then, for him? Could he have been imagining that, also?

Or had she measured him against this – this Alex and found him the lesser of the two?

Oh, Tom was the lucky one! A solid woman like Florence was what a man wanted! A woman who knew her own mind, instead of –

He pounded his knees with his fists. Timid, short-sighted fool that I am! To assume that she would be there, waiting, ready whenever I was ready! Instead of making sure, instead of saying, that last night on the front steps –

He went into the bathroom and was violently sick. Then he came back and sat for a while, staring at the wall. After a time he picked the letter off the floor and ripped it across, ripped it over and over, and flung the shreds back on the floor. His arms felt heavy. A great weight descended and he threw himself down on the bed.

Someone pounded at the door. Martin opened his eyes into weak, departing sunlight.

'Are you in there? Open the door. Where've you been?' Tom cried. 'Didn't you hear the squawk-box? They've been calling you for an hour!'

'I didn't hear. I don't seem to be feeling well.'

'Sit down. I have to talk to you.' Tom's long, ugly face was suddenly sad, like Lincoln's face.

'What's the matter?'

'First tell me what your trouble is. Are you really sick?'

'Yes. No. I've had a kind of blow, that's all.'

Tom studied him. 'Is it anything you want to tell me about?' he asked softly.

'Mary's being married in England,' Martin said, looking at the floor.

'I'm sorry! Oh Martin, I'm so sorry!'

'I know you are.'

'You don't deserve it – '

A fire engine clanged in the street below. When it had passed, the silence was absolute.

After a minute Tom spoke. 'I have to hit you again, Martin. Have to hit you when you're down.'

Martin looked up. Distress furrowed Tom's cheeks, furrowed and creased them.

'What do you mean?'

'Your sister telephoned. When you didn't answer, they told me instead. Your father's had a stroke.'

CHAPTER SIX

He slid the flivver into the shed. Dean, their old, brown, calloused horse, thrust his head out of the stall. He'd outlived his usefulness and Pa was simply saving him from the glue factory. Hideous thought.

Martin entered the stall and laid his head against the hard, rippling shoulder. Its living warmth gave comfort. He felt such loneliness! With Alice married and gone, with his mother herself in need of strengthening, there was no one to talk to. And after all, what was there to talk about?

Should he talk about Mary? No use in that. It was over and done with. Strange how chemistry worked, how the flow of man's desiring could be extinguished by time and troubles as a fire is quenched.

Talk about his father, the withered flesh, the tottering walk? What is there to say about a life that's running out? Just running out, like this horse's life, old Dean's.

Anybody coming in would think he'd lost his wits, standing here like this. And abruptly repelled by his own sadness, Martin straightened and went into the house.

'Pa gone up to bed this early?' he asked.

'No, he had his supper and went to his desk in the office.' Jean lowered her voice. 'It seems to help him, sitting there looking at old records and things. I suppose he feels he's busy. Martin?' Something in her tone made him look up. 'Martin, I didn't know he'd taken a new mortgage on the house, did you?'

'I? No. He's never talked business affairs with me.'

'Well. The original mortgage had been paid off before you went to high school . . . I don't understand.' His mother's lips trembled. 'How could he have worked so hard all these years and we still have nothing? It just seemed to go as fast as it came in. It's not as if we'd had any luxuries. Well, yes, we did buy the new parlour suite last year; the old one was really a disgrace. And we put new linoleum down. But I wouldn't even have done that if I had known.'

He didn't answer, there being nothing to say. She set his plate on the table, poured coffee and, attempting cheer, sighed, 'Well, what's done is done I guess. No use bemoaning it.'

If there is anything pathetic, Martin thought, it is penury in old age, the spectre of dependency. Old age must be hard enough without that.

From the kitchen table he could see into the parlour, where above the brown imitation Chippendale sofa, hung the new photograph of his parents, taken fortuitously only a few months before Pa's stroke. Alice had wanted it taken. Ma had resisted, but Alice had pressed. It was only because she was moving away, she had said. Privately she had told Martin of her feeling that something was going to happen.

'You couldn't have known Pa was going to have a stroke,' he had argued.

And she said no, she certainly hadn't known that. She had simply felt that *something* might be going to happen and she wanted the photo before it was too late. So they stood for all time together in a gilded oval frame, the mother wearing a silk dress and a gold watch on a neck chain, the father in his dark good suit, looking, for him, unusually dapper and spruce. He would never look that way again.

'You saw Ken Thompkins today?' Ma inquired now.

'Yes. He won't last the night. He's been vomiting from a strangulated hernia since last Wednesday and they didn't call till today. His wife thought it was colic.' Martin could hear the exasperation in his own voice. 'My God, what pitiful ignorance! I thought as a last hope we could rush him to Baker for surgery. I would've driven him the seventy miles myself, but he wouldn't go. Says if he's going to die, he wants to die at home.' And Martin threw out his hand in a gesture of hopelessness, tipping the coffee cup.

His mother rose to wipe the spill and handed him two letters. 'I forgot. Here's mail for you.'

Martin propped the letters against his water glass, reading over a lifted fork. Tom wrote that he had opened his office.

He had got privileges at a good hospital. Florence was keeping her job, and they were gradually furnishing the house. Martin must somehow get down to see them.

The second letter was from Dr Albeniz. He was holding Martin's place open. He understood the circumstances, but hoped Martin would be able to set things in order at home within the next few weeks.

'Something wrong, Martin?'

'No. Tired, that's all.'

'I don't know what we'd do without you,' his mother said. 'It would be disaster, plain and simple. Isn't it the hand of Providence, though, that if this had to happen to your father, it waited until you were finished and ready to take his place?' She stood frowning a little, wiping and wiping the spot, now dry, where the spill had been. Then becoming aware of his gaze, she brightened. 'Oh, I hear my raccoons at the trash! They're almost tame, coming for their bread every night. I used to be annoyed with them, but your father taught me – You remember your pet raccoon, Martin? You were only about seven or eight when Pa found it along the road. Remember?'

He was not fooled by her brave prattle.

'Pa's doing better, you know,' he said gently.

'Martin, you mean well, but I'd rather have the truth. I see him going downhill. Give me the truth: What's going to happen?'

'Ma, I don't know. I'd tell you if I did. I'd be surprised if he improved any, but he could go on no worse than this for years. Or he could have another stroke or a coronary tonight.'

Her eyes widened. 'Oh, it isn't fair! He was so good to everyone!'

The night-bell rings. Sleet clatters on the windowpane. Pa creaks down the stairs and out of the door; the motor coughs in the garage. The time is two-fifteen . . .

'No,' Martin said, 'it isn't fair.' (Not if you believed in just rewards, which he didn't and his mother did.)

Presently the collies began barking in the yard, subsiding as they recognized a familiar voice.

'Sounds like Charlie Spears,' Jean said. She opened the door. 'I thought it was you! Why, Charlie, what have you got there?'

Charlie Spears came in and set a carton of groceries on the floor. 'Thought you might use some extras from the store outside of your regular order. A few delicacies for Doc. Doc Senior,' this with a nod to Martin. 'He was always partial to bananas, and here's Scotch marmalade, herb tea, water biscuits and some of that there smelly foreign cheese. I never liked it myself, but then, there's no accounting for taste, as they say.'

Jean flushed. 'Charlie, you're too good to us. You shouldn't, really you shouldn't. We're doing fine and – '

Charlie looked up sharply. ''Twasn't charity, Missus. 'Twas because Doc was always real good to me and he's a friend.'

When he had gone, Jean said, 'People have been so kind. Sometimes it's hard not to cry, they've been so kind. It's one of the rewards of this kind of life. So you see, it isn't all hardship, Martin.'

'I know that, Ma,' Martin said firmly.

There were shuffling steps in the hall, and his father appeared in the doorway. 'Who was that?'

'Charlie Spears. He brought you a package of goodies.'

Enoch glanced at the carton without interest.

'I'm bored,' he said petulantly. 'Nothing to do here all day.'

'You'll just have to learn to kill time,' Jean told him, 'until you get to be yourself again.'

Enoch stared at her. 'Kill time! That's the worst thing you could have said. It's time that's killing me. Well, I'm going up to bed. Good-night, folks.'

He struggled slowly up the stairs. It was difficult because the banister was on the right and it was his right arm which had been weakened. Once when he faltered, Martin rose to help, but his mother waved him back with a signal.

'He doesn't want to be helped.'

And Martin knew that this understanding was born of thirty-four years of life together.

So they sat, the wife and the son, not speaking, stirring the coffee in their cups. Chink. The spoon struck the cup, then ground around the sides again. Chink. Once more the collies barked, this time at the front of the house. Martin got up and went to look. There was nothing to be seen in all that darkness except the band of light that slid from the open door. Then his nose led him to the basket of apples, to the sharp, fresh scent of Greenings.

'Martin, what is it?'

'Somebody's left apples on the porch. There's no name. That's odd.'

'Not odd. People do that lots of times when they can't pay and Pa's written them off. They feel they want to give whatever they can. No, leave them there. You can carry them to the root cellar in the morning.' She went back to the kitchen.

He sat down on the porch step next to the apples, with a dog on either side. A fox barked from the wood lot across the road. Low on the horizon, just above the trees, Orion shone. You couldn't be Pa's son, he thought, without having learned something about the constellations. The sky looked lonely, the universe larger and more lonely than at other times and in other places.

If he could hear some music, it would be a comfort, he thought, remembering the soaring voices and soaring strings. All the lights! All the life! Why couldn't he just accept?

Alice had gone with Fred to live with his parents in Maine and she, a woman with no place of her own, was not complaining. Although, who knew how she really felt about it? Her letters were always cheerful. But then, Martin wasn't given to talking much about his feelings, either.

'You're letting the cold air into the house.' Jean stood in the doorway. 'I'm going to bed. You coming up, too?'

Martin and the dogs went in. 'Soon. I thought maybe I'd go over some things in Pa's desk.'

'Oh, I wish you would! If he had only let me take care of things! I always wanted him to, but he didn't believe in a woman doing all that. I know the bankbooks are somewhere in the desk. I guess you can find them.' She hesitated. 'I don't want to bother him by asking how much money there is, as if I expected him to die.' Tears stood in her eyes, puddled there, but not overflowing. 'So it would be a good idea if you'd look things over. Only don't stay up too late. You need your rest.'

The old rolltop overflowed with paper. Out of childhood came the recollection of his mother's exasperated voice: 'If you would just once let me straighten this mess up, Enoch!'

Under a pile of prescription blanks, old postcards, letters, calendars and samples of medicine in cardboard containers, lay a marriage certificate and birth certificates, Alice's and Martin's own. Also Enoch Junior's, Susan's and May's. Why on earth had Pa kept those? Here was the mortgage agreement, which should be in a safe deposit box in case of fire. Here was the disability policy, small at best, but invalid now at age sixty-five, just when you were most likely to need it. Martin swallowed outrage. And here were three savings-bankbooks, tossed in the muddle. He opened them and added the sum. Four thousand, four hundred eighty-three dollars and seventy-six cents. He rummaged incredulously for another book, but there was none. This was it. This was all Pa had, after a lifetime of labour.

He sat in a kind of stunned despair. The pity of it! Four thousand dollars and this modest house, an upended box devoid of comfort or grace, that needed every kind of repair anyway. How often had he not heard the story, told with pride, of how this house had been acquired?

'I had my eye on it, at the crossroads, and only three and a half miles from Cyprus. The bank was glad to make the loan. I had a good reputation already, and I'd only been in this country six years.'

So then, this house and a basket of apples left by a grateful patient. And who would take care of them now, except their son?

It must have been hard for his mother. He remembered the time Pa had dropped a hundred and twenty-five dollars. He'd had the money stuffed in his pocket on his way to town to pay bills.

'I even made you a leather purse,' his mother had

mourned. 'Why don't you use it?'

And Pa had been ashamed. 'I forgot.'

There were the times he had actually given money to patients. 'They had nothing,' he would say, and his mother's lips would grow tight and thin, as though she were fastening them together with a pin. She'd been afraid to speak, having never got over the honour of being married to him. If she ever had regrets, she had not admitted them, probably not even to herself. True to her stern beliefs, she would accept without complaint whatever burden the Lord might see fit to lay upon her.

For a long time Martin sat, then abruptly reached for a piece of paper and a pen. He could have poured out pages of his grievous disappointment, but nobody beside himself cared about that. Each man bore his grievous disappointments alone. So the pen slipped rapidly across a single sheet of paper.

'Dear Dr Albeniz. Thank you for waiting until I could reach a final decision. I appreciate your patience and your understanding . . . grateful and honoured by your offer . . . impossible because of my family situation . . . regret. Very good wishes.'

Short and sweet. He put his hands over his face. His sadness was so vast it emptied him. He was hollow, floating in chill grey sadness, in shreds of vapour, fog and whispers. Everything that had been so bright and pulsing had just quietly slipped away, fallen from his outstretched hands. Gone. All gone.

A great wind rushed past the house. Wind of the world, carrying a hundred million hopes away. Not just mine. Remember that.

And rolling the top down on the scattered papers in the desk, he went upstairs to sleep in the maple bed which had been his ever since he had outgrown a crib.

The year hurried towards its close. The lakes froze; a thin film of dimpled ice hardened and thickened. Among the neighbours Christmas preparations made a pleasant bustle as tins of peanut brittle and home-made fudge were carried from house to house. Pine sprays with red bows were hung on front doors and small boys careened down the hills on their Flexible Flyers.

Christmas morning brought a sugary, fresh fall of snow. Shortly after six o'clock, Martin was called out. When he got back it was almost time for dinner. Pa looked up questioningly.

'Anything important today? Anything I ought to know?'

'I think I've finally persuaded Mary Deitz to have the goitre operated on.'

'She's had that goitre fifteen years! Cut, cut, that's all you young fellows know how to do.' Pa was having one of his cranky days.

'I'm not the one who's going to do it, more's the pity.'

'Hmph. You were telling me something the other day about something in the – the ventricle . . . I don't remember. What was it again?'

'The vertriculogram, you mean?'

'Yes, that's it. How does that work again?'

'Well, it's – you remove the ventricular fluid and you inject air through a hole in the skull. Then you can tell by X-ray where the air has moved within the brain. That's putting it very simply, of course.'

'Hmph. I daresay there's good in a lot of this new stuff. But these fellows don't know everything, Martin. Just because they fasten their names on to some high-sounding articles, don't let them fool you.'

'No, Pa, I won't let them fool me.' He looked so small and old, standing there. And also, in a dreadful way, he looked childish.

'What'll happen when you fellows have divided up the whole human body among yourselves, hey? One'll study the left ear, the other will study the right knee! Why, there won't be a doctor among the lot of you fit to treat a whole patient!'

Pa had used to say, 'You will see such marvels in your lifetime, Martin!'

But now illness and the hidden envy that can corrupt old age had changed him into someone else. And his son's heart ached.

The Christmas table was set in the dining-room which was

on the chilly side of the house. Pa felt the cold. 'I don't know why we had to eat in here,' he complained.

'I'll put the electric heater near you,' Martin offered.

'No, wait, I'll get it,' Jean said. 'You carve the turkey, Martin.'

That had been his father's job. All those years of Christmas and Thanksgiving turkeys, of Easter hams, eaten in this room! It would be Martin's job now, so he guessed he'd better learn. Strip the leg off first, take apart at the joint, now cut the wing. Now slice neatly from the breast.

'My, that's expert,' his mother said heartily. 'Enoch, will you say the grace?'

'Let Martin do it.'

'For what we are about to receive, Father, we thank Thee,' Martin murmured.

The platters passed between the three of them. Pa's plate was mounded with creamed onions, turkey, mashed turnip, mashed potatoes and cranberry sauce. He had not lost his enormous appetite. Silently, voraciously, he ate, gazing with abstracted eyes at the sideboard array of Jean's best cut-glass bowls and her 'good' dishes.

'Those dishes were given to us when we were married,' Jean said suddenly. 'And do you know, there's only been one broken, and it wasn't done by me. It was one of the neighbours helping clear the table. That's why I never like anyone to help me. Even if they don't break things, they chip them.'

There was a silence. Martin tried to think of something to say.

'I do wish Alice were here,' Jean remarked.

He understood that the remark was partly an expression of a real wish and partly an effort to break the silence. He tried to co-operate. 'Do you suppose she'll have a chance to visit before spring?'

'I shouldn't think so. The roads are awfully bad and the train connections are dreadful. She'd have to travel all the way east to Boston, and then come west again.'

'I imagine she'll do it all the same,' Martin guessed.

'Oh, she might at that. She's a good daughter, Alice is.

And I know she wants to see her father. Anybody like to try my mincemeat? I brought two jars up from the cellar. It's so good the next day with cold turkey. Enoch! Enoch! What is it?'

Pa's hands clutched at his chest. 'I don't feel well.' He pushed his chair violently away from the table. 'I have a terrible pain. Terrible!' he cried, very loud.

And while in an instant of dumb shock they stared at him, he stood up, stretched tall and reaching, stiffened, buckled at the knees and toppled. His face struck the edge of the table with a dreadful, tearing sound. Then the chair broke, splintering as Enoch and the chair both crashed to the floor.

'Oh God!' Jean screamed. 'Oh God! Enoch, get up! Martin! Enoch! Get up!' Her cry was to repeat itself in Martin's ears for the rest of his life, and Christmas was to be marked with the memory of it forever.

Enoch was laid out in the parlour between the two front windows. People came with proper grave faces, bending to the widow, who, her first spasms of weeping past, sat quietly acknowledging their hushed sympathy. They looked down at the dead man in his dark suit and his secret dignity: *I have gone beyond your small concerns and I know what you cannot know*. They stood looking with embarrassment and fear. They walked risen on the balls of their feet, and with the same grave, tragic faces, left the room.

They stood in knots on the porch, on the walk and in the road, hailing one another, greeting briskly.

'Want a lift home, George?'

'Say, when'd you get the new car?'

Alone in the evening, Martin went back into the room. It was not his father's face that moved him most, it was his hands. Wasn't that strange? Yes, his hands, folded on the chest where the undertaker had arranged them, waxy and larger than life. Were they really that large or was it because of something the undertaker had done? Hands, that marvellous circuitry of brain to hand that can curve to catch a ball, clench to a smashing fist, or open to touch with gentle palm. Marvellous, marvellous. My father's hands.

And somewhere out of his most cursory readings in psychiatry, Martin remembered: Was it Freud who said that the greatest blow to a man is the death of his father? All the knotted, complicated web of memories, resentments, comfort and confidence, humour and wisdom and stubborn foolishness – everything, all of it that made me and that I shall carry through my years lies here. You try to make some order out of it, and there is none. It ends in this.

My father, you've gone so far away. I think that if I talk loud enough, surely you will hear me. I can't understand why it is that you can't hear. You lie there, but you've gone. Everything's *stopped* in you. It terrifies me, this death of yours. I've seen death so often by now, but not your death. There are things I would like to have talked to you about when you were yourself and well. In so many ways Ma has been the head of the household, for somebody had to try to manage things. But you were always the heart. You were the heart.

In the piles of letters that arrived during that next week, there came a note from Jessie Meig.

'Father and I were so sorry to learn of your father's death. He was a kind, old-fashioned man. He will be missed. If you ever have time, would you come to visit us? Would the Sunday after next for tea at four be all right?'

He whipped the letter against the table's edge. Be damned if he would walk into that house again! What did they think of him, for God's sake? Why should he want to visit there? A small fury surged in his chest, and then receded. Very likely they weren't thinking anything. Then he felt foolish.

He looked at the letter again, at the blunt black strokes: an unusual script, individual and strong, rather like Jessie herself. He wondered what life was like for her now in that house with her sister gone. Not that they had been that warm towards one another! Still, a sister was a sister. He was tempted to accept. Admittedly, and not unnaturally, he was a little curious. Why not? But on second thought, he decided he really didn't want to go.

A few weeks later his mother reported, 'Jessie Meig

telephoned today. She wondered whether you had got her note.'

He was ashamed of his rudeness. Perhaps he had been more than rude? Perhaps even terribly unkind, rejecting the well-meaning, outstretched hand? Then he had a mental picture of Jessie, seated in the enormous wing-chair, almost curled within it, as though she felt protected by the wings. He had forgotten how small she was, and he thought: Out of pure decency, I ought to go.

So, on the following Sunday afternoon he strode up the walk between the iron deer, stood under thawing icicles on the porch and entered the house he had never expected to enter again.

CHAPTER SEVEN

Jessie put the remainder of the lunch into a bag and capped the Thermos. 'Do you want to drive, Martin, or shall I?'

'It's your car. You drive.'

Summer had barely peaked and already the first small signs of its wane were beginning to appear. Blueberries, powdered with pale dust, were thick along the roadside. Queen Anne's lace stood stiff and starched in the fields.

Ever since winter's end, Jessie had been going along with Martin on his far-country house calls. He wasn't quite sure how the habit had been formed; he thought vaguely that it might have been her father who had suggested it. At any rate, that negative, inhibiting person had been surprisingly cordial during these past months.

'It'd do you good to get out more,' he had said.

Certainly that was true. Jessie's need for companionship was visible enough. Martin understood, because the same need was in him. He missed good talk, that quick comprehension which comes when the associations and the bent of mind are kin. Most of his boyhood friends had dispersed; those still here at home were married and there was no place for Martin in their households. After five close years, he felt the loss of men like Tom and Perry. It seemed sometimes that in all of Cyprus the one person to whom he could really talk was Jessie Meig.

The father went upstairs in the evenings leaving the library to them. Martin had come to take his place opposite Jessie at the chessboard. She usually beat him! There was music on the radio; there was pleasant comfort.

'You're worried about something again,' she said now. 'I can always tell.'

'I am. It's that place we stopped at before lunch. I'm still feeling sort of sick about it.'

'The woman with the cough?'

'Cough and nausea. She's lost sixteen pounds in the last

two months. I know it's a malignancy. I'm so sure I'd take a bet on it.' He shook his head in recollection of the dreary young woman with the delicate face. 'I told them she needs to go to the hospital for tests. I was as emphatic as I could be without using the word "cancer". I said she must go, that there was no choice. The husband kept saying, "She's just weak after birthing and she'll be all right". *He* assured *me*! And anyway, the hospital was out of the question. Who would take care of the kids? Then he followed me outside and told me he'd be careful, he knew she'd had too many kids too fast. She wasn't strong like some women. He'd see she had no more. Oh, she'll have no more!' Martin said grimly. 'She won't be alive nine months from now.'

'Trouble started in the ovaries, I suppose.'

'Why, yes, I've a pretty good idea it did. But how do you know? Were you guessing?'

'You told me something once about another case that sounded like this one. I would never want to be a doctor, but still I do like to listen to you and I do remember things.'

'And I – if I couldn't have been a doctor, there's nothing else in the world I would have wanted to be.'

Around a bend, they were slowed almost to a stop by a wagon with an enormous load of hay. From the top of the pile a woman called cheerfully, 'Hi, Doc!'

'That's good fodder you've got there,' Martin called back.

'Yes, and we'll be needing it before you know it. The older I get, the shorter the summers get.'

'Just don't throw that back out again unloading!'

'They like you, Martin,' Jessie said when they drove on.

'I like them.'

In his few short months of practice he had been touched a dozen times with powerful emotion and the emotion of power. In their houses, in the beds where the fevered lay with brilliant eyes, they turned to him in trust. Touching their sick flesh, he could feel their engulfing gratitude and admiration. Something swelled in a man then: might one call it a kind of love? And yet he knew, although they did not, that what he did was often not enough and should be better.

'Most illness is self-limiting,' he mused aloud now. 'Fluids, bedrest and warmth will cure most ailments in a matter of days. But what bothers me, Jessie, is the other kind. This morning's case, for instance. I'm stymied, battling distance and lack of facilities and ignorance. The patients' ignorance and my own. Mostly my own.' And he repeated his thoughts aloud, 'What I do could be done so much better!'

'I'm sure it could,' Jessie said.

On those infrequent times when he had expressed such doubts to his mother, her standard, uncomprehending reply had always been: 'Oh, you belittle yourself, Martin.'

'It must be marvellous to know and do!' Jessie cried vehemently. 'To be your own person! Why do people think women don't want that too? They think you're some sort of oddity if you want what a man does, the same freedom to stretch your thoughts and learn things. You know, if I were whole, I would defy all that and try it anyway. Some women do and always have. George Sand, for instance. I've read her novels and they aren't very good, but that's not the point. She was a free woman. That's the point.' Her hands were tense on the wheel. And she finished furiously, 'As for me, every thought I have, every breath I take, is influenced by this damned hump.'

Martin tried to change the subject. 'The next place we come to used to be the Brook farm. My father would tell me every time we passed it how, back in the nineties, when he made calls in a buggy, they had a big mean dog that would lie in the tall grass beside the road and jump out at the horse. One time it made Pa's horse bolt, and the buggy turned over in the ditch. Pa broke his arm.'

They passed the Brook farm without event. Silage corn was tall in the fields and cattle chewed dreamily in pasture-shade. A man, recognizing Martin, waved a paintbrush from a ladder propped against the Grecian pediment of his house, on which the facade of the Parthenon or the temple at Sounion had been reproduced in native wood. Pa, the classics student, had never failed to remark on things like that or on the names of New York State towns: Ithaca, Syracuse, Rome. And Martin's thoughts drifted on with his father.

'Pa used to carry a wire fence cutter with him on winter calls. The road got snowed over so often, he'd be driving through fields without knowing it. He used to fold a newspaper under his vest to keep warm. Sounds like a hundred years ago, doesn't it? But it wasn't so long ago, really. Say, doesn't that look tempting?'

In Gregory's Pond, the confluence of three streams, a few small boys were swimming.

'Why don't we bring our suits sometimes?' he proposed. 'Oh, I forgot, you don't like to swim.'

'That's not true. I really do like to.'

'But you said – '

'I only said so because I didn't want you to see me in a bathing suit. Now all of a sudden, I wouldn't mind. Maybe because you're a doctor. But I wouldn't be ashamed any more.'

'Jessie, there's nothing to be ashamed of!'

'Well, not ashamed exactly. It's that I think people will find it – disgusting,' she said, so low that he barely caught the word.

' "*Nihil humanum mihi alienum est.*" You said you remembered your Latin, didn't you?'

' "Nothing human is alien to me",' she said quietly, and after a moment, 'Thank you.'

'You ought to put a higher valuation on yourself, you know.'

'I suppose I should. But then, so should you.'

'What do you mean?'

'You ought to be doing what you *want* to do. Something more important than what you're doing.'

'But what I'm doing *is* important. These sick people are important.'

'Of course they are! But you're one of the movers, the advance guard, Martin. Listen! There are people who sing in the chorus, and we need them. Then there's the tenor lead, and we need him most of all.'

'Maybe you overestimate me.'

'Oh, I despise false modesty! What's that magazine sticking out of your bag? You've had it there since last week.'

'This?' He drew out a copy of *Brain*. In a moment of high hopes he had taken a subscription to it. 'Oh. There's a fascinating article this month about an operation for the removal of the frontal lobe. I'll lend it to you if you want to read it.'

'I wonder what a person is like after that?'

'From what I've read they're recognizably "normal". They do lose some – mental energy, I guess you could call it – desire to figure out new undertakings, and so on. But I guess that's better than the alternative.'

'Incredible! The whole business is, delving inside the brain.'

'Yes. I used to watch Dr Albeniz operate – It seemed almost magical to me.'

'Isn't he the one who wanted you to train with him?'

'Yes.'

'It's been horrible for you to give it up, hasn't it?'

'Well, not easy.'

He would have to stop thinking about it, learn to accept reality and cultivate patience. He'd never had much patience and that was another flaw in him.

'I'm sorry I brought it up just now,' Jessie said soberly.

'That's all right.'

'It's not all right. It's like taunting you with your impossible dream, and that's cruel.'

'I'm not the most deprived person in the world, after all.'

'No, but you are depressed more than you should be.'

Was it so evident then? And he was always so careful to be briskly cheerful!

'Oh, you don't show it. You needn't worry about that. But I've told you, I'm queer that way. I can sense hidden things in people.'

Astonishing girl! For it was true. Melancholy, sticky and grey as cobwebs, had been clinging to him.

'There's something I've been wanting to say to you, Martin. I haven't done it because you're so reserved and I – '

'Reserved? Is that how you see me?'

'Of course. Don't you even know that about yourself? What I wanted to say is: I hope you have no thought that I'm running after you.'

He was embarrassed. 'Of course not.'

'Most people wouldn't agree, but I always think that men and women can be good friends. So I just wanted to set you straight, in case you might be thinking I was fool enough to think otherwise. These last months have been wonderful for me. You understand?'

'I understand.'

The little car spun along. Jessie's keen face frowned on the road. Then she turned back to Martin.

'I've been wanting to ask you something else, too. Were you terribly in love with Fern?'

Ah, but this was too much!

'In love with her?' he answered curtly. 'I scarcely knew her!'

'There's no reason to be angry.'

'I'm not angry!'

'Offended, then. It was a natural question, wasn't it? Why all this so-called "tact" and secrecy?'

No matter how blunt or shocking, this outrageous girl would say it! Yet, he thought, I am a supersensitive cuss and I know I am; my pride will be my downfall.

Then Jessie said more softly, 'I'm sorry. I went too far just now. It's none of my business, after all.'

'But what made you think – '

'What made me? Because Fern is – Fern. If I hadn't had my own problems, I would have loved her myself.' Jessie sighed. 'As it is, I've almost hated her. I was rotten to her when we were children . . . Once I bloodied her nose, then when she hit me back they punished her, even though I'd started it. I have some mean memories, I can tell you.'

He began vaguely, 'Well, children – '

'Of course,' she interrupted, 'it's not bloody noses any more. It's just feelings. As if she could help the way she is any more than I can help the way I am! I've felt so guilty sometimes, I've been sick with it.'

He didn't want to listen. And he wondered whether this girl would be stripping herself before him if he hadn't been a doctor. People seemed to think that if you were a doctor you would welcome every possible confession.

'I've begrudged her very existence. Even her name, I've begrudged her that, too.'

'Her name?'

'Yes. It sounds so cool and full of grace. "Mary Fern". "I'm lovely," it says. "Mary Fern". While I, I'm "Jessie Gertrude". It's a black woollen-stocking's name. As if they took one look at me when I was born and gave me a name ugly enough to suit.'

Jessie shifted gears to climb a hill. Then she said, 'Fern's the total sentimentalist, you know.'

Martin didn't answer. Below them the valley spread its wide, green peace. Jessie was spoiling the afternoon.

'Mother worried so about her! She used to say Fern would rather *suffer* than destroy her idea of perfection. For instance, she would never get a divorce and come home if she were to make a bad marriage. That would be an admission of defeat. Did I tell you she's pregnant?'

'No.'

'They didn't lose any time, did they? But I'm glad for her, I really am. Alex is awfully nice; they've a marvellous house and a flat in London and he's really giving her encouragement with the art thing, for whatever it's worth. It should be a very good life for her at last, not having me to keep her from going places.'

'Don't dwell on that, Jessie. Things probably weren't nearly as bad as you're making them.'

'Yes, they were . . . You know, I've never told these things to anyone before. Do you think I'm a rotten, nasty person, Martin?'

'Of course I don't.'

'I swear to you that I really, deep inside me, want everything to be good for Fern. Do you believe me?'

'I believe you and I think you're wonderful,' he said gently. 'Even with that sharp tongue of yours.' He smiled. 'You're perceptive and honest. I'm glad I know you.'

She answered with untypical shyness, 'Are you? Then I'm glad, too, because it's the same for me.'

*

The second winter began. Still winters of the north! A branch cracks, snow sifts and falls sighing to the ground. For five months the ground is white and the spruce-covered hills are black. In the morning before you see it, you can smell the fresh snow that has fallen during the night. You hear the ringing silences of evening.

Martin's mother said suddenly, 'You ought to be married.'

A flush spread up her cheeks. She must have been thinking the words ever since they had left the supper table and not meant to speak them with such startling abruptness.

'There's no girl around that I want to marry.'

'You haven't tried to find one, have you? All you ever do is work or go to play chess with that Jessie Meig. It's no life for a young man.'

The telephone rang and Martin went to answer it. 'Hello?'

'This is Donald Meig. I was thinking maybe you could run over tonight. Can you? There's something I'd like to talk to you about.'

'Yes, surely, I'll be right over,' Martin said, with some surprise.

Half an hour later he was in the familiar library.

'Excuse us, Jessie, will you?' Meig said. 'I've a medical matter to discuss with Martin.' He closed the double doors firmly. 'Have a brandy. It'll warm you. You're wondering why I called you.'

Meig sighed, and Martin waited. 'You have problems. I have problems. Or I should say I have one problem. Yes. But I'd like to talk about yours first. I know you're not satisfied with your life here.'

Martin felt ashamed. Jessie must have talked, making him look like some sorry malcontent. So he defended himself.

'I feel I've been doing a fairly good job, learning practical things that I needed to know.'

Meig waved him aside. 'Nonsense! Platitudes! You're not the average run-of-the-mill country doctor, and we both know it. So let's get to the heart of the matter. You've had some spectacular offers.'

'One offer.'

'All right One spectacular offer. Jessie tells me it was the opportunity of a lifetime, and you've had to pass it up. Is that true?'

'True.'

'A damn shame! The door opened to the future and then shut in your face for want of a few dollars!'

'A great many dollars, I'm afraid.'

'All relative. What's a fortune to one man is pennies to the next. And compared with what you might earn if you could have this training, it actually is only a few dollars.'

Surely the man wasn't offering to lend him money? Martin felt a peculiar distaste.

'It's not because of the dollars, however many, that I would have taken the training,' he protested.

'I'm aware of that,' the other man said shortly. 'You've heard of Hugh Braidburn in London, the neurosurgeon?'

That was almost like asking whether one had heard of Darwin or Einstein! 'Of course. He's co-author of the textbook. Cox-Braidburn.'

'Well, I'm acquainted with him. His father-in-law was the head of our plant in Birmingham. We sold the plant about ten years back, but the contacts are still there. As a matter of fact, Braidburn had dinner with us on his last trip over just before my wife died.' Meig sipped the brandy thoughtfully, twirling the snifter, tilting the little amber lake. 'I could get any favour I asked him for.'

On a table behind the sofa stood a photograph that Martin had never seen before. Framed in silver, Mary held an armful of calla lilies, a lace veil swirling to her feet. He tried to decipher her expression but could see only the calm, reflective smile of the traditional bridal picture.

'I said,' Meig demanded, 'what do you think of the idea?'

'Excuse me. I wasn't – I didn't quite understand.'

'Good God, man, pay attention! I asked you how you'd like to spend a couple of years in London studying with Braidburn.'

What sort of a charade was this? To study with Braidburn? Why, even Dr Albeniz would be awed at the thought of it!

'Like it, Mr Meig? It would be – it would be paradise! But it's impossible!'

Meig laughed. It struck Martin that he had never seen the man laugh until now, hadn't ever seen his teeth.

'It's not impossible at all. I told you I could get any favour I asked him for.'

Yes, yes, Martin thought, I suppose people like these always do know somebody who will do them a favour. It's a chain, a network all over the world. If I had a voice and wanted to study for the opera, he'd know the best voice teacher in Italy, one who didn't take any more pupils, but he'd take me. And he became aware that his heart was beating very fast.

Meig leaned forward now, lowering his voice. 'Of course, I can't expect you to understand without giving you the whole story. So now let's go to my problem. I have angina.'

'I'm sorry. I didn't know.'

'Nobody does. I go to a doctor in Albany because I don't want anyone around here to find out. Most especially not Jessie. I mustn't frighten her.'

'If you'll excuse me, do you think that's wise? If anything were to happen to you, it would be harder for her not to have been prepared, and Jessie is nothing if not a realist.'

'You know her rather well, then.'

'We've had a lot of talks this past summer and fall. I can tell you I think she can cope with things far better than most of us.'

'She's a bright girl. Both my girls are. They're like their mother. Soft, too. Especially Fern. Curious about everything. Music. Pictures. Books. Jessie's got all that but not as soft. She's got a little of me in her.'

Jessie would be amused to hear that. 'Father's a Babbitt,' she'd told Martin once, not unkindly. 'He calls Uncle Drew "arty" because he collects books, although he does make allowances since Uncle Drew is rich, after all.'

Now Meig looked away at a point on the wall above Martin's head. 'Damned injustice! My wife never drew a happy breath after Jessie was born.' He looked back at Martin. 'It's been hard, all around, very hard. We weren't always fair to Fern, either, I suppose, keeping her away from lively places where young people meet each other. But we were always torn between her and what was best for Jessie.'

Martin moved restlessly. All of a sudden, it seemed to suit this cool and haughty man to confide in him! All of a sudden, and why? And what did it have to do with neurosurgery in London?

'Now let me tie all this together. I have angina, I have a daughter who will be alone in the world on the day I die. Fern has a life of her own now in England, and there are a couple of relatives in New York who also have their own lives. So what's to become of Jessie? That, young man, is my problem.'

Martin was silent.

'When I'm gone and she's lonely, some clever operator will think she has millions, which she hasn't, and he'll marry her. After a while he'll leave her. Oh, there's little you can tell me about the world! I've seen it all.' Meig stood up, poured more brandy and sat down again. 'If I could only see her well and wisely married before I die – Marriage used to be, and in Europe among some groups even today, still is, a family contract. It's a sound, planned arrangement involving friendship and mutual interests. And that's not bad as a foundation, when you consider it carefully.'

Was it possible he was going to say what Martin thought he might be going to say?

'Well, I've turned this over and over in my mind for a hundred hours, and I want to make an honest proposition.' Meig took a deep breath. 'Marry Jessie.'

Martin felt his mouth drop open.

'I'll see to it that you get the best medical training in the world. I'll subsidize you until you can support yourself. And I'll give you enough to maintain your mother. She won't have to know it comes from me. She can think you're getting paid over there and it'll save her pride. I understand all about pride, you see. Yes, marry Jessie, and make a life for yourself.'

One couldn't just get up and stalk out of a man's house.

One couldn't tell him he was out of his mind. Martin was stunned.

'You don't have to give me your answer now. Think it over. Take plenty of time. On second thought, not plenty, because I don't know how much time I've got, and I'd like to close my eyes knowing that she's cared for and protected by a man of decent character. I'm a keen judge of people, and I would put my life's savings on this table in front of you and leave the room.'

'I appreciate that, Mr Meig. But I have to tell you that I hadn't thought of marriage for years yet. As you say, I am – at least I hope I am – a responsible man, and marriage isn't something that one just – '

'Martin, let's do without diplomacy, shall we? This is a time for plain talk. You're thinking, and I don't blame you, that Jessie Meig isn't precisely what you had in mind when you thought of choosing a wife. I'd be a fool if I didn't know that! But I also know, and you do too, that burning love affairs usually go up in smoke anyway. Look at the divorce rates if you don't believe me! Now, Jessie is an unusual human being. You've said so yourself. She's intelligent, she's good company and she thinks the world of you. Anybody can see she does. She'd be a trusted companion all your life.' He paused. 'And she'd have reason to be grateful to you.'

Martin winced and Meig saw it.

'Yes, I did say "grateful"! What's wrong? But you'd be grateful to her, too, wouldn't you? Because without her you'd spend the rest of your life here, going to waste.'

Martin stood up to get his coat.

'Will you at least think about it?'

'I understand what you've said, Mr Meig, but – '

Meig waved him aside. 'Your impulse is to say "no, absolutely no". You think if you accept, you'll be selling yourself. Dishonouring yourself. Isn't that so?'

'I feel – ' Martin began and was interrupted again.

Behind the strict, rimless glasses the eyes were shrewd. 'Sentimentality, Martin, sentimentality!'

Martin had one foot out of the door.

'Of course she doesn't have the remotest idea of what I've

been saying and must never find out, whatever you decide.'

Martin was horrified. 'No need to worry about that!'

'Very well, then. Just give it some thought, that's all I ask.'

It was such a cold night that, unless you knew better, you could lose an earlobe. In spite of the arctic air and all the layers of woollen cloth that he was wearing, Martin sweated. The shame of it! He looked back at the house, wondering which of the second-storey lights came from Jessie's room. And with flashing insight, he thought he could feel how it would be for her, proud as she was, if she could know what had just passed between her father and himself.

The proposition was, of course, unthinkable. Yet it had been well-intentioned, born of desperation. That this arrogant, private man should have revealed himself like that to a stranger! What must he not have seen in that stranger? Ambition, obviously, but much more also: loyalty and kindness and honour. No question about that. He trusts me, Martin thought. Then his thoughts veered.

He dares to think I can be bribed!

Don't be a pompous ass, Martin; he didn't mean it that way!

It's a bribe, all the same!

He's terrified and wants to see his house in order. A human being has revealed his sorrow before you, Martin!

But the thing's impossible. And now a fine friendship has been spoiled for good. How can I feel free in that house any more?

It was the most weird encounter, weird and sad! The wind rushed and the night was inexpressibly lonely. The planet was small and shrivelled with the cold. And he went to bed thinking of loneliness.

For two weeks he stayed away. Then it occurred to him that such an abrupt disappearance would be a cruel hurt to Jessie. And indeed, it had been.

'I thought maybe my father had made you angry the last time you were here,' she said, looking anxious.

'No. Why should you think that?'

'Because he can be so superior and cold. He antagonizes people.'

'Well, he wasn't. Anyway, I don't antagonize so easily.'

'That's not true. The truth is exactly the opposite.'

'You're right, as usual,' he admitted, and she laughed.

Seated as usual in the great wing chair, with her cheeks gone pink from the fire's heat, and the pinpoint sparks of gold in her eyes, she could have been so lovely! If only – And he wondered whether anyone would ever marry her. Would anyone ever love her? Respect, admiration, companionship – these would come easily in all the virtuous ways through which human beings relate to one another. And surely even tenderness could come. But love?

She said softly, 'You're very quiet, Martin.'

'Sorry. I didn't mean to be.' He brought himself back into the moment. 'By the way, I finished *Main Street*. I meant to return it tonight, but I forgot to bring it.'

'Did you like it?'

'Yes. It has the ring of truth. Depressing truth.'

'I've something else for you, quite different.' She ran across the room to the shelves. She always ran. Did she think it made her less visible to run?

'Here. It's Roland's *Jean Christophe*, a beautiful story of a musician in Paris. Especially good for you.'

'Why for me?'

'Because it's a story of a struggle. Always, even when he was a child, he knew he was going to be a composer, a great one. He faced everything – loneliness, poverty, rivalry; but he never gave up.'

'And did he win in the end?'

'Read it.' She forced his eyes to meet her own. 'You're a tenacious man, you know? You'll get what you want. I feel it in you.'

A sudden brightness came into the little face, a fervour so glowing that it seemed he was seeing past the frail barrier of her forehead, seeing deep into her with shocking clarity.

She loved him.

Good God! He hadn't intended that! Hadn't intended to weaken or mislead this vulnerable small girl! What had he done? How had this come to be? Clumsily he flipped the pages of the book she had put into his hands.

'Seems like something I'll hate to put down,' he said.

'Yes.'

Did he deserve to feel such guilt and shame? Truly he hadn't been aware that this was happening. Nor perhaps had she. Well, it would have to be stopped, that was all. Brought abruptly to a halt before any more damage was done.

He simply wouldn't come here again.

And swiftly, with such grace as he could summon, he escaped from the house.

There are days on which troubles accumulate and peak. One oversleeps and there is no time for breakfast. One is late for the first appointment and for all the others after that. It rains on the wet snow; then the rain turns to sleet and the roads turn to ice. It is March and one is sick of winter, but there are weeks and weeks of it still ahead.

The office was crowded all the morning with coughs, sore throats and a rampant case of measles that should have stayed home instead of polluting the waiting room.

The last case in the afternoon would have broken Martin's heart if he had allowed it to. Elsie Briggs was thirty-four, unmarried and the youngest of a large family. Hers was the old story of the daughter who stayed home to take care of her parents, wearing herself out for the senile and incontinent, locking herself away from life behind four dismal walls. And Elsie Briggs was finally breaking down. They would be taking her to the state hospital on Friday because there was nothing else to do with her. There was no out-patient care; there was no place other than the bleak state institution. Martin shuddered. In this mood he closed the office for the day and went to the car.

Ordinarily, he would not have answered a summons fifteen miles north in the mountains, especially in weather like this. But these were old patients who had bought a remote farm and moved away. Their parents had been his father's patients. Pa would have gone, he told himself grimly.

Sliding and struggling up the hills, each one more steep than the last, the flimsy car shook through fierce crosswinds. The windshield wipers clacked. All was grey: dim fields, grey air, steady snow. After two miserable hours, he pulled into a yard to find what he had expected: unpainted boards, a ramshackle porch, no light poles. If anybody needed cutting or stitching he would turn the car to let the headlights shine into the room. Rural poverty like this in the twentieth century!

In the bare kitchen stood a huddle of five runny-nosed babies and a thin mother, terrified because her husband was sick. Who was to tend to the man's work?

The man had pneumonia. Martin left medicines and a sheet of instructions.

'Keep taking his temperature regularly,' he told the woman. 'Can you get out to a phone to call me tomorrow?'

She was concerned about his bill. 'I can't give you anything now, Doctor, but I'll be at my sister's right near your place in a couple of weeks. I'll bring it then.'

'Don't worry about it,' he said gently, knowing quite well that he would never be paid, knowing also that he wouldn't want to be paid. For who could touch dollars that would deprive these children of something they needed? And heaven knew, they must need everything from oranges to shoes!

So he left to slide and slip, downhill this time, the fifteen miles homeward. In the city or under some better system – though God knows what system in places as remote as these – this patient would be taken care of in the hospital. At least, somebody would see him tomorrow. In this weather he surely couldn't get back soon enough. And this frustration, along with so many others, nagged him as he drove.

I don't know anything. I'm not an expert obstetrician, cardiologist or orthopaedic surgeon. I'm not an expert anything. That arm of Wagnall's that I set last week wasn't done right. I know it wasn't.

My father's kind hands lay folded over his black vest in the coffin. He gave the best care he could. He tried. My God, he did! And that's better than nothing, better than no care at all! A man has to be satisfied with it. My father was satisfied.

Quite without warning, not fifty feet ahead of the car, a

tremendous limb, almost a quarter of a giant elm, split from the weight of ice and crashed on the road. In pounding panic, Martin swerved. If he'd been a few feet further along, all his problems would be over! And he laughed at his own macabre humour. Indifferent nature! Savage world!

The wind whipped the trees as he carefully skirted his near-disaster. March was the most dismal month of all. Yet his father had loved it, had liked to talk of the stately cycle of the year, its rhythm and its grandeur. The road curved around the lip of a plateau from which, through beating snow, he could see a spread of white fields and hills, folding back to the mountains out of which he had just come. Grand, yes! Eternal. Majestic. All the orotund words. A man might well stand in awe of it. He understood that deeply. But everybody wasn't meant for it, and he hated it, hated the loneliness, the monotony, the awful cold. He had never said it aloud before, but he said it now.

'I hate it.'

And he could have wept.

Six miles from home in sleet as slippery as grease, the car slid off the road. He swore, then rocked the car, trying to get traction. He revved the engine over and over, to no avail. At last he got out. It was so cold, thirty below he'd guess, that his lungs burned with the small pain of each indrawn breath. The hairs prickled in his nostrils. Taking the shovel from the back seat, he tried to dig. The snow was so hard that the tip of the shovel bent backwards. He sighed.

'Goddamned junky old car! Goddamned winter!'

Suddenly recalling Pa's advice, he got the burlap from under the front seat and placed it beneath the rear wheels. Then he started the engine. It roared and whined. The wheels spun furiously. It's rubbing the tyres to a thread, Martin thought. But at last they caught hold and the car lurched back on to the road.

When he crept into the yard an hour later, the house was dark and he remembered that his mother had gone to an afternoon at the church, followed by a supper. She had left his meal on the coal stove in a covered dish. It was stone cold. Then he saw that the kitchen fire was out. The house smelled dank and musty. He ran down to the cellar where the furnace stood like a hungry monster beside a hill of glossy coal and flung the door open.

There was no fire here, either. The monster hadn't been fed and ashes were thick in the grate.

Blasted boy! His mother had arranged with Artie Grant to tend the fires today while she was gone, but obviously he hadn't come. He went back upstairs to the rear porch for kindling wood. Each ice-encrusted piece had to be dislodged by sheer force. Now, back to the cellar with newspapers and matches. But first the ashes must be cleaned out. Martin's head pounded as dust from the ashes set off a fit of coughing. He sweated and shivered, shovelling the ashes out, then shovelling the coal in. Last he shook down the grates, making a lonely rattle in the empty house. From the head of the stairs the collies stood observing him, while he watched the fire take hold.

Finished in the cellar, he went back up to the kitchen. His mother had just come home. For an instant she was framed in the doorway, her pretty eyes anxious. She wore her old, black 'good' coat; the black feather on her hat was turning green. Humble. That's how she looks, he thought. Mean word. Humble.

'Goodness, look at you! You're all over ashes!' she cried.

'Yes. Where in blazes was Artie Grant?'

'He's usually so dependable! I guess the weather was just too bad for him to get here.'

'It was, was it!' Martin was furious. 'Wasn't too bad for me, though! I only travelled thirty miles round trip to Danielsville and back!'

'Martin,' his mother said mildly. 'Martin, you're tired and hungry.'

'Of course I am. Why not?' After a day like this one, was it too much to ask for a house that was warm so that you could at least rest when you came in?

When his supper was ready Ma sat down in the rocker near the table. 'That shutter keeps banging. Hear it? The hinge is loose. If I get a new hinge, will you put it on some time?' And without waiting for him to answer. 'Your father never cared about things like that. Never cared about things at all, you might say. The world of ideas, that's what he lived in, all that he cared about,' she reflected, sighing a little. The light fell over her head, over a smooth streak of grey that lay like a ribbon on her still-dark hair. She was talkative tonight. 'Yes, he was a student of the world. He read everything. I'm sorry I never had much time, and now it seems to be too late. I'm out of the habit of reading.' She rocked: creak, creak. 'Anyway, I would never have been like him. I do like things so much. I like *having* things. You never knew that about me, did you?' she asked shyly, as if she were making some astounding confession.

'It's no sin to like things, Ma.'

'Do you know where I always wanted most to go? I used to wish I could go to Washington, to see the Lincoln Memorial and the Capital and all that. But we could never seem to get away.'

'You could go now. It's outrageous that you should have to think twice about having such a small pleasure.'

'More than twice. We don't have the money to spare. You'll be needing a new car by summer. It's a wonder this one has lasted as long as it has.'

Never in all the years Martin had known his mother had she expressed any desires. It hurt him now to hear her. Yes, and made him strangely angry, too. He felt a whole jumble of restless feelings.

'Your father was so content. He'd sit here rocking by the stove when the front room was too cold to go over his records, and he never complained. Sometimes he'd read aloud about places far away. Places like Afghanistan or the Amazon. And I'd ask him, "Don't you wish we could go there?" "I am there in my mind," he'd answer.'

'I'm not like him,' Martin said.

'That's true. I've never known anyone like him.'

In the hall the old clock struck with a tinny bong. Ashes tinkled in the stove. His mother coughed, a thick phlegmy cough that she hadn't been able to get rid of all winter. It wasn't her fault, surely, but it was exasperating. And he had a sudden projection of himself on long, dull, winter nights like this one, sitting in a shabby room like this one with a faceless woman: not his mother, of course, but a woman who would be his wife, since inevitably a man acquired a wife.

The future was a dull road going endlessly uphill, downhill, uphill, stretched through an unchanging landscape; at last, when one no longer hoped for any change, one would come to the last hill and just drop quietly off into the unknown. Life would have passed, never having counted for very much, or not what one wanted it to count for, at any rate. It would have gone by without colour, without sparkle or aim.

But all the time, in other places, some men would have been doing what they wanted to do! They learned, they lived, they moved ahead! And there came again that old sense of rushing time which had haunted and beset him since adolescence. He was already twenty-eight! Without meaning to, he smashed a fist into his palm and sprang up as if he had been shot. There was such tension in his solar plexus that he had to move, he had to –

His mother looked up. 'Where're you going?'

'I don't know. Just out.'

'In this weather?' For it had begun to sleet again.

'I've been in it all day. I'm used to it.'

'Oh, I forgot to tell you. While you were down cellar, Jessie Meig telephoned. Odd for a girl to telephone a young man, don't you think so?'

'No. Just natural and honest.'

'Her sister didn't do it, did she?'

No, Martin thought, she never did.

'It's not even very clever, if you ask me. She must be a strange girl, that Jessie Meig.'

'Why do you always say "that Jessie Meig" as though you had something against her?'

'How could I have anything against her? I don't even know her.'

'You know she's crippled, and that's what you've got against her.'

'Martin, I don't understand you sometimes! You're so

blunt and bluff lately, so outspoken! You've no tact any more.'

'I'm outspoken, I'll admit.' It came to him that indeed he was more candid than he used to be, that he had learned it for good or ill from Jessie. 'Say what you mean and mean what you say. What's wrong with that?'

'Very well, then. I can't for the life of me understand what you can see in a poor, crippled girl. It's pitiful, of course it is, but here you are, a tall strapping fellow, and you could get any girl you wanted if you set your mind to it.'

'I've told you, Ma. She's a friend, one of the best I've ever had outside of Tom, and there are things she understands about me that even Tom doesn't. How she's managed to know so much about the world, living the way she has, I have no idea. And I like being with her. What more can I say?'

His mother looked surprised. 'Why nothing more, I should think.'

And he went on, vehemently, 'Because she has a few misshapen bones, is she any less a woman? Is she to be put away as damaged goods, returned to the manufacturer, because of that?'

His mother was silent.

'By the way, what did she want?'

'Just to know why you'd been staying away and whether you might want to come over this evening.'

Twenty minutes later Martin stood in the Meigs' library. It went very quickly. His mind had simply made itself up, and he didn't have to think about words. The father grasped Martin's two hands in both of his.

'You won't be sorry. It's probably the wisest decision you'll ever make.' There were tears in his eyes and at that moment Martin began to like him. 'God bless you both.'

Jessie's answer to his question was surprisingly calm.

'Are you sure you know what you're doing?'

'I'm sure.'

'Because I don't want to be an albatross around your neck. I couldn't bear it.'

'You will never be that, I promise!'

She had a pretty mouth and when she smiled, two charming dimples appeared at the corners. Taking her face between his hands he kissed her gently.

'I'll make life good for you,' he said.

He meant it, with all his heart.

BOOK TWO

THE WEB

CHAPTER EIGHT

Fern always teased Alex that she had married him because she loved his house.

'Well, naturally,' he would answer, 'how could anyone help but fall in love with Lamb House?'

Among its oaks and orchards it lay as though, like them, it had been planted there; so far-sighted had they been, those Elizabethans with a sense of home and long generations.

Through diamond-paned casements one looked south towards the village of Great Barrow. Little Barrow lay three miles to the west. On the tilted slope above the valley, pear trees flowered and the hills rolled back into a haze.

Fern turned from the easel. The spaniels, sprawled with noses to the grass, raised their heads in question. They had followed her across the Atlantic and shadowed every move she made.

'No,' she told them, 'I'm not finished yet.'

And she raised her eyes to the living picture beyond the easel. In the upper left-hand corner lay a green square dotted with pinpoints of white which seemed scarcely to move, although they were live sheep on the Ballister farm. Everything was small and perfect, as in a meticulous Book of Hours. The valley was the merest hollow in the swell of the land.

'As if God's finger touched, but did not press, in making England,' she said aloud, and was pleased with herself for quoting Elizabeth Barrett Browning. She had been studying the English poets from Chaucer to Eliot, for if one were going to live in a country, she believed, one ought to know its poets.

'Now that I know you well enough, I'll confess,' Alex's mother had told her only a few weeks before. 'I wasn't very happy about having an American daughter-in-law. So many American girls are simply not ladies; I can't help saying it. But you are, and so very charming, Fern! Everyone says so.'

They had been standing in the upstairs hall, which, like the great one downstairs, was blazoned with family portraits: squires in eighteenth-century breeches and lace cuffs, clerics in grim black, an admiral with a three-cornered hat, two cabinet members – Tory, nineteenth-century – and over one fireplace, the original Elizabethan with beefy face and sleepy eyes to whom this manor had been given for favours rendered the Crown somewhere in the West Indies. They were all Lambs.

Alex's mother came from a decent undistinguished family of school teachers.

'Naturally,' Alex said with some amusement but no unkind- ness, 'all this ancestor business means more to her.' His late father, though, had been bored and sometimes irreverent about it.

On a table in the angle of the stairwell stood a group of photographs in silver frames.

'That, of course, is Edward the Seventh as Prince of Wales,' the elder Mrs Lamb had informed the younger.

Fern had dutifully bent to read the scrawled inscription.

'My husband often went on shooting parties in Scotland with His Royal Highness.'

'Went whoring with His Royal Highness too, I'll wager,' Alex had remarked in private.

'I had this photo of Susannah put up here in the hall while you and Alex were on your wedding trip. It used to stand on the piano in the drawing-room, but I should think that too conspicuous, not fitting, now that Alex has married you.'

Fern had murmured that she wouldn't have minded, which was true. She felt no jealousy, although her mother-in-law apparently expected her to. The girl was dead, after all. Here she sat for all time in her patrician simplicity with hands on lap and a pearl rope looped around the little finger. The one memorable feature of her neat face was a timid expression in the prominent eyes. Could she perhaps have had some foreboding that she was going to die and leave her week-old boy?

'To tell the truth, I was never very happy about Susannah, although she was English to the bone.'

Perhaps she had only been intimidated by this mother-in-law!

'You are far prettier, you know.'

What an unnecessary, heartless thing to say!

'It's a good thing Neddie has no idea about his mother.'

'He'll have to be told I'm not his mother.'

'Why, yes, some time, of course. But he does love you, Fern.'

'And I adore him.'

Sometimes there is immediate bonding between two human beings. It has no connection at all with age or circumstance. It is simply there.

'You've handled him splendidly, everyone says so.'

She knew it was said she was 'marvellous with Neddie', making no difference between him and her 'own' infant girl. They didn't understand. Neddie *was* her 'own'.

'He's not been jealous of the baby at all! Usually they carry on dreadfully when a new baby comes into the house, or so I hear. Unfortunately, I never had more than one. You're sure you're not rushing things in that respect, Fern?' This last had been spoken with a glance, a light progression of the eye as it blinks in its rhythm and recovers from the blink, towards the mid-section of Fern's body, where the new swelling was just barely visible. 'After all, Emmy's not a year yet.'

'The doctor says I'm quite healthy.'

Fern's own patience surprised her. Two years ago she would have had to swallow exasperation; now she was learning to see beneath the surface of people and things. Behind this pallid face with its indrawn lips, behind the accent – which, even here in England, was a fairly blatant imitation of the royal family's accent – she saw a lonely woman who had striven foolishly all her life.

So she said gently, 'If this one's a boy, we shall name him Alex, of course. Will he be the fifth or the sixth?'

'He will be the sixth Alexander Lamb. Should you want

me to come a week or two ahead of time to plan for the christening, I'm sure I'll be able to manage it. And I can stay on afterwards, as long as you like.'

Poor soul! She was waiting to be invited to live with them at Lamb House. But that, Fern thought, I will not do. She's perfectly well-housed at Torquay with all the other prosperous widows. No, that I will certainly not do.

'You know,' Mrs Lamb had complained, 'it's Neddie who should have borne the name. Don't you think it's disgraceful that Susannah insisted on naming him for her father? True, her father had died that year, but even so, the first-born son should be named after his father.'

'Well, anyway, he looks like Alex,' Fern had assured her, although it was probably not true. Neddie would be narrower and darker than Alex. But it was what the older woman wanted to hear.

Pregnancy, like love, she thought, can be calming to the nerves. The doctor said some women became euphoric. This inner radiance then, this vitality and warm contentment with her own body, the home and the people who surrounded her – this must be euphoria. And, taking up the brush, she corrected some greens with a stipling of gilt where the sun had glazed them.

A little group came in sight around the corner of the house: Neddie, running ahead of the nurse who was pushing Emmy in the perambulator. Fern held out her arms and the little boy ran into them. She put her face down on his crisp hair which smelled of pine shampoo. It pleased her that this child who had been shy with strangers had so readily accepted her and loved her.

He wiggled free.

'Shall we have music again, Mummy?' he asked.

'Mummy's busy,' Nanny Hull admonished.

'Later this afternoon, darling. We'll put a record on.'

'The singing man?'

She laughed. 'Yes, yes, the singing man.'

Neddie had come into the room when Alex had a Caruso recording on the phonograph. Without making a sound, he had sat down to listen, and then had waited while Alex wound the phonograph again to repeat it.

'And will I have yellow cake, too?'

There had been a cake with yellow icing that day, and now they were turning into a ritual, the singing man and the cake.

'You'll have cake, if you promise to eat your supper. You mustn't stuff on sweets,' Nanny said.

'Of course he mustn't.'

The baby Emmy was asleep. She was blonde and already long for her age. She would be large-boned, as if she belonged entirely to Alex and not at all to her mother. With curiosity Fern touched the pink hand that lay curled like a shell on the blanket. I don't know her yet, she thought. Everything is closed up, a gift in a glossy box. It is delivered at the door, and one can only guess what is possibly inside. But it is all there, and there's little we can change.

Still, at the same time, we could teach her anything, couldn't we? Mandarin Chinese, if we wanted to, instead of English? Everything is so confusing. I feel light-headed.

'Have you had a bit too much of the sun, ma'am? If you don't mind my saying so, you ought to put up your work for a while today. You've been at it since noon.'

The woman spoke considerately and probably sincerely, except for her use of the word 'work'. She couldn't possibly conceive of what Fern did as 'work'.

'Yes, thank you, Nanny. Perhaps I shall.'

'It's fearful hot today.'

Funny what the English called fearful heat! It couldn't be more than eighty. Still, she obeyed, as Nanny drew the wicker lounge chair into the shade and plumped the cushions.

'There you are! A nice bit of nap will do you good. I'm to take Neddie down to his pony and he'll go for a ride with Mr Lamb.'

Fern closed her eyes, letting the drowsiness of pregnancy have its way. She was so catered to, so loved and cared for! How many women with two children had leisure to go all deliciously relaxed and limp? One could feel so guilty thinking about one's unearned privileges.

Old Carfax, stirring in the perennial border, struck a stone with his hoe. He was being careful not to wake her. He was a wiry little man, pasty-skinned in spite of a life out in the weather. For thirty years he had been tending this garden: it was an extension of his back, of his roped and sinewy arms.

Fern opened her eyes just as he stooped to remove a thread of weed which would have marred the perfection of the rosebeds. She watched him move on through the perennials: violet steeples of campanula, gold coreopsis, dusty dark-blue globes of echinops. Fragrance of stock and musky spice of phlox hung in the sweet air. Behind the border stood a solid wall of yews, still wet with last night's rain.

'The yews are as old as the house,' Alex had told her the first time he had brought her here. 'We've a priest's hole on the third floor behind a false wall. I'll show you. Part of the family was Catholic, you know, but it got to be too dangerous for them, I suppose, and we've all been C of E for two hundred years at least. They also say Cromwell slept here, but I don't know whether that's true.'

'It's like all those houses at home, where Washington's supposed to have slept while he was chasing you or you were chasing him.'

They had been sitting on the stone bench, the one where Carfax had just now set a flat of Michaelmas daisies. They'd sat there talking for an hour or more, then quite suddenly Alex had asked her to marry him and as suddenly she had accepted.

Yet they had really been leading up to that moment from the time they had been introduced in the winter. Aunt Milly had pursued her purpose with utmost tact, to be sure! And ordinarily Fern would have been outraged by any such 'scheme', but because she herself was so strongly drawn to Alex, she hadn't objected.

He was delightful. It was, quite simply, good to be with him. It was heartening – was that the right word? Yes, heartening was a very good word, she decided. There was a kind of crinkling good nature in his face even when he was being earnest, and she had told him so. She was not used to men who laughed. Certainly Father had done very little laughing!

He had a fine curiosity about practically everything. At dinner he could listen to Uncle Drew's talk of securities and German reparations. He could ask pertinent questions of a guest concerning blight-resistant roses. With a cricketer he talked scores and plays. One felt that he could manage anything. And he had a certain reserve; Fern was comfortable with that. Travelling through Europe, she had had to fend off too many young men on dark hotel terraces. To a girl whose life had been unusually reclusive, that sort of thing could be flattering at first, but after a while one got tired of having to decide between accepting sticky kisses when one felt nothing for the man or, by resisting, risk being labelled 'prig'. But Alex had been satisfied to go slowly, sensing her wish to feel the way, to move as a river flows, deepening to the place where all the streams gather in a final rush, which would be the more marvellous for having come gradually.

So she had read, and so she believed.

Obviously he was affected by his responsibilities. He had inherited a substantial business in maritime insurance; but unlike many young heirs he had not turned it over to managers; he ran it himself. The greater responsibility, of course, was to his child.

She remembered the day he had first brought Neddie to the hotel. They had been on the way to the zoo. She had opened the door and there they had stood, the tall man and Neddie, who was just two. She had knelt, putting out her arms, and the little boy had come quite willingly, while she murmured the things adults do.

'What a fine big boy you are! And is this your bear? How are you, Toby Bear?'

She had been fourteen, almost grown, when her mother died. The loss had seemed to mark her more than any other happening in her life until then, and perhaps that was why she had been so moved by Alex's child, when he put his hand in hers.

'Strange,' Alex said. 'He's usually quite timid with people he doesn't know.'

Alex's eyes had been very soft and in that instant Fern had known he could be trusted.

All during the late winter and early spring they saw London together. Alex had friends in a variety of circles: business, music, society and art. They ate with a pair of school teachers in Soho and dined at Claridge's before the opera. They walked in the parks and on streets which Fern had visited with Jane Austen, with Thackeray and Galsworthy. And, as so many Americans do, she fell in love with the grand, old, mellow city.

In a mews near Curzon Street Alex had a flat furnished, as she was later to learn, like Lamb House. Oak and yew were seventeenth-century; mahogany was eighteenth-century; the landscapes were nineteenth-century. Here was the progression of the family, marching through history.

Alex had discerning taste. She told him he ought to be in some business having to do with the arts – antiques or a picture gallery. He had been pleased.

'But maritime insurance is more lucrative. I can always buy art. Some day I'll be buying a Meig, you know.'

'You've never seen any of my work. How can you say that?' she had replied.

'Just a feeling I have about you.'

They had been having dinner at the flat, so he was a host being courteous and that was all. Yet she could remember everything that had been said.

She had sighed. 'I'm so confused in my mind. I wish I knew whether I had any potential.'

'There's only one way to find out. By doing. It's a shame you haven't had more encouragement.'

'More? I've had none at all.'

Except for Martin Farrell's. He, admittedly knowing nothing about art, had nevertheless urged her to struggle on. And sitting there across the table from Alex, she had become aware of the letter in her purse which had arrived from Martin just that morning.

It had been written in a state of joyous excitement. She, with her own hopes, had understood that a door had been flung open for him, a wide and generous entrance to the future! And she was very, very glad for him.

But there had also been a faint sense of shame. She had

thought, all the weeks of that hot, lovely summer in Cyprus and especially on the last night, that something was growing – that given time, perhaps when she came home . . . She had obviously been mistaken. Three years of further study! Very likely he wouldn't marry until long after that.

Women, herself included, tended to be foolish about doctors, as about pianists or romantic actors, whom young girls pursue and old ladies adore.

Foolish. Foolish.

'London suits you,' Alex had remarked abruptly.

And looking out at the shine of the expensive street, she had reminded him: 'I'm also a country person.'

'What you need,' he'd said, 'is to have a home in a quiet country place where you can paint, yet be near enough to the city for first-rate classes.'

And he had reached across the table to press her hand.

Not long afterwards they had driven to his village. It had a cobbled High Street, a chemist's and tobacconist's and an ancient church.

'There's where the Lambs are christened, married and buried. That's the lichgate. They used to rest the bier there, but now we trim it with white flowers for brides. There's the riding club where I keep three horses. It's only a stone's throw from home, and it's just as easy to stable them there. Do you ride? Yes? Oh, there's nothinglike riding just after dawn when everyone but birds and roosters is still asleep!'

So they had rounded the corner of the lane and come upon the house, drowsing in hazy, filtered light. There it lay, sturdy, secure and most of all so brightly cheerful. It seemed like a place Fern had always known. It seemed as if there could be no deeper joy than to stay here with this gentle, loving man, in this golden peace.

Promptly then, cablegrams went out to Father and Jessie at home. Letters went back and forth across the ocean. Lists were written and arrangements made. Aunt Milly rejoiced. Alex's mother rejoiced. An engagement solitaire was bought at Asprey's.

Fern sent instructions home. Father must bring the photograph of Mother in her room. They must crate and ship her books and all her paintings. They were to bring the sterling which had been put aside for her, Tiffany's *Audubon Birds*. ('Animals, naturally,' Jessie had remarked, with her usual tart humour, which happened to be accurate, for Fern had also asked them to bring along her collection of dog etchings as well as the two spaniels, who would have to remain for six whole months in quarantine.)

The wedding was held at Lamb House. Just as Alex had said, the lichgate had been trimmed with white flowers. They had ridden back from the church in a carriage, also decked with flowers. Neddie had worn a powder-blue velvet suit and had his picture taken with the bride and groom, while old ladies wiped their tears.

Everyone in the village had been invited. There was champagne for all in the great courtyard square and there was dancing indoors under the enormous chandeliers. The dining hall was illuminated by silver candelabra as tall as a man. The vermeil dinner service, taken from the vault for the occasion, glittered between bowls of old Carfax's prize roses in bridal pink and cream.

'Positively medieval,' Jessie remarked. 'I didn't think they still did this sort of thing.' Then more softly, she said, 'But it was beautiful, Fern, and I shall want all your photos to remember it by.'

The honeymoon was a voyage to India. For Fern Meig, who had never been anywhere and had so longed to go 'beyond', the very thought had been intoxicating. In the eyes and ears of her mind she saw and smelled enchantment: red lacquer, gold thread, frangipani and patchouli, jasmine, burn and blaze.

Unfortunately, Alex had been seasick most of the time. She had felt sorry for him, not only on account of his physical misery, but because she saw he was humiliated.

Then at the end of the sixth week, she too became a victim, but for a different reason: she was pregnant. It must have happened almost immediately, on the night they spent ashore at Gibralter, visiting some friends of Alex's father. That, and the few other nights they had slept on land, had been the only normal ones on the trip. So it had been rather a queer honeymoon! Poor Alex! Thank goodness, though, for his sense of humour; he had finally been able to make a rueful joke of it.

Now, with Emmy not yet old enough to walk, she was pregnant again, and still having spells of nausea, so that on many nights she had to disappoint him. But he was considerate and patient. Not all men were, she knew.

He was patient in other ways, as well. He had taught her how to run the unfamiliar household. He had taught her about bills and bank accounts, things difficult enough to master in a strange currency, especially hard for her who had never handled money at all. He'd been so good about all that! And so good about her work. True to his promise he had arranged for the best classes in the city, in particular an outstanding class in oils with Antonescu. For the first time she had been able to feel she was learning.

'Well, how are you doing?' Alex came round the house and laid a hand on her shoulder.

'Painting or stomach, do you mean?'

'Both.'

'Stomach's queasy unless I remember to keep a sweet cracker in my pocket.'

'Biscuit.'

'Well, some day I will remember to call a cracker a biscuit. I promise. How was the ride?'

'Marvellous. After this baby we'll go every morning when I'm home. And when I'm in London you should go with Daisy or Nora or somebody. I took your mare out just now for exercise. I'm rather too heavy for her, though.'

There wasn't an ounce of extra weight on Alex. He glows, she thought; from his boots to his bright hair and outdoor skin, he shines as if he had been gilded.

'We'll make a rider out of Neddie, too. You should have seen him on his pony this afternoon.'

'He wasn't scared at all? He's only four, Alex!'

'That's the time to start. And he loves it.' Alex examined her picture. 'You know, you've got the perspective on the hill just right! Do you realize, incidentally, that you don't imitate any more? You're developing a style of your own.'

'Maybe. Antonescu says I still pay too much attention to detail, though. It should sweep more, it should feel more careless. I understand what he means, but it's not easy to do it.'

A bicycle bell tinkled up the drive. In a moment Mrs MacHugh from the village would appear around the curving shrubbery, bringing the afternoon mail.

'I'll get it,' Alex said.

It was past time for a letter from home. Of late, Fern had been troubled by thoughts of home. Aunt Milly had written that Father had seemed unusually tired on her last visit to Cyprus. There'd been a history of heart trouble among the men in the family. If Father were to die, what would become of Jessie? And Fern had a vivid recollection of her sister sitting with the cards spread out for an elaborate game of solitaire; the little face, surrounded by arabesques of curls and lavish folds of scarf, was proud and lonely.

She stood abruptly and walked to the front of the house, where Mrs MacHugh, having just handed the mail to Alex, was turning the bicycle back down the drive.

'Letter from America! Two of them! Looks like one from your father and one from Jessie. The rest – just advertisements and an invitation from the Mercers.'

She sat down on the step to read. The note from Jessie filled just one page.

'I shall be in England a week after you receive this.' In England? But how? But why? 'Read Father's letter. He will explain it all. He can do a better job of writing than I can just now.'

Prick of pin, quiver of apprehensive chill as when a running cloud covers the sun. Tiny shudder as when a jangling note is struck on the piano. She opened her father's letter and read it quickly through. Then she read it again.

'Oh no!' she cried.

'Oh no what? What's wrong?'

Fern laughed. The sound was harsh and queer.

'What is it?' Alex repeated.

She gave him the letter, then leaned back against the doorpost, fighting a sudden heaving of nausea.

'Well,' he said, 'this is news, isn't it?'

'I don't believe it!' she cried.

'Why? Is it all that strange?'

'For goodness' sake, don't you think it is?'

'Well, I suppose one mightn't actually *expect* Jessie to marry, and yet she – '

Fern sat up. The wave of sickness had subsided.

'I think it's – I think it's disgusting!'

'I don't understand. Do you know the man, by the way?'

'Yes, he's a doctor, as you read. A country doctor. It's – farm country, hills, something like Scotland. Yes, it looks something like Scotland,' she said irrelevantly.

'But do you *know* him? What is he like?'

Fern swallowed, as if a lump of some tough substance stuck in her throat. 'It's hard to describe him.' She shook her head, frowning. 'He is a very intelligent man with a wide-ranging mind. A quiet man with a lot of restless energy. But that's contradictory and complex – '

'We're all contradictory, some of us more than others. Anyway, if he and Jessie love one another, I don't see why you call that disgusting.'

'She may be in love with *him*. I've no doubt she is. But as for him, well, could you be in love with Jessie?'

'I'm not, so I can't answer for myself. That doesn't mean some other man couldn't be. And I did like her a lot, you know. I thought she had wit and heart.'

'He can't love her! It's impossible.'

'You don't know his feelings, Fern. You really ought to be glad for them. For Jessie.'

'Did you read the whole thing? They're taking a flat in London. He'll be working here for the next three years.'

'So then he won't be a country doctor, after all, will he? They'll have a whole other life.'

'Yes, a whole other life.'

Alex got up and drew Fern to her feet.

'Let's go in. I need to shower and change. Then I want tea. Yes, you ought to be glad for them,' he repeated, climbing the stairs.

Fern lay down on the bed. Water rushed in the bathroom

shower, fogging the mirror on the open door so that she saw herself in a blur. Lying there in the middle of the enormous bed she looked forlorn and she felt ashamed. Why should she begrudge Jessie this miraculous deliverance?

Whenever she thought of her sister she saw her small and huddled, sometimes even crying with a lump on her forehead that was Fern's fault. Jessie was a measurement, a symbol of deprivation and unfair disadvantage.

Her thoughts went to Martin. 'A quiet man,' she had told Alex a few minutes ago, 'with a lot of restless energy.' She might have added more: a sensitive man, perceptive, tense, reserved, intellectual, kind, proud, ambitious – yet not one of these words, even the word 'ambitious', made clear how he could have married Jessie.

She was bitterly angry.

'After they're settled in,' Alex said, rubbing himself dry, 'we'll give a party for them.' His eyes crinkled with friendliness. He liked parties. 'We'll have a little band and string lights in the trees. Welcome to England and all that. What do you think?'

'Lie down here with me,' she said.

'I thought you didn't feel like – '

'I only meant, hold me. We don't have to make love unless you want to.'

He drew her head down to his shoulder. 'You don't feel well. I can wait. There's more between us than only that, I should hope.'

Yes. And she thought: I do wonder what all the mystery is for? One gets the idea that it is the purpose of everything, this entrance of the man into the woman, when actually it is such a quick thing, not at all like the fuss that's made over it. What's really best is to be held and loved, to wake up in the night and not be alone. To be cared for as Alex cares. He's done so much for me. I've grown so much with the things he's taught me.

Her hands went to the rounded hill below her ribs. The baby fluttered for the first time. Its new life, thumping, had knocked at the door. How wrong of her to feel anger or anything but thankfulness and – and gladness! She had everything. Everything!

'Have a nap,' Alex said. 'We've an hour before tea.'

The sky suddenly had gone dark and chilly. A gust of rain battered the windows. He drew the coverlet about them both, while her head still rested in the curve of his shoulder. So warmed, her tremors eased.

Ah, foolish, she thought. Alex is right, it is no business of ours! As long as we're here together, with Ned and Emmy and whoever it is that's stretching and turning inside me now, why should I care what other people do?

In a few minutes, she drifted into the sweetest sleep.

CHAPTER NINE

Martin stepped outside into a fragrant morning; the air was damp on the skin. Here in England June still had the feel of spring. It was a long walk to St Bartholomew's, but he enjoyed starting his work day at the hospital with the vigour and well-being that came after exercise. And with this sensation of well-being he crossed through the park and turned down the Mall.

It had been, beyond expectation, a good year. He smiled, still warmed by the hour he had spent since he had got up, in the pleasant flat above the square of chestnut trees and sycamores. Jessie and he had breakfasted at the bow window that overlooked all the bird-filled greenery. His last sight before leaving was of her puttering over some last-moment touch on the little room which had been readied for the baby who was due right now – perhaps even today!

He hadn't really planned to have a child this soon. But apparently Jessie had! She would be an excellent mother, he reflected. He hadn't thought much about that until now, but on these solitary walks all sorts of thoughts streamed through one's head . . . Yes, she would be excellent, with all that energy, remarkable energy for so small a body. Well organized, too; everything was planned out beforehand so that the actual doing seemed always to be easy. He marvelled at this ability of Jessie's to manage things, and could imagine her directing in her capable, cheerful way a household of children. *Cheerful.* That was Jessie. If you had to think of a single adjective that above all else described her, *cheerful* would surely do as well as any.

Suddenly he recalled the day they had moved into the flat; it was a furnished sub-let, drably decorated; it had been raining that afternoon and the drabness, combined with the pelting rain, had depressed him so that he'd almost wanted to turn around and walk out – he who never really cared that much about possessions or the appearances of things! But what wonders Jessie had done with those rooms! She'd filled them with flowers, inexpensive daisies in bright-blue glass bowls. She'd hung travel posters on the walls, delightful scenes of golden places: the Fountains of Vaucluse and Venice and Segovia. She'd become a devotee of the flea markets: one day she'd come home lugging a tarnished, wretched old pot that turned out to be a splendid silver tea kettle. She'd been so pleased with herself! She knew how to enjoy the hours, Jessie did, and knew how to stretch her mind. She'd stretched his mind, too, leading him through every gallery and museum in the city. They had gone to Elizabethan plays and the ballet and of course to the opera that he loved so well, and rummaged through old bookshops . . .

In the fall they'd gone to Paris; there had been a neurological conference at the Salpetriere; they'd walked their feet off down every alley and into every corner. Christmas week had been cele- brated in Rome. They had seen palms growing in Cornwall. They had travelled to Ulster and visited the stony village where Martin's father had been born and a long line before him had died. Martin had been immensely moved by its loneliness and dignity. Yes, it had been a remarkable year and he had Jessie to thank for it.

Not that he hadn't had some trepidation at the beginning! Once having passed the first shock and splendour of the opportunity with Braidburn, he had come to the awareness that in England he would see Mary again; the thought had plagued him all the way across the Atlantic Ocean. He had felt – he hadn't known quite what it was he had felt, other than a decided discomfort and a wish that he might somehow avoid the whole business, which was, of course, impossible.

They had been driven straight to Lamb House. It had been one of those grey-green English afternoons, half-way between rain and heavy mist. The sky had been filled with noisy birds, starlings and rooks; the country looked soft, he had thought.

'I like this kind of day. I've grown used to it,' Mary had said, answering some comment about the weather.

Queer that he should remember such a slight remark!

She had been standing in the doorway when they drove up. The boy Neddie had been on one side and a tiny girl, just able to stand, had been on the other. And he had wondered whether she was aware of the picture she made, blooming with her two children and her pregnancy.

Yes, he remembered that day. They had gone walking about the grounds. Naturally, Jessie had described Lamb House beforehand, but no description could have done justice to it in Martin's mind. He had had no frame of reference for such a place.

Intending nothing, truly intending nothing by the trivial words, he had remarked, 'This is a long way from Cyprus, isn't it?'

And with unmistakable anger, Mary had repeated, 'Yes, isn't it?'

Surely she couldn't have been jealous of Jessie? After all, she hadn't wanted him for herself! So it had come to Martin's mind that she must be resentful over the marriage because she thought him some sort of fortune-hunter. This idea had stung him, and still would have done so if he allowed it to. For he was, after all, living on another man's money, wasn't he? And living well. Perhaps, then, he did look like a – a fortune-hunter?

But not for long! Jessie's father would be repaid for everything. They would live better yet on what he, Martin, would provide. His wife and children would depend on no one else but him.

Fortune-hunter! And what of Mary's motives? Ah, but that was unfair! Alex was a man to be desired by women, a kindly, generous, intelligent man who happened to have wealth. Martin himself could surely have been bitter at the sight of him, not because he had any remnant of desire for Mary – she had rejected him and that was the end of that! – but because of normal resentment towards the winner. Instead he had come to like Alex. You couldn't help but like him.

Occasionally, still, he could remember his first anguish over Mary, how painfully and slowly it had ebbed into anger and how the anger had finally seeped away into nothing. Oh, there was some small disturbance yet – embarrassment, that was all. He was still and probably always would be so damned touchy! A regular prickly pear, he was.

But he was forcing himself to get over this embarrassment. Mary too had evidently got over it, or over whatever it was that had made her so cold when he and Jessie had first arrived. Perhaps she saw now that he was working hard, and would get somewhere in the world and was in the meantime making a good life for Jessie.

So the relationship between the two couples was cordial enough, although it was not a close one. Every now and then they met in town for dinner or theatre. Two or three times Martin and Jessie had been at Lamb House amid a bustle of guests and children. Jessie declined the last few invitations and he had concurred. He really didn't have the time to spare; he wasn't his own master as Alex was. Besides, the Lambs' was a different world. Alex, the Englishman, naturally had friends in many circles. Jessie and Martin, strangers both, were very slowly enlarging their little group one by one, or rather, two by two. Alex and Mary ran an expensive establishment; she was busy in the domain of art; he had countless business obligations. Their lives were complicated. The Farrells' life was simple. And they were satisfied with its simplicity.

'You're happy, Martin, I can see,' Jessie liked to say, not questioning or doubting, merely taking pleasure in his pleasure, and expressing the euphoria which had bloomed with her pregnancy. He, in turn, took pleasure in seeing that euphoria, and in the calm, fine trust between them . . .

He looked at his watch and quickened his walk. He was due in the operating room at eight. This was Mr Braidburn's day. 'Mr' – funny English mode of address to a doctor! And now Martin's mind leaped ahead, away from his own concerns, towards the hospital where he had spent the larger part of this past year. Even when he was away from that building, his heart was still in it!

'What happened to the Eldridge girl over the week-end while I was away?' he would ask himself. 'To the iron worker with the third-degree burns who'd got a piece of steel in the brain?' And his memory would go back in time to the story Pa had told so long ago of the scalded child in the farmhouse kitchen. Poor Pa! He'd had the will to help, but not the tools. Now Martin had those tools in hand.

There were just three young Americans and half a dozen Englishmen working in the wards and clinics, examining and selecting the patients to be discussed on the following day. Often Martin wondered how much these patients understood, as they were wheeled in before the instructors and assembled students. Most of them were simply too frightened to understand very much, he thought, which was just as well. God pity them: the paralysed; the afflicted with their jerking limbs and senseless laughter; the soon-to-die.

Most of them were poor and inarticulate, struggling for words even when they must know clearly enough what they wanted to say.

'Doctor, will I die? Will I walk and talk and be a person?'

Their shabby imitation-leather pocketbooks, clasped stiffly on their laps, were sad to him. He dreamed of his mother. She had owned that same kind of shabby black bag. He dreamed that it was lying on the kitchen table at home. His mother was crying, 'I've lost my pocketbook,' and he was telling her, 'Why, here it is, Ma. Don't you see it?' But she only kept on crying and wringing her hands. The poor moved him so.

He pitied animals. So soft he was! He must learn to hide it! In the laboratory he worked on monkeys and dogs. It made him sick to touch their fur, to win their trust only to terrorize them later. Yet it had to be done. How else to learn what cells do after a stroke or how brain wounds heal? How else to learn anything? Fortunately, Evan Llewellyn, wiry dark Welshman, great neurophysiologist and patient teacher, was kind to the creatures. He kept suffering to a minimum. Otherwise Martin could not have stood it.

It was a privilege when he was allowed to share a small basement laboratory with Llewellyn. Jessie, having overheard Martin talking about microscopes, had bought him a beautiful Zeiss, and there with Llewellyn and the Zeiss, during long afternoons and often late into the evenings, he laid the foundation of all he was to know about the pathology of the cell. He was becoming increasingly convinced of what Dr Albeniz had said about the unity of all brain study: surgery, neurocytology, and even psychiatry were parts of a single discipline and ought not to be separated. The practitioners in these divisions must know what the others were doing.

'Too many neurosurgeons blunder into the brain,' Llewellyn declared.

He was nearly eighty, with cheerful eyes and a face remarkably unlined. 'Never stop learning,' he would say. Whenever he was challenged for coming in on holidays or Sundays, he had an answer. 'When you stop working, you're dead, or might as well be.'

Martin thought: That's what my father used to say. And a truer thing was never said, he added to himself, as he rounded the corner and made his way to St Bartholomew's door.

Braidburn talked as he worked, his steady voice instructing and explaining. This was the third hour and he was tiring. A drop of sweat stood on his forehead; a nurse stepped forward to wipe it before it could slide.

'Look here. The size of an orange.'

Martin blotted seeping blood with gauze. A year ago he had been puzzled at first sight of these absorbent squares, each with its dangling black thread. Now he knew so much; also he knew how much he did not know. And he remembered his fear when a brain was first exposed beneath his own hands, when he was first permitted, under supervision, to take the knife.

'Sponge,' Braidburn ordered.

The patient was young. Martin had seen him first at the clinic, waiting on a bench with his wife and a couple of whining children. He had a wizened city face, a clerk's face, respectful and scared. Relating his symptoms, his mouth had twisted.

'I can't seem to stand up straight. I feel like vomiting. The headache's splitting and my eyesight's queer.'

Through the ophthalmoscope Martin had observed the haemorrhaging retina and the enlarged head of the optic nerve.

'See anything, Doctor?'

'Well,' he'd answered kindly, evasively, 'we'll need to take X-rays, you know. Then we'll see about straightening you out.'

He had known then what the pictures would show: a tumour in the left lobe; slow growing, he would guess. Also, he had thought, or felt, that it would be non-malignant; he had not voiced the thought to anyone. There was something odd about the appearance of the person when malignancy was present. Again, that was only a feeling he had. Pa used to have feelings like that about patients, too. But Pa had often been wrong.

This time Martin had been right: the tumour was benign and encapsulated. A little thrill went through him, remembering the pale wife and children. Also, he was pleased with himself.

'The rest is up to the gods,' Braidburn said now. 'We've done all we can.' He looked up. 'Close the flap, Farrell, please. Jasper, assist. I've finished.'

There ought to be applause, Martin thought. Some of his fellow students complained that men like Braidburn were arrogant and difficult. Braidburn in particular had been labelled 'manic-depressive'. But he was merely a man of moods. Martin loved him, as he loved all these men and loved this place.

A few hours later, he had just taken a seat at the bench downstairs with old Llewellyn when the telephone rang. Martin spoke a moment and hung up.

'My wife's at the hospital in labour.'

'Hurry up, then, what are you waiting for?' Llewellyn cried.

Martin tore upstairs and started to race towards the taxi-rank. Mr Meredith intercepted him.

'Llewellyn called upstairs. Get in. We'll drive you.'

So it was that Martin went in a limousine to the meeting with his firstborn.

Meredith was considerably silent. Martin wondered what he could be thinking. Perhaps the same thought that he himself had been stifling and that now had abruptly shot up again from some buried place in his consciousness. It had been foolhardy to permit a pregnancy! What if the child were like its mother? How terrible and cruel! The child would despise them, and rightly so, for having brought it into the world. And Jessie – poor Jessie – would be destroyed by guilt. Martin shook with fear. All the day's contentment shivered away.

Meredith was saying, 'I met Fleming once. Looks like anybody else. Penicillin will absolutely revolutionize medicine . . . although some patients are allergic to it. But I shouldn't bother you with medicine today, should I?' He tapped Martin on the knee. 'Just watch that Achilles' heel.'

'What?' Martin asked in confusion.

'We all develop one, you know. The moment the child is born. Whatever happens to it after that will happen to you, every cut and bruise. Ah well, here we are. Good luck.'

At the desk they told him Jessie was already in the delivery room.

'Make yourself comfortable in the waiting room. We'll call you as soon as we know anything.'

The waiting room was vacant except for a woman reading a book. When Martin entered she put it down and he saw that the woman was Mary Fern. She smiled.

'You were operating, so Jessie called me when the pains came very suddenly. I've been with her until just now.'

'Thanks awfully. Is she all right?'

'Very excited. Very happy, between pains.'

Martin sat down, took a magazine and couldn't read it.

'You're reading the same words ten times over and you don't know what they mean,' Mary observed.

'I know.'

'Try a picture magazine, it's easier.' She added gently, 'I know you're a doctor, but when it's your own baby, I suspect you forget you're a doctor, don't you? So let me tell you, it's not so bad having a baby. She'll be all right. She really will.'

'Thanks again.'

'I'm glad I happened to be in town. We're staying in overnight.'

It occurred to Martin that he hadn't been alone in a room with Mary since – since Cyprus, and seldom enough even then. This thought created an intimacy in the commonplace, impersonal room. Absurd! He smelled a slight fragrance: her perfume. When she turned a page he heard the faint jingle of an ornament on her gold bracelet. For some reason the sound was irritating. He wished she would go home. Then he was ashamed of himself, and spoke to her pleasantly.

'The country must be beautiful this month.'

'Yes, it's heavenly. But you're making conversation. You don't really feel like talking now. Don't bother about me, please . . . I'll just sit here and read.'

The stillness was oppressive. An hour ticked by. At every passing step in the hall he looked up, thinking it was for him. Mary looked up too; they exchanged anxious glances. She returned to the book, rustling the pages. The bracelet jingled. He wished again that she would leave.

Her presence, as he sat there with nothing to do but let his mind wander, brought him a mean recollection. At a luncheon table when he had first arrived at St Bartholomew's, Henry Barker had all unknowingly humiliated him. Barker was Braidburn's associate, a garrulous, informal man, rather un-English. Martin remembered every word he had said.

'To tell you the truth, when your father-in-law wrote to ask a favour of Braidburn, I thought probably a loan was being called in, a return for old friendship, you know. I can't say whether Braidburn thought the same. We had no idea we were getting a gifted man. For you are that, Martin! I look forward to meeting your wife. Only the other day we were talking about our visit to America with the Braidburns whenwe met your wife and her family. A lovely child she was, about fourteen, I should think. Tall for her age, with the most extraordinary blue eyes. I never forgot.'

Martin had said evenly, 'That was Mary Fern. She's married to an Englishman, and they live in Oxfordshire when they're not at their flat in town.'

Mr Barker had been confused. 'Oh? How many sisters are there, then? I seem to remember only two.'

'There are just two. I married the other one.'

Why did he remember, keep remembering, such things? Why did he not expunge them like a chalk scribble on a blackboard? Just wipe them out?

Mary stood up. 'I'm supposed to meet Alex's mother and bring her home for dinner.' She looked at her watch. 'Will you think it awful of me if I leave you?'

'No, no, go ahead. And give my best to Alex.'

'You'll call me the minute you hear? We'll be at the flat all evening.'

'Of course.'

He watched her go down the street. She still had that slight sway in her walk. Her skirt swung gracefully. It was funny, a few years ago women all wore dresses to the knees. Now their skirts were three-quarters of the way to the ankle. How quickly one grew accustomed to change!

'Don't you think Alex has done a lot for Fern?' Jessie had asked recently.

He had answered that he didn't know what she meant. But he had known. Lamb House, status and freedom had made a woman out of a girl.

He watched her as far as the corner. A man turned to look after her as she passed; struck, maybe, by the blue eyes in the dark face? A mere accident of colouring and charm, and men, poor fools, were beguiled!

But what should all that matter to him? And he felt abruptly angry. It did not matter! His life was filled. He had his work, his home and now a child. And the child would be normal! Of course it would! By the law of averages it would; he ought not to have let himself succumb to any morbid thought that it could be otherwise, or to morbid thoughts of any sort. Such thoughts were wasteful and therefore stupid, and he knew better.

Think of bright things, good things, purpose; think not of

the past, but of the years to come . . . I'll come back again to Europe one day, he promised himself. I must see Epidaurus and the Temple of Aesculapius. I'll bring my son with me! Yes, my son! I'll teach him and show him things I never saw, never had. I'll give him things I did have, too. My father's arm would rest around my shoulder, drawing me to his heat when it grew cold. We'd sit on the steps and watch the sky light up from the first solitary spark to the streaming of the Milky Way. My father and I. Now my son and I. He'll be tall and easy, not tall and rigid like me. He'll have broad shoulders. I can hear his voice, its first deepening when he starts to become a man. This is what life is all about –

A man in a surgeon's white coat was walking towards him. 'Mr Farrell?'

Martin stood up with a question on his lips, afraid to ask it.

'A healthy child, and your wife is all right, too. Just coming out of anaesthesia. You may see her now.'

They entered the elevator. 'We had to do a Caesarian section,' the other man said. 'Tried not to, but there wasn't enough room. The spine, of course.'

Martin followed him down the corridor. He was struck with the oddity of himself in the role of follower. Was this how people felt towards him, waiting for his words to fall?

'I would not recommend having any more, Mr Farrell.' Sober eyes admonished Martin. 'I'm very, very serious about that.'

'I understand. Certainly not.'

The man switched to sympathy. 'You've had a couple of bad hours.'

'Yes,' Martin said, and to his own shame was suddenly aware that his terrors had not been first for Jessie, but for his boy, his son. He wondered what anyone who could know that would think of him.

He went in to Jessie. Her face was white as the blankets, but her eyes were triumphant. Filled with tender contrition, he stooped and kissed her forehead, and stroked her damp, curly hair. Murmuring, she closed her eyes.

'She'll sleep now,' the nurse said. 'Would you like to see the baby?'

At the nursery door he was shown a bundle wrapped in a pink blanket. He remembered that he hadn't even inquired the sex of the child and he felt a draining disappointment.

'A lovely girl,' the nurse said.

He stared at the baby. She was unmarked by struggle through the birth canal, and she had long dark hair.

The nurse was jovial. 'You could almost braid it, couldn't you?'

He knew he was supposed to respond with the usual comic, awkward pride of the new father. But there was only a sinking in his chest. His little son! And this was the last chance.

The baby opened her eyes. It was impossible, of course, but she seemed to be staring straight back at Martin. For more than a few moments they regarded one another. Then she yawned, the pink mouth making a perfect O, raised her hand and dropped it in exquisite relaxation.

'She's bored with our company,' the nurse said laughing.

Against all rules, Martin put his finger into that miniature palm. At once the miniature fingers curled around his thick one. How strong she was! Already reaching out to life and grasping! The tiny thing! He felt a lump in his throat. The tiny thing!

And she was perfect, without a flaw. A rush of gratitude went through him; he felt the old warning tingle of rising tears. At the same time he wanted to laugh. Perfect, without a flaw! Beautiful, too, with a straight little nose, strong curved chin and thick lashes, lying now on cheeks whose skin was fine as silk. His girl.

'What will you name her?' the nurse asked.

He had to think a moment of the name they had selected for a girl.

'Claire,' he said, between the laughter and the tears. 'Her name is Claire.'

That night he sat down and wrote a letter. 'Darling Claire,

On this the day, almost the hour of your birth, I want to tell you how I feel before any of my thoughts can slip away. We don't know each other yet, but already you are part of me, like my hand or my eyes. I wouldn't have believed it possible. I love you so . . .'

CHAPTER TEN

Sometimes Fern thought of the bed as a kind of throne, raised as it was on a shallow platform in the middle of the long wall. Everyone came to her here, where she leaned against fresh white linen pillows under a canopy upheld by carved mahogany posts. Neddie and Emmy climbed up to be read to; the baby Isabel was placed here in her arms to be fed.

Alex had said, 'I read once that home is where the furniture has stood in one place for a century. You're sure you don't mind moving into a house that was furnished long ago by other people?'

She had not minded, as long as she could have her books from home: art books, history, poetry and books her mother had read to her when she was a child. They all stood now on shelves in the yellow sitting-room across the hall. Everything else in Lamb House had been there before her, except for the bed. She had not wanted to lie with her husband in the bed where his parents had conceived him. So the original had been taken down and stored away. In a London antique shop she had found a replacement almost like the first, but without any personal, known history and therefore, new.

Sometimes she thought of the bed as a ship, a great safe ship floating all night on a quiet sea until morning. Waking early, she would open her eyes in the familiar haven of the lovely room, into which first light shook itself through white, trembling curtains and dappled the copper bowl of orange roses on the table. And for a few minutes she would lie quite still, feeling that fine brightness of the spirit, that tranquillity of the flesh, which is called, for lack of any more apt definition, 'well-being'.

But all this was of the past.

For months now, she had lain most of the time alone in the bed, on sheets gone cold and pillows crumpled by her restless, sleepless head. Alex slept on a narrow cot in the dressing-room next door. He had first begun to sleep there during the winter when he'd had the flu. Its aftermath of coughing had lasted for weeks. Then, in order not to wake Fern after late meetings in town, he had kept on using the cot.

She was finding it impossible to talk about. That was puzzling, because Alex and she had been able to talk about anything. Women in particular had often remarked, with some curiosity and much frank envy, on this free and lively interchange of theirs. It was such a wonderful thing to be able to *talk* to a husband! Their husbands came home from work and read the newspaper –

Given, then, a relationship like this there ought to have been no reason why she could not have said: 'What's wrong? I want to know.' Yet she could not bring herself to say it.

Instead, humiliation knotted in her chest; she felt a prickling, inhibiting, sense of shame. She was perfectly aware that this was only false pride and a wife ought not to have false pride. Yet she had it.

One day she bought a book about married love and left it on the table at the foot of the bed, next to the folded London *Times*. Alex riffled through it and put it back.

'Good Lord,' he said, 'you'd think people never could have got married and lived together without having somebody write a book of instructions for them!'

The remark was so unlike him, to whom open-mindedness and intellectual curiosity were essential virtues, that Fern was astonished and said so.

In answer he laughed and went back to *The Times*. And she, rebuked and made foolish, said no more.

'By the way.' He lowered the paper a few minutes later. 'At the Bakers' dinner Malcolm said you were the most striking woman in the room.'

'Very nice of him.'

'Well, you were! You should always wear either white or blue.' He yawned. 'I'm wrung out. I could drop right off to sleep. Had a meeting about the blasted German insurance today Terence made the report and you know how long-winded he can be. If you want to read some more, I'll sleep in the dressing-room.'

'I don't want to read any more,' she said flatly.

The darkness had a hollow feel, as if she were alone in a cavern. How could everything have changed so quickly? Briefly Alex stroked her shoulder and brushed her earlobe with his lips.

'Good-night. Sleep well,' he said tenderly.

In a minute he was asleep. She *willed* him to turn back to her, but her will had no effect. Yet, if he had turned and opened his arms, she would not have come into them. For was she to exist only to satisfy his odd whim? What could he be thinking of? And didn't he wonder at all what *she* might be thinking?

Rain spattered the leaves close to the windows. Rain again! No wonder the English drank so much brandy and so much boiling tea! The dampness shuddered in her marrow. She got up to take another blanket and lay wide awake while the rain quickened and darkness deepened in the hollow cavern.

There was another woman: there had to be. Who, then? That cousin of Nora's, she of the false voice, chirrup and chirp? She had a very convenient flat in London. Maybe even Nora herself? Shameful to think that of one's friend; kind, strong Nora. Still, one never knew; one heard incredible things. That Irish girl, Delia somebody, who won the jumping trophy at the horse show? She was dark and the women he admired were always dark ones. The girl couldn't be more than eighteen. She had the most absurd way of stretching her eyes, slanting them up at a man even when he was no taller than she. Alex had danced with her at least five times at the Elliots'.

Maybe it was none of these at all. Maybe it was someone he had known before they were married, some woman he couldn't have married, because she wouldn't have been a proper mother for his child.

She must find out. She would find out.

Alex sighed in his sleep and turned over; one relaxed arm brushed Fern's rigid shoulder. He smelled of cleanliness, of shaving lotion and Pear's soap. And she slid away, out of touch.

Her mind sped. He'd gone riding with Delia last Thursday afternoon. They were out two hours, at least. She would have gone, too, if he'd asked her, but when she got back from errands in the village he had already left. And when she went down to the stable to saddle Duchess, they were just coming in.

'We went all the way to Blackdale. It was marvellous!' Delia cried. 'You should have been with us, Fern.'

Yes, I should.

Her hair falls like black silk . . . It's not possible. Things like this happen to other people. Like auto accidents and cancer, they happen to other people.

On a Sunday afternoon in dark and threatening autumn weather, Alex stood up suddenly and stretched.

'I've a yen for exercise. I think I'll take Lion for a canter up to Blackdale. Not far.'

'Not far! An hour and a half there and back. And it's going to rain.'

She knew she sounded critical and cross. But he answered pleasantly.

'I'll be home before the rain comes, I think. And if not, I shan't mind.'

'Well, suit yourself. I've no wish to get soaked.'

'Shouldn't want you to,' he said, still pleasantly.

He had been gone half an hour before her thoughts took clear shape, and a decision was made. What sort of fool did he take her for? A country canter in this weather? And he'd been on the telephone three times before lunch today.

From the closet she pulled a mackintosh and rain hat, for the rain had begun. Then she went into the hall and called softly up the stairs. 'Nanny? Let the children have tea without us this afternoon. I've an unexpected errand.'

She would be waiting for them at the stable, standing in the lane as they rode up. She would smile, smile dangerously, and then see what Alex would have to say.

But afterwards – what would come then? She couldn't think that far ahead. Vague images of daring courage came to mind: of those men who last summer had gone up the sheer face of a mountain in the Himalayas. The vertigo! The horror of falling! Could they have felt such panic in the pit of the stomach? No. They wouldn't have been able to do it if they had.

Step forward. Get through it. The rest will follow.

She walked swiftly. There was no one on the road, the villagers being either at the radio or sleeping Sunday dinner off. Even the clattering crows of autumn had taken shelter from the wet.

The fools! They would be soaked! Unless they knew of some place to hide away in – she couldn't imagine where. There was no one about in the stable yard, either. The horses had all been taken indoors. From the little office next to the tack room where Kevin, the head groom, had a desk and kept his records, came an oil lamp's weak glow. It wouldn't do any harm to wait inside with Kevin. She would still be able to hear them trotting up the path. Let Kevin hear or think what he might.

The window was next to the door so that, standing with one's hand on the knob, one's face was almost pressed against the pane, and one's eyes were drawn into the room. Something caught Fern's attention before her hand had turned the knob.

A cot, covered with a plaid horse blanket, stood opposite the desk along the further wall. Someone was lying on it. She leaned forward. Blinked. Stepped back. Leaned forward again. Frowning, she flattened her nose on the wet glass. It was like looking into an aquarium. The shape on the cot – no, there were two – the shapes slid, pale and slippery, like great, gliding fish, underwater creatures twisted in some unfathomable embrace. And for a minute or two she stood there, failing to understand. She saw, yet did not grasp the meaning of what she saw.

Then a face came into view. It moved into the path of the lamplight. It was a face and a bright head that she knew . . . Alex spoke. She saw a flash of naked white as Kevin sat up.

And she understood.

She gave a harsh cry and clapped her palm to her mouth and fled from the shaft of light into the shrubbery. She heard Alex crying, in a voice of terrible alarm, 'Who's there? Who's there?' And she ran.

Crouched and stumbling in the failing afternoon, under a sky grown eerie as moonlight, she ran, hidden from the public road behind hedges and walls. A bramble ripped her leg. She fell. Pebbles ground into her palms. She had a crazy thought that someone was pursuing her.

'Oh my God!' she gasped. Her heart beat so! It beat so! It was too terribly hurt! And she put her hand to her chest. Was there some stoppage there? Even at her age, the heart could stop, couldn't it?

She reached the house and banged the door open. A child, hearing her steps, called from upstairs, but she raced to her room. She threw the soaked mackintosh and hat upon the floor and lay down upon the bed. Her throne! Her ship! She was dizzy, sick, delirious. It was all unreal! Untrue! She had not seen, could not possibly have seen it!

Yes, she knew of such things, but very vaguely, for there was nothing in print except for some sparse definitions in the dictionaries. A girl in school had overheard her brother talking. There had been tittering, shocked laughter, so that dimly and half-comprehended, a conception of something awful and unnatural had been formed. She had been perhaps fifteen when these things had happened. And she knew now very little more than she had known then.

If only her heart would stop *pounding* so! It felt as though a volcano were swirling and burning in her, as if she were too full to contain the swirling and burning.

Downstairs the front door opened and then was closed with the muffled thud of solid wood. Footsteps sounded: Alex's familiar tread. He came in and stood beside the bed.

'So it was you,' he said softly.

Fern's dry, scared eyes stared up at him.

'Well, now you know.'

She kept on staring at him. He looked the same. The strong shoulders in the handsome riding jacket, the humorous tilt to the eyes, were the same.

'Why?' she whispered.

He shook his head. He sighed.

'I'm sorry. Oh God, I'm sorry.'

New terror passed over her, a terror like the cold wind of abandonment. She was alone. Alex was not Alex any more. Then who was there?

'I thought it was Delia,' she whispered.

How much better if it had been Delia, after all!

'You thought it was Delia? That rattle-headed, empty fool?' He laughed.

There was no mirth in the laugh; it was only bitter, nervous, agitated. But the sound of it, and the look of his easy stance, with the riding crop in his left hand and his right hand thrust into the jacket pocket, were too much. Everything burst in Fern. Everything that had been held back for months, added now to this, burst open in one long, wild, frenzied scream. It rose and filled the room; it emptied out into the dusk.

'Stop it! Stop it, Fern, stop it!' Alex cried.

She wasn't able to. Her mind was working clearly; she understood that this was hysteria, her only experience of it. What she had read of it was true. You slid down and down and down, hearing from some far distance your own appalling screams. Over the edge you went, over the edge.

She was struggling for air. And struggling up, she ran to the window to push the casement wide.

Alex, misinterpreting, pulled her back and pinned her on the bed.

'You fool! I'm not worth killing yourself for!' He opened her collar. 'Quiet! Quiet! Whatever's happened, it's not the world's affair . . . People can hear you.'

She wept now, beating the bed with her palms. 'I don't care who hears! Let them!'

'You'll terrify the children. You care about them, don't you?'

The children! Ah yes, the children! And this, their father.

'Take some,' Alex said. A decanter and small green glass

for his nightcap stood on the tray. He filled the glass. 'Take some,' he commanded again.

She twisted away. 'Don't put your hands on me!'

'All right. But please. Talk to me. Let's talk together.'

Silently now, her thick tears rolled as smooth as glycerine.

'I know how innocent of the world you are. I can't expect you to be anything but horrified. And I'm so sorry, Fern. Oh my God, just so sorry!'

She thought, I can't stay here. I can't. For one mad instant she saw herself walking out, just walking out, leaving everything behind – this house, the children, her pictures – and most of all this loathsome man. She saw the strapped trunks and the suitcases waiting in the hall. On the top of the pile lay the patent leather travelling case which had come with her from home. The car waited in the driveway. Neddie, Isabel and Emmy stood at the foot of the stairs, their bewildered eyes asking why she was leaving them.

Alex was speaking softly, soothingly. 'At least, though, you must see that Kevin's no threat to the marriage, as Delia would have been.'

'Threat to the marriage? What marriage? If I could walk out tonight, just walk down the road in the mud; if there were a train going out, a train to anywhere, I don't care where, I'd go now. I'd go this minute.'

'You're forgetting something.'

'Forgetting?'

'Your children.'

'They'll go with me wherever I go.'

Alex shook his head. 'No,' he said. In the straight-backed chair beside the bed he sat erect, as if in the saddle, except that one knee was crossed high on the other thigh. This easy posture alarmed her, as she recognized something she had seen before, although it had never yet been directed at her. It was an iron will, in casual disguise. It was determination, not to be diverted.

'What do you mean? You're not fit! Do you think you're a fit father to rear a family? Why, any court would – '

'Any court would if any court could. But it would be your word against mine. Whose do you think they would believe?'

He got up, walked the length of the room and strode back. 'Whose word? They would say you were a demented, vicious woman.'

'I'll find a way! There has to be a way for truth to make itself known. This is a civilized country.'

Alex held up his hand. 'Wait. And if you were able to prove it – you wouldn't be, but for the sake of argument, let's say you could – then of course, this being a civilized country, I would be relieved of my post. How do you think we should all live then? If you have any idea that inherited wealth alone supports us, you're terribly mistaken. You know very well what's happened to investments here since the crash in America. I *need* to work, Fern. Keep that in mind, if you care about your children.'

'Then I'll simply take them and go, that's all. You can't very well set a guard over us whenever you're out of the house.'

He raised his eyebrows. 'Where will you go? Your father's been almost wiped out in the market and his factory's running on one cylinder. He'd hardly welcome a returning daughter and a brood of children, would he?'

She wiped her eyes roughly. 'Alex, tell me, if you can, why? Why?'

'Why what?'

'Why did you marry me? Or marry anyone?'

'I thought it would work. I wanted it to. God, how I wanted it to! From that first time at your aunt's dinner . . . Fern, you were the loveliest thing I'd ever looked at. Everything, everything about you, your voice, and the quietness in you, and all the life . . . You think like me. We go so well together. I wanted it to be so good for us.' His face twisted as if he were going to weep. 'My heart aches for you; I wish I could love you as you ought to be loved. Oh my God, how I wish I could!'

'In the name of decency, then, will you give me a divorce? On any grounds you want. Any.'

He shook his head.

'Alex, for God's sake, why not?'

He wept. His tears repelled her.

'Why not?' she repeated.

'I would never see my children again.'

'I would let you see them. I swear I would.'

'I want to live with them, as much as you want to live with them.'

'You have no right! You've forfeited the right.'

'It's the point of view,' Alex said, bringing himself under control. 'Society's point of view. In the society of ancient Greece, if you were living there, you would see this differently.'

'I'm not living in ancient Greece.'

'Well but, listen to me, I'm a good father. You know I am. This other thing – this has nothing to do with it.'

'You disgust me,' she said.

'Is that all you have to say?'

'I want a divorce. That's what I have to say.'

'No, Fern, no. Freedom, yes. Live as you will. I'll ask no questions. But the house stays as it is.'

The rain shines on the window. The pale bodies twist like sea creatures underwater.

A shudder rippled down Fern's back and contorted her face. Her teeth began to chatter.

'When you're more calm in the morning, I'll explain to you – '

'I don't want explanations,' she cried. 'Just get out! Get out where I don't have to look at you. Get out!'

When he had left the room, she crept under the blankets. It was fearfully cold. She remembered a hot beach in Florida years before, walking on the sand with her mother and Jessie, picking up shells. How good to be so young, to know nothing!

A bird twittered in the blackness and a breeze puffed. It was the subtle stirring of the earth that comes just ahead of the dawn. She remembered that they had had no dinner last evening. Her dry eyes ached. She would be appalled to see them in the mirror, and at the sight of her own stricken face the tears would start again.

What am I going to do? she thought.

The door opened. Past the window the black had turned to grey. She could see him as he approached the bed, and she stiffened. He was still dressed except for his boots and the coat of his riding habit. Like her, he had been awake all that long night.

'Fern, can't we even try to be reasonable about this?'

'Reasonable!' she cried scornfully. 'You really like that word, don't you?'

'It's a good word, one of the best.'

She didn't answer. She felt hopeless, burnt out.

'I'll fix a room across the hall. I'll spend more time in town. I should anyway. The business needs it.'

Fern got out of bed and walked into the bathroom while his voice followed her.

'Plenty of couples live this way. They rear their children, they're good to one another. Share things – everything but sex. It's not ideal – but it happens. I could give you names that would surprise you. Some of the artists you most admire. MPs. You've even been in their homes. Why, I could tell you – '

'I don't want to hear their names!'

And on the icy tiles she knelt down, something she had not done in years, not since passing through the religiosity of early adolescence. Yes, once since then, on the night her mother died, she had knelt then and prayed: God help me, please. So now on her knees she murmured again: God help me, please. But she had been reared in a household of sceptics, and nothing moved inside.

When she realized that Alex was standing there watching her, she struggled to her feet.

'You find this theatrical, I suppose?'

'No, I've done it myself on occasion.'

'And did it help?'

'No.'

She picked up the bathroom glass and threw it at him. Falling short, it smashed on the floor, scattering its pointed shards with a tinkle.

'Damn you,' she cried, 'get out! Get out of my sight!'

When Alex had gone, Fern got down again on her knees in

the splintered glass and cried and longed to be dead.

Alex's mother, accepting a second portion of pudding, remarked, 'I'm sorry to have missed Alex. If I had known he was going to be busy in town all week, I'd have postponed my visit.'

The women sat together at one end of the long table. The three days' visit had been interminable for Fern. Ordinarily it would not have been hard to endure, for by now she was used to Rosamund. (Such an odd name for this woman! 'Rosamund' should be young and careless; these Alex's mother could never have been, even in youth.) But she was far too desperate to cope with small talk, although she made the effort.

'You'll stay for dinner, won't you? We'll have it early. You'll have plenty of time to catch the evening train.'

'No, I'll take the five o'clock. Thanks anyway. I'll be back next month for Neddie's birthday, though.'

By next month, Fern thought, it may all have been too much. Perhaps I shall have fallen apart by then. Can't you see what's happening?

Rosamund whispered, 'Fern, you're not expecting again? You don't mind my asking? But you do look a little peaked.'

'Oh no, no I'm not.'

Rosamund laid her hand on Fern's arm. The heat of her hand came through the woollen sleeve. Her warm breath smelled of minted mouthwash.

'I used to envy my friends who had daughters. I used to say, "A woman needs at least one daughter." But you know, I don't say it any more, not since I've had my daughter-in-law. In this slipshod, devil-take-the-hindmost world, I can rely on you. You're so good to me! I tell everyone.'

This undeserved, pathetic praise caused disquiet in Fern. What had she ever given, after all, to this poor woman, so hungry for affection? Visits and presents, perfunctory, expensive knick-knacks that one picked up without effort or thought.

'Fern, will you come up while I pack my suitcase? There are some things I want to show you.'

In the few days of her occupancy Rosamund had made the room her own. There was a clutter of magazines on the bedside table next to a photograph of Alex's father. On the round table in the bay window lay an elaborate, interrupted game of double solitaire, and this last spoke to Fern. As Rosamund gathered up the cards, it spoke of Jessie, of long evenings and long silences.

'In my spare time,' Rosamund said now, 'I've been making a surprise for you. I thought you might like this.'

And she placed on Fern's lap a heavy picture album covered in dark blue velvet, embroidered in silver thread: Alexander Lamb V.

'I'd intended to keep it for your Christmas present, but I'm too impatient to wait that long.'

Fern turned the pages. There was Alex at three months, lying naked on a fur rug. Here he sat in a high chair, there in a rowboat. Wearing an Eton jacket, he stood between his parents. 'Smile!' the photographer had commanded and Alex had smiled. The label read, 'First Day at School'. Here, some years later, he was on the soccer team.

'Can you tell which one was Alex?' and as Fern pointed to the wrong one, 'I thought you wouldn't be able to tell! Wasn't he chubby? But he has such a large frame! I wonder that he stays so thin now, with the meals you serve.'

'We don't eat this way all the time. And of course, with all the exercise, especially riding, you know – ' She stopped.

'Well, I wanted you to have it.'

'It's beautiful,' Fern said. 'Thank you so very, very much.'

'Wait. I have something else.' From her bulging handbag Rosamund withdrew a silk purse on a drawstring. 'I've been meaning to give you these, and now is as good a time as any. That's my mother's garnet bracelet. It's eighteen-carat. Not that I'm boasting, but so much Victorian jewellery isn't real gold, so I thought you ought to know. And my ruby ring. Try it on. It'll fit your little finger.'

Fern was frightened. 'You mustn't do this!' she cried. Wasn't it odd that these things should frighten her? 'I can't possibly take all this away from you.'

'You're not taking; I'm giving. Who else will I leave my

things to when I die but to you?'

'Yes, but leaving them is different. You've plenty of time yet to wear them and enjoy them.'

For the second time that day Rosamund laid her hand on Fern's arm. Fern looked down at the blunt arthritic fingers.

'Child, the ring won't even fit me any more. I want you to wear it. The ruby's small, but it happens to be flawless. I was always so proud of it.'

'I don't know what to say,' Fern began.

People who trusted you, who were good to you, controlled you. You were helpless before them. This woman expected to be loved. She assumed that her son was deeply loved. She weighed you down. The air in the room became as it was in her own home – heavy with habit and obligation. In Rosamund's parlour the mantel was cluttered with snapshots from old holidays, with Christmas cards and theatre programmes. It was like living in a museum or an ossuary.

'I don't know what to say,' Fern repeated.

'Don't say anything! I'll have more for you the next time I see you. My husband was so generous towards me! They're good men, the Lambs. We're lucky, you and I. Alex is a one-woman man like his father. You'll never have to worry the way so many do these days. And did even in my time, too; oh yes, they did! What some of my friends put up with! Because of pride, of course, and also for the children's sake. What's a woman to do? I often think of Lucy Hemming. She's dead now, so I can talk. Walter Hemming kept a singer, pretty enough in a common way, took her to the best places where all Lucy's friends could see them. Disgraceful! But you're crying, Fern! Have I said anything? What is it?'

Fern stood up. She had to get out of that room.

'Nothing. It's foolish of me. I was just touched at your giving me so much.'

'Why, my dear, you are soft-hearted, aren't you?' Rosamund was pleased. 'Just enjoy them. I'm so sorry I missed Alex. Kiss him for me.'

She thought, rushing down the hall. that she wouldn't be

able to stand much more. There had to be someone she could talk to. Someone.

She longed for her mother. It was humiliating that, at this age and herself a mother, she should feel such need. If only her father were a man one could go to! But you could never talk to him of *interior* things. He had always been concerned with externals: proper appearances and material goods. He would never understand this. She could even imagine his fury, an outrage almost childish. There would be no rational analysis from him, no comfort. Her mother would have given comfort even though she might not have known what was actually to be done.

As for talking to Jessie, the roots of alienation were too deep. Perhaps alienation wasn't the right word; indifference might be a better definition. Or unease? Whatever the term, things were as they were.

Since the birth of her child, Jessie had drawn further away. Within the real world she had made another world into which few were admitted and these mostly old people, or women who, because they were dowdy or scholarly or both, were no threat to Jessie. Fern saw this clearly, pityingly. And she wondered what place Martin had in that little world. Her mind, opening the door of his and Jessie's bedroom, retreated in shame and closed the door at once.

So she couldn't go to her sister. They hadn't even seen each other since they'd had an American Thanksgiving together and now it was almost February. No, not Jessie.

Who, then?

And she knew even as she put the question and denied the answer – because the meeting would be awkward at best and probably futile as well. She knew nevertheless that the answer was Martin.

Why? There was a subtle coolness between them. She still felt discomfort in his presence, although not what she had felt when he first arrived in England. Certainly she wasn't angry any more. She had made herself behave like a mature, accepting woman. Perhaps, she reasoned, Alex had been right. People looked for different things in marriage and, after all, theirs was not the first such marriage. Martin was most tender with Jessie. And quite mad about the little girl! A lovely child, she was. A firebird. Quicksilver. Curiously, she reminded one of Neddie. Emmy and Isabel would be large, placid women, easy to live with. Martin had been so wonderful with poor Emmy that time they happened to be visiting and she broke her arm. A gentle doctor. Alex called him a born physician. Rare. Strange, but the doctor and the man seemed *separate*.

The man didn't reveal himself except when he talked about Claire. When one overheard him from the far end of a table or a room, he was usually talking about her. But more of the time he didn't talk at all. She didn't remember him as such a silent, private person. At home in Cyprus she had thought him spirited and eager. How things changed! But she herself had changed since then! One could call it learning or ageing. No matter. But Martin was kind; that hadn't altered. He would surely listen to her. He could be trusted. Maybe he would even know some way to help her. Was there any help?

A coal fire burned in the grate. The walls were covered with black and brown books bound in frayed and powdering leather. Everything in the room was very old; it looked like Sherlock Holmes's office on Baker Street. Actually, it belonged to Mr Braidburn. Martin had explained that he sometimes saw patients here for Mr Braidburn when he was away.

Fern kept looking around the room, aware that Martin also was considerately looking elsewhere, giving her time to calm herself. There was a Turkish carpet. There were heavy curtains, printed in dark red and tan. The room was warm. One could forget that it was on the ground floor of a hospital, that on the floors above people with hideous things growing in their heads lay dying. On the desk there was an open folder with a pen beside it. But Martin had written nothing and said nothing, only listened.

Now he said, 'You were beginning to smile a moment ago. Why?'

'For some reason or other, I was remembering the day you

told me my eyes don't belong in my face.'

He didn't answer.

'I think of myself as having been very childish for a girl of twenty.'

'Not childish. Inexperienced, which is quite a different thing.'

He lit a cigarette and leaned back in the chair. She was conscious of every sound, of the little scrape of the match and the creak of the chair. A small pain flashed through her temples.

She said abruptly, 'People don't know anything about each other when they marry. It's absurd. It's all artificial. We go to the hairdresser. He brings flowers . . .'

'Yet you must have loved him.'

'I didn't know anything about him, as you see.'

'The part you knew, you loved. Didn't you?'

'Why did you say that?'

'I think – you wouldn't have married him otherwise. Would you have?'

She felt as though she were undergoing an inquisition. He was *pressing* her. Why? And she passed her hand wearily across her forehead.

'I don't know. It's just the time, the place. Feelings rush over us. It's just – tricks. Yes, tricks.'

'You shouldn't be bitter. Shouldn't deny the feelings you had. That is, if they were true ones.'

He laid the cigarette in the ashtray from which smoke rose in a straight column towards the ceiling. Raising her eyes with the smoke, she saw that he was looking at her for the first time since she had come into the room.

'Were they?' Martin asked.

'I'm sorry. Were they what?'

'Your feelings. Were they true?'

'Yes, yes. I don't know.' These last weeks she had grown thinner, and her rings were loose. She twisted them. She faltered: 'If you had asked me before all this, I would have said "Yes, I loved him." Now I think it's possible I thought so because I didn't know what I was missing.'

Martin got up and went to the carafe that stood on a table.

'Would you like some water?'

When she declined, he poured a glass for himself and stood with his back to her drinking it slowly. His back, his shoulders, even the way he stood, were subtly different from what they had been three years before. They had the look of authority. She was thinking that when he went back to his chair and spoke again.

'Are you saying that you were comfortable with Alex because he made no approach to your sexuality? Is that what you're saying? Is that one of the reasons you married him?'

'You've no right to say that!' she cried, in immediate anger.

'Why haven't I? I'm a doctor. You asked for my opinion.'

'That doesn't give you the right to humiliate people.'

'If you feel humiliated, I'm sorry. That wasn't my intent.' He spoke quietly. 'But you don't have to stay if you don't want to hear me.'

'All right. Go on.'

'You've said yourself, often enough, that you were very young for your age. That means you had no knowledge of sex and as yet apparently no real need of it. Also, what little you knew about it you feared. And I think you still do.'

'Do you mind telling me what you're driving at?'

'What I'm driving at is that you're not hurt because you've been deprived of sex and love. You're hurt because your life's been turned inside out.'

She wanted to slap him. In her need she had come to him for aid and comfort; he was giving her scolding and scorn. Tears started. Biting her lip, she controlled them.

He stood up again and went to rearrange some books on a table. He was strangely agitated. Then he came back and sat down.

'I'm sorry. I'm not being fair to you. I sounded angry, I know.'

'Yes, you did. Why?'

'I don't know why. One doesn't always understand oneself.'

'"Physician, heal thyself",' she said with bitterness. And

quite suddenly she saw before her, not the man of authority who had risen when she had entered the room a while ago, but the young man in the shabby suit at the dinner table in Cyprus, a youth with something burning and bright in his face, and with a certain pathos. She spoke gently, now.

'We're quarrelling – '

He collected himself. 'Mary, I don't want to. I want to help you.'

'You still call me Mary,' she said irrelevantly.

He lit another cigarette and leaned down to replace the pack in a desk drawer. When he raised his head he had resumed the professional manner: kindly, seasoned and firm.

'I want to help you,' he repeated. 'You're scared to death.'

She twisted her rings. 'I don't know where I'm going, don't understand anything. I have no patience with the children, can't work, can't paint, can't bear to look at Alex – he disgusts me.'

'Tell me, Mary. What do you know about homosexuality?'

'Not very much.'

'There have been times and places in which it was an honoured form of love. Did you know that?'

'They didn't teach us that in history class! But I suppose I knew.'

'Some of the world's best minds – Leonardo, Michelangelo. Even Shakespeare, they say – "How like a winter hath my absence been from thee?" That sonnet was probably addressed to a boy. Does that shock you?'

'Maybe, a little.'

'Well, the Church says it's wrong, of course, but – '

She interrupted, 'I wasn't brought up with much religion.'

'I was, though. I've had to discard a lot of it and yet the core – ' He stopped. 'What I wanted to say was, the Bible also tells us not to judge. And that I believe is right. Not to judge.'

She was silent.

'People hate anything different from themselves. There are people who hate Jews without ever having known one, or else having known one bad one.'

'This is different.'

'Not really. All the goodness that was in Alex – isn't it there still?'

'I don't know.'

'You do know.'

She sighed.

'He's not *wicked*, Mary! And let me tell you, he suffers. It's obvious he can neither change himself nor accept himself. If he could accept himself it would be easy for him. But this way, it's very hard. Can't you see how hard?'

'I haven't thought about it.'

'Well, think about it. Maybe you'll come to understand.'

'My father never would!'

Martin smiled slightly. 'I'm sure he wouldn't.'

'When I found out about Alex,' she said slowly, 'it was as if a trap-door had opened up and I'd been dropped, just dropped, out into the weather. Violently. I'd been living all my life in a cocoon. Tell me now. Tell me. What am I to do?'

'No, you tell me.'

'I?'

'Yes. You tell me what is the most important thing you have to do from now on.'

For an instant she wasn't sure of his meaning. Then it came to her with a rush. 'To take care of my children. Is that what you meant?'

'Of course.'

She smiled warily. 'That certainly isn't all one gets married for.'

'People marry for many reasons. Because they're lonely, or need a particular kind of understanding or a companionable mind. Many reasons.'

Now he was looking straight at her again, dropping the professional manner as one slips out of a sweater and leaves it on a chair.

'Please, don't say anything to Jessie, will you?'

'I don't discuss other people's confidences.'

'Excuse me. I should have known better.'

'And excuse me. I was pompous and rude just now.'

Neither spoke for a moment. Then Martin began.

'Work. Work is always the salvation, Mary. You have a gift. Use it. Fill your days with it.'

'No,' she said. 'I've no true gift. Father was right about it. It's only a very little talent that I have.'

'You can't be sure yet. Give it time.'

'Time! I'll have plenty of that – '

'You'll need a great deal of courage. But I think you have it.'

'Thank you.'

He added thoughtfully, 'A very good thing, although maybe you can't see its importance right now, is your home. As long as you have to stay there and have no choice. There's great comfort to be had from "place". It doesn't happen to be like that for me, but for some people it's – as they say – the essence. It's true for you, isn't it? And Lamb House is the place?'

'Yes,' she said. 'I walk around sometimes just *touching* things. There are certain trees, an old sycamore where I can sit and feel the world breathe. One can feel such peace among trees.'

Suddenly she was very, very tired. They had said everything there was to be said and gone as far as there was to go. She rose to leave.

'Wait. I'm giving you a prescription for sleeping pills. Just half a dozen. Take one only if you need it badly.'

'I shan't kill myself, you know!'

'If I thought you had such an idea, I wouldn't give them to you at all.'

He stood up, but did not come from behind the desk or offer to shake her hand. It crossed her mind that he hadn't touched her when she had come in, either, and that perhaps in spite of the professional kindness, he really disliked her after all. She put the prescription in her handbag and thanked him.

'Perhaps I haven't helped you, but I did try,' he said.

'It's helped me to talk to you. Yes, it has.'

'I'm glad.' He might have been expected to say, 'Come back any time if you need me again', but he did not, and so she repeated her thanks with a correctness to match his own, and went out.

On the rattling suburban train, she fell asleep. She had always been one of those rare, contrary souls for whom sleep in time of trouble was a psychological escape, and there would be no need for pills.

When the train swayed around the last curve before the home station, she woke up. Martin had been right: there was comfort in 'place'. The High Street gave cheerful assurance. The butcher, florid and garrulous, came out on the step to remark, as always, upon the weather. The seed store had hung out its little packets of nasturtiums, delightful scraps of orange and yellow silk with a sharp enticing perfume after rain. Fern thought wryly: But they are usually covered on the underside with black pinhead bugs. It is the underside that surprises.

Neddie came around the house. 'Guess what?' he cried.

She widened her eyes, responding to his gaiety, his dare. 'I can't guess. What?'

'We had ice cream at Rob's house. It was his brother's birth- day.'

'You did?'

'Yes, and it was chocolate.'

He pranced, jiggling the green pompom on his woollen cap. Oh my heart, my darling! How could I ever leave you?

'Chocolate!' she repeated brightly before, remembering some other errand, he sped away around the corner.

The house enfolded her. She went slowly up the stairs, sliding her hand on the smooth old banister. At the top she paused before the photo of Susannah.

'There was never any love between us,' Alex had told her, after the first month or two. He had been ruefully amused, making a joke of it. 'That's when I found out that the books in her family's library had false backs. Only, I found out too late.'

Had Susannah also found something out too late? But the cool face told nothing.

Alex, coming upstairs a moment later, knocked on the

frame of the open door. 'May I?'

'Yes, come in.'

They faced each other, Fern at the closet where she had been hanging up her coat, he in the doorway.

Then, astoundingly, he said, 'You've seen Martin.'

'What? What makes you say that?'

'You know I sense things. You've told him everything, haven't you?'

'Yes. Are you angry?'

'No. What did he say?'

'I don't know exactly. That is, it's hard to remember.' She stammered. 'I suppose – he tried to explain, to help me understand.'

'I'm very grateful to him. I've always liked him, anyway.'

She raised an eyebrow.

'Don't be nasty! I was referring to intelligence, compassion, humanity.'

She saw that Alex had imagined mockery in her expression. 'I only meant, you don't know him well enough, do you, to feel much of anything towards him?'

'I told you I can sense things. I judge people very quickly. For instance, I know that he's in love with you. I've known it for a long time. He's the man you should have married.'

'Don't be absurd!'

'Haven't you seen how he always manages to leave a room the minute you enter it?'

'What on earth are you saying?'

'You mean you haven't noticed?'

'No, I haven't,' Fern said tightly.

'Well, it's true.'

She turned away. 'I've got to get this hot dress off. It's miserable.'

In the dressing-room she put on a robe. That pain again, the little pulses in her temples! She touched them lightly. He oughtn't to have said that about Martin! There were enough terrible things for her to think about already without adding more. She had mountains to climb! Mountains! And anyway it wasn't true! Martin was responsible, and serious; he wouldn't – Suddenly, involuntarily, she gave a little cry.

'Are you all right?' Alex called.

She came back to the bedroom and sat down. 'It's been a hard day, and I'm worn out.'

Alex knelt on the floor and took her hand.

'Fern, I'll be the best friend you ever could have.'

He moved his cheek until it rested on her limp hand, and she could feel his tears. She wanted to draw away, yet did not; they sat unmoving through an expectant silence.

At last he raised his head. 'I've been through hell,' he said.

'Have you?'

'Don't you believe me?'

'I believe you.'

'Hell for you, too. I know that, Fern. I hope . . . I don't ever want you to think that I – that what I am has anything to do with you. It's just me.'

Silence again.

'It didn't work with Susannah. But then, she was a sharp-tongued bitch, and I thought it might have been partly her fault. I hoped it would be different with you. And I tried, Fern, you know I did.'

She was seeing herself objectively. She was looking through a telescope, to the end of a long, long corridor of time, during which she would mature into understanding. It was as though she were looking at some other woman, surely not at herself, who would have to endure a purgatory of fruitless, unending analysis, while anger and pain would slowly evaporate like salt in the sun, leaving – leaving what? A desert?

Alex spoke again. 'I try to remember how it began. My music teacher, perhaps? He had strong fingers. Supple brown hands. I couldn't stop looking at them.

'And there was a boy in school. Lewis was his name. He sat at the next desk. He also had brown hands and thick, beautiful hair. Strange, troubling twinges went through me, very slight, I remember, very puzzling. Little devils, sitting with hot pitchforks somewhere at the pit of my brain.

'I didn't understand yet. You were supposed to have girls' pictures in your room, a snapshot of your own girl, or actresses, all breasts and thighs and glossy mouths. I kept thinking maybe I just wasn't growing up as early as boys usually do, that pretty soon I'd get to be like the others. But I didn't know, and there was nobody in the world I could ask, least of all my father . . . And then suddenly I was in the last form and during the long vacation a lot of chaps went up to town and brought some girls over to somebody's flat. And the girl I was with – ' now Alex was almost whispering – 'the girl laughed because I – I didn't want to. She laughed. And the news got around when we were back at school. It was a huge, splendid joke! Except for Lewis. He came to me, and we talked. He was so fine, so decent, so different from the others . . . He became my only friend, and I was his. In a way you might say we suffered together.'

He looked down at his hands, turning them over and back, as if they could offer him some explanation.

'There are memories, so minute and sharp they ought to have been absorbed years ago, but never have been. A burly ruffian with hairy ears and a shattering voice, saying, "Alex pees sitting down." Why isn't it possible to forget things like that? Why should a boor's taunt have power to torment you a quarter of a lifetime later?'

So that's the way it is, Fern thought. She had not wanted to be so moved. She had wanted to keep the hard anger, to hold the insult which had been dealt her, to hold them both fast and neither weaken nor give in. But give in to what?

In these few minutes, night had come, and from the triangle of sky that filled the upper corner of the window, there poured an iridescent afterglow. It fell upon the man's bowed head. Feeling her gaze, he looked up.

'Fern, everything I have belongs to you and the children. I don't mean just things, this house or money. I mean caring. My devotion. I can't help what I am. I'll have to go on just quietly being what I am, you know. But I'll never ask what you do with private portions of your life. I'll never ask.

'So we could live here, couldn't we, with our children, and be happy in other ways?'

'Happy!' she cried silently.

And Alex repeated, 'Couldn't we?'

In the simplicity of the words and in his face she saw, not

so much a plea for pity and understanding, as a kind of wonder that they two were here like this, having learned what they both now knew. That much she saw, and also she saw disbelief, as when a man has been wounded, so she had read, and stares at the shattering, not able to believe that he is himself and the wound belongs to him.

Then pity came, after all, and she bent down to rest his head against her shoulder, rocking and swaying as if he were a child and she his mother. Or as if she were the child, panicked and lost, and he her comforter. Or as if he and she, strangers just met, survivors of some awful cataclysm, some rage of nature, avalanche or quake or firestorm, must cling together out of need and then, because of common humanity and common trust, must stay.

BOOK THREE

PASSAGES

CHAPTER ELEVEN

No self-respecting institution at home would have put up with so ancient a building, Martin reflected, as he prepared to leave for the afternoon. In America this would have been torn down, or more probably abandoned for a new building in a newer part of the city. These steps on which he stood to regard the blossoming day had been laid down in the eighteenth century. The wings to right and left of the central structure were Edwardian, darkly bulbous, with beetling fenestration. It amused him to imagine that they looked like the women of their era, stout in bombazine and bustles.

'Making your plans for the day?' Mr Meredith drew on gloves and tucked his umbrella under one arm.

'Great plans. I'm going to the park with Claire.'

'Taking a bus?'

'Later. I want to walk a little before I catch it.'

'Fine. I'll go part way with you.'

Through speckled sunlight and shade under the lime trees, they fell into step. Each man was sturdy with well-being and aware that the other was the same. A small boy came galloping with an enormous Borzoi on a leash. A young woman in a petal yellow suit came out of a house, carrying a sheaf of tulips wrapped in green tissue paper.

'Splendid weather,' Meredith remarked with a sigh of pleasure.

Martin said, 'I can't believe I've been here three years.'

'Does it seem longer to you or shorter?'

'That depends on mood. Longer or shorter, it's been wonderful. It's opened worlds for me.'

'I must say you've taken good advantage of it. Your cytology paper is impressive, Mr Braidburn tells me. I confess I haven't read it yet. I'll have to wait until it's published. You're going to the conference in Paris next week, of course?'

'I wouldn't miss it. Dr Eastman's coming over from New York and I'll have a chance to see him again.'

'Have I congratulated you on your association with him? Great fortune for you.'

'I'm indebted to Mr Braidburn forever. After all, when Eastman wrote that he was looking for a new man, Mr Braidburn could have recommended any one of half a dozen others, and I know it.'

'What have you been offered, may I ask? Full-time association?'

'Yes, on a trial basis, naturally. If things work out well, why then it will become permanent.' Martin's voice trailed off. The whole prospect had an air of unreality. Everything had gone so smoothly, one deliberate step after the other.

'You've got just two months more, haven't you? You must come for a week-end in the country with us before you leave. Well, I turn off here. Enjoy your afternoon.'

Glancing after him, Martin thought: Funny, in the beginning, the formal manners, the bowler hats and accents put me off. He smiled, recalling some of those first impressions.

They had taught him much, those men: Meredith, Braidburn, Llewellyn and the rest. All those dark winter afternoons under electric lights in the pathology lab! Those early mornings watching Braidburn in the O.R.! And the lunchtime discussions on clinical neurology; the diagrams drawn on the backs of menus; the questions; the arguments! Yes, he would take good memories back with him.

From the top of the double-decker bus, he enjoyed the panorama of the city. How the northerners of this foggy little island worshipped the sun! This was the first real warmth of the season today and here they were already, stretched out wherever there was a plot of grass, turning their pale faces to the light. Here came the Victoria and Albert Memorial, a wedding cake in stone. He had a glimpse of a deerhound on a stone frieze, pursued by men wearing classical togas. Absurd! A large stone lady perched on a kneeling elephant; an elaborate necklace fell between her naked, spherical breasts, and that was absurd, too. But the breasts were exquisite. He stared at them until they were out of sight. Now came the turn into Kensington High Street and a few blocks to walk home. He got off and began to hurry.

Claire was dressed and waiting for him. They started for the park, she riding ahead of him on her tricycle, jangling its bell. Her dark curls just touched the velvet collar of her tiny coat. Jessie dressed her in fine taste, but then, Jessie's taste was always fine. He couldn't take his eyes from Claire. And he wondered whether she would ever have any comprehension at all of what she meant to him. Her bright voice, her vigour! There was such a softness in him! That nothing, nothing, should ever happen to this child! No one ever hurt her! And although he knew that this cherishing of a child was the most universal emotion known to man, still it seemed to him, no doubt foolishly, that what *he* felt must be unusually intense.

How irrational life could be! Now, with the way lying clear before him to support a family, he could have but one child. Alice had sent snapshots of her three, the girls not nearly as pretty as Claire. Fred taught at a village school in the potato country; it must be a struggle for them. Yet Alice was about to have another child.

Once in the park, past the Round Pond and the ducks in the Serpentine, Martin led the way to the statue of Peter Pan. (He had read the story to Claire; Jessie said it was too advanced for a three-year-old, yet he was sure she had understood it.) And, finding a bench, he settled down to watch Claire riding back and forth on the path.

Not far from the statue they were taking pictures for a fashion magazine. Lanky and lean, the models posed smartly with arched back, thrusting pelvis and long, striding legs. Their purpose was ostensibly to seem indifferent and aloof. Yet sexual invitation was written on their lovely, haughty faces.

Under a spreading bush a couple lay in uninhibited embrace for anyone to see. And it was said that the English were 'cold'!

Martin breathed deeply. A tart, bitter fragrance blew from behind him: out of dark earth had come an explosion of huge geraniums, blazing and blooming like none he had ever seen at home. And these also were sexual in their exuberance.

Primeval, burgeoning spring! Fragrance and moisture of new life, bursting, reaching, wanting. Wanting so! Until it – it hurt!

He became aware of his heartbeat. It happens now and then· you hear your own heartbeat and suddenly, for no reason that you can explain to yourself, you are reminded that some day it will stop. The sturdy, steady heart will flutter and gallop, will flutter and slow. There will come a final beat. And the amazing little pump, which has been serving without an instant's rest for all your years, will halt.

And now the old, familiar melancholy seeped in Martin: the veil, the cloud over the sun, the shade drawn down on the day which had been so blithe and charming up till a moment ago. And he remembered that this melancholy had been lying upon him for many months past.

There had been such cheer when Claire was born! So much purpose and joy! What had happened to them? And when? But it was impossible to set a time, to say 'There, that's the moment we began to be unhappy.'

Back in Cyprus it had seemed remarkable that Jessie could be possessed of such practical good humour, so much realistic common sense, such strong optimism. 'Wholesome' had been his word for her then, often a priggish word when misused, but actually a fine one, meaning 'healthy' and 'whole'. Now that wholeness had split. How? Why?

There had been 'scenes'. He hated them. It might be supposed that no one enjoyed them, although maybe some people did, dramatic types who flaunted emotion to gain attention. But Martin cringed at the thought. And Jessie was always miserable afterwards. Yet they happened, again and again. They were very hard to live with.

A few weeks before they had gone to see *Giselle*. A new ballerina had been dancing, an exquisite girl who was being talked of all over the continent. A dream of a girl – unforgettable. Her dark red hair, caught in a tail, fell tossing to her shoulders. She rose *en pointe*, her white arms reaching in a perfect curve, her mauve skirt drifting – Splendour and grace to catch at one's throat in awe and linger, smiling, on one's lips!

And all the while Jessie had been watching, not the dance, but him.

Coming into the bedroom later that night, he had caught her standing naked in front of the mirrored door. She had turned on him furiously.

'Why don't you knock? Do you have to come in here to stare at me?'

'I wasn't staring at you! But for heaven's sake, I'll look away if you want me to.'

'Yes, do! It's a lot more pleasant for you to look at anyone else but me, I'm sure it is. Ballerinas, waitresses – almost anyone but me.'

Wanting to be patient, he had yet said the wrong thing. 'Jessie, can't you try not to think about yourself? Other people really don't pay all that much attention to your – '

'To my what?'

'Your – disability.'

'You can't say it, can you?'

'Say what?'

'Hump!' she cried. 'I can say it well enough! H-U-M-P. Hump. Go on. Say it!'

He sat down wearily, covering his eyes with his hands.

'You didn't think I heard,' Jessie said, 'that time in Vienna in the shop where we bought the porcelain tea set and the saleswoman said to you, "You'll be glad you bought it. Your mother will love it." She thought I was your mother!'

'Oh, if you're going to let a shopgirl's stupid mistake haunt you like this, what can I say to help you? I want to help you, Jessie,' he said gently.

So he had tried and in the end, when she had exhausted anger, she had apologized, in shame.

'Oh, you are patient with me, Martin, I know you are! I ought to be grateful for what I've got, and I really am. It's just that when we're out together – you have no idea how I steel myself to go places with you! I feel the thoughts in the air, the messages passed from one to the other. And I know what they'll say after we're gone, how the women will talk on the telephone the next morning.'

For a week or two after that particular time they had gone nowhere, except on Sunday to a country inn where they had sat on a high-backed settle near a fire and watched the locals play Shove Ha'penny. No one had paid any attention to them. For those few hours it had been as it was when they rode around Cyprus on house calls, talking about the state of medicine and everything else under the sun. He understood now that these things had interested Jessie because she could hide behind them: they were not about *her*. But she couldn't hide in anonymous places forever. She must know that.

Could he ever think of her as other than a poor bird with a broken wing? Her strength had been deceptive: the bird could flutter bravely in the cage but the wide world frightened it. Then his mind closed, unwilling to confront yet another analysis.

He looked for Claire. She was safely pedalling down the walk, her short legs working like pistons. He looked at his watch, which was a handsome one, last year's Christmas gift from Jessie. She was always buying things for him, caring about his clothes – he himself cared almost nothing about clothes – seeing to it that there were books on his night table, making plans for the office he would have. Next year at Christmas they would be in New York and he would be earning. He would have to find some splendid present for her, something, even, that he couldn't afford. A ring? She had slender fingers. A sapphire?

Now memory made one of its implausible and senseless associations. Mary wore rings. Mary still wore that curiously fashioned topaz ring. Only a few weeks ago, coming home earlier than usual, he found that she had dropped in for tea, something she hadn't done in half a year or more. She had risen as soon after Martin's entrance as decent manners would allow. He had been aware of that, every nerve in him had been aware of her. And he had observed that she still wore the topaz ring. White lilacs circled the brim of her straw hat. Her shoes were delicate. He had seen that her eyes avoided him, looking past him towards the wall, or resting on her hand, the one with the ring, which lay on the arm of the chair.

He concluded that she was embarrassed before him. People often were after they had revealed their intimate miseries. He had only seen her perhaps six times since that day, more than a year ago, when she had sat before him and told, with more dignity than most women would have been able to muster, the story of wreckage. He had, for a bad few moments, been harsh with her that day; for some reason he had wanted to hurt her; and at once he had been terribly ashamed and tried to make amends. He hoped he had made them adequately.

There had been no way to find out, or to find out how she was faring at all. From the outside, seen at a Thanksgiving dinner or a Christmas party, everything looked handsome enough, with a patina of wealth and charm and family unity.

'Fern would never get a divorce,' Jessie had remarked once, a long time ago. 'It would shatter her image of perfection.'

But that wasn't true. She would have got one if she could have.

And he wondered about many things: whether Alex had any idea how much he, Martin, knew of the Lambs' affairs; whether Mary had someone else by now; whether she lay alone at night and how troubled she might be because of it –

Surprising, though, how one could get used to being 'alone'. He had thought of himself, and indeed had been, a man with strong and frequent sexual needs. Yet now a very little went a long way. Lying down at night next to Jessie's immaculate, light body, he could fall instantly asleep. When a man has worked under pressure all day he is too tense to want anything but sleep, he told himself – and at the same time knew this for the rationalization it was.

Oh, it ought to be otherwise! It ought to be the core of a man's life, its force and heat!

If only he could get rid of the images that lay on his brain as though they had been printed there! Mary, in Braidburn's office, struggling against tears. Mary, proudly pregnant, standing at the door of Lamb House. Mary, in Cyprus, painting three scarlet birds on a wire fence. Fantasies! Soon, if he didn't curb them, he would become obsessed by them again as once he had been. Foreboding and alarm began to flutter in him now. It was humiliating not to be able to direct his mind at will . . .

Claire climbed up on the bench between him and a proper British nurse who was tending a baby in a perambulator.

'Read to me,' she commanded.

He opened the little book which he had thrust into his pocket before leaving home and she explained earnestly, 'It's about dinosaurs. This one is Allosaurus. He eats vegetables.'

'And very good for him, too.'

'I hate vegetables.'

'I know. That's why I said what I did.'

She laughed. Only three, and she could already share a joke with him!

'Shall I read about him, or about this one?' he asked.

'This one. He's Tyrannosaurus Rex. He eats people. Look at his teeth, Daddy.'

'Oh, he's fierce all right,' Martin agreed. 'We'll read about him, then.'

When he had finished, she went back to the tricycle.

'That's a bright little girl, sir,' the nurse remarked.

'Thank you.'

'A child with spirit. She knows what she knows.'

Martin dutifully praised the baby in the perambulator.

'I often see your little girl here with her mother. This is my favourite place in the whole park.'

'It's a beautiful spot.'

So this woman had seen Jessie, too. The nurses must have gossiped: 'The child's mother – poor thing . . . No, not the father . . . Very odd, really.' He could hear them. Then he felt ashamed. Good God, he was as bad as Jessie! People did have other things to talk about, after all.

'You'll be going back to America soon, I hear.'

'Yes. In the fall.' He corrected himself. 'The autumn.'

'I expect you'll be happy to go home.'

'Yes, home is always best, isn't it?' Martin answered tritely

The sky was what one called 'mackerel', spotted and clouding over towards a sudden English shower. He stood up and called to Claire. Holding the child's hand, he guided the tricycle across the street.

'Home is best,' he had said. Yet here he had had perhaps the best years of his life. Here he had grown furthest and swiftest towards what he wanted to be. 'Why don't you stay in London?' people often asked. For it was a civilized place. Always he would remember its moist, foggy air and its mild light lying on greenery and grey stone.

New York, on the other hand, was aggressive. The searing summers drained your strength. The tearing February wind, blowing off the rivers, was fierce enough to spin you around in your tracks. And all the time, one was battered by noise of traffic and hammering rivets. If they were not tearing something down, they were putting something up. A restless, unsettling place!

Yet he had felt its lure and power from the very first. There was no place like it, so challenging, so – alive! It called to him; it dared him to do his best. Yes, time to go back. Time, too, for Claire to know she's an American. She speaks now with a pretty bird-like chirp, the accent and inflection of the English upper classes. So that's another reason to return. But the true reason, the real one? The answer struck Martin like a slap across the cheek. Because it will put an ocean between *her* and me.

'It's *Otello* tonight, isn't it?' he called from the shaving mirror in the bathroom.

Jessie didn't answer. When he came back into the bedroom, she was sitting at the window, looking out into the street.

'Why, you're not dressing! We haven't got all that much time!'

'I'm not going to the opera,' she said.

'Not going! What's wrong?'

'I've nothing to wear.'

'What can you be talking about?'

'About having nothing to wear. I refuse to go out any

more in makeshift clothes.'

'You always look fine,' Martin said, too heartily. 'That white lace cape-thing you bought – '

'Capes! Scarves! Creeping in, crouched under a cape!'

Swallowing impatience, he said reasonably, 'I don't know anything about fashions, but perhaps a good dressmaker – '

'I'm tired,' she interrupted, 'of having you ashamed of me.'

He almost shouted: 'I have never been ashamed of you, Jessie!'

'If I looked like Fern, you wouldn't have to be.'

'I am not ashamed, I tell you!' He was so weary of having to cope with this again! Maybe in the morning when he felt fresher he would do better, but not now at the end of the day. He sighed and recited, 'Actually, you do look very much like Mary. You've said so yourself.'

'Why will you keep on calling her Mary?'

'She likes the name.'

Jessie's mouth twisted. 'You know, Martin, you don't fool me. You never have.'

'What in blazes are you talking about? Who's trying to fool you?'

'You never say, "I love you". Do you even realize that?'

'I'm not much for words. Maybe that's a fault. Yes, I guess it is. But actions are something else, aren't they? How do I treat you? You should ask yourself that.'

'You've been – exemplary. You made a bargain and you've stuck with it to the letter. Honourably. You couldn't get my sister, so you took me.'

As it is said, the best defence is a good offence. 'I am not, positively not, going to stand here – ' and catching a glimpse of himself in the mirror, with one half of his face covered in shaving lather, Martin felt ridiculous and irritated with himself. 'You're making trouble where there is none, Jessie.'

'Don't fence with me. Father warned me before we were married. People don't know how shrewd Father is, because he's close-mouthed when he wants to be. But he knew it was Fern you wanted and he warned me not to marry you. He was right.'

'He warned you?' Martin was totally confused.

Jessie twisted a handkerchief. She began to cry. Two red blotches appeared on her cheeks. 'Yes, yes, he only wanted this for me after I convinced him. Maybe he wanted to be convinced, I don't know . . . You were, after all, a solution for me, weren't you?'

He was stunned. For a moment there was no sound in the room.

'Why am I telling you this? I'll be sorry tomorrow – '

Anger surged in Martin and quickly died. After all, what difference did it make now who had or had not conceived the marriage?

'I loved you, Martin. We were alike in a way; we were prisoners. Your prison was poverty and mine was my body. And I thought – I thought perhaps we could make each other happy. It would be a kind of trade-off.'

He stood in a fog. Thickly it settled, a heavy weight of hopeless fatigue, so that it seemed he could never make the effort to move through it.

'I thought – oh, I gave it hours of thought, believe me – I thought, although you didn't love me, as you might have loved Fern if she hadn't gone away, or loved some other woman, still you liked me tremendously. I knew you did. I believed we could manage with that. It's been done before.' And Jessie looked up half timidly, half in defiance.

Prison, she had said and it was true, except that he had already escaped from his and she never would.

'Jessie,' he said softly, 'Jessie . . . You're wrong. You think I don't love you . . . but I do.' And that also, in its way, was true.

A small doubting smile fled across her face. 'Don't, Martin, I'm too smart for that.'

He made a helpless gesture. 'Then I just don't know. If you won't believe me – '

She sighed. 'It's my own fault. I took advantage of your need. It was my fault.'

'Who's talking about fault? We're here, now, today. And we have so much – ' Suddenly his energies revived and he began to speak eagerly. Holding his fingers spread, he counted, 'We have a home. We have friends and will have more. We have a beautiful child. We can't allow this sort of thing to go on, for her sake, if for no other reason.'

'That's true.'

'Well then?'

She stood up and lay her head in the hollow of his shoulder. 'I'm drifting. I'm floating with nothing to hold to.'

He put his arms around her and held her gently, as one holds a troubled child. 'You have me to hold to.' He stroked her hair, the jaunty curls on the sad, bent head. 'I wish I could make you feel the way you did when we used to ride around on house calls. Remember how we'd talk and talk? You had ideas about everything in the world.'

'I felt I was a part of things then. It's different here. You're gone all day climbing up in the world, and I'm left out.'

'But this is what it was all for! It's what you wanted, isn't it?'

'I know. I planned the whole thing, and at the start I was happy; I was! But now it's all got complicated . . . I don't make any sense, do I?'

'Well, plenty of people don't make any sense. But you'll climb out of the slump. I'll pull you out of it. Now let's hurry, shall we? How fast can you dress?'

'I don't want to go tonight, Martin. Truly. You can go without me. I won't mind. And I'll be all right. Really.'

She expected him to stay with her, he knew. And, pity or no, he felt suddenly perverse. He wasn't angry, he wasn't being stubborn; he was simply weary of yet another 'scene'. Moreover, he had wanted to hear *Otello*.

'All right then. I'll go,' he said. 'Have a good sleep. You'll feel different in the morning.'

The singers had taken their final bows, and the departing crowd moved slowly through the lobby. Alex Lamb touched Martin on the shoulder.

'Hello there! Where's Jessie?'

'Didn't feel up to par tonight. She went to bed early.'

'Come back to our place for a spot of supper. It's my birthday and some friends are coming.'

'Well, I really ought – '

'Come on, you can spare an hour or two for your brother-in-law. Jessie must be asleep by now, anyway.'

The Lambs' table was bright with iris and narcissi, flowery porcelain, laughter and wine. The women were so lovely! Even the older ones had a pearl-glow, not from the candlelight, but from something within. And in Martin, too, a subtle warmth began to stir.

'Fern hasn't been able to shake the cough,' Alex was speaking to someone at the far end of the table. 'The children had it first, and it's gone from one to the other. So I'm insisting she take a week on the Riviera to get over it.'

'You're not going?'

'I can't. There's too much on the fire at the office. But she'll be happy on the beach with a pile of books.'

A woman called, 'That's the most splendid necklace, Fern! I've been meaning to tell you all evening.'

Everyone turned to look at the necklace; a filigree of gold and garnets, it rested as in a velvet case on Fern's naked shoulders; the heavy pendant lay on white silk between her breasts.

'Her present for my birthday,' Alex explained; with the smile of a fond husband.

Observing that smile and Mary's answer, Martin felt, among all the converging streams of his emotions, a current of soft compassion. Of all the people in that room, he was almost surely the only one who knew the truth. How capricious, how reckless was life! Once he had seen it as a steady journey: for some a dull plod, for others a march of triumph, but in any case something with direction, that one *controlled.* He had, of course, been very young when he had thought so.

For nothing he had done or willed had brought him to where he was now. And where was he now? Quite simply, he was a man in love, a man obsessed with loving, filled with it, driven by it. Something had forced him to love this woman from the first moment. And never, in spite of all his self-denials, had he ceased to love her.

How was it possible? Who could say? It was, after all, the

human condition! A natural phenomenon: a simple thing! But light and water were simple things, too, as long as one didn't try to explain them.

And, sitting at that festive table, Martin had now a sense of total recall: the white room with her pictures on the wall; her face raised to his when he came in; that incredible blue gaze; the paint spot on the sandal. The moment, arrested moment, in which everything had changed although he had not known then how much.

But she? What of her? He had no way of knowing, dared not try to find out. And he thought of her, living her sham; he thought of Jessie – and he thought his head would burst with futile thinking. The warmth and sparkle seeped out of the room, seeped out of his spirit.

Someone was addressing him. 'So you'll be leaving us, going back to America, I hear?'

'Yes, soon,' he replied.

Someone remarked to Fern, 'You'll miss your sister.'

She made some acknowledgement. Glancing up at the sound, he caught her gaze. And a strange thing happened: she did not turn away. Eyes normally move towards the sound of voices; they come to rest on one face, then another; they flicker over a table and across a room. But hers did not. They fastened on Martin's eyes and held there.

Talk bubbled around the circle as wine bubbles in a glass; still the eyes held to each other. His – his heart was in his eyes, that's all he knew. Hers – hers had such a look . . . He wanted to believe it, had to believe it. Unmistakably it said: If you want me, I shall not refuse.

Wild, tremendous, reckless joy surged in him.

His right-hand neighbour, an agreeable, grey-haired lady, looked concerned. 'Is anything wrong?'

'Wrong?' he repeated confusedly.

'You put your fork down so abruptly, I thought you weren't feeling well.'

'No, no. I just remembered something, that's all.'

'Well, as long as it was something happy,' she said brightly.

The talk kept on swirling. He did not hear it. At last people pushed their chairs back and left the table. Then someone put music on the record player. Dancing began in the hall.

From the arc of the bay window in the drawing-room a balcony projected, a little space affording room for no more than two or three to stand and look down upon the square. Mary leaned against the railing. When he stepped behind her she did not move.

The square was still. It was late; distant traffic only murmured now, as distant water rushes in a country place. Light globes hung among the trees like white balloons and a powerful scent of wet earth rose from the shrubbery.

'Who stole my heart away? Who – ' The little tune floated with a poignant sweetness from the room at their backs.

In the tiny space among the potted plants their shoulders touched. Still neither of them moved. Someone inside turned a lamp on; the beam of its light fell over a blossoming azalea in a tub, turning the white buds rosy, the colour of flesh.

'My God,' Martin said. He was shaking.

She looked at him.

'What are we going to do?' he asked.

'I don't know.'

'We have to do something about it. Don't you know that?'

'Don't,' she whispered. 'I'm starting to cry. I won't be able to turn around if someone comes.'

He understood that tenderness would bring more tears. So he waited a minute or two and then spoke quickly.

'I'll be in Paris at a conference next week. I can leave after the second day. Will you – '

'Yes . . . Yes.'

'Where will you be staying?'

'At the George the Fifth . . .'

Voices passed and passed again in the room behind them. Still they stood, hostess and guest, looking out at the lovely night.

'Darling,' Martin said. It was the first time he had said the word aloud. 'My darling Mary.'

CHAPTER TWELVE

They had six days. Eastward through the Provençal spring they drove, past olive orchards and round hills dressed in lavender. On cobbled squares they parked the rented car and drank cassis while old men played boules. They came down out of the hills to the sea on a morning when light showered from the sky and broke into a hundred thousand sapphires over the bay.

How beautiful, oh God, how beautiful!

And they came to a white town, to a house with tall, blue-shuttered windows, where the air smelled of lemons and everything glittered in the sun.

'We're here,' Mary said. 'Menton.' She laughed. '"*Glücklich wie Gott in Frankreich.*"'

'What does that mean?'

'It means "Happy as God in France." It's one of the few things I still remember in German.'

'Do you remember enough French to ask for a good room?'

'We already have one.'

'Then shall we go upstairs right away?'

'Do you want to?'

'You know I do.'

Light, coming through the blinds, drew bars of dusty gold across her thighs. Outside it was still afternoon, but within the tall old room dusk had settled.

She made a little sound, an indrawn breath, part sigh, part cry. He turned in the bed and put his lips on the soft hollow where the sound had caught in her throat. His thudding heart had slowed; now it started up again. They had been lying in that sweet peace which follows the ultimate attainment. Surely no other woman in the world, he thought, had ever or could ever – Over and over they had dissolved and merged and become one. There were no words for it. All the millions of words that had been written came down to nothing.

In the evening, they sat and talked. They went back to the beginning.

'What did you really think, Mary? Didn't you *know* I wanted you? Why didn't you come home? Why did you marry Alex? Tell me. Tell me.'

'Oh,' she said, 'what had I seen or known? I had never been touched by anyone. Yes, you touched me . . . I thought when I came back from Europe, we'll see each other again and after a while – '

'But I was dying for you, Mary!'

'But your letter! You were so proud and glad about Doctor Albeniz – '

'You remember the name!'

'I remember everything. I understood then that your work would always come first. I thought perhaps I had imagined the other – about me. And I felt ashamed. Then that same week I met Alex.'

Martin was silent. Yes, of course she would have welcomed Alex then, with all his cheer and strength, with all the colour and movement of the life he offered! Offered without postponement!

'I understand,' he said.

'Would your work really have come first, Martin? Would you have asked me to wait three years?'

He wanted to be completely honest, both with her and with himself. 'I don't know. I've thought about it, foolishly I suppose, asking myself whether you would have waited for me, whether I would have given up the offer if you hadn't been willing to wait or what I would have done if my father hadn't died. My God, what a tangle it was – and is!'

'And I,' Mary spoke so low that he could barely hear her, 'I wanted to get away from that dim house. Would I have waited three years more? I don't know. You can't imagine how I wanted to get away and – and live!'

'I can,' Martin said.

'Yet I ask myself, was it really as bad as all that? I've told you before, one has no right to be a fifteen-year-old romantic when one's twenty.'

'You've made up for it,' he said gently.

'Oh yes, I'm a hundred years older!' She clasped her hands under her chin; her rings flashed in the darkness. 'How easily one throws oneself away! As if one could replace oneself and all the lost days. I would do differently now.'

'You can't be sure of that. We torture ourselves, all of us do, with questions that can't be answered.'

'I wonder,' Mary said, 'whether my children will ever wonder about me some day and ask whether I've been happy.'

'That's a strange thought.'

'Not really. I often think about my mother. You would have liked her, Martin. She was so different from Father. I never knew why they married. I think he was overawed just because she was so different from him. Sometimes at the table she would talk, and I knew he wasn't even listening. He didn't care about any of the things she loved.'

Martin looked down into the trees. The dark pines and her evocation of old memories were suddenly oppressive.

'Don't,' he said.

'Don't what?'

'Talk about sad things.'

'I didn't mean to be sad. You do the talking, then.'

'No, I'd rather hear you. I don't know you enough, Mary. I should need a lifetime to know you and I won't have it.'

'Now you're the one who's talking of sad things.'

What's to become of us, he thought, now that we have begun something that can't go on and also can't end?

He roused himself. 'Come. We'll go down and walk on the beach. It's too beautiful to waste a minute of it.'

In Nice they walked on the Promenade des Anglais, while a stream of smart, snub-nosed Renaults went by. Stepping quietly in the hush of grandeur, they looked at shop windows and marble lobbies. From a terrace they observed a nineteenth-century panorama: wide effect of water and gauzy sky, of sails, white dresses, pillars and balustrades. Sprightly music played and no one, Martin saw, noticed that the musicians had threadbare cuffs.

'Let's go back to Menton,' he said abruptly.

'You're a funny duck! We just got here!'

'Do you mind? If you really do, I'll stay.'

'No. We can have a country lunch if you'd rather.'

'Then I'd rather.'

At a market in a walled village on the Grande Corniche they bought food: cheese, fruit, bread and the shrivelled black olives of the region. On the side of the road they stopped to eat.

'Better than all that splendour,' Martin remarked.

'It made you uncomfortable?'

'Yes, that sort of thing's a snare. A doctor must never let himself forget ordinary people. It's only too easy.'

'For you, do you mean, or for anyone?'

'I'm no different from anyone else. Or maybe I am. I want beauty terribly, and beauty in this world can be expensive.'

'I think you're too hard on yourself.'

'That's what Jessie always says.'

Mary looked away. Her face was sad. 'I'd managed for at least two hours not to think of her until just now.'

'We're not going to hurt her,' he protested. 'Neither of us wants to or will.'

'But I'll know when I look at her, or at you, or at myself.'

He closed his eyes, shutting out the noon brightness. He thought aloud. 'We couldn't have helped it – the whole thing, from the beginning.'

'I'm so sorry for us all!'

'For Alex, too?'

'No, he's as happy as possible, in his circumstances. You know,' she said, 'I've accepted all that . . . Did you ever think I really would?' There was a spiritual beauty in her face as the sadness ebbed into grave calm.

'Yes,' Martin said, 'I did think you would. I remember, on the day we met, how compassionately you spoke of Jessie.'

'But to be truly compassionate, one needs to have suffered. One needs to have been alone. I know that now. I didn't then.'

'Mary . . . tell me, is it terribly hard for you now, the way things are?'

She was silent for a while. He did not interrupt her silence.

Then she said, 'You might say it's as if I were a widow, living with a kind of brother. Not the worst fate in the world, I suppose. Thank God, I have my children and my art, such as it is.'

But if she didn't have the children, she would be free. Yet, if she were free and he not free, how would he feel about that? Guiltily, Martin repressed the selfish thought.

'Listen to me,' he said. 'We're over-analysing. Let's just accept, instead. What's past is past. There's nothing we can do about it now.'

She stood up. 'You said we mustn't spoil our days here, and you were right. So, no more talk! Let's go back to the beach and pretend we have all the time in the world.'

Three more days. For long hours they lay in a hidden hollow of the beach, under the escarpment of the hills out of whose rocks these ancient villages had been carved. On a promontory, like a finger thrust out into the sea, the tearing wind had bent pines into the attitude of prayer. But in this windless hollow the warmth was kindly, the air was like silk on the skin and the sand like silk.

He took her hand. It seemed to him that strength flowed from one to the other through their hands. And he thought that ultimate joy would be to lie forever in this sun, to float in this sea – for was the sea not once our home? – and to wake in the first light with this woman next to him.

Coming back to their room one day they found the maid cleaning. 'I saw you walking yesterday,' she said. 'M'sieur and Madame looked so happy.' She spoke with the awkward boldness of one who is naturally shy. 'I watched you laughing, and I felt happy, too. I'm going to be married on Saturday.'

'Oh,' Mary cried, 'we shall be gone by then! Is he the

young man who waited for you at the end of the drive last night?'

Blushing, the girl nodded. 'You could have come to the wedding in my village. It's not far from here.'

Mary reached into the closet for her dressing-gown, white silk embroidered with red Chinese poppies, 'I want you to have this,' she said and, as the girl protested, 'No, I want you to. I've been so happy wearing it. It will bring you luck.'

'I wonder what sort of children they'll have,' she said when the girl had left. 'She, with her round face and pug nose? The boy is thin and has a craggy nose. He looks gentle.'

'You wonder about everything, don't you? You're probably the most curious person I've ever known,' he answered, smiling at her.

There was a radiant joy in her eyes. He saw that for the moment her spirit was unencumbered. He wished it might always be so . . .

'I would like to have gone to that girl's wedding,' Mary said.

'Why would you?'

'I saw a country wedding here once. The bride was a farm girl in a home-made dress. After the ceremony she laid her bouquet at the feet of the Virgin in the side chapel. I think they pray for many children, I'm not sure. I would pray that I had chosen the right man . . . Afterwards they drove away in an old car with daisy streamers tied on. It was very touching . . . I cried.'

Could it have been like that for us? Martin wondered.

One more day. In the afternoon they went walking inland. Everything drowsed. Birds were silent. Houses with closed shutters lay sleeping in the heat. Plane trees in long alleys were quiet in the windless air.

'Siesta time,' Mary said.

'I know. But we can't waste it.' And he said, 'I've never made love on the grass.'

She laughed. The sound was happiness, and this happiness was beautiful to Martin, seductive and yet pure.

'Why wonder? Let's find out.'

They walked on past a field where cows rested in the shade, then climbed a fence into a dark little grove. Still the world slept; there was no one in sight. Behind a curtain of living green they lay down, in the hush and murmur of the breathing meadow.

The last day. Late in the afternoon Martin came out to the terrace and paused in the doorway. Unaware of his presence, Mary sat with bowed head. She had changed into travelling clothes; their neutral tan was sober in the pastel afternoon. And this sober colour, the curve of her skirt and her bent head created a melancholy which, if you were able to translate them into music, would quiver into a minor chord and die on the air. He stood there looking and looking. There was something in his throat. He kept swallowing, but it wouldn't go down. Then she saw him.

'The bags are downstairs,' he said.

She nodded.

'They've taken the car. We'll get a taxi to the station.' He sat down and took her hand. It lay limply in his. 'There's time for something to eat,' he said.

'I can't.'

'But you must,' he said and asked the waitress for a tureen of soup.

And he sat there wishing, wishing that they were just beginning, that they were going away somewhere, to Afghanistan or Patagonia, where they would shed everything: names, past, everything.

'What have we done?' Mary whispered.

'Nothing,' he said. 'Nothing to hurt anybody, since that's what you mean.'

'Nobody?'

'No. Alex wouldn't care and Jessie will never know.'

'And what about you and me? What is to become of us?'

Below them lay eternal blue, azure and turquoise, blue upon rippling blue. He stared out over the water.

And Mary repeated, 'Tell me, what's to become of us?'

'I don't know . . . I'll think . . . There must be something.'

'Oh God!' she cried.

'Dearest. Dearest. Don't.'

She turned her face away.

The waitress came back with the tureen. 'Careful, it's hot! Shall I bring a salad?'

'Madame is not feeling well. This will be enough,' Martin said.

'So now we just get on the train and go back,' Mary cried. 'Nothing more? And that's all? I'm twenty-eight,' she said, and he understood that she meant, 'I'm too young to settle for "nothing more".'

The wheels of daily living turn regardlessly. So he paid the bill and tipped the waitress, checked in his pocket for the train tickets and summoned a taxi.

The train clattered northward. At a rural stop, a couple with three children entered the compartment; the youngest was asleep on the father's shoulder. The man's face was tender; his hand cupped the small head.

When a rag doll dropped to the floor from the girl's sleeping hand, Martin picked it up. And he remembered Claire, who slept with a doll in a tattered orange dress.

At that same moment Mary said, 'Emmy and Isabel have dolls like that. Alex bought them in France.' Her lips trembled.

If Mary's children were mine, Martin thought, and Claire belonged to Mary –

She laid her head on the back of the seat. He remembered that she had told him how she found escape in sleep. Rest then, he thought, drawing the shade to keep the light from flickering on her face. Her breasts rose and fell under the tan silk. He remembered their perfume. If they had been alone in the compartment, he would have put his head next to hers. But now these strangers were here, sitting like monoliths on Easter Island. Every time he looked up, he met the curious eyes of these innocent strangers, and he hated them.

All through the long trip to England, to the parting place, his thoughts went round and round like a poor blinded mule at the threshing floor. There must be a way . . . There is no way . . . There must be a way . . . There is no way . . .

They were astonished to be met at the railroad station in

London by Alex Lamb. Even before the train had come to a halt under the glass roof and the iron fretwork they saw him scanning the carriages, then running towards them.

'Nothing wrong with the children, it's all right!' he called. When they came up to him he lowered his voice. 'But you have damn well made a mess of things! All hell has broken loose.'

'What? What are you saying?' Mary cried.

'Good Lord, Fern, I don't mind! But dammit, if you had only told me! Then I would have known what to say.'

On the platform, surrounded by luggage and hurrying feet, they heard the story.

'You see, Jessie got the idea that it would be jolly to call the hotel in Paris and let Claire talk to her father. And the concierge told her – ' Alex turned to Martin. 'He told her that you had left. Or rather, he said that Monsieur and Madame had left, that he himself had got them a reservation on the Blue Train for Nice.

'So then Jessie, having thought that over, telephoned my house and asked for Fern. And I said, quite naturally, that you'd gone to Nice for a week's rest from the children and me. How could I have known? You really ought to have told me!' Alex repeated.

'Jesus Christ!' Martin cried.

'I hope you're not upset about me,' Alex said. 'You've been told that I'm not likely to play the role of outraged husband. Jessie, of course, is something else.'

'How is she now?' Martin asked.

'Now? I really couldn't say. She was rather bad off when I saw her on Saturday. I went right up to town to talk to her, but it wasn't any use. She and the child left Monday on the *Leviathan* for New York.'

CHAPTER THIRTEEN

The double doors of the familiar library had been slammed and the curtains pulled tight, trapping Donald Meig's anger in the shadowed room. His words beat the walls like fists.

'You Goddamned scum! Her own sister! I wouldn't have cared if it had been anyone else! What the hell! I wouldn't even have blamed you all that much. But to shame the family that took you in and – No, let me talk! If it weren't for me, you'd be doling out aspirins and driving thirty miles in the middle of the night for two dollars – if and when you could collect.'

Martin trembled. It had been a hard voyage through ferocious seas, with the ropes up in the corridors and the passengers vomiting in their cabins. After disembarking, he had rushed at once to the train. Now, tense with a poisonous mixture of humiliation and foreboding, he stood before a man who appeared to have gone mad with rage. Meig's eyes glittered like the glass lumps in the deerhead on the wall.

'All right, Mr Meig. You've said it a dozen times and I've answered you. I'll answer just once more: It was terribly wrong. I have no excuse.' He threw out his hand. 'Still, I ask you again: I want to go upstairs and see Jessie. After all, this concerns her more than anyone.'

'Jessie doesn't want to see you. Jessie wants a divorce. And you – ' Meig levelled a forefinger as though it were a pistol – 'you are going to give it to her. You are going to make no problems. Do you understand?'

'That's between Jessie and me. We have a child.'

'A child? Yes, you damn well have! And my English society daughter might have remembered that she's got a house full of children herself. Oh, a wonderful pair, the two of you! My God, I've seen degrading things in my time, but nothing lower than this! His wife's sister – '

A door in the hall above closed with a thud. Running feet,

a child's feet, crossed the floor.

'At least I want to see Claire,' Martin said.

'No. No. You've seen all you're ever going to see of Claire. Listen to me! I've consulted lawyers, all last week I spent with lawyers, and do you know I have it in my legal power to keep you away from that child forever on grounds of moral turpitude? Do you? And I suppose you think Dr Eastman would take you on as an associate when the tabloids got through with you! A doctor and his sister-in-law! Juicy reading! The public would drink it up! And I'll do it, make no mistake. I'll do it if you throw one obstacle in my way. I'll ruin you and I'll ruin Fern, too. I want nothing more to do with her. No, you've seen the last you're ever going to see of Claire.'

Martin's stomach churned. He hadn't eaten all day, and his head throbbed. Feeling sick, he stared at the glass lumps in the deerhead.

'You're an unforgiving man, Mr Meig. Haven't you ever heard of a second chance?'

'An axe murderer doesn't get a second chance, and that's what you are: an axe murderer. You've axed my family. You've driven two sisters apart and robbed me of Fern and her children. Yes, I know it took two of you, but you're older. You're a man and a doctor. You had the greater responsibility. And when I think that you owe me everything you are!'

'As far as that goes, you needn't worry.' Martin spoke quietly. 'You'll get back every cent with interest.'

'Oh, interest, is it? Make it five per cent. It's the going rate. That's all the more reason, then, why you'll get out of here without any fuss. Go to New York and pay me what you owe. After that, we want no more to do with you.'

The train was full. He rode back to the city, smothered by a haze of cigar smoke and the roaring jollity of a crowd celebrating repeal. Bracing his head in the corner between the seat and the window-glass, he closed his eyes.

His child. His Claire. He thought he would lose his mind if he couldn't see her.

Her curls, finger-wound, lie on the collar of her yellow coat.

'Allosaurus eats vegetables,' she informs him seriously.

'You couldn't get my sister,' Jessie says, 'so you took me.' Her face is swollen with tears.

She would be most unlikely to feel compassion.

Suppose he were, somehow, to contest the divorce?

It wouldn't work and he'd have been destroyed for nothing.

What did that mean – 'destroyed'? And why should he care? He only wanted his daughter. His child.

Jessie's child. She'd come full circle, Jessie had. Out of that house of gloom he had taken her, and back to it he had sent her. Oh, not wanting to! Wanting truly – and he examined himself, for the hundredth time turning a searchlight into the darkest corners of his spirit – truly to cherish her as he had so carefully done until that night on the balcony at the Lambs' house.

Oh, wasn't it strange, that if he had had some common affair of the streets, the world would have shrugged and pretended not to see?

Mary Fern. The night wind rises, rattling the palms, and we go inside together. She comes through a door at noon with an armful of marguerites; she drops them on a table. She laughs –

The train jolted towards the city and Martin dozed. He dreamed that he was walking on some great avenue, Fifth or Park, that he went to call on Dr Eastman and found the doctor staring at him in horror and dismay because he had no trousers on.

In fact, Dr Eastman welcomed him. 'I've been looking forward to this ever since we met in London,' he said graciously. 'I'm forty-eight and overworked. It will be good to have you share the burdens.'

He was a tall man, looking younger than his years, with the long, handsome face that seemed indigenous to old American wealth. Did the wealthy breed handsome children through a process of selection, or did handsome people find it easier to grow wealthy? More importantly, though, one could sense good nature in Eastman, which was fortunate, because people who looked like him were often frosty and stood on their authority.

So he emerged from the meeting with some tentative confidence in one area, at least. He began to walk fast, striking hard at the pavement. Early in life the patterns are set so that, mechanically, one follows in their grooves. When Martin Farrell is distressed he walks, or else sits down somewhere to listen to music. He flexed his hands. They were his capital, all he owned, they and the new knowledge in his head, gain of the years since he had last walked in this city.

Gains and losses . . .

'Loss,' he said aloud, without meaning to, so that a child trundling a toy on the walk looked up at him. And the word sounded in the air like the sorrowful whistle of a train going past in the country night.

Through shreds of moving cloud, a needle spire appeared and hid again. It was the great building of the Empire State. When he had left for England, only a few years before, it had been an enormous wound in the earth, and he had a new young wife who believed in him. And no child. And no broken love on the other side of the Atlantic. No ache of longing. No remorse.

Change. Much change.

Often he wondered how they would appear to him, those first few years, after they had passed and he could look back on them. There had been such a piercing in his vitals that he had sometimes been certain he could not survive it. He had sat with his wretched head in his hands, thinking, always thinking . . .

The wrongs he had done, not wanting to! The lives touched by his life and damaged by the touch!

Alex wrote twice to him. A large-minded man, Alex was, realistic enough and selfish enough to look after his own interests first, yet decent enough to include others in the scheme of things.

He wanted Martin to know that Fern was enduring. She was most terribly distressed about Jessie: all her life she had been so careful of Jessie! Alex was doing his best to hearten her; she must paint again and go to classes; must see friends and go riding; fortunately, the children were demanding and could fill her days.

It would not be necessary, he wrote at last, perhaps it would even be unwise to write again. He trusted that Martin would understand.

Martin understood.

And he wrote to Jessie. He thought of her, sitting in the old familiar chair in the old shadowed room while their child slept upstairs. The tone of her reply was calm enough, but the denial of all requests was firm and final.

'We will leave things the way they are. You have many possibilities ahead of you. I have only Claire.'

And that, too, Martin understood.

In the end it was work that saved him. Purposely, he exhausted himself. In the office, thanks to Martin's long hours, they were seeing far more than the doubled number that would have been expected by the addition of one other man. Eastman remarked that Martin worked like a demon.

As the months increased, inevitably and mercifully the memories blurred; they always do. Now and then he had an unexpected vision of Lamb House in soft fog; or a vision of blue Mediterranean glitter; or of steam puffing from the locomotive at the railway terminal in London. The last thing he had seen was her back in the tan travelling dress hurrying away, leaning on Alex's arm. We never got to say good-bye, he thought.

And sometimes still, a woman with a swaying walk would pass on the street; foolishly, knowing quite well it was not she, he would turn around and stare.

Sometimes a child passed, a girl who would be – and he would estimate the time – about the age of Claire. And if the child happened to have dark curls he would wonder whether Claire still wore hers long and how tall she was and whether she remembered him at all or ever spoke of him or missed him.

So, close the chapter, Martin. Close the book. It stands on the shelf and you can reach it any time and read it over if you wish. But it is better not to.

CHAPTER FOURTEEN

The picnic had been cleared away, the remains of water-melon and potato salad stowed in the kitchen and the last of the children put to bed. Now, in the pleasant somnolence that comes when one has over-eaten, they sat on Tom's narrow porch, watching the slow approach of summer night. Across the street a garage door rumbled and shut with a thud. A girl's voice rang out once and ceased.

Perry spoke out of the darkness in the corner. 'If I didn't know New York was just across the George Washington Bridge I'd think I was back in Kansas.'

'I've come to love small-town life,' Flo said. 'I never thought I would.'

'I'm not surprised. I should say you and Tom were made for it, both of you,' Martin observed.

Flo had been born middle-aged, predictable and kind. He could feel the warmth of her, as if she had reached out and touched him. As for himself, he had easily assumed the role of bachelor uncle, coming out here on holidays and Sunday afternoons with toys for the children and pastry from the French bakery near his apartment. Bachelor uncle! Well, there were worse things to be.

'I wish you'd stay for the rest of the week-end,' Flo said. 'You'll miss the fireworks tomorrow.'

'Can't. Eastman's leaving tonight to join his family in Maine and I'm on call.'

'You surely don't have many emergencies!' She meant, it can't be like Tom's life; people call him out any old time.

'You'd be surprised. We get gunshot wounds, all kinds of nerve damage. And car accidents, of course, especially on holiday week-ends. Tell her, Perry.'

'It's a fact,' Perry said. He mused: 'I was thinking, we go back a long time, don't we? Ten years since med school! It doesn't seem possible.'

'Say, Martin,' Tom added, 'do you ever see anything of

your first hero – what was his name?'

'Albeniz, you mean?'

'Yes. Albeniz.'

'Not much. He still works at Grantham Memorial and I'm at Fisk. My first hero, did you say? My only one, on this side of the Atlantic.'

'Why? What's the matter with Eastman? Not a hero?'

'No. I suppose that sounds strange, though.'

'He's a great surgeon,' Perry said quickly. 'You've got to admit that, Martin.'

'I do admit it! He could operate on me any time, but – '

'But what?' When Tom got hold of something, he held on doggedly.

'I don't know, really. Something subtle. Oh, maybe I'm being entirely unfair. Maybe it takes the edge off heroism to be so damn rich!'

'I read in a society column,' Flo said, 'his wife comes from the Harmon Motors family.'

'A lot of us were invited to their place in Greenwich over Decoration Day,' Martin said. 'It looked like a movie set – butlers serving drinks around the pool. Didn't seem like a doctor's house at all.' And he added somewhat sheepishly, 'I had a good time, though.'

'That's a helluva long way from emergency relief!' Tom said. 'We only get a dollar a call, you know, but at least you're sure of the fee. Only thing, I wish patients wouldn't get scared in the middle of the night and call three doctors at once. We usually meet on the stairs and have to toss to see who gets the call, and then the losers have lost sleep for nothing. Oh well, we keep our heads above water and that's something!'

'Speaking of Albeniz,' Martin began. He hadn't talked about him in a long time, and suddenly for some reason he wanted to. 'Albeniz was a prime mover in my life. He made a difference in it. And the thing that bothers me is that, outside of his own hospital, you don't hear much of him. He doesn't get his just due at all.'

'And why would that be?'

'I don't know, really.'

'Yes, you do!' Perry said. 'It's simple; he doesn't write enough or travel to meetings to blow his own horn. He doesn't play the social game, either. There's an awful lot of that, in a big medical centre, you know.' He spoke earnestly, explaining to Tom. 'I never realized how much! Hospital committees, racquet and tennis clubs, golf – that's how you build a consistency.'

'Sounds like a bunch of stockbrokers, not doctors!' Tom's old indignation flared. 'If you want to become rich, you don't belong in medicine. You can always go in for real estate or wholesome plumbing fixtures for God's sake.'

'Remember what Wong Lee used to tell us? You can't crusade against the world, Tom. You'll only bang your head on a stone wall.' Perry stood up. 'Listen, I've got to pick up my girl. Do you mind if I run? I'll just make it.'

Martin looked at his watch. 'I might be going soon, too. By half past, anyway.'

They watched Perry stride across the grass to his car and drive away.

'Salt of the earth,' Martin said.

'Always was.'

'He's rising to the top, too. One of the best anaesthesiologists around. You feel secure with him there.'

'Listen,' Tom said abruptly, 'I want you to do me a favour. I've got a three-year-old boy I'd like you to see. I could have him over now. They're only a few blocks from here.'

'Tom,' Flo protested. 'It's a holiday! You've no right to put Martin to work.'

'Martin's a doctor, and this might save these folks a trip into the city.'

When Martin had examined the boy and the parents had taken him away, Tom asked, 'Well, what do you think?'

'There's a positive Babinski on the right. There's got to be some sort of lesion in the cerebral cortex.' He paused, collecting his impressions. 'It could be a tumour, a congenital defect in a blood vessel or – '

Tom interrupted. 'In any case, you ought to see him this week.'

Martin hesitated and Tom urged, 'No delays, Martin, please.'

'Of course not . . . They've got no money, I suppose?'

'Hardly! The father delivers for a laundry.'

'Eastman would see him as a clinic patient, then. Or I would, since he'll be away for the next few weeks.'

'So?' Tom waited. 'You can handle it, Martin.'

Something in Tom's voice and his respectful silence while the little boy had been examined touched Martin poignantly. Here in this simple office, so like Pa's except for more modern furniture – a flat-topped desk and leather chair, an electrocardiograph and sterilizer – stood the friend who had started out with him, who had done just as well as he had and who must now turn anxiously to him for help. It made him feel apologetic about knowing more. He hoped Tom had no such feelings about it.

'You know,' Martin said, 'between ourselves, I'd rather you sent him to Albeniz's clinic than ours.'

'For Pete's sake, why?'

'Maybe this is disloyal of me, but I owe you the best, and I can talk honestly to you. Eastman's clinics are perfunctory. He's in too much of a hurry to do a real job. The private practice is just too big, and that's the fact of it.'

Tom shook his head in disapproval.

'I can't complain because – well, I can't.'

Tom's eyes seemed to bore into him. 'You were saying about the clinic?'

'I was saying – Tom, send the kid to Albeniz! People come from all over the city to present cases and ask questions. He's a *teacher*.'

'Do you ever go there any more yourself?'

'Not for the last year or so. It's impossible for me. We're too busy – ' One day on impulse he had made what he told himself was a social visit to Albeniz; in truth he had some vague hope that Albeniz might offer him an association. But Albeniz worked alone in his modest office, which had never been very busy. Money, apparently, didn't interest him that much –

'God, look at the time! Let me just say thanks to Flo

and then I'll rush.'

Tom followed him to the street. 'Oh, you've traded in for a Nash! Rumble seat and all! This is a nice little boat.'

'Don't use it much in town. Got it mostly for when I run out to see you.'

Tom's hand went to Martin's shoulder. 'There's a lonely look about you, Professor '

Martin smiled. 'I know. I ought to get married. You are, and Perry will be next month and everybody is. You've been telling me that since the first year in med school.'

'Yes. And you don't listen.'

Martin wiped the smile off. 'You're forgetting, I've been married.'

'But that's over,' Tom said gently.

'Well, I'll give it some thought one of these days. My love to the kiddies.'

He turned the little car towards the George Washington Bridge. The week-enders had departed long since from the city and traffic was light. He drove slowly. A sudden tiredness, wholly emotional, washed over him. Visits to the Horvaths were usually an antidote to the weariness which could befall a man who had to grind through a heavy routine week after week. In their simplicity, Tom and Flo gave comfort. They were bread and butter; they nourished and soothed.

Their house was a cheerful place, with its heartening, practical bustle and no time or need for introspection. This time, though, the visit had not quieted him.

Leaving them, he had felt a kind of evanescent melancholy in the region of the chest.

Envy of Tom? No, no! He would require, when at last he should be settled in life, something quite different from what he imagined Tom and Flo possessed in one another. And he wondered as he crossed the bridge, where the river ran silver under the evening sky and the downtown towers were pink and all the city's scruffy soil was concealed for the night, whether Tom might ever feel he wanted more or whether everything had indeed turned out as neatly as he and Flo had planned and packaged it.

So it might have been for me, he thought with sudden

wrenching, if it hadn't been for Mary. Mary Fern. In England now, the sun would soon be rising. And probably rain would fall before the day was over. It almost always did. She would collect her paints and easel and go inside. She would stand at the door, taking delight in the sound and smell of the rain.

Swerving, he missed an empty hearse by inches. An omen or a warning? Smiling wryly, he pulled himself back to the present time and place. He had come full circle now, back to the days of Greenwich Village and the Harriets. He wondered where his particular Harriet might be. A respectable wife and mother, he supposed, home in Wilmington, North Carolina, and remembering Martin only vaguely, if she did at all.

Now there were others. There was Muriel, who taught school and was separated from her husband: no entanglement there. There was Rae, a clever girl who called herself modern – meaning without illusions – and Tina, supervisor at a hospital far out in Queens. One never got involved where one worked.

Once last year he had come close to another sort of girl, very young and cheerful, with charming freckles on her nose. He could perhaps have committed himself, if her parents hadn't objected because he was divorced and had a child. So it had ended before it had begun, which was just as well because he hadn't really wanted it very much, anyway.

Surgery began at seven. When, in the early afternoon, Martin and Eastman got back to the office, the waiting rooms were already crowded. Three secretaries juggled appointments at the telephones. The examining rooms were filled. Records and files in their manila envelopes were piled on the desks.

The patients, terrified under brave, assumed calm, were led in.

O Excalibur, the magic sword! He carried the magic sword, and it was knowledge.

Turning the car left off Riverside Drive, he drove eastward past the brown, Romanesque monument which was the Museum of Natural History. Now the city's poor were ambling homeward from their holiday in the park. A beggarly decade, this of the thirties, a time of meagreness and grief. He wondered whether the forties would be any better: they were always saying prosperity was just around the corner.

Yet, in medicine, the thirties would be remembered as years of rich discovery.

The pace was accelerating, as his father had predicted it would. Already the sulphonamides and penicillin had changed the face of disease and routed the horror of infection in surgery. He could feel a palpable excitement on entering an operating room, knowing how greatly increased was the chance of success. A patient wheeled in on the stretcher was an unopened gift package, he thought suddenly. A preposterous concept? Not at all! For if one could send that patient home, able to walk and to talk, his words coming sensibly and clearly, why then, wasn't that a gift to yourself, the doctor? The most splendid gift of all? There was nothing like it, nothing in the world!

He was fortunate to be working with Eastman. The man's technique and speed were marvellous. And Eastman liked him. There was, of course, no reason why he shouldn't, for Martin not only worked well, but he worked hard. Still, those qualities were no guarantee of anything. Many an association broke up because of nothing more than some obscure difference of personality. He remembered that year in medical school when it had seemed that Dr Humphrey, the anatomist, had been his enemy from the very first day in the classroom. Just didn't like the cut of my jib, Martin thought. It was hard when, very young, you first learned that there were people in the world who didn't like you. But then, there were people *you* didn't like! Women with nasal whining voices; all people who lick their lips between words, their wet tongues slipping in and out like snakes' heads; sloppy people who forget things and come late.

We're all hard on each other, he reflected. Jessie's father never liked me. He used me. I never liked him, either, although for a while I tried to. And I suppose you might say I used him, too.

He had been hoping to 'use' Dr Eastman, not for any

benefit to himself, but for that idea which was coming to seem more and more imperative of late. Working in that laboratory on cell pathology and neuroanatomy, he became aware that the idea was never absent from his thinking. So on a resplendent spring afternoon, walking from the hospital to the office, he had spoken of it to Eastman.

'We'll never abolish useless, even dangerous surgery, until the surgeon knows more neurology. In England Mr Braidburn's been trying for years to found his own separate institute. Unfortunately, they can't raise funds over there. But in this country, depression or not, it seems to me there's still a lot of untapped wealth. One only needs to get the right people together.'

'I daresay. Raising funds is a hard business. I'm afraid I'm too middle-aged, too busy and tired to embroil myself in it,' Dr Eastman answered, fending Martin off.

He had persisted. 'Dr Albeniz used to talk about it when I was in med school. About true progress coming only when all the neurological specialities are joined in one discipline under one roof.'

'Albeniz is a fanatic, Martin. He's exceptionally talented and as fanatic as a monk. For him there's no world beyond the hospital.' Eastman laughed. 'I believe he'd sleep there if he could and if his wife would let him.'

It seemed to Martin that Eastman had spoken too carelessly, as though the subject were of small importance. That anyone should speak so lightly of a man like Albeniz astounded him.

Eastman, reading disapproval in Martin's face, had admonished him good-humouredly.

'Don't be so solemn, Martin! You're advancing and making a damn good living. What more do you want? Leave well enough alone.'

Yes, he was advancing. He owed no man! Donald Meig had got every cent back with interest. A cheque went out each month to his mother. He lived in an excellent small apartment, half-way between the office and the hospital. There he had everything he wanted – four walls of books, green plants and some Shaker furniture. Pure line, no clutter, only space and quiet and a good record player. He had surprised himself with how little he had wanted after all.

Yes, he was fortunate. He had a coveted place and no right to feel unrest.

After putting the car in the garage he walked home through a gritty, warm night breeze, telling himself how fortunate he was. When he entered the apartment, the telephone was ringing. Over the wire came the familiar, short command.

'Dr Farrell? You're wanted in emergency.'

'An auto accident way out on Long Island,' the resident reported.

'A young girl. They're bringing her in now.'

Rows of heads in the emergency waiting room turned curiously, and he lowered his voice.

'It was a wedding party, riding from the church to the reception. The girl was a bridesmaid, the bride's sister, I think.'

Martin grimaced. 'A rotten memory to keep!'

'They ought to be here soon. We'd been trying you for half an hour before we got you.'

'Sorry. You tried Dr Eastman? He mightn't have left yet.'

'Yes, he had. We called you next.'

The wait took Martin back through years to his own stint in emergency. Hurried, harried nurses and interns kept method and order. Two little boys, wounded by firecrackers, were brought in. A mother with a sick, swaddled baby expostulated in an un known, foreign tongue.

The ambulance wailed, and Martin started up while the doors swung open, and a stretcher rushed past carrying a blue-grey man, having a heart attack. Not for him. Then the siren wailed again, and this time it was for him.

From under the blanket trailed the blue silk skirt of a summer dress made for rejoicing. The contrast of this dress with the bloodied young, blonde head of its wearer was outrageous and obscene. And he thought how absurd it is that in one careless, brutal instant a life can be deflected from its peaceful course.

Having made his light-fingered, swift examination, and ordered X-rays, he stepped out into the corridor, still sick with this absurdity, which had never struck him so forcefully before.

A man wearing striped trousers and a dark coat with a carnation in the lapel, some proper uniform that was not a part of Martin's life, came up to him.

'My daughter,' he began and stopped.

Martin took his arm and led him to a bench. He looked into an anguished face.

'Mr –'

'Moser. Robert Moser.'

'I'm Dr Farrell, Mr Moser. You want to know what we found,' Martin said gently.

'I want you to answer one question, Doctor. Will she live?'

'We'll do everything we can to see that she does.'

'I'm a man who wants the truth, doctor. No soft soap.'

'Well, Mr Moser, we are doing X-rays now, but I can tell you already that your daughter's skull is fractured in several places. And there's almost certainly extensive pressure on the brain. Just how much damage, we can't tell until we look.'

'Then you'll have to operate?'

'Yes. Right away.'

'There wouldn't be time to get my wife here? She – they've given her a sedative, and my chauffeur is driving her in. I came in the ambulance, but she would want to see Vicky.'

'I don't think we ought to delay. We've got to relieve the pressure.'

'I see.' Mr Moser stared at the floor. His lip went twitching towards his left cheek. He looked up.

'Dr Eastman should be here any minute, shouldn't he?'

'No, sir. Dr Eastman's out of town. I'm his associate, and I'll be taking charge.'

The twitching ceased and the lips firmed. 'You're very young. How long have you been with Dr Eastman?'

'Four years. Before that I trained in London. I'm perfectly qualified, I assure you.'

'Excuse me, but your assurance won't be enough. This is

my daughter's life. You're positive you can't reach Dr Eastman?'

'Positive. He's gone to Maine. He's a sailor and will be gone for two weeks.'

Mr Moser stood up. He was of equal height with Martin. They were almost toe to toe, as in a confrontation.

'Maine isn't the moon. He could come back.'

'Not in time, Mr Moser.'

'I'm a trustee of this hospital, do you know that?'

'I didn't know it.'

'I want an experienced man. I've no wish to insult you, Doctor, but I've no time to waste on amenities, either. I ask you to give me a list of neurosurgeons on a par with Dr Eastman.'

'We don't have yardsticks to measure doctors,' Martin said, and immediately regretting the hot-tempered reply, amended it. 'But I can name some competent surgeons for you. There's a Doctor Florio on the staff, and there's a Dr Harold Samson.'

'I'll call them.'

'I can do it for you.'

'I'll do it myself.'

Martin waited. He could see Moser in the telephone booth, dialling, hanging up and dialling again. He felt a strong current of compassion and at the same time anger, at the stinging rejection. What did the man think he was doing on Eastman's service? Polishing shoes?

Mr Moser came back. 'Neither one of them is home. What do you doctors do, abandon the city because it's a holiday?'

Martin didn't reply.

'That's all there are? There must be dozens of neurosurgeons around!'

'You said you wanted the best.'

'Well, give me second best, then.'

'You're looking at one right now.'

'You're pretty damned impertinent, you know that? Dr Eastman ought to be told about you. I asked you for another name, or I'll call my internist and ask him, although God knows where he is tonight.'

Martin controlled his anger. 'There is a man . . . He doesn't work here at Fisk, but he has privileges here, and I believe he'd come.'

Mr Moser sank on to the bench. He looked as though he had used his last strength.

'His name is Albeniz. It's in the book.'

'Damned foreign name. I can't think how to spell it. You call him for me.'

Dr Albeniz listened to Martin's brief summary. 'I would come for you,' he said, 'but it's impossible. I'm in bed with a cold and fever. Why don't you do it yourself?'

'I'm willing to, but the father wants someone better qualified.'

'You're perfectly qualified, Martin.'

'Not well enough, he thinks.'

'Well, if he can't find anyone better and won't accept you, you have no more responsibility in the case. Tell him so and let him go where he wants.'

'I'll do that,' Martin said.

When he came back from the telephone, Mr Moser had put his head in his hands and his shoulders were shaking. Martin stood over him.

'I can't get Dr Albeniz,' he said quietly. 'He's ill.'

Mr Moser did not raise his head. 'Then go ahead. I can't do any more. Go ahead with whatever has to be done and God help you.'

Martin wasn't quite sure, as he walked away, whether that had been a prayer or a threat.

Midnight lay beyond the windows when Martin entered the operating room. At the edges of white light, the world was gloomy green. Green walls and rumpled cotton. Green, refracted from the bottles in cabinets. Green, the sterile cloth on the table where, glittering like silver at a palace banquet, lay the tools: knives, drills, forceps and mallets.

Perry looked up, waiting, his eyebrows rising like parentheses above the mask. He had been fetched out of a movie theatre where he had been with his girl. Martin was thankful they had found him. There was something reassuring in the sight of those familiar eyebrows.

The assistants waited. A nurse put a second pair of gloves over Martin's first pair. A fine calm came to him: I can do it.

On the girl's naked skull, brown coagulated blood clumped in dark beads along the crooked wounds, like branching rivers on a map. Such strange thoughts he had, selecting a knife from the service row! His eyes narrowed; he could feel them tightening and sharpening. His lips pressed shut. And he brought the knife down, into a spurt of fresh, red blood, which was at once sucked up and sponged away. Down through the scalp the knife sliced, until the scalp was folded back on glistening bone.

Electric drill. Press hard, down through the bone. A drop of sweat starts on his forehead under the cap. Alertly, a nurse steps up to wipe it away. He remembers having seen the gesture in London. Braidburn sweated, but Eastman never does.

The drill stops. He moves it slightly and applies it again. He is drawing a pattern, a small circle on the skull. Press hard. Careful, careful, not to penetrate the brain beneath the bone! Complete the circle. Now he has made a disc of bone; lift it out and ease the pressure on the brain: that is the object. He is aware of voices, movements in the room, whispers and the swish of rubber-soled shoes. The clock lurches. A half-hour ticks.

He asks Perry, 'Everything all right?'

'Everything okay,' comes the answer.

Down now to the dura mater. 'Steel blade,' Martin commands and it is handed to him. He flicks out the disc of bone and holds his breath, dreading, waiting for haemorrhage and gush of blood. No! For an instant, he is relieved. He calls for his magnifying glasses. When these have been strapped around his head, he peers in, and holds the breath back in his lungs again. He is conscious of his own heartbeat.

From the force of the blow, the smash of bone on metal, a splinter of that bone, needle-sharp, has pierced the pia mater. He perceives a leakage of the spinal fluid and sighs. Dietz, the senior resident, is peering in, too. Now he draws away. Dietz's eyes are very black – the rest of his face is hidden, but his eyes convey to Martin that he has seen and understood. It is somehow comforting to feel the comprehension of this intelligent young man. It is comforting to be surrounded by the whole quick, skilful team.

And carefully – oh, every movement is so tense, precise and careful – Martin eases, pries the needle-point of bone – he is almost panting now – and retrieving it securely between the bright tips of the forceps, hands it to the waiting nurse. He sighs, a deep, long involuntary sigh.

Now there is nothing to do but withdraw and wait. He has done all he can. The leakage will cease of its own accord or it will not. The meninges will heal without infection, or they will not. There will be a scar, that much is certain, and the scar will perhaps be normal, or it may not. It may cause epileptic seizures at some later date, or it may not.

So he sutures the scalp. It is all over. Then he stands and looks down at the girl, while they wrap her head in folded white cloth: Hindu hat, lacking only a forehead jewel.

Her lashes lie on her childish cheeks. The purity of the unconscious face strikes him to the heart. He rips the gloves off and walks out and is terribly, terribly tired.

The parents were waiting in the outer hall. He was sorry that they had come to him before he could change his clothes, because their daughter's blood had spattered on him and he saw them looking at it.

'We've done what we could,' he said, knowing it was not enough to tell them.

Moser opened his mouth to ask a question, but then the mother began to weep, and he led her away; it was a relief to Martin because he did not know what he could have answered if they had pressed him.

After he had changed his clothes, he thought of going home. But also he wanted to look at the girl again. He knew there would be nothing to see tonight. She would be unconscious far into the following day. Still, he wanted to see her again. So he went to the coffee machine and had a cup and then another, before going upstairs.

The family had taken a suite, and she lay in the centre of a large white room like a carved stone queen on a tomb: a long white ridge under white covers, with calm white eyelids.

'Can I get anything for you, Doctor?'

He hadn't noticed the nurse sitting in the corner. 'Just tell me the time, please. My watch has stopped.'

'A quarter past two.'

'You'll be here till seven?'

'No, sir. This isn't my shift. I go off at midnight ordinarily, but the supervisor asked me to stay.'

The pitch and tone of the girl's low voice attracted his attention, so that he strained through the weak light to see her. What he saw was the full body of a Venus and a mild young face, too round for beauty.

'Have I seen you before?' he asked.

'I don't think so. I only came two weeks ago from Mercy Hospital.' She stood beside Martin looking down at the unconscious girl. 'I've got her bridesmaid dress hanging in the closet. Her mother said, "Throw it out. I never want to see it again." But I couldn't do that. Doctor, what's going to happen to her?'

'You know better than to ask that,' he chided gently.

'Well, of course I really do. But this has really got to me tonight.'

He saw brimming tears, and he went on as gently as before, 'You mustn't let a case do this to you, or you'll be torn up all the time, won't you?'

'I know. I'm not at my professional best.' She gave him a rueful smile. 'Sometimes I go so far as to think I wasn't even meant to be a nurse! I take things too personally. And I wonder, are other people like me? You for instance? You see this kind of thing all the time. What do you do about it? Can you just forget and go on to the next one?'

'I don't forget. I store it away with all the other evils that happen in a lifetime, and I learn not to take them out or look at them too often.'

'I'm not always like this. Heavens, I wouldn't want you to think I was! I just haven't much resistance right now. You know the way you are after you've had the flu, for instance?'

'I know,' Martin said.

When the relief nurse came, they walked down the corridor together. In an island of light, a charge nurse worked on charts; beyond that island lay dark blue shadow.

'And have you just got over the flu?' he asked.

'Not the flu. A broken engagement. That's why I transferred, to change my luck. Superstitious, I suppose. Would you like some coffee?'

'I don't need a third cup, but I'll take one anyway.'

There was no use going home now. He had office hours at nine, and three hours of sleep would be as bad as none at all. He followed her into the cubicle where the coffeepot stood on a table.

A night-time chill came shivering through the window. The girl drew a sweater from a hook and warmed her hands around her cup. The sweater had a name tag: Hazel Janos.

'That's me. Hungarian. People never pronounce the name right.'

'My best friend is Hungarian. Tom Horvath. He taught me to eat palachinken.'

'I make good palachinken, with cherries and sour cream.'

He sat back and observed her. She had very white skin, the kind that burns painfully at the beach. Her brown hair was too fine and soft. She would be one of those women who always had trouble keeping it in order. Right now, pinned under the starched cap, it was tidy. She looked particularly clean. He wondered why nurses always did: surely they didn't bathe more often than other people did?

Resting her chin on her hand, she looked out into the night sky. The outline of a rooftop made an isosceles triangle at the lower end of the window. She sighed.

'I'm curious about you,' Martin said.

'Why?'

'You're all knotted up, aren't you?'

'Yes.'

'Want to tell me about it? Or shall I mind my own business?'

'You really want to know?'

'Only if you care to tell me.'

So often people told him of their quarrels and debts and

loves, and he usually wished they wouldn't. But now, for some reason, he wanted to hear this girl talk. Why? There was nothing remarkable about her, unless a lulling voice and a very female softness were remarkable.

'There's not much to tell. It was only another case of a girl who wanted to get married and a man who didn't.'

'I see.'

'Walter lost his job almost four years ago. I told him we could live on my salary till things got better. My folks have three rooms on the top floor where we live in Flushing and they'd have fixed them up for us. But he wouldn't sponge, he said. So we just argued and argued and one day I gave him an ultimatum and I lost. That's it,' she finished quietly.

'Perhaps he'll think it over,' Martin suggested.

'No. He's gone to Kansas City. He has a brother there, and maybe his brother will find a job for him, I don't know. I think he was just tired of things here, of all the wrangling and of me.'

'He just needed to get away to a new place. I can't blame him, really. The juice seems to get out of things when you have to wait too long for them.'

'That's true,' she said. Then she added, 'I'm twenty-eight and a virgin. Do you suppose that could have been my mistake? I sometimes wonder.'

Her candour touched Martin. 'I honestly don't know,' he said.

'Maybe in my heart I didn't trust him. Oh, why am I telling you all this? Because you're a doctor and people think they can say anything to a doctor that they wouldn't say to anybody else?'

Oh Lord not again, he thought, and answered, 'I think people feel that way.' He sensed that she was waiting for some positive statement, something that would be a comfort so he searched for something and came up only with a cliché. 'Time heals everything, they say.'

'Do you believe that, honestly?'

'No,' he said.

She laughed. Her lips curved back on strong even teeth and the laugh changed her face. Comely, he thought. That's the word. Comely.

'I'm not laughing because anything's funny. I think it's because I feel better for having told you. You're the only person I've told besides my father and mother.'

He reflected, 'I never do remember why laughter and tears are related. One of my professors in a philosophy course spent a week on lectures on the subject, but for the life of me I can't remember what he said.' He bent forward, clasping his hands around his knees. 'I have a little girl,' he said suddenly, surprising himself. 'I haven't seen her since she was three years old, and she's seven now.' And why *he* should be talking like this to *her* , he had no idea. 'Her mother and I are divorced and she has custody. I thought maybe she would relent, let me see the child. I've asked often enough.'

'And?'

'And lawyers answered, reminding me of the terms of the divorce.'

'But that's so cruel,' Hazel Janos said softly.

'Yes. The divorce was.' Not Jessie, he meant. There was no cruelty in Jessie. He could understand her position quite well. And he sat still, thinking about that which would have been impossible to put into words and was yet so clear to him.

The girl said, 'I rather thought there might be something else besides what they say about you.'

Martin looked up. 'What they say about me?'

'Well, of course, you must know that people – that nurses – talk about doctors, especially about the young, unmarried ones.' She flushed. 'But they say good things about you! That you're awfully gentle with your patients and really care, that even when you're cranky with the nurses sometimes, you're sorry afterwards. They all like you.'

'That's not what you meant before, when we were talking about divorce.'

She said timidly, 'They think you must be a chaser because you're not married. But I didn't think you were.'

'You didn't?'

'No. I felt a quietness in you. And maybe some sadness.'

It isn't sensible to talk about your private life, especially where your work is: a snobbish concept, maybe, but of proven prac-ticality all the same. And even as he was thinking so, Martin began to speak.

It was almost as though someone else were talking and he were listening. Slowly and thoughtfully, he heard himself say aloud the names of people and places which he had scarcely used since they had passed out of his life: Menton. Mary. Jessie. Lamb House. Claire.

The night wind blew hard here on the fourteenth floor, so that Hazel drew the sweater closer. Her eyes never left his face.

'That's the whole story?' she asked when he had finished.

'The whole story.'

'And it's over between Mary and you?'

'Yes,' he said harshly.

He was angry with himself. Why had he spilled everything out to a stranger? All day he had been feeling a foggy sadness, and now, having been on his feet almost twenty-four hours, he had simply been carried away by fatigue. Damn, he ought to have gone home to sleep instead of sitting here pouring his heart out! He stood up. It was five o'clock. A milky light had risen at the windows.

'I'd better get home to shave and change before I go to work. By the way, when do you go back on duty?'

'At seven tonight.'

'Then this was your time to sleep, and I've kept you up.'

'I wouldn't have stayed if I hadn't wanted to.' She touched his arm. 'I just thought – you're probably sorry you told me so much. You're worried I'll talk about it all over the place. But I never will. You can trust me.'

He looked down into a face so gentle that it pained him: it was like looking at a wound. One saw such faces on lonesome children, on certain rare old men and sometimes on women of radiant goodness.

'Yes,' he said, 'I trust you.'

Eastman moved back from the respirator, stepping carefully between the oxygen tank and the tubing. In the transparent box which had been trundled over the bed, Vicky Moser lay unmoving, except for the slight rise and fall of her chest. He beckoned to Martin and they went out to the corridor.

'For the sake of my blood pressure, I had to wait a whole day before I could talk to you, Farrell,' he began.

'I don't understand!'

'You had no right to take the knife to Vicky Moser!' Eastman's words were precisely separated, cut apart, as if he were teaching English to a foreigner. 'You had no authority. What made you think you had?'

Martin was dumbfounded. 'But you were out of town! And I *am* your associate!'

'You made no real effort to reach me. As a matter of fact, I had gone to my sister's house in Westchester before starting for Maine in the morning. I could have been back here in little more than an hour.'

'How, in all fairness, could I have known that?'

'Well, in all fairness, perhaps you couldn't. Certainly, though, you could have called some other chief, couldn't you?'

'Dr Florio and Dr Samson were called and couldn't be reached.'

'What about Shirer, then? These are prominent people, Farrell. Moser's a trustee. You don't fool around with people like Moser. I shouldn't have to tell you that, for God's sake.'

Anger began to boil up in Martin, but he answered coolly. 'In the first place, sir, I don't care a damn about prominence. In the second place, I didn't recommend Dr Shirer because I consider myself a better surgeon than he is.'

'What? Shirer has been on staff here for thirty years! And you compare yourself with him?'

'He's been doing mediocre work for thirty years, Dr Eastman.'

'Oh, I suppose you consider my work mediocre, too?'

'Of course I don't. But there are some procedures I *can* do as well as you can, and this was one of them.'

'It was, was it?'

'Yes. I knew I could do it. I wouldn't have undertaken it otherwise.'

'I call that arrogant. I don't know what you call it.'

'I call it confident.'

Eastman's cheeks reddened. 'I'll want to talk about that again, Farrell. I'm not sure you and I can get along in the future unless certain things are clarified.'

In Martin the anger now boiled over. He had done a thorough job! If it didn't work out, if the girl should die or should live and merely vegetate, why then, it would have happened anyway! It would have been 'fated', 'ordained', whatever that meant. I truly and honestly know my limitations, he thought.

And he said, with a calmness that surprised himself, 'I don't think we will get along, Dr Eastman, unless you give me the respect and freedom I deserve.'

For a second Eastman stared at him; then, without replying, he turned about and almost ran down the hall.

For three days they poured glucose and oxygen into Vicky Moser. She was now Eastman's patient; Martin had been removed from the case. He wondered what was being whispered about the hospital. No doubt the news had filtered down to the newest student nurse on the floor. Nevertheless, he went in to look at Vicky. Hazel Janos was there one evening, but she made no comment, only watched while Martin pulled Vicky's eyelids back and found no change. The pupils were still enlarged and made no move under the pinpoint shaft of his pencil-light.

On the fourth day came momentary hope when normal breathing resumed, and she was taken out of the respirator. But still she lay inert, unresponsive to touch or light or the sound of voices.

Once, in the elevator, Martin saw her parents, two people grown abruptly small and old. The mother huddled and shivered, although July blazed outside. When they saw Martin, they turned away and he understood that they were holding him responsible and would always hold him so.

At the office he continued to hold regular hours. Eastman did not come in. Obviously, he had interrupted his vacation only for the Moser girl. It seemed to Martin that the secretaries looked at him with curiosity and compassion.

Probably they had been told he wouldn't be with them much longer.

And for Vicky Moser the days rolled slowly through their routines: feeding tubes, spinal taps, antibiotics, anti-convulsive. If she lives, Martin thought, she may not be able to talk. She may not be able to move. Or she may be able to talk only nonsense and move with the violence of an animal. Even though officially the girl was not his patient, in his mind she was so still. With him she had entered the desert, so to speak, and he must see her out of it.

Whatever happened, they would say it was his fault. Eastman would see to that, had seen to it already. And it wouldn't be his fault. *Still, what if it were?*

He began to pray: O God, don't let her die; she's only eighteen. Strange that he should pray! He had had no interest in religion for years, being neither for it nor against it. He wondered whether his beseeching was not perhaps some sort of theatricality, watching himself at humble prayer in a fine old tradition, without believing a word of it. And then he remembered his father's rounded cadence in the mouldy green parlour before winter breakfasts and he felt like crying.

O God, don't let her die!

At the hospital, late one afternoon as he was about to go into Vicky's room, Martin met Eastman coming out.

'Anything you want?' Eastman asked bluntly.

'Just to know how the patient is doing.'

'My patient,' Eastman said, 'is doing badly. I plan to operate again in the morning.'

Martin was appalled. 'Operate again? But why?'

'Self-evident, I should say.'

'I would guess there's haemorrhaging, which ought to subside. If you ask me, we should give it some more time.'

'I'm not asking you. I'm of the opinion that there are splinters in there, and I'm going back for them.'

'Doctor,' Martin said earnestly, 'let's put personal feelings aside for a minute. I give you my word there are none. I removed them all.'

'Damn it! You couldn't have!'

No stranger would have believed that this man could ever

have been genial. His eyes were hostile; his lips folded inwards, making a gash across the chin.

'I'm having X-rays in the morning, naturally, but I can tell you right here and now what they will show.'

He swung around. His shoes slapped the floor smartly all the way to the elevator.

When Martin went into the room he saw at once that there had been no change. The very air felt cold, as if some chill were issuing from that poor body, as in a crypt where the dead have lain for centuries. He stood a moment, shuddered, and he went downstairs again, out to the searing street. Here were the smells of life – gasoline and dog-droppings and a sugary whiff from the open door of a bakery.

Why had she not revived? There were no splinters, he knew there weren't. *Still, suppose there were?* Eastman was going to operate again, and she wouldn't be able to take the shock. If she died –

He thought of the times he had been present when a family received the news of death. A husband, a mother or a child dies; some people can accept such loss in wordless despair; others scream, protest that it can't be true. It was the most terrible errand a doctor ever had to carry out, and one never would, never could, get used to it.

That night Martin scarcely slept. At five o'clock he got up and walked through echoing streets to the hospital. He half hoped Hazel Janos would be there, then recalled that she went off duty at midnight. A bulky, middle-aged woman in white was dozing upright in the chair beside the bed.

'Is there any change?' he whispered, and the woman answered, 'None.'

Gently, Martin raised one eyelid, then the other, and turned his flashlight on. There was no contraction of the pupils. He sighed.

Then he lifted the blanket, reached for a limp arm and stroked it. Was there, or did he imagine a very, very faint withdrawal of the flesh, a reaction to his touch? He felt a swift rise of expectation and as quickly stifled it. He pressed harder. Was there a movement, the merest fraction of movement?

'Did you see that, Nurse?'

She turned up the light and leaned over the bed.

'Here. I'll show you.'

Again Martin pressed the arm, and now he was sure he saw a slight withdrawal.

'Did you see it? Did you?'

'Yes. Yes, I think I did. Oh, Doctor, do you think possibly –'

And the two of them, the ageing woman and the young man, stared at each other across the bed.

'I don't dare hope,' Martin said. It may mean nothing at all, he told himself, only a reflex, a flicker in a dead brain. It probably does mean nothing. Yet he hoped.

At seven the shifts changed and a new nurse came. He heard the two women whispering in the corridor outside the room as he stood watching by the bed. Still the girl lay, the marble effigy on the tomb. At eight o'clock orderlies arrived to wheel her below for X-rays.

'I hear they're going to operate again,' the nurse remarked with curiosity. She had a handsome, cold face. Martin didn't answer. Hazel Janos would *care,* he thought suddenly.

At eight-fifteen Mr Moser entered the room, stopped when he saw Martin and frowned. 'I thought you were off the case.'

'I am. This is purely unofficial. I'm humanly concerned to see how my work turned out.'

Mr Moser sat down next to the nurse. They spoke in such low tones that Martin couldn't hear, but he wasn't supposed to hear. He was to be excluded.

At the window he looked down to aimless scurry and hurry on the street below. From this height human beings were no more than water beetles on a pond. Awesome to think how in each one, that man lifting the trash can, that one inching his car into a parking space, raged a private, daily struggle with the universe!

When Dr Eastman came in, Martin did not turn around.

'We shall have to operate,' he heard Eastman say in his quiet voice of authority. 'There's undoubtedly a splinter in there, maybe more than one. We'll know, of course, as soon as the X-rays come up.'

In the room there was total silence. Martin, still standing at the window, felt eyes on his back. At eight-fifty a technician came in with the X-rays.

'Thank you, Mr Poole,' Eastman said formally.

Now Martin turned around as Eastman held the X-rays to the light. The brain was a grey-and-white intaglio on the plate. Spare, Martin thought, like modern art. For a long minute or two Eastman studied it while Mr Moser, puzzled and afraid, peered over his shoulder.

At last Martin spoke. 'Well, Doctor?'

Eastman pursed his lips. 'Perplexing. Perplexing.'

'What is?'

'There's nothing. Unless – '

'Unless what?'

'Well, no splinters – that I can see.'

A strange sound, part laugh, part sob, forced itself from Martin's throat. It was almost inaudible, but Eastman heard it. He looked over and then quickly away.

So I was right, Martin thought. But still, still there could be infection, couldn't there? We were absolutely sterile, and yet one never knows.

When the door opened and the patient was brought back, the little group reformed around the bed. Eastman was silent. The others waited for him to say something.

And Moser said softly, 'My wife is falling apart.'

Eastman nodded. 'I know.'

'What do you suggest now, Doctor?'

'I've been thinking – another set of X-rays. There's got to be something there. I'm still convinced. The ventricles aren't swollen, the – '

'Look at this,' Martin said.

'At what?' Eastman said coldly.

Martin turned the flashlight on. 'The pupil. She reacts. And this morning I thought I saw – '

'Yes, what?' the father cried.

'It may have been nothing at all.'

'What did you see?' Moser asked. 'What did you see?'

'I'm not sure. I don't want to give you false hopes – '

He pinched the girl's arm. He thought her lips moved but he couldn't be sure. And he stood there, stroking, then gently pinching, then pressing that thin white arm. And all the time, without seeing it, he felt Eastman's gaze upon him, scorning and challenging.

Mr Moser sighed. 'Nothing. Nothing,' he murmured.

'I don't know. I feel – ' Martin began.

What he felt was a slight, slight reflex in the arm.

'I don't know,' he repeated.

And Vicky's lips moved. A little sound, a breath, the faintest groan came into the silence around the bed. Martin bent over the girl.

'Are you Vicky?' he whispered. The dry lips moved again, barely touching each other.

'Are you Vicky?'

The eyes flew open. For the first time in days they opened to the light; for a few tense moments they were blank, then subtle recognition gathered there.

'Have you been sick?'

She nodded. Her head barely moved on the pillow, but it was unmistakably a nod.

'You're going to get well now, Vicky.'

She stared at Martin. Her eyes strained to understand.

'Yes, you are. Do you know I'm a doctor?'

Again she nodded.

Martin thought – he thought his heart was in his throat.

'There's someone here to see you,' he said softly. 'Look,' and he motioned to Moser.

Moser leaned over the other side of the bed.

'Is this your father?' Martin asked.

It was a long minute. 'Is this your father?'

The girl's eyes struggled to focus. The whole face struggled to come back from a far place. There was no sound in the room, no breath, no rustle, as the three men waited, their faces furrowed with their tension.

And finally, finally, into that agonizing silence came a word, very low, but audible and clear.

'Daddy,' she said.

*

Bob Moser grasped Martin's hands. 'I was half out of my mind, Dr Farrell! For God's sake, you can understand that, can't you? If I was hard on you, if it was unforgivable, try to forgive it, will you? I'll never forget you till my dying day. I – we – all of our family – we'll never forget you.'

So much emotion, so much gratitude, were both overwhelming and oppressive. As quickly as he decently could, Martin fled.

Eastman caught up with him outside of the solarium. 'I don't mind telling you, Martin, this has been one of the worst experiences of my professional life. I just went off the deep end. It looked so bad there, just so bad.'

'I understand,' Martin said.

'I'm sorry if I was unjust to you. I sincerely am. I was wrong and I admit I was.'

There was embarrassment in another human being's discomfiture. And Martin fidgeted. 'That's all right. As long as it's turned out well.'

'Turned out well? The girl's going to come out of this and what can you add to that?' Eastman beamed. Light twinkled on his glasses; his teeth twinkled in a large, affable smile. 'So let's forget the whole business, Martin, and take up where we left off.'

Martin began quietly, 'I've been doing some thinking, Doctor.'

'Yes?'

'And the sum total of it is – that I really want to go it alone from now on. It's been a fine opportunity, working with you, and I've appreciated it, but – perhaps it's a matter of temperament – I know I'd rather work alone.'

'Martin, you can have all the freedom you want. That's what you're telling me, isn't it? I understand your position. I give you my word that from now on it will be the way you want it.'

Martin shook his head. 'Thank you, Doctor, but I've made up my mind. I can wait a few weeks until you find another man, of course. I'm sure there'll be a dozen knocking at your door to take my place.'

'Don't be foolish. Don't cut off your nose to spite your

face just because you're piqued.'

'It's not pique. I'd been mulling it over long before this, without knowing I was doing so.'

'There's a Depression out there, in case you haven't noticed.'

'Oh, I've noticed, all right! But my wants aren't very many. I feel I can manage.'

'You're making a great mistake, Martin!'

'I hope not. But I have to try.' Martin put out his hand. 'Thank you for everything, all the same.'

He walked on past the solarium. Wheelchairs stood against the walls. There was a rich smell of flowers; hospital bouquets were wistful, belying the very nature of flowers. He went on past stretchers in the corridors and visitors waiting in the lobby for admission cards. The loudspeaker called with urgency: 'Dr Simmons – stat, Dr Feinstein – stat.' My world, he thought.

Hazel Janos, powder-white from cap to shoes, was coming up the steps. Her eyes widened and brightened when she saw Martin.

'I think our girl's going to make it,' he told her jubilantly. 'She spoke this morning, recognized her father.'

'Oh,' Hazel cried. 'I'm so glad! I prayed for her.'

'Say a little prayer for me, too, will you? I've taken a big leap. I've left Eastman and I'm on my own.'

'I will, but I don't think you'll need prayers. You've got success written all over you.'

'Have I? Strange, I don't feel that way about myself. I don't especially want it, either, if it means being another Eastman.'

'You'd never be like that. You're soft inside.' For a moment she looked frankly into his eyes; then, flushing, turned away as though she had been too intimate and went inside, through the revolving door.

Martin ran down the steps. It might not be so easy, after all, to make his way without Eastman's protecting hand. But it was time, as he had said, to try.

And he felt more free than he had felt on a very long time.

CHAPTER FIFTEEN

We remember more than we think we do. We understand more of what we see than we are credited with understanding. Years after the fact, one day things fall into place and we say, 'Ah true, ah true! I must have known that, really, when I was only five or six or seven.' Flickering as interrupted dreams, the voices – indignant, earnest, mournful – sound again behind shut doors and across the lawn. Sudden tendernesses and secret glances repeat themselves in a dim landscape at the back of a stage, behind a gauze curtain.

The child knew her mother was different from other mothers, from other people. How? When did she first perceive this shameful difference?

The child knew that her father had gone away and that there was something terribly wrong about that. She thought she remembered great height, someone bending down to her, always bending, and being picked up and hugged. There had been a statue in a wide green place, and they two had stood in front of it. There had been a tiny glass boat, hanging on a Christmas tree. She had put out her finger to feel the pointed masts. Gold walnuts hung on the tree. There was a huge glass ball, lavender, so smooth you wanted to stroke it or else to crumble and scrunch it, like that.

'You mustn't break it,' her father had said.

It was he, wasn't it? Who else could have said it, then?

Dogs had come barking. The house had been full of dogs And there had been children, some vague girls and a boy, quite big, who called the jumping dogs away. But she had been frightened, and her father – who else could it have been? – had picked her up and told her not to be afraid.

She asked her mother about this memory, but her mother had forgotten. Her mother had forgotten everything, it seemed, and although she always answered questions patiently, the answers never told anything. So after a while, Claire stopped asking.

One day at a friend's house after school, an old woman said, 'And you're Claire Farrell! I knew your grandfather. He was a good doctor, a good man.'

'My grandfather? He's not a doctor. He's sick at home. He stays in bed most of the time, or on the sofa in the sun parlour.'

'Your other grandfather is the one I mean, child. Your daddy was a doctor here, too, but he didn't stay very long.'

In the bottom drawer of a cabinet in the library, Claire found the photograph albums. Some of them were very old, bound in shabby red velvet with tarnished metal clasps. The people in these were strange; their wide skirts looked like lampshades. The men had full beards and solemn eyes. She could recognize none of them.

But there was another album, a black one with a broken spine. Here the pages were loose, and some of the pictures slid out of their pointed corners. These were familiar people: Grandpa, looking much the same as now except that his hair was dark; and Mother as a little girl, twisted even then. It was strange to think that a little girl could look like that. Here she was again, older this time, with a dress-up dress on and a pearl necklace, standing next to a laughing girl, much taller than Mother and not twisted. Claire carried the album to where Grandpa sat in the sun parlour.

'Who's the pretty girl with Mother? That's our porch they're standing on.'

'That's your aunt, Mary Fern. We don't talk about her any more. We don't think about her. You'd best go put that away.'

'Why? Is she dead like Grandma?'

'No, she's not dead, but she might as well be.'

'Why?'

'Because she was wicked. She did bad things.'

'What bad things?'

'Stealing, for one. Taking things that didn't belong to her.'

When Mother came in, she was very angry. 'I will not have you talking to the child like that, Father,' she said. It seemed to Claire that she was shaking.

'Why not? She might as well know the truth.'

'At six?'

'She can start getting used to the idea. When she's older, she'll have been prepared for it.'

'Never! Never, do you hear? It's my business, my trouble! Mine to decide how much of it I want to have known and talked about, whether all of it, or some of it, or none of it. And don't let me ever, ever hear you say one word to that child again, Father. I mean it, I mean it!'

Old Bridget, who had been listening from the kitchen, said to Claire – (but she was half talking to herself, Claire knew; she used to mumble in the kitchen: 'The breadknife now, where did I put it? Oh, I am so sick of these rheumatics, my poor legs!') – old Bridget said, 'Yes, that's what happens when you get old and sick. She would never have got away with talking to her father like that before.'

Mostly, though, Mother was nice to Grandpa even when he was cross. She always said she was sorry for him because he was old and sick. Maybe she could be very sorry for sick people because she wasn't made right and knew how it felt.

When you walked behind her you could see how one shoulder stuck up so much higher than the other and how the crooked edges of her bones stuck out from under the collars and scarves and all the clothes she wore.

Why didn't she look like other mothers? Why did a person have to have a mother like her?

Yet she could do things the other mothers couldn't do. She could make anything with her hands. She made a patchwork quilt for Claire's bed and silk flowers for the bowl on the hall table. She sewed a Tinker Bell costume for Claire to wear in *Peter Pan*. It was all feathery white, with hidden, tinkling bells that had come from a theatrical costumer's in New York. The teacher kept talking about Claire's costume. She didn't say so, of course, but it was the best costume in the class. Some of the other mothers had used nothing better than crepe paper. The pirate hats didn't fit and kept sliding off.

Today was the final dress rehearsal. Everybody was

standing in the schoolyard after lunch waiting for the bell to ring. The teacher was on the steps watching her first-graders. She wore a dress with little flowers all over it. She had pink nails and a new ring like a pearl button, only it was a diamond engagement ring. She was going to be married next month as soon as school was out. Claire wished Miss Donohue was her mother.

They went inside and ran through the rehearsal. The teacher said it was practically perfect. Claire felt so beautiful and so clever, tinkling her bells. And suddenly, when they were just about to take the costumes off, something came into her head, something from that time long, long ago.

'I really saw Peter Pan once,' she said. 'There's a statue of him in the park in London and I was there with my father.'

Jimmy Crater scoffed. 'You did not! There isn't any such statue!'

'There is so and I saw it.'

'You're a liar.'

'I am not. Go ask Miss Donohue.'

'Why yes,' Miss Donohue said. 'Peter Pan in Kensington Gardens. It's famous. Now, who'll help me stack this scenery in a safe corner till tomorrow?'

'There,' Claire said, 'I told you.'

'Ah, you're full of baloney.'

'Am not.'

'You never even were in London.'

Now a little circle of allies and enemies gathered around Claire and Jimmy Crater.

'I was born in London!' Claire cried triumphantly. 'I lived there with my father and mother. I ought to know where I lived!'

'You haven't even got a father,' Andy Chapman said.

'I have so. Everybody has a father.'

'Oh yeah? Where is he, then?'

'None of your business.'

Under the Tinker Bell ruff and fluff, Claire felt the rising heat.

'Hasn't got a father, hasn't got a father!'

Claire stuck out her tongue. 'You're mad, Jimmy Crater,

because I can knock you down. I'm bigger and stronger and I'm a girl, but I can knock you down!'

Jimmy's fists went up, prize-fighter fashion, churning under his chin. Andy, the ally, thrust his up towards Claire.

'Come on! Fight then!' they taunted.

'I don't want to fight, but I can if I have to!'

'Ah, you're scared! You haven't got a father, and your mother's ugly, and you're scared!'

Claire's fist struck Jimmy's nose. When he fell, chairs clattered. Andy shoved Claire. They all fell, ripping the Tinker Bell dress down the back. It made a sound as if the cloth were screaming.

Miss Donohue came running. 'Boys! Boys! Oh, how awful! What's happening here?'

Claire got up. 'Look,' she said. 'Look what they did.'

Miss Donohue turned her around. Her cool fingers fiddled with the cloth at Claire's back, pulling and smoothing.

'I'm sorry, Claire. I'm so sorry. I'll sew it for you, dear, it won't show on stage, I promise. Claire, where're you going? You can't go, school's not out yet!'

But Claire had already gone. Out of the room, out of the building, around the corner she fled.

The streets were empty. Mothers were inside the houses, getting dinner ready. Fathers were away at work. No one would have seen her even if she had been weeping. But she was not weeping. She would not cry. Rage clenched her fists. If Miss Donohue hadn't pulled them apart, she would have beaten those dirty boys!

She took the long way, but she often did that, to pass the houses of her friends and those she had peopled with imaginary relatives. The yellow house with the privet hedge belonged to her best friend, Charlotte, who was at home with a cold. If she had been there today, she would have helped Claire fight. Charlotte's house was nice to be in, much nicer than home. Sometimes Claire was invited there for Sunday dinner. They had scatter rugs in their parlour and hall, and after dinner Charlotte's father and mother would roll them up and dance to the victrola. They called it doing the tango.

Charlotte's father said he would teach it to them when they were older.

The brick house with the rose garden belonged to an old lady who was always doing things to the flowers. She carried a straw basket and wore straw hats. She always smiled and said hello to Claire, and even though she was old, she was pretty. Claire liked to imagine that this woman was her grandmother. She liked to imagine going to that house on Thanksgiving. There would be aunts and uncles and cousins at the table.

The Hendersons lived across the street from Claire's house. Every Thanksgiving, Claire's mother would look out the window at the cars driving up to the Hendersons and say, 'My, they're having a crowd this year!' Then she would turn and go sit at the table with Grandpa and Claire.

Sometimes Claire would go to the kitchen after dinner and have a second dessert with Bridget, who could be very jolly when she wanted to be, but often wasn't. Mother said Bridget was cranky because all the other help had been let go, so she had everything to do herself. Anyway, she was getting old and would soon be going to Florida to live with her niece in a warm climate. And then they would have to find another maid because, afford it or not, Mother certainly couldn't be expected to take care of a big house like this herself. That's what Aunt Milly said, anyway. Mother said she could if she had to. She said you could do anything if you set your mind to it. Aunt Milly said Mother was a wonder, but she was too hard on herself.

Claire liked it when Aunt Milly came to stay a few days. She had a nice, chuckling laugh and always brought good presents, besides. She was visiting them now, sitting with Mother on the front porch. There was no way to get into the house without their seeing her. So she slid through the shrubbery, under the mulberry bush. If they saw her, there would be fuss and questions: Why had she left school early? Why was the costume torn? Her mother would scold and scold, as if it wasn't all her fault in the first place. I hate my mother, Claire thought.

The mulberry bush was like a little private house with soft

green walls. You could sit there by yourself and think, could swallow the lump in your throat until you didn't feel like crying any more. You could listen to interesting conversations on the porch or watch ants building a nest. They were building one now, marching in a long procession through the tunnel they had made. Each one was carrying something, a seed or a dead bug. One of them had a piece of leaf bigger than itself! Uncle Drew said there were rooms underground at the end of the tunnel where they stored their food and kept their babies. He said it took them days to build all that. You could wreck it all, squash it with your foot, in a second if you wanted. But that would be mean. Poor things.

'Claire, is that you? What are you doing?' her mother cried.

'Sitting under the mulberry bush.'

'I can see you are. But what are you doing there?'

'I'm watching ants.'

'Ants! For heaven's sake!'

'Why not? They're a whole lot better than dolls!'

'Well, come on out, will you? Goodness, your Tinker Bell costume! It's all torn! And your face is scratched! What happened?'

'I had a fight with two boys.'

'Oh my,' Aunt Milly said. 'Oh my, I'm surprised! A dear little girl like you!'

'No, no, Aunt Milly,' Mother said. 'Claire, do you want to tell me what it was about?'

'No,' Claire said. *It was about you, Stupid. All your fault.*

'Well, but you know you mustn't get into punching fights. Girls don't do that.'

'Why can't they? Why can boys do everything? It isn't fair.'

'But you don't want to be a boy, do you?'

'No. I want to be a girl who can do things boys do.'

'It doesn't work that way.'

'Why?'

'I don't know. It's just the way things are.'

'Then I don't like the way things are.'

'You will, though. You'll grow up and be very, very

pretty. And a wonderful man will come along and want to take care of you.' Mother stroked Claire's hair back from her forehead. 'Come and we'll put peroxide on that scratch.'

She followed the lopsided back upstairs. The little bells tinkled sadly. No man was taking care of Mother except Grandpa, and he didn't count. No man like Charlotte's father danced with her. Because she was ugly, that was why, just as Jimmy Crater said. Claire's eyes filled with tears, and this time they leaked over.

'Ouch! You're making my eyes sting with that peroxide!'

'It's not this little bit of peroxide, you're crying.'

'I am not crying!'

'Yes, you are. Is it because the costume's torn? It's too bad, but I can fix it. I'll have it ready for you in the morning.'

'I'm not going to school in the morning.'

'Not going to be in the play?'

'I don't want to be in the play.'

Mother shook her head. 'I don't believe that,' she said gently.

If her mother had been angry, Claire would have been angry right back. She had no fear. But sympathy brings more tears; already she had learned that much about her own emotions. So she stood there with her small chest heaving, an ache in her throat and a stinging behind her eyes.

Mother looked away. She seemed to be looking all around the room: at the floor, where bright spots flickered as the wind moved in the new-leaved maple at the window; at the walls and the ceiling; everywhere except at Claire. Then, in that same quiet voice, she spoke.

'I won't be coming to the play tomorrow, either, or to the picnic afterwards. I've too many things to do at home.'

But that's not true, Claire thought. She wanted to come! She's been talking and talking about it. Then why?

Her mother seemed to be thinking of something, making up her mind, the way she did when she was deciding on turkey or lamb or on whether Claire might go to Charlotte's house or not. She was so quiet for such a long time that Claire was suddenly afraid. Maybe her mother was going to cry? Mothers weren't supposed to cry; if mothers cried it meant that something must be terribly wrong and bad, something that would make you feel lost –

At last her mother spoke, her voice was strange, not like any of her ordinary voices: scolding or in a hurry or simply telling something.

'Oh, you've had a bad time, a terrible day, haven't you? I know, I know! It's awful for you because I look so queer next to the other mothers. And you have no father. You can't even say he's dead, can you? Like the McMath children, whose father died and everybody went to the funeral, so they knew.' Now she looked at Claire. She grasped her shoulders and held them hard. 'But I'll make it up to you. I owe it to you and I will. I don't know how, but I swear I will.'

The words were almost angry, but Claire knew her mother wasn't angry. It was scary in a way, yet in another way it was like the times her mother put bandages on cuts and made things all right, and was so strong.

'Come to the play tomorrow,' she said suddenly. 'I want you to.'

'Do you truly? You don't have to say so if you don't mean it.'

'I want you to,' Claire repeated.

CHAPTER SIXTEEN

Sky-glow came through the slatted blinds, marking the walls in zebra stripes. The city sky was never truly dark; the city never truly slept. A truck ground gears; a tugboat hooted on the river; pigeons clattered on the window-sill. Martin looked at the clock. It was five in the morning and he had set the alarm for six. This had been happening to him of late, this early waking, with troubled mind alert and turning. Softly, he slid out of bed into chill air, drawing the blanket back around Hazel's shoulders.

In the other room he went to the window and looked down on to the street. A couple in evening clothes got out of a taxi; the woman wore long, rich furs. For a moment or two, as they crossed the sidewalk, he could hear their bright voices. From a private house in the formal, nineteenth-century row on the other side of the street, a man emerged and got into a car. He was carrying a suitcase. A woman stood in the doorway, waving good-bye to him. Was he leaving early to attend the funeral of a relative in Boston, or embarking for adventure in Calcutta? The mystery of other lives, the barriers between them and his own life, the uncertainties of all lives, saddened Martin always, but more so in this dimmest hour of the night.

Kahn, the cat, climbed out of his basket, stretched, and coming to Martin, rubbed between his ankles in an S-curve, then sat back to regard him with a calculating stare. It was as if the creature felt his tensions. Its eyes glittered, two green light bulbs implanted in smoky fur. A child had placed the kitten on his desk one day when it was small enough to fit in a man's hand. He bent to stroke it, and the animal purred its pleasure. Then, having had enough, it walked off into the bedroom and leapt to the bed at Hazel's feet.

Light turned mother-of-pearl now at the edge of darkness. From where he stood, Martin could just discern the curve of

Hazel's arm and the long spread of her hair on the pillow. Wild September brown, he thought: she was so warm, so absolutely warm! Most women had cold hands and feet; not she. Her body had deep curves, tempered a little to modern taste: powerful, rosy thighs, great firm breasts, strong shoulders. What dogged generations of survival it took to produce that vigour!

And yet the rest of her – spirit, psyche, whatever you wanted to call it – was total contradiction. You had only to catch her unaware to know that. Innocence, he thought, as intrinsic as the whorls on the fingertips. She did not even know that her flesh was voluptuous! How would you describe her? A simple person? She had such pleasure in small things – a row on the lake in Central Park, a movie and ice cream afterwards. She took the complications out of living. She was restful. In her presence you could feel that people were good and the world a hopeful place.

And yet – and yet she was not happy. Her tears, or rather the traces of her tears which she always tried to hide, disturbed him, and he would feel obliged to question her, although he knew the reason quite well.

'It's nothing,' she would say, denying because she was afraid of driving him away. She wanted him to marry her. She loved him: her twining arms when they lay together, her beating heart against his chest – she loved him.

She had scruples. It cost her much to do what she did not believe in doing, and to hide it from her family, besides. He had met the family twice. Grimly, he recalled the noisy immigrant home in Flushing: the parents; the sister; Rudi and Ernest, the huge brothers; all the other brothers and sisters-in-law. Hospitable, honest people, they were frankly impressed with the American doctor. They liked him. But they were strait-laced, too, and wouldn't take kindly to this at all if they knew. No, not at all.

Why hadn't he married her? Why was he holding back? Waiting for that old first longing, the sweet obsession? But perhaps the obsession was something one did better without. Four years since . . . He went into the kitchenette to heat water for tea, having acquired the English morning habit.

Tea worked against the seeping cold on days like this. In the refrigerator stood a covered bowl of goulash, left from the previous night's supper, and a dish of cucumbers in dill sauce. Hazel was a home-maker, maker of a home. Such strange, delicious foods she provided! Such warmth in her kitchen, such fragrance of rich cabbage soup and cinnamon-scent of pudding!

Once, in some context or other, he had said to her, 'Food is a way of giving love, you know.'

And she had answered, 'What difference does it make? Psychologists only put names to what everybody's known all along.'

She had a way of coming to the heart of things. It had occurred to him momentarily that that was a trait of Jessie's, too, but then he had realized that in Hazel it was just naiveté, which was certainly not like Jessie at all!

'It's so beautiful!' Hazel had remarked the first time he'd brought her to his home. And she had walked around the two plain rooms, looking and touching. She had been impressed by his books and his father's medical diploma from Edinburgh, written in Latin and festooned with ribbons and seals. She had admired the etching of the Parthenon, to which, in a rare moment of semi-extravagance, he had treated himself.

'You're giving your plants too much water,' she had informed him. 'It drowns the roots. That's why the leaves look yellow.'

He remembered everything of that first time. She had known he was going to take her to bed. Wanting it, she had also feared it. And he thought, as he very often thought: *Poor women. One can be so sorry for women.*

He felt much tenderness for Hazel, and believed he saw her clearly. She was a woman afraid she would never be married, or would have to marry some beefy fellow like her brothers. She was afraid of growing fat, like her mother. Afraid of being overdressed or underdressed; of having had insufficient education and not recognizing music or having read books that other people had read; of not possessing the virtues of the refined middle class.

At Christmas, Martin had brought his mother to the city for a week's visit. Christmas had been tinctured with a bitter taste ever since his father's death, and he had hoped to enliven it for her with the glitter of theatres and restaurants. One evening he had brought Hazel to the hotel for dinner, and his mother had immediately liked her.

'There's a girl who could make you very happy, Martin,' she had told him.

Yes, his mother would see that! It had occurred to him lately that Hazel was quite like his mother – except, he thought ruefully, his mother, being of a different generation, was far less forbearing. (She had never asked about Jessie or what had happened. She was a lady, brought up not to mention painful subjects and not to want to hear about them either.)

On a spring Sunday he had taken Hazel to Tom's house. And afterwards Tom and Flo had got on to the subject, too. Why didn't he marry her? You didn't find women like Hazel on every street corner! What was he waiting for? But he had fended them off with a feeble joke about Tom's being Hungarian, like Hazel. He wouldn't let anyone pin him down, and wouldn't pin himself down.

Certainly he was doing well enough to support a family – not splendidly – but who except for a glamorous few in this sombre decade could think of splendour? He was doing surprisingly well. His name was appearing more and more frequently on the operating schedule at Fisk. He was acquiring a bit of a name. Among the younger general men he had made friends; they played handball with him and biked in Central Park on Sundays; they referred their patients to him because they respected his work. Also, they approved of his fees, which were surely more reasonable than Eastman's!

And remembering Eastman's ornate house, his office with its Circassian walnut panelling and its Oriental carpets, Martin felt a certain satisfaction. His own office in a modest building on a side street was functional. There were no excessive costs to pass on to the patients. He had time to spare for teaching, good teaching, and research. In a couple of years he might even be needing a second man, someone who might want to work with him on his dream of a neurological institute – his pipe dream.

Having drunk the tea, he went back to the living-room, closed the bedroom door and put the new record player on very softly. Mr and Mrs Moser had given it to him on the anniversary of their daughter's operation, along with the happy news that she was playing tennis again.

He lay his head back while daylight crept and the Bach *Magnificat* sang. God, to be able to say it all as those old masters had said it! All the splendour, the beauty, the love! One wanted it so, and sometimes found a bit of it, and then lost it.

My life is half over, he thought. I'm thirty-seven.

On the bookshelf at his elbow stood a small framed snapshot of Hazel standing in front of a hydrangea bush. She was holding Tom's and Flo's newest baby.

'That becomes you, Hazel,' Tom had said and Flo had frowned at him. The frown meant, 'Don't embarrass the girl, for goodness' sake!' In the eye and ear of his mind, he recalled the day: Tom's dowdy, cheerful Dutch colonial, the scuffed woodwork, the tricycles and high chairs and all the noise. Why did it ache in him, in him who loved order and serenity and quiet?

In the park where he sometimes walked with Hazel on Sundays, a father and a little boy came to sail a toy boat. Other fathers slid and shouted at ball. And he would stop to watch them. Machismo, was it? A man wanting a son? Yes, yes, as old as time, that was! But a daughter, a daughter was – and he thought of Claire again. Not an hour passed on any day without some glancing thought of her. How much of him could she remember? Slipped from his hold, forever lost and gone, like Mary.

The music stopped. Carefully, he slid the record back into its cardboard case. I am overwhelmed with loneliness, he thought. Overwhelmed with it.

Hazel coughed. It was almost six, and she too must rise and go to work. She wasn't one of that spoiled lot that men complained of, telling in the locker room how their wives nagged when an emergency spoiled a dinner party. No; Hazel was solid, kind and durable. And in her flesh also, a man could find the oblivion which ends in ease.

She loved a wedding! He smiled to himself. She had invited him to her brother's wedding; the ceremony had moved him more than he would have thought possible. The bride was nineteen and pale at first under the lace cap, but afterwards rosy as a child, and Hazel's eyes had filled, thinking – how well he had known what she was thinking!

'You'll have no trouble with the word "obey",' the minister had said, 'although it is becoming the fashion to omit it.'

Well, he wouldn't try to force 'obedience': Hazel needn't worry about that. How glad she would be! And how glad he, to be what he had never been: the giver. Giver, firstly, of material things. And don't, he thought grimly, don't ever sell that short. Would he ever forget the hard years, his mother's dread when the bills arrived? No, don't sell it short, for the peace and calm it brings. So he would be a giver of that peace and calm. Something swept through him, a fine resolution, a purity of hope.

He opened the bedroom door. Full daylight lay now over the bed. Her face was half buried in the pillow, but she heard him come in and stirred, and gave him her lovely, curving smile. He lay his cheek on the warm, spread hair.

'Wake up,' he whispered. 'Wake up. I want to ask you something.'

CHAPTER SEVENTEEN

Nineteen thirty-seven was the darkest year, the lowest year, when the stone struck the bottom of the well and sent a dismal echo. Jessie sat before the desk where bank statements, tax bills and accountants' reports were spread. Oh, the darkest year, in which Father's heart had finally given out and the Websterware plant, after three-quarters of a century, had closed its doors!

She raised her eyes from the papers to rest them, having been at the desk since morning. A monotonous winter rain poured from the sombre sky, pitting the broken ice and mushy snow on the lawn. Where the snow washed away, soaked earth lay exposed like soft brown pudding. This was the fifth month of winter. It had come early, yet when had it not come early in this part of the world? And she thought, looking out upon the bleak day, that June could never have been in this place and would never come to it again.

Place where I was born, you have grown cold to me. You have a stranger's face. Once I belonged here and was intimately known (in London, or any other place, I was a sojourner, an observer). The genteel, passing on a Cyprus street, looked considerately into my face and never allowed their eyes to fall upon my crooked shape. The workmen in my father's factory would quickly tip their caps and turn away. Now they are unemployed and don't tip their caps, certainly not to me. My taxes are in arrears. There is really no excuse, Depression or no, for the mess we are in, Claire and I. Something could have been salvaged! How many times I told Father, I warned him, to cheapen the line to fit the times! Who buys copper pots, fit for the kitchens of aristocrats, in times like these! Better if he had given more thought to business instead of ranting these last few years about Martin and my sister!

I remember the night I couldn't stand it any more. I told

him I wouldn't listen to another word and when he kept on, I threw a lamp across the room. I had never done a thing like that in all my life and I despise vulgarity, but I did it.

In the morning Father said, 'I hope you will apologize.'

The pieces hadn't yet been swept away. It was a hideous lamp, a Greek goddess with a fixture growing out of her head, ugly and expensive, like everything we own. Yet when I saw it shattered on the floor, I was terribly ashamed. But I would not apologize.

'No,' I said, 'I was driven. You drove. I've told you I don't want to hear any more about Martin.'

And Father at last was silent.

I feel so sorry for Martin. Isn't that strange? *Sorry for him? Sorry for Fern?* But I knew about them from the very first, that's the reason. When they stood together in this dim house, in the corner next to the potted palm, I knew. When they came walking out of the orchard at Lamb House, I knew again. They might not have known, or wanted to, but I did. Those eyes of hers! Lapis lazuli, someone said. Just two eyes after all, and if they had been brown or grey, would that have made a difference?

Still, it would have been no good for Martin and me even if Fern had not existed. Oh, we would have stayed on and eked out a life, but what good would it have been? I'm too proud for that. Does it seem strange that a woman who looks like me can indulge herself with pride? Pride's a luxury, isn't it? But that's the way I am.

Yes, I cried my tears in the beginning, cried in bitter shame, in outrage and loneliness, even in despair: what was I to do with my life? Life, though, has a way of answering that; grief passes as other trouble comes to take its place.

So: I don't hate, but I don't love any more, either. Let them live and prosper, far from me. Certainly my sister prospers in her English garden. And Martin? Well, let him make of his career what he can, and he will probably make a good deal of it.

But the child – the child is mine.

Across the hall, Aunt Milly had been fiddling with the radio. What ever could she have done with her time before the thing was invented? Kate Smith's hearty voice cheered her; Amos and Andy, amused; the tribulations of King Edward and Mrs Simpson enthralled her. Now, though, she switched it off and came to the door.

'Jessie, aren't you through yet? Why don't you give yourself a rest?'

'I have to go over these figures before the tax people come.' She felt a wry smile stretching her cheeks. 'They're coming here instead of my going to the Town Hall, as I rightly should. Deference to my crippled state, I suppose. Or else in memory of the glory that was once the Meigs'.'

Aunt Milly's rosy old face puckered. 'Jessie, I wish you'd let me help out. That's why your uncle sent me up this week, to see what we could do. We can't do a great deal, it's true, we've been hit like everyone else, but I'm sure we could manage something.'

'No. Thank you, but no, Aunt Milly. I've got to stand on my own feet. Temporary help wouldn't solve anything, anyway. I'd only be worried about paying you back.'

A car door slammed and Jessie peered out the window.

'They're here. Two of them. Donovan's from the tax office and the bald one's Jim Reeve, the new mayor.'

'Would you like me to stay for moral support?'

Jessie shook her head. Poor Aunt Milly, whose very maids had always ordered her about, to give support?

'No, dear. You go read in the parlour. This won't take very long.'

'After all, you're now years in arrears,' Donovan said. He had the placid manner of the overfed, but his voice was not as mild as it had been half an hour earlier.

'I suppose I'm the only one in town who is!'

'Of course not. But that's got nothing to do with this case.'

'Naturally,' Reeve added, 'there are plenty who've fallen on hard times. But sooner or later they're bound to go to work again and be able to pay up. In your situation, though – '

Jessie felt herself stripped naked before these men. Sweat gathered under her arms and on the palms of her hands.

Four generations of Meigs had lived in this house, and during all those years no men such as these could ever have been invited to sit down in the parlour. Yet now, in the arrogance of their picayune power, they had come to tell her they had the means to confiscate the house itself! And enjoyed the telling too, without a doubt! Donovan, whose nails were dirty, was unconsciously picking at the brocade braiding on the sofa, loosening the strands. She opened her mouth to chide him and stopped; the thing was hideous anyway.

'I will not let you sell my house for taxes,' she said instead, surprising herself.

'Now really,' Donovan began, 'we came here to talk sense. We don't want to argue. This is no pleasure for us, I assure you.'

'Oh, it's a pleasure for you, all right! You can't flimflam me! It's the best fun you've had in a long time. But let me tell you something. I'll burn the house down before I let you take it away.' She caught her breath. 'Don't look so amused. I know quite well I'd be arrested for arson. But that wouldn't help you, would it? And what worth is a vacant lot in these times?' She turned to Reeve. 'Listen, I happen to know you've had your eye on this house. You'd like to live in it.'

Reeve had a nervous twitch and now his eye jumped. 'I don't know where you could've got that idea. I never – '

'Come on, come on. Let's not waste each other's time. This is a small town and word gets around. I know your wife wants this house. Very well, then. Give me a fair price, and she can have it.'

There was silence. Donovan lit a cigar, and Reeve stared down at the floor. Then he asked, 'What's a fair price?' His eye had gone quite wild and there was a hot flush on the crown of his head.

'Twenty-eight thousand dollars. That's what the Critchleys got down the street. Theirs is a twin house to this one.'

'That was a year ago. Prices have fallen since.'

'Twenty-eight thousand dollars,' Jessie repeated. 'Less the back taxes.'

Then Donovan said, 'You're forgetting. We can take the house for taxes and put it up for public sale.'

He owes Reeve a favour, she thought instantly.

'Public sale!' she said with scorn. 'You don't expect me to believe that? You think you'll get the house for half-nothing, don't you?' She lowered her voice. 'Listen here, my great-grandfather gave employment to half the people of this town. Where did your father work, Mr Reeve?'

Reeve smiled slightly. 'At Webster's.'

'And your grandfather?'

Reeve sighed. 'At Webster's. What's the point of all this?'

'The point is that you wouldn't be mayor, you probably wouldn't have gone beyond eighth grade, if it hadn't been for that job. You'd be raising potatoes, and you wouldn't have the faintest chance for a house like this.'

Donovan took out his pocket watch. 'You still haven't got to the point.'

Jessie breathed deeply. 'Well, I'm getting to it. You either give me a fair price for this house, or I go to the newspapers and tell them you've got a private deal to take it for taxes and buy it cheap yourself. Then you'd have to put it up for public sale, and I'd get a decent price after the tax lien had been paid. And you'd have a lot of explaining to do.'

Donovan put his watch back in his pocket and looked at Reeve with a silent question. Jessie stared out the window, watching the rain, listening to its thirsty gurgle in the gutters. Maybe it won't be so bad to get out of here, she thought. Except that, for the life of me, I don't know where I'll go.

Presently Reeve said, 'I'll bargain with you. I'll give you twenty-five, less the taxes.'

'Twenty-eight, Mr Reeve. Take it or leave it.'

'Twenty-six and that's overpaying.'

'It's not and you know it. Twenty-eight, Mr Reeve.'

Reeve got out of the chair. 'Twenty-seven and not a cent more.'

She saw that he had gone as far as he would go and thought quickly: So, a thousand less. I didn't expect to get what I asked, anyway. That's how business is done. She held her hand out.

'We'll shake on it, then. And good luck to us both.'

Aunt Milly trembled. 'Jessie, you were marvellous! I couldn't help but hear. Oh, to tell the truth, I listened at the door. I was so worried. I don't know how you did it. I couldn't have, not in a million years.'

'It only worked because there were two of them. Reeve obviously thought over what I said about the newspapers. He's in a worrisome position, after all. There've been rumours that Donovan's brother-in-law, the contractor who built the new high-school gym, gave them a kickback. So naturally they don't want the papers to have anything else to probe into. The timing was right and my little stratagem just happened to work, that's all.'

'You were so splendidly furious, Jessie!'

'I was furious, all right. I've been half-crazy with worry and angry over being worried. That's how I was feeling when those two walked in, so I just took it all out on them.'

'Well, you were splendid,' Aunt Milly repeated, adding, 'But where will you go?'

'Believe it or not, I haven't the faintest idea.'

'Oh, dear heaven!' Aunt Milly murmured. Her chubby hands clasped and unclasped. 'Your father – I know he was troubled about the way things were, but I'm sure he never dreamed the plant would actually shut down! And your mother! When I think of her, so delicate and cared for, I'm just so upset . . . Don't you think you really ought to ask for help now? For Claire's sake?'

'If you mean I should go to Martin, you can save your breath. We made a bargain: a painless divorce in return for his not coming near us ever again.'

'But – ' Aunt Milly argued faintly, 'times change, and you know he'd want to do everything he could for the child; you know how he adored her.'

'Yes, and I don't intend to re-awaken the whole business just because I need money. It's a closed chapter.' Jessie's voice quavered, and she thought: It's been a terrible day; I could just lay my head down and cry. She steadied her voice. 'I have to be independent. I have to.'

'Only one more question. I don't know why you never

wanted to tell me, but do you ever hear from him?'

'In the beginning I did, but not any more.'

'You know he's married again? I heard quite by accident from a woman who lives in the same apartment house.'

Jessie made no answer. A burning soreness which had been absent a long time spread in her chest. Aunt Milly lit another lamp, drawing an amoeba shape of sickly yellow light on the floor. The glass eyes glittered in the deerhead on the wall and the room wavered in gloom.

'God, I hate this damned room!' Jessie cried suddenly. 'To think we spent most of our lives in it!'

'You're upset, and no wonder. Come out on the sun porch and unwind a bit. Then we'll talk about what you're going to do.' The clear little voice chirped kindly, 'Goodness, what you've done with this porch! It's like sunshine even on a day like this.'

The old wicker furniture and the floor had been painted. A round indigo rug with a scalloped ruby border lay in the centre of the floor. Ferns flowed out of hanging baskets at the windows. A brass Indian jug held knitting needles and wool. The room had the boldness and cheerful confidence that is unconcerned with fashion; because everything in it was inexpensive and of purest taste, it looked like a rich man's simple country retreat.

'I'm glad you got rid of those depressing palms. Uncle Drew always said they belonged in a funeral parlour. And the rug is handsome.'

'I hooked it myself. Have to have something to do in the evenings besides read.'

Aunt Milly looked thoughtful. 'It's really different, Jessie! Original and bright. Somehow it belongs to this century. Do you know what I mean? I do believe you're an artist, my dear!'

'I'm certainly not an artist.'

'Well, I think you are!'

Jessie closed her eyes. The adrenaline having poured, exhaustion now followed. Nevertheless, her thoughts spun.

At least there would be some money from the house: a respite of sorts. But it was no permanent solution. Oh, if she were a man, she would have been educated for something! But being a woman and a cripple – loathsome word, although the euphemisms were no better – you were supposed to stay home and be taken care of. Yes, but what if it didn't work out that way? What then? I could have run the plant much better than Father did, she thought. I'm not being conceited, either. I know my defects well enough! I'm sharp-tongued; I tend to be bossy. I've got to watch that. But I know I could have run the plant much better than Father did. I can handle people, I'm not afraid of them, at least not as much as to let it show. And I've always had a head for figures.

'I never liked it here, do you know that?' Aunt Milly startled the silence. 'I always felt sorry for your mother, gay as she was, having to hibernate in Cyprus. It's only a factory town, plopped down among the farms. Fine if you're a farmer or you work in the factory, but otherwise there's nothing here. Especially for you, Jessie. Let's speak frankly. Small towns like this are narrow-minded. They put people in slots. You've always been that "poor Meig girl". And now you're poorer than ever.'

'What are you driving at?'

'I think you ought to leave, that's what. You have nothing in Cyprus except memories. And some of those you'd be better off without.'

Always, there was perversity in Jessie. She had never really liked it here and yet since it was, after all, home, she felt obliged to defend it.

'We had some good years before Mother died. You forget,' she said stubbornly.

'I know, but they're over. You know what? You ought to come to New York.'

'And what would I do in New York, tell me that?'

'For one thing, Uncle Drew and I would be there, so you wouldn't be entirely alone. And you know what else? I think you should go into the decorating business.'

'Decorating! For heaven's sake! You think that's easy? I couldn't just put a sign up and open the door!'

'Well, of course not. But you do have marvellous taste.

And you've always made a hobby of antiques; you must have taught yourself a lot.'

'I've had no training! I couldn't possibly – '

'You could take courses towards a degree while you were working. It's been done.'

'And where would I find customers?'

'I could start you off. I know two people already. There's a Mrs Beech who has a little summer place in the Berkshires. A room like this one would appeal to her. Then there's a friend of mine whose daughter's being married. They're pretty strapped financially, but I know you could fix an apartment for her without spending too much.' Aunt Milly held two fingers up. 'That's two, possibly a third. And those women would recommend you to their friends; that's how it would grow. Jessie, I believe you could do it.'

For the moment, Jessie had nothing to say. The idea was so foolish, so daring, that no sensible answer could weigh against it. On the floor near her chair, Claire had left a half-done jigsaw puzzle of George Washington at Valley Forge. Thoughtfully, Jessie studied it, then leaned down and fitted a piece of mad Anthony Wayne on to his horse.

'You'd have the money from the house to start with,' Aunt Milly urged.

True. And perhaps with very good management and very good luck, it might work. As Aunt Milly said, it had been done before. No. No. It was crazy!

'The world isn't waiting for me, for Jessie Meig,' she said.

'The world isn't waiting for anybody.'

That was true, too . . . To be one's own mistress! Never to have to ask anybody for anything! Imagine it! Ah, but it was crazy, impossible –

'It would be a whole other environment for you, Jessie. Cosmopolitan people are so much more tolerant. You wouldn't be an oddity, if that's what you're afraid of. A thousand circles criss-cross the city with all kinds of people – foreign, artistic, old money, new money – all kinds.'

True. True. And there were such fine schools in the city. Enrichment. Small classes. Claire at Brearley or Spence. That bright, busy mind being fed. Expensive, but what could be more worth working for?

Here the tail went on to the horse; there went a piece of an officer's tri-cornered hat; a gilt button; a section of split-rail fence. After long minutes, Jessie looked up. A kind of daring, scared excitement raced through her, catching in her throat.

'You know, Aunt Milly, you may be right! And after all, I don't have a wealth of other choices, do I?'

On the final morning, she rose early and threaded her way through cartons and barrels to the kitchen. For the last time, she put the coffee on and in a kind of mental fog, waited while the water purred. Two pairs of mourning doves, coloured a rosy fawn in the first light, were at the feeder. Fern's favourite birds, she thought, with a little stab of memory, and stood there listening to their plaint until, something having startled them, they flew off with a squeaky rattle and twitter.

From the farms a quarter of a mile away, a rooster cried its clarion command to the sun and was answered all around the countryside with jubilant and pompous yawp: Behold the day! The old and peaceful, common sounds of home!

'I'm a teary mess,' she said aloud, 'and I don't want to be. I can't afford it. I've got to make sense and order. God, how do I know I can?'

For the last time, she went outside to walk around the house. The gravel crunched and the wet grass was fragrant. Above her rose the tower with its gingerbread carvings: carpenter-Gothic was the style. Its attic had been emptied of three generations' flotsam: Grandfather's moth-eaten billiard table, a chewed wicker puppy-basket and Father's gold-tipped walking-stick from his dapper youth. Also Fern's bridal photograph, which Father had tossed there when Jessie came home.

She went into the house and stood in the bay window where the minister had married her to Martin, she knowing all the time that it was wrong.

So he had married again! A beauty this time, a beauty like Fern? A woman whose naked body he could adore, not pity or shudder at? And what of Fern, whom certainly he had adored? Who loved her now? Did he, still? And if so, why then – Dammit, enough of this! You'll get nowhere, Jessie! Some things are for you and some things are not. Haven't you learned that yet?

Six o'clock. She went softly up the stairs. Outside Claire's door stood a carton of books with ice skates and a child's tennis racket on top. A terrible, crazy panic started in her. What if anything were ever to happen to the child? What if she had died during the night? Oh God! She pushed the door open and went in.

Claire's long legs lumped the blanket almost as far as the end of the bed. Normal! Tall, straight and perfect! Her mother's affliction, thank heaven, was no inherited thing, but only one of nature's little miscalculations. Like an albino elephant.

The small hand gripped the corner of the pillowcase. Such a vigorous child, she was, curious and determined! Not the easiest to rear, but a treasure. A treasure. She shall have everything, Jessie thought, all the joys: dresses, dances, lovers and trips to the stars. And they will all come from me. Damned if they won't.

She leaned over and touched the child on the shoulder. 'Come, darling. Time to get up. Time to go.'

CHAPTER EIGHTEEN

From her place at the breakfast table Claire couldn't see the back yard, but she knew that the skimpy forsythia had stretched weak yellow strands over all the board fences between Park and Lexington Avenues. In their own yard, a few scattered hyacinths, left over from what must once have been a lavish garden, had poked through the hard earth. Sparrows chittered and fought. They always grew more strident as spring approached.

Jessie mused across the toast and cereal. 'Some day I want to do the whole yard, build a terrace and plant trees. Oh, what treasures these old brownstones are! Just look at those tiles! You'll never see work like that again.'

Blue tiles covered the fireplace wall. Painted on each was a musical instrument: violin, flute, drum or horn – ten in all, before the pattern was repeated. Claire had counted.

'Portuguese,' Jessie said. 'The man who owned this house before the bank foreclosed was a music critic or professor, I think. Poor man.' She sighed. 'This room must have been his study.'

Every day Jessie just walked around admiring things: the ten-foot ceilings, the pineapple newel posts, the pegged floors.

'This house was built with love,' she would say.

Claire was bored by such preoccupation with the house. The only thing she really admired was the dumbwaiter on which the meals were hauled up from the kitchen. They ate on the third floor because the dining-room was occupied by the business.

Jessie reflected now. 'Funny, I had to pay about as much for this little place as we got for the big house and one and a half acres back home. You know, I've been thinking. I may rent a proper shop over near Madison Avenue. I saw one that's fairly cheap. And the business really needs more space.

Then we'd have the whole house to live in.' She sighed again, but this time it was a satisfied sigh. 'You know Mrs Brickner, the one who comes with the Pekinese? She wants me to do an apartment for her in Palm Beach. Things haven't gone too badly for us, have they, Claire?' And, without expecting an answer, Jessie picked up the *New York Times*. 'It's not polite to read at the table, but breakfast is different,' she said.

Claire had expected her to say it, since she did so every morning. She waited for her mother to hand over the second section.

'Here, you read, too. You ought to know what's going on in the world, now you're in fifth grade. Yes, look, the ad for that store is in again. Maybe I'll ask your Uncle Drew what he thinks. Or maybe I'll just go ahead myself and take it. These bad times can't last forever, can they? And I could be ahead of the game with a long lease at low rent. Anyway, the people who have been coming to me don't seem to be suffering from the bad times, I must say.' The paper crackled as the pages were turned. 'You know, sometimes I wake up and for a minute I think I've just been dreaming about these last three years.'

Claire didn't hear the rest. Out of all the thousands of black letters on the spread page, her eye had fastened on a handful, the few that spelled a name: *Dr Martin Farrell*. First there was something boring about speeches at the Academy of Medicine, then a short list of names. *Dr Martin Farrell* stood out from the rest as if it had been printed in red.

This name was never spoken at home. She had not thought about it for a long time, either, not since she had been quite young. The image 'father' came to mind when it did, without specific features, in a sort of blur made up of largeness, tobacco smell and harsh wool. Her concept of 'man', came, naturally, from the men she knew: friends' fathers, the school principal, the doctor and the dentist, with something also of Uncle Drew, a pale figure who sat back while Aunt Milly did the talking and who, in a restaurant, added up the bill and paid. Of course, there had been Grandpa, but he was dead, and she had been only six when he died in his upstairs room with its sour smell. These, then, were the models out of which 'father' was constructed and it existed in some vague recollection, some old sense of loss, long ago.

Surreptitiously, she passed her hand over the print: *Dr Martin Farrell.* It must be the right one. There wouldn't be two, would there?

'It's eight-fifteen,' Jessie said suddenly, lowering the *Times,* 'and you haven't finished your breakfast.'

Claire picked up the spoon and began swallowing cereal. Something had fixed itself in her head, something so hard and solid that it was surprising that she had not thought of it before. She drank the milk and got her coat. Jessie tied her tartan scarf and kissed her forehead.

'Be careful at the crossing,' she admonished, as she did every morning. 'You coming right home after school or going to Carol's house?'

'Carol's got a cold. I'll come home,' Claire said.

She went downstairs. From the front hall, you could look into the shop, which took up the whole first floor. Along one wall were dark shelves with shining objects on them: a marble head of Shakespeare, a clock with a gilded face, candelabra and a porcelain tureen with blue roses on it. Pieces of beautiful cloth were spread like fans on the backs of chairs. There were old, carved chests of drawers and many little tables. There were lamps and pictures and a crimson velvet sofa. All of these things were for sale except her mother's desk with its tidy, stacked papers and its telephone. Aunt Milly and Uncle Drew said Mother was very clever, and it was astonishing what she had managed to do in only three years. Yes, her mother was very smart. But she was not thinking of her mother.

She hurried down the front steps between the two stone urns, each with its evergreen like a toy soldier in stiff salute. Under the bay window was a neat, small sign: Jessie Meig, Interiors. It still bothered Claire that her mother's name was different from her own. Sometimes people asked about it. Her mother said it didn't matter, that here in the city divorce wasn't anything to be shocked about. Claire knew that was true. There were three other girls in school whose parents were divorced, so it was not at all the way it had been in Cyprus. Still, for some reason, it bothered her this morning.

She went down Sixty-seventh Street swinging her bag of books, arrived at school, sat at her desk and went to lunch as on any ordinary day. But a curious excitement stirred in her all that time.

The subway swayed and roared. She had never been alone in it before. She had copied the address out of the phone book, shown it to the man in the change booth, and been told to take the Lexington Avenue line, get off at 125th Street, then walk two blocks east and one block north.

This was adventure! Being alone and going somewhere was adventure. She thought of Boadicea, blonde and bold with her crown, commanding troops against the Romans. She thought of an Indian princess with coarse black braids as glossy as a horse's tail, riding in prairie wind towards where the Rockies rose.

Suddenly in the window across the aisle, her own reflection flashed. With the green school skirt hanging below her hem and the plaid wool scarf around her neck, she bore no resemblance to Boadicea or an Indian heroine, either.

Suppose he didn't want to see her? Suppose he had a lot of other children by now and hadn't told anyone about Claire? He might even be terribly angry! Yet something drove her on. She had the directions firmly fixed and didn't even need to read them again. It puzzled her, when she climbed back up to the lofty afternoon, that all the people on the streets were Negroes. The boys jostling home from school and the women carrying grocery bags were all black. It didn't seem like New York at all. But she walked briskly, found the correct address, and sure enough, there was a sign in the first-floor window: Dr M. T. Farrell.

She rang the bell and a tall, black man with curly white hair, wearing a white coat came to the door. He seemed surprised.

'I'm looking for Dr Farrell,' Claire said.

'I'm Dr Farrell. Come in.'

She wasn't sure what to do next, but she said politely, 'I'm looking for my father, Dr Farrell.'

The man smiled. 'Well, it's too bad, but it seems you've come to the wrong place.'

She had worked up so much courage and energy and now this! All the courage and energy oozed away like air from a balloon.

'Sit down,' the man said, 'and let's see if we can straighten this out.'

In the cramped, vacant waiting room there were four rows of wooden chairs, one against each wall. Claire selected a chair in the middle of a row. The doctor sat opposite.

'Suppose you tell me about it,' he began.

'Well, you see, I haven't seen my father since I was three and I'm not sure what he looks like. But his name is Dr Martin T. Farrell. I think the "T" stands for Thomas. I'm almost sure it does.'

'Now that's a coincidence, isn't it? Because I'm M. T. Farrell, too. But my name is Maynard Ting Farrell.'

'When I looked you up in the telephone book, it said "M. T. Farrell".'

'Yes, I use initials, I don't know why. I just always have. Why don't we get the telephone book again? Perhaps we'll find Dr Martin.'

He had a soothing voice. Coloured people have nice voices, Claire thought.

'Yes, yes. This must be it. Dr Martin T. Farrell. It's just five lines below my name. You skipped it when you were looking.'

She giggled with relief. 'That was stupid of me, wasn't it?'

'Not stupid. You must've been in a hurry or had a lot on your mind. Where do you live?'

'On East Sixty-seventh Street.'

'You know, you could have walked to where you were going. It's only seven blocks.'

'Oh!' Claire said.

'Does your mother know what you're doing?'

'Of course she doesn't! But I wanted to see my father. You're not going to tell her?'

The dark man looked at her for a moment. 'No,' he said

gently. 'I'm not going to tell anyone. Have you got a nickel for the subway back downtown?'

'Oh, I have a lot of money. I get fifty cents a week. Look, it's in this pocket.'

'Well. Just stick it deep down while you're on the street and only take the nickel out when you get to the subway. Why are you staring at me?'

'I was thinking how nice you are,' Claire said, 'and that you look like chocolate with whipped cream on top.'

'Why, that's a very pleasant thought, isn't it? And you remind me of the opposite – vanilla with chocolate on top.' He opened the door. 'Now, you'd better start before it gets dark.'

On the stoop he stood looking after her. 'Good luck, good luck!' he called.

The people you meet! Claire thought. It's a strange world. One minute you're lost and feel like crying and the next minute you feel so friendly.

Street lamps came on just as she arrived. The dusk was shadowy. She felt afraid. What if it were the wrong place again? The apartment building looked like the ones where many of her friends lived: white stone with a green awning that reached from the door to the kerb. A doorman with brass buttons opened the door and directed her.

This waiting room, like the other, was vacant. But unlike the other, it had a carpet, pictures, lamps and magazines. A lady with a permanent wave sat behind a small desk. She looked annoyed in that well-mannered way people have when they are in a hurry and you are delaying them. She was probably getting ready to go home. Claire marched right up to the desk.

'I want to see Dr Farrell,' she said, holding her fear in.

'Have you an appointment?'

'No. I only just decided to come.'

'Well!' the woman said, with a deep, indignant breath. 'Well – what is it about?'

'A personal matter,' Claire answered. Mother sometimes said that on the telephone.

'I'm sorry, but I can't take up the doctor's time unless you will state what – '

She felt a sudden strengthening of nerve. *I don't like this woman and she doesn't like me.*

'Just tell him – just tell him that Claire is here. He'll know who I am.'

He hadn't cried out or jumped up and squeezed her, which was a relief. It had occurred to her on the way that he might do that and she didn't want that, although she could not have said why. He had started to get up and come around to the front of the desk, but then he had sat down again, as though he hadn't been able to get up. His face had gone very pale. She had seen how white it looked against his dark blue suit. Now it had gone red.

From the opposite side of the desk, she regarded him furtively. She didn't want to seem to be staring at him. She didn't want to meet his eyes. It felt – it felt too *sudden,* meeting his eyes as she had had to do when she came into the room. Yes, too sudden. So she kept glancing at him and then quickly away at the wall of books to the left. Her hands were twisted together in her lap and the palms were wet. She took a handkerchief out of her pocket and wiped them.

He was medium. He was neither very young like her friend Carol's father, nor bald and tired like some of the other fathers in the houses where she went to play. He had nice hair, brown and thick. He didn't wear glasses and he looked, she thought, like a doctor. Perhaps it was because he wore a dark tie. Doctors always seemed to wear dark clothes; at least Dr Morrissey did whenever she had the grippe and he came to see her. Yes, he looked like a doctor and he was her father, her real father, sitting here.

A cry came out of her. 'I feel scared!'

He answered softly, 'Yes. Yes, I know.'

'No matter how calm you make yourself on the outside, there's nothing you can do about the inside, is there?'

He replied with a question. 'Does your mother know you're here?'

Why did people always have to ask that, as if your mother

had to know or be told every time you took a step or spoke a word or ate a mouthful?

'No. I came from school by myself.'

'From school? You go to school here in New York?'

'Yes, of course, since second grade. I'm in fifth grade now. I go to Brearley.'

'You live in New York?'

'Yes. We didn't have any money in Cyprus and we came here so Mother could earn some. She went to school and she has a degree now. A.I.D.'

Her father took a handkerchief from his pocket and wiped his forehead. Then he took a drink of water from the pitcher on the desk. She could see he was very upset. She didn't see why he should be *that* upset.

'Tell me about it,' he said.

'Well you see, Grandpa lost all his money and then he died and the factory closed and we couldn't afford to stay in our house any more. So Mother learned to be a decorator and Uncle Drew and Aunt Milly got a lot of customers for her and then more came and Uncle Drew says she is a very smart woman.'

All these words with which Claire had lived so long in her mind, sounded aloud with a moving sadness. She had never felt their whole meaning until this moment. Her voice quivered, telling the story. At the same time, it was pleasurable and dramatic to be part of such a story.

'Your mother ought to have to come to me. How could I have known? I would have given you money.'

'She wouldn't have taken it.'

'How do you know that? Did she say so?'

'She didn't ever talk about it, but I knew just the same. She doesn't like you, does she?'

On the desk lay one of those paperweights that you turn upside down so that snow falls over a country village and a white church with a steeple. Her father played with it, turning it up and back, up and back again.

Then he said, 'No, I suppose she doesn't. I'm sorry about that, too, because I like her. And you I love, Claire. I've never stopped loving and thinking of you, every day of my life. Every day,' he repeated, putting the paperweight down with a thump and looking at her, looking straight into her eyes.

She looked straight back. 'Why don't we live together, then? Why did you go away? I used to ask and ask and I never got any answer, so I stopped asking. But somebody really ought to tell me.'

Now her father raised his eyes and looked at the wall behind her, above her head.

'The simplest thing I can tell you is that people sometimes change. First they expect to be happy together. Then they find out they've made a mistake and aren't happy, so it's just better for each to go his own way.'

'That's not the whole story,' Claire said impatiently, feeling the old indignation at being put off. 'You haven't really told me anything at all.'

Her father sighed. 'You're right. I really haven't.'

'Then why don't you?'

'I don't like to say this because you seem so much older than ten, but – '

'Ten and half.'

'Ten and a half. Perhaps you really aren't quite ready to understand it. Sometimes I don't even understand all of it myself.'

'I think I know why. It's because Mother is – has a hunchback. She looks funny, so you didn't want to live with her any more.'

Her father got up from his chair. 'Oh no! Oh no! I can't help what else you may think, but you can't be allowed to think that of me. Never, Claire. Never. Your mother is a wonderful woman, and I knew when I married her that – '

'Then it's because you wanted to be a famous doctor. That's why you went away.'

'Who on earth could have put that idea in your head?'

'Nobody. I'm only trying to figure things out.'

'Well, that isn't true, either. Besides, I'm not famous.'

'Aunt Milly says you are, almost. She says you will be some day.'

'Your Aunt Milly talks about me?'

'Only sometimes when Mother's not there. Once we went to a movie together and afterwards to Hicks for a soda, and Aunt Milly said it was wrong to hide things from a child and never talk about you, as if I had no father and never had had one. She says it's wrong to keep so much hatred.'

'It's not a question of hatred. Not that simple.'

Her father turned around and stood facing the window, which was odd, because there was nothing to see outside except a courtyard and walls. Anyway, it had got dark by now. Then she realized that he was crying.

'Are you crying?' she asked, and when he turned to show that his eyes were wet, he smiled and said, 'It's all right for a man to cry sometimes, you know. It's nothing to be scared of.'

And he came and laid his cheek on her head. She sat very still. He whispered. She felt the warm breath on her head.

'I hope you haven't been too sad about all this.'

'Oh no. I mean, it's not the very worst thing in the world that you went away! It's happened to some of my friends, and they get along fine. Only sometimes, well, you know, sometimes I get in a thoughtful mood about life. With me it's usually around five o'clock when I'm getting ready for dinner. Isn't that odd? Then things go around in my head and I feel bad for a while. Mother says I think too much, anyway. Maybe I do.'

'Tell me, can you remember anything at all about when we lived together in England? Can you?'

'Not very much. Just odd things, here and there. I remember the Christmas you gave me Reginald. We were in a house, not our own, because it had stairs. You took me down on your shoulder and you gave me a doll with a lace dress. You said it was from Santa Claus. I believed in him then. And still, I don't know how it was, I knew that that present wasn't from him. It was from you.'

'You named her Reginald.'

'Yes. And there was a man – I guess he had been invited to Christmas dinner – who laughed when I told him my doll's name. He said Reginald was a boy's name, and I couldn't name her that. But you said I could if I wanted to.'

'I remember.'

'I wonder whose house it was. There were children there, bigger than I. One was a boy, I think. And it must have been a country house because there was a lot of snow outside.'

'Yes, it was snowing.'

'The dining-room was down a long hall, and the Christmas tree was in the hall,' Claire said proudly.

'Yes. Yes, it was. I'm amazed that you can remember all that.'

'Whose house was it?'

Her father said slowly, 'It belonged to your aunt, Mary Fern.'

'I thought it might have! She's Mother's sister, isn't she? And why is she a secret, too? Why will Mother never answer a question about her own sister?'

'I can't help you, Claire. I'm sorry.'

'I wish I had a sister. I hate being an only child. Hardly anybody I know is an only child.'

Her father said quietly, 'You have a brother.'

Astonished, she cried, 'I have?' And, following his glance to a photograph which stood on a bookshelf near the window, she saw a woman holding a little boy on her lap. The child wore a short suit, and he had a toy duck or chicken in his hand.

'That's my brother? That little boy?'

'Yes. His name is Enoch, after my father. Your grandfather.'

It was too much. It was almost overwhelming . . . Then she thought of something.

'I know about your father. Home in Cyprus sometimes people told me he was their doctor a long time ago. That postmaster told me and our maid Bridget said so. Is that your wife in the picture?'

'Yes. Her name is Hazel.'

Claire considered that. 'What shall I call her when I visit your house?'

'Let's ask her what she'd like, shall we? But then, your mother may not allow you to visit, you know.'

'I'm going to, anyway. I really do obey almost all the time, but this is different. Besides, if you want me to come, I'll obey you. You have a right to say what I may do, haven't you?'

'Not really, Claire.'

'Why not?'

'Well, because – well, I haven't ever done anything for you up till now, have I?'

'You can start, then.'

'Oh, I want to. Is there anything you need? Tell me.'

'I don't need any *things*. Mother's making a lot of money. Well, not a lot, but enough. Every time she fixes up somebody's house, they tell their friends, and then the friends call her.'

'Remarkable. A remarkable woman.'

There was a silence before her father spoke again. 'And are you interested in decorating, too?' But it was as if he really didn't care to know and was only saying something polite to fill a silence.

'No. I don't care about doo-dads like that.'

He laughed. 'Doo-dads! Where did you get such an old-fashioned word? Your grandfather used to say that just the way you said it now.'

Proudly Claire affected carelessness. 'Oh, I don't know. I read it someplace. I read a lot. I've just started *The Count of Monte Cristo*.'

'Ah yes.'

'But what I like even better than reading is science. Leaves and bugs and all that. It's my best subject. I'm going to be a doctor.'

'You are? And when did you decide that?'

'Oh,' she said, still feeling that proud carelessness, 'about a year ago.'

'But you'll marry and have children when you grow up.'

'Not if it interferes with being a doctor. Did you know we were all descended from monkeys?'

'Yes, in a way. It's not exactly like that, though. It – '

But her thoughts came rushing, and she had to interrupt. 'Tell me, do you believe in God? My grandfather did. He even got angry when I asked him once. But Mother isn't sure, and I wondered what you thought about it.'

'Well, I think, the more we learn about the universe, the more we have to believe in some design. It can't all be just an accident, can it? So in that way, I call the plan God, and I believe. But that's not the same as the bearded old king with a crown and a throne.'

'The anthropomorphic God,' Claire said quickly. Her father blinked surprise.

'I read that in the *Times*, and I looked it up in the dictionary. You didn't think I knew it, did you?'

'No, I didn't. I have a lot to learn about you, I see.'

'Do you know what I'm thinking of now?'

'I can't in the world imagine. You keep my head spinning.'

'I'm thinking of the clock with the gilded angels. I suppose talking about God reminded me of angels. It came from Switzerland. Don't you remember?'

'I never saw it, Claire.'

She flushed. How stupid. How unthinking. Of course, it had been long afterwards.

'I'm sorry! It was Grandpa who bought it for my birthday, just before his first heart attack. He was sad that year.'

'Was he?'

'Yes, I think he was sad because nobody liked anybody any more.'

Father was silent again for a little, and then he said strangely, 'You're only ten.'

'Ten and a half. You keep forgetting.'

'Yes, yes. Ten and a half. Enthralling Claire! You always were. Enthralling.' And he kept looking at her.

When the desk clock rang six chimes, he jumped up.

'Your mother will be worried sick about you! We've been sitting here, not thinking of the time at all. Come, I'll walk home with you.'

Claire drew her coat on. 'Better not come near the house, though.'

'I'll only walk to the corner and watch until you're inside.'

When he had got his own coat, he came and put her head on his shoulder. Then he lay his cheek on top of her head again. She did not ordinarily like close contact, having had very little of it. Her mother seldom gave more than a good-night kiss, and Claire had long ago sensed that this reluctance of Jessie's had something to do with thinking that people might not welcome her embrace. So this was the first time she had ever known the actual feel of someone else's emotion; it was more intense than any words that could have been spoken. And she held very still with her head on her father's shoulder until they heard the traffic start far off on the avenue. Then he let her go.

'God keep you. God keep you, Claire,' he said.

Jessie stared into the darkness past the window. Claire waited. After the furious preliminary scolding, having come home past six o'clock and frightening her mother to a frenzy ('I was about to telephone the police!') they had sat down in the little room with the blue tiles and Claire had told the whole story. Now, dry-mouthed and scared, she waited for anger and punishment. Her mother scarcely ever punished, but then Claire had never done anything as monstrously daring and defiant as this.

Jessie laughed.

First her mouth opened with the sort of disbelief that comes after some particularly crazy practical joke. And then she laughed out loud. 'Good God!' she said. 'Good God!' And then, 'Well, I guess I've no real right to be furious. It's just the kind of thing I would have done.'

It couldn't possibly be going to end as easily as this! Nevertheless, Claire's heartbeat slowed.

'So, then, how is he, your father?'

How was he? That was another question you couldn't answer, like some of the other questions grown-ups asked: 'How are you doing in school?' 'What are you doing with yourself lately?' But some sort of answer was expected.

'He said I was "enthralling".'

'Did he?' For an instant Jessie looked pleased. Then she pulled in her smile and looked sombre again. 'And so, what did you think of him?'

Another question you couldn't answer! But Claire thought of something. 'I thought he would be older.'

'He looks – he looks well then?'

'I guess so.'

'What did you talk about?'

'A lot of things. He has a little boy I saw his picture.'

'I see.'

'His name is Enoch. That was my other grandfather's name. Did you know?'

'Yes, certainly I knew. And now you'll be going back to visit, I suppose.'

Something forlorn had come into her mother's voice, something hollow and sad, like an echo. Claire looked up quickly, but Jessie was just sitting there as usual, with the pearls glimmering in her ears and the crocheted scarf about her shoulders that she wore every night because she said the house was chilly. Melancholy seeped like shadows in the room.

'Don't you want me to?' she asked.

'You can imagine I'm not happy about it. But you'll do what you want, anyway.'

'I wish you wouldn't mind too much, though.'

Jessie didn't answer that. Instead she asked, 'You've been thinking about your father for a long time, haven't you?'

'How did you know?'

'I didn't until now. But obviously I should have known.'

'I'm sorry I scared you,' Claire said. 'We got talking and forgot to look at the clock.'

'Well, next time let me know where you are, that's all.'

Her mother stood up. She was so small! Claire was about half a head taller.

'It's time for your bath, and you haven't done any homework,' Jessie said.

At the door, Claire turned around. 'Mother?'

'Yes, Claire?'

'Don't worry. I'll still love you.'

'I won't worry.'

'Things will be the same. This won't make any difference.'

'Of course, dear. I know it won't.'

But of course, she didn't know it. And Claire, trudging up the long stairs to her room, didn't know it either. For it could never be exactly the same again. It wasn't just the two of them, any more.

CHAPTER NINETEEN

Martin moved his chair back from the table. 'Well, this was a great dinner. Had enough?' he asked Claire.

The devastated Sunday roast stood in its cooling gravy on the sideboard with the peas, the sweet potatoes, the home-made rye rolls and the apple pudding. He ate too much, as his father had before him. He resolved to watch it.

'I'm stuffed,' Claire said. 'You're a better cook than our maid, Aunt Hazel. You can cook better than any maid we ever had.'

Hazel smiled. 'If you still want to take Enoch to the park, Claire, you'd better start. It gets dark and cold early.'

'I want to go to the park,' Enoch said at once.

'I'm ready. I'll just get my pea jacket.'

'All the buttons are off it,' Martin observed.

'Not all, only three. How come you noticed? Mother's always noticing, but I didn't think you would.'

'You think I'm blind in one eye and can't see out of the other?'

'Give them to me. I'll sew them on,' Hazel offered.

The three stood watching while she sewed the buttons. Her soft hair kept falling over her forehead. Whenever she pushed it back, she looked up at them and smiled.

'You're really so nice,' Claire told her. 'You know, my friend Alice's parents got divorced, and her father's new wife is nasty and Alice hates her, but I certainly don't hate you.'

'That's too bad,' Hazel said. 'About Alice, I mean. I'm glad you don't hate me, though.'

'I was supposed to wear my good coat today. It's rose-coloured, sort of, and has a grey fur collar. Mother made me buy it, but I don't like it.'

'Your mother has beautiful taste,' Martin said. 'You can learn something from her.'

'I know, but I'm not interested in things like that – clothes and keeping my room neat and stuff. I'm just not interested.'

'There. That's done,' Hazel said. She bit the thread off between her teeth. 'Now you look better. I'll get Enoch's snowsuit on. Be sure to hold his hand very tightly; he can slip loose before you know it.'

'You can trust me,' Claire assured her.

'She likes coming here,' Hazel observed when they had gone. 'I guess it's fun for her to be with Enoch. Her own house must be very quiet, I suppose.'

'I suppose,' Martin answered.

'She really is an odd character, Martin. In a wonderful way, I mean. So – different.'

'That's true.'

'Do you ever think you would like to see her mother?'

'Not particularly.'

Hazel wanted to talk about Jessie, to probe in dark places. But the truth was that, yes, he would have liked to see Jessie, to talk about Claire, to find for himself whether the sore had healed at all. However, Jessie did not want to see him.

'Well, I guess I'd better clean up the kitchen. You going to work?'

'Just for an hour before the Philharmonic comes on. I've a few patient reports to check.'

He had fixed up a room for himself and his personal treasures: his desk, his books, records and the little radio on which he listened to the Sunday broadcast of the Philharmonic. The rest of the house was Hazel's, the woman's province in which he did not interfere. She had done with it as she liked, and the result Martin would have characterized, if asked, as cosy: somewhat tasteless, but inoffensively so. There was a clutter of pillows and fringe and draperies in cloudy colours which tended to cloud his mood. Old rose, reminding him of rotting flowers, and tans like stale tea stains. In Martin's little study the walls were white. The dark floor was bare around the edges of an old Persian rug patterned in gold and cream like sun on sand. There were no curtains, only shelves of plants, so that from his desk he could see the sky, and this gave him freedom and lightness of heart.

Someone last spring had sent them an azalea in a wooden tub. The flame-coloured petals had fallen, but the shining leaves thrived, and it would surely flame again in season. Hazel had nurtured it. She had a green thumb.

The afternoon was murky and still. He looked down to where, three floors below, bare gingko trees stood in a row along the kerb, each one enclosed in its low fence of wire scrollwork. Claire, holding Enoch by the hand, had just crossed Seventy-third Street and headed towards the park. He watched them, the tall, curly-headed girl and the little waddling boy, until they turned the corner. Tenderness filled his chest. That they might know grace and mercy all their lives! Their flesh was so soft. He yearned to them: more to the girl than to the little boy? No, no! How could he? And after all, one couldn't measure. They were different, his feelings, neither more nor less, just different.

He suspected – he was almost certain – that Jessie could not be at ease with this new development. He hoped her resentment was not too acute. He suspected she would not have let Claire know if it were. At any rate, Claire never said anything about it.

She had invited herself to dinner this Sunday and Martin had asked, 'Doesn't your mother want you to have dinner with her on Sundays?'

'She has a cold and has to stay in bed, so I'd have to eat alone anyway.'

He tried to fathom their relationship, and concluded that Jessie, pragmatic as always, had adjusted to living with a good, but strong-willed, very adult child. In short, Jessie would know when she was beaten! It took rather a good deal to beat Jessie, too, Martin reflected now, with a touch of amusement and more than a touch of admiration. The world had not confounded her yet. Professionally, she was doing very well. Hazel reported that at one of the hospital auxiliary meetings, some of the women had mentioned Jessie's name as though they were impressed. An extraordinary twist of fortune!

Extraordinary, too, that after all his own despairing, fruitless efforts, his daughter, without any act or effort of his, should have been returned to him. His entrancing daughter!

His mother had come to visit again for her birthday. Meeting Claire for the first time, she had wept.

'She's different from the others, from Alice's girls,' she had told Martin. And he had asked her in what way.

'It's hard to say, exactly. More curious, for one thing. And very strong. Yes,' she had repeated after a moment, 'yes, very strong.'

As Jessie had done, Claire would say whatever came into her head. She had been like that when she was three, he remembered. (Enoch, at three, was still a baby.) He was thankful that what came into her head caused no disruption in the life of his household. She had with frank simplicity liked Hazel at once, and Hazel, loving soul, had liked her. Hazel would be especially charitable, he knew, because Claire was a 'victim of divorce' and because her mother was crippled. Hazel tended to think in clichés. But they were kind clichés.

He was thankful that, for whatever reason – most probably her own pride – Jessie had said nothing to Claire about the truth of their divorce. Some day, inevitably, he supposed she would have to know and he dreaded the prospect of being diminished in his daughter's sight . . .

Ah well! Sufficient unto the day, et cetera. He pulled out his writing pad and a pile of reports. A reminder had been propped against the book-end: 'The Mosers have invited us for next Friday dinner. Are you free? Shall I accept?'

As it happened he was free, yet he knew that if he had not been he would have made an effort to become so. The Mosers were amiable and decent people. They were all gratitude. Vicky was in fine health: Martin was given detailed proof of her fine health at every meeting. Moser wanted to believe in Martin's special genius, a belief that was as ill-founded as his first refusal to believe in Martin at all. But it was difficult, even impossible, to change a layman's opinion of a doctor, once he had formed it. And generally he formed it on the strength of something read in a popular magazine, or on the experience, probably misunderstood at that, of a relative or friend.

'An acquaintance of mine has a son,' Moser had been saying recently, 'out in Dayton, Ohio. Same situation as Vicky's was, after an accident. And the surgeon botched it. He's a useless lump of flesh, poor boy. An outrage.'

'Well,' Martin had said, feeling an obligation towards the unknown surgeon who had probably not botched it at all, 'it might have been a different thing entirely, you know.'

'No, no, it was the same thing. It only made me realize more and more what we owe you, Martin. Yes, it was the hand of God that led us to you. And nothing you or anyone can say will change our minds.'

He hoped the dinner would be nearby at a hotel. It would be a long drive out to the Mosers' Long Island place on a winter night, after having worked all day. Still, Hazel liked to go there. It was no average experience, of course. You turned in at the great iron gates, travelled half a mile up a driveway between immense walls of shrubbery and were greeted by a servant at the top of a flight of steps. Double doors opened on to an octagonal hall. You walked on pastel carpets through lofty rooms filled with mirrors and brocade furniture, past a polished mahogany library whose shelves were filled with uncut leather-bound sets and silver golf trophies. Through the casements you looked out on terraces descending to the Sound at the base of a shallow bluff.

'It's an English manor house,' Mrs Moser liked to explain. 'Elizabethan. We had an architect who was famous for English design.'

Mrs Moser had come from Iowa and married Mr Moser long before he became president of his tool and dye company. She wore many diamonds, but she was a simple person, somewhat intimidated by her husband and his status. Hazel felt comfortable with her.

Martin started at the top of the pile of reports, read through one and wrote corrections in the margin. His mind wandered: too much dinner, or maybe just the Sunday let down after a week of split-second activities and meals on the run. His mind went back to the Elizabethan manor. The Mosers would not have recognized a real one or liked it if they had. He thought of Lamb House.

Why was it that, on days when he was with Claire, he thought more of – of *her*? Were they at all alike? Not the eyes, for Claire's were dark. Never in any other human being had he seen just that pure and lucid blue. But there was something, some joyous movement of the head, something in the child of eleven that reminded him they were of the same flesh, after all.

No, Martin, no.

In the kitchen, Hazel was singing. 'I hear music when I touch your hand,' she sang, and the sound was sweetly, faintly mournful, like herself. She wanted so much to make everything between them perfect. By preference she read romances and women's magazines, but the better to resemble Martin, she made herself read whatever he had just been reading, and asked him to discuss it afterwards. He often did and found her comments apt. She was not especially fond of music, either, but would go with him to the opera and had bought a book to learn about it. She was convinced that all the other doctors' wives were educated, although he had told her that was not true, and in any case it didn't matter, because he was satisfied with her as she was.

What Hazel really liked was domesticity and the company of women like herself. Flo had become a trusted friend, and that pleased him; it would have been hard on him and Tom if their wives had disliked one another. Also, she liked being with her family, especially her sister Tess, whom Martin bore only because she was Hazel's sister. Tess was an incessant talker, and her voice was excruciating.

Hazel knocked on the door. She always knocked on the door when he was working, although he had told her she needn't.

'I thought I'd remind you the concert will be coming on in three minutes. You get so busy, you might forget.'

'Thanks. But I wasn't busy, I've been daydreaming.'

'About what?'

'About what a good year it's been.'

'I'm glad. If you want me to listen to the concert with you, I'll stay. I won't talk, either.' Her eyes were innocent, holding more innocence than Claire's, by far.

He said fondly, 'Only if you want to. You needn't pretend with me, I don't mind that you don't like music.'

'I want to try to like it, Martin, so we can share it together.'

Try to like it! Mozart and Bach, their celestial mathematics! The glory and the peace, like stroking fingers, like quiet hands.

'All right,' he said and turned the dial.

There was a buzz and scratch of static. A voice rumbled. Then it came clearly.

'At seven fifty-five this morning, a large force of Japanese planes attacked the United States naval facilities at Pearl Harbor, inflicting great damage on Ford Island, as well as at the Army Air Base, Hickham Field. Casualties are mounting – '

'My God!' Martin cried.

'A large number of Army Air Corps planes was destroyed on the ground. Winging in over Oahu, Japanese torpedo and dive-bombers destroyed hangars, docks and – '

Hazel's hand went to her mouth. She always covered her mouth when she was frightened. 'Does it mean – ' she began. They stared at each other and her broken question hung unanswered in the air.

Ask anyone who was alive on that day and is old enough to remember what he was doing and where he was at the moment he heard the news, and he will answer you with a kind of awe in his voice.

'We were on our way to the beach.'

'I had just taken the roast out of the oven.'

'We were getting dressed for my brother's wedding.'

So these two also would remember the day that shook the world, that changed the world for them, as for their countrymen, and indeed, in the end, for all men everywhere.

The last thing Martin saw before he turned the bedside lamp out was his uniform hanging in the closet with his sober civilian suits. The suits looked queer, like relics of some other man or life. He felt he would walk awkwardly in them if he had to wear them and it had been only half a year since they had been his daily garb.

The room was strange, too, this room in which they had conceived their child and spread the Sunday papers on the bed, and warmly covered, had lain listening to the wind. Home on a three-day leave, he thought it might have been better not to come, not to be reminded of what he had already grown unused to and would not have again for no one knew how long. Or ever? The last medical contingent to go overseas had been torpedoed in the North Atlantic. Young Prescott had gone down with them, and for some reason – he had not known Prescott well at all – but for some reason he could recall his face most vividly, plump and soft, eager to please and worried. His wife had been pregnant with their fourth child.

From down the hall came a sharp little cry. Hazel sat up and waited for the cry to be repeated, but it was not. 'Enoch's dreaming,' she said.

What did a three-year-old dream about, this gentle baby with his mother's anxiety already written in his eyes?

'Martin,' she whispered into the darkness, 'how long will you be at Fort Dix?'

'Dear, I haven't the least idea.'

'But it's a staging area, isn't it?'

'Hazel, please.'

'I know you're not supposed to tell anything, and I understand why, but – ' She clung to him. He could feel her lips moving against his neck. 'Martin?'

'Yes, dear?'

'I'm trying not to cry. I'm so ashamed of myself.'

'It's all right to cry. I don't want to leave you and Enoch, either.'

How old would Enoch be when he came home? And Claire, whose years with him had been so few? And in how many rooms, how many houses all over this land were men and women lying awake tonight, holding back the hour of departure?

'Martin? You won't be angry if I ask you something?'

'Of course I won't. Ask me.'

'It's something we've never talked about. I really haven't ever thought about it before, except that now – well, if you should go to England – I mean. I'm not asking whether you are, but it does seem possible from all one reads that you will be going there – '

He knew, he knew what was coming.

'Well, suppose you should be sent to England. Would you ever want to see her again? Mary?'

It was the first time in years that anyone had spoken the name aloud to him. Now, in the column of air where the door stood ajar and the hall light intruded upon darkness, suddenly the name took shape and hung there in a curlicued script, coloured, he thought, a kind of silvery green! Mary: Mary Fern.

'You know that's over,' he said softly. 'Long before I met you. And now we're married.' He tightened his arms around her. 'Weren't you once engaged to someone else? I could be jealous of that, couldn't I?' He didn't know why he was talking so much. He was prattling and it was absurd.

Hazel said faintly, 'Not really. But that was different.'

Of course. They both knew it had been.

'We are married,' he repeated with emphasis.

'Yes, we are truly, aren't we?'

She picked up his hand, laid the palm to her cheek and kissed the palm. So soft! And he was responsible for this soft life! Why did women, good women, and it seemed to Martin that the women he had cared for were all good women, make a man feel as if he held their lives in his hand? He'd better be worthy of this trust! He wanted to, and he would be. He would cause no pain and no tears, ever. No, never, never.

Deep into the night he lay, long after she had fallen asleep, listening to the little puff of her breath, tensing for another cry from their child. The pallid light of his last day was already sifting out of the sky before he slept.

CHAPTER TWENTY

First he put the lamp out, then pulled the blackout curtains aside. The windy autumn night was Elizabethan, Shakespearean. He half-expected to see the witches of Endor come sailing over the woods, or horsemen in cloaks come clattering up the road.

The outline of the main building was inked against the sky. Once it had been a sanitorium for the nervous diseases of wealthy Englishmen, casualties of the peace. Now it had been turned over to casualties of the war. Martin stood a few minutes listening to the soughing wind, then sighed and went back to his desk to write.

'Dearest Hazel, I'm in the country, about half an hour out of London. (Omit that, the censor won't allow it.) It's good to be on dry land after what they say was one of the worst crossings ever. What it could have been like on a smaller ship, I can only imagine. It was bad enough on the Queen Mary. (Omit that, for heaven's sake, take everything out after "ever".) I am a good sailor, I discovered. I was born in a flood and survived. There is an affinity between water and me. One jokes about seasickness but it is no joke, I can tell you. (Poor guys piled high, deck upon deck or bunks stacked one above the other, vomiting their guts out.) There really ought to be some sort of medication for it. I daresay there will be one day.

'For those of us who stayed well, it was an exhilarating experience. (Exhilarating? Without lights we zigged and zagged across the ocean. Dark ship, dark ocean. I went out on deck where the silent watches were posted, hoping for clouds to cover the infernal brilliant moon. Exhilarating!)

'I have to tell you a funny story. (Keep it light, keep it cheerful. Besides, it *was* funny.) I shared a suite, the bridal suite maybe, with two men, one a dermatologist from Des Moines, good-natured, a sort of jokester; the other, a psychiatrist, wasn't a bad sort either, except for being somewhat pompous and all-knowing.

'Well, the psychiatrist assured us that seasickness is a mental state, that if you don't want to be sick, you won't be. You know the sort of talk some of them can go in for. Anyway, on Thanksgiving Day we met the worst of the storm, waves over the topside portholes, ropes up along the corridors. Our psychiatrist, claiming a slight headache, elected not to go to dinner. He looked sallow and faintly green, like the tinge on a cauliflower. My friend from Des Moines thought it would be kind to bring a tray back for him, but when we got to the room, he was flung out on the bed like Raggedy Andy.

' "Look what we've brought," Des Moines said. "Didn't know whether you like dark or white, so we got some of both. And a great stuffing – better than Mother used to make, better than my mother's anyway. Cranberry relish, pumpkin pie with ice cream – why, what's the matter?"

'The psychiatrist waved us away. His eyes were rolling.

' "Come, come, you're not seasick. Bring yourself under control, man! It's all in the mind! Try some creamed onions."

'I got the basin just in time to save the carpet.

'So here I am, and very busy. We have a first-class hospital with every piece of equipment you can think of and some you can't. The worst wounded are brought here. (Change that "wounded" to cases. At Oran the Vichy French fought the American landing like tigers. How especially hard to think that the terrible wounds on these boys of ours were inflicted by Frenchmen! Sad and mad. But then the whole business of what men do to one another is and always has been sad and mad.)

'Dearest Hazel, I wish I were more articulate. But then they always say doctors are non-verbal people, don't they? Whether true or not, it's true of me. You will just have to imagine how it is for me without you and Enoch. And, of course, my Claire.

'You have been so understanding about her. I know there are women who wouldn't welcome her as you do. Have I told you, have I thanked you enough for it? If not, I do so now.

Now I'm going to end this, read your letter again, and go to bed.'

He picked up Hazel's loving scrawl.

'My darling. You asked me to tell you what kind of big present you should bring me when you come home. *When you come home*. I read those four words over and over. I'll tell you: I shall want another child. There's nothing else I want. (She never asked for things. Other men here had already been up in London to spend their pay on earrings, silver tea-sets and Lord knows what else.)

'Oh my darling, we all miss you so! Enoch gets to look more like you every minute. (He doesn't. He looks like Hazel.) I have gone back to nursing. You said you wouldn't mind. I'm on the seven-to-three shift. Josie is still with us, and she'll get Enoch off to school in the morning after I leave. Then I'll be with him from three on, so you see, I'm not going to neglect him.

'I do have a good feeling, though, about helping out. The hospitals are so dreadfully shorthanded. Also, I shall be earning money, so we won't have to dip into savings, and there'll be a head start for you when you come back.

'Your mother is well. I spoke to her on the telephone, and I won't forget her birthday.

'I went to hear Ezio Pinza in *Boris Godunov*. I'm really learn- ing about opera. I do wish they sang all of them in English, though.

'Claire comes every other week or so. We've become good friends, I think. But it's no effort on my part, so don't thank me. You know, Enoch will do things for her that he won't do for me? Last week he was sick and I couldn't make him swallow his medicine, but when Claire arrived, he did it for her. I asked her whether her mother knew how often she stopped here after school, and she said, "I don't tell her, but I'm sure she guesses." And then she said, "She'd just as soon not hear." Imagine such insight at her age! She's a lot older than her years. Sometimes I almost feel she's older than I am. Certainly, she's more determined.'

Smiling to himself, Martin got Claire's letter out again, and skimmed the pages.

'Dear Daddy, I'll be going into eighth grade in September! Brearley is a great school, but the science class is very babyish. I don't mean to say I'm so smart, but one of my friends has a sister in high school, and I can understand her biology book. I'm in a big hurry to be a doctor. Will you like that too?

'Do you ever pass the place where we lived and the park where I rode my baby bike?

'Aunt Hazel is very nice to me. Of course, that's only because I'm your daughter and she loves you. I think it's hard for her, living alone. She says she has trouble balancing the cheque book. If everything wasn't always so mixed up, I could ask Ma to teach her. Ha! Ha!

'Are you staying anywhere near that house in the country that belonged to Aunt Mary Fern, and does she still live there? I still can't imagine why she's such a big secret when she's Mother's sister.'

Martin put the letter away. That child! Ferreting and probing, persistent and blunt as ever her mother had been.

Someone had left a touring map of the British Isles in a drawer of the desk. Merely out of curiosity, because Claire had asked the question and he had nothing better to do, he unfolded the map. Lamb House was sixty-odd miles away, a long distance over the twisting lanes that in this country passed for roads. Not that it mattered. Long or short, it did not matter. He put the map back and slammed the drawer shut.

Occasionally, one panicked. How many years might this war not go on? One had a confusion of emotions as the wounded were brought in: thankfulness that one was not lying destroyed on a stretcher, and then shame that one was not. Argue as you might, and it was true that you had no choice (a neurosurgeon belonged behind the lines, not aiming a gun at Rommel, the Desert Fox), the shame was there. Even Tom, a first lieutenant in the South Pacific, was facing danger under fire, while he, Martin, was safe in this first-class place, not very far from the Eisenhower headquarters at Bushy Park. Also, guilt was there. Out of the suffering of the maimed, he was being educated, increasing his skills. And this disturbed him most of all.

Under a shrapnel wound he discovered a proliferating prior growth, which, without the wound, would have gone undiscovered. Having written about this oddity for a professional journal back home, he received a flood of letters and some publicity, which had not been his intent. He was deeply, perhaps unreasonably, troubled about things like that.

He spent long hours with his patients, hours when he could have been eating or sleeping. Some of them touched him so, that he thought they would live inside him for the rest of his life.

A boy from a tobacco farm in North Carolina, a chubby kid no more than nineteen, told him, 'You know, Doc, I was sure I was going to be killed in this war. I never thought about anything like this.'

'This' was a shattered arm and a ruined face. Martin had been more successful with the arm than the plastic surgeons had been with the face, although it was no fault of theirs. Their repairs were masterly, but still they were repairs. On the left side the patched cheek had the tight, immovable gloss of patent leather, while out of a raw socket glared a glass eye fixed in its glitter; the right side crinkled with speech and its eye could still weep tears.

'Tell me, Doc, will people be – well, will they know me when I get home? Tell me the truth, Doc, please?'

Martin said what he could. 'I didn't know you before, but they've done a splendid job. And of course, it will improve as it heals.'

'Do you think – this is probably a dumb question, but – well, if you were a girl – I mean, do you think that girls will – '

Girls will shudder and pretend and be very, very tactful, at least most of them will, I hope.

'Sure, sure. Why not? You're a kind of hero, son, and don't you forget it.'

Could he tell these young men the truth of what he felt, that their wounds were a personal affront to him? An outrage? We are outraged when vandals destroy a painting, but *this*?

Sometimes men weep. They turn away so that I will not see. And sometimes they don't turn away. I pat a hand or a shoulder. I'm awkward. 'I know,' I murmur, 'I know.' But I don't know. How can I, whose turn hasn't come? How can I really under- stand a twenty-five-year-old man whose genitals have been shot away?

There is a kinship of pain so worldwide now, Martin thought, that it has almost become a part of the natural order of things.

A few months more, and he would have been here a year. His life had evolved into a routine, a continuing order, as if he were a bank clerk or an insurance salesman, except that his work was to mend the dreadful wreckage of the war. When the working day was over he would wash his hands and go to dinner or, now and then, up to London for a night out. It was absurd, surrealistic. The only remedy was not to think about it much. Just go ahead, he supposed, and do what you can and take your promotions. He was a full colonel now, as if he were on a battlefield, where, in a certain sense, he was.

Long afterwards, Martin couldn't recall where he had been going, only that he had been hurrying down a London street, and then, suddenly looking up, had seen in a gallery window a watercolour on an easel: three red birds sat on a wire fence. He stood quite still.

It's not the same, he thought, collecting himself. That other had a background of snow, and this picture was dark green, full summer. Yet the resemblance was unmistakable.

He went inside. A genteel elderly lady came forward and he asked about the picture.

'It's a nice piece, isn't it? Rather better than most of them here.' And seeing that he seemed surprised, she explained, 'We've turned the gallery over for the month to an amateur exhibit and sale. It's part of the war effort, the proceeds going to needy children. Would you be interested in that one?'

He stammered. 'It looks like one I've seen before. Is the artist perhaps – '

'I can look it up for you. Wait, here it is. *Three Red Birds.* A Mrs Lamb. A lovely person; she's given us quite a few things, as a matter of fact. She works in charcoal, too. This head of a child is hers. Now it, I think you'll agree, really is rather good.'

That must be Ned, Martin thought. He'd be a young man now, eighteen, fighting for England, no doubt. But here he was only about ten years old, with his chin held between his hands. The hands were poorly drawn. But the eyes had life and spirit; the mouth suggested humour. And Martin stood, holding the sketch and feeling – he didn't know what he felt.

'It has a certain quality, hasn't it? It could have been sentimental, but isn't.' The woman smiled. 'It's the sentimental things the public wants, of course. Although why not, when you come to think about it?'

'Yes, why not?' Martin echoed.

Apparently the woman had a need to fill up silence. 'Most of this amateur work is pretty bad. But sometimes you find a person who's almost got it, whatever "it" is. I've dealt in art for thirty years, and usually can tell the real thing when I see it, although for the life of me, I can't define it! Now, this woman comes very close. She may have it, or she may not, I'm not sure.'

'I'd like to buy it,' Martin said.

'Which? The head?'

'No, the birds.'

'Oh. Well. How very nice. The lady will be so pleased. She brought it in from the country just last week.'

On the train returning to the hospital, he had a strange sensation that he was carrying contraband and people were staring at it, staring through the paper. For a moment he thought of leaving the parcel on the seat.

When he got to his room, he propped it against the wall in a corner without unwrapping it. Why the devil had he bought the thing? There it stood, making a disturbance in the room. There were enough disturbances in the world without any more.

It was three days before he took the picture out of its

wrapping and held it to the light. In the lower left-hand corner, she had placed her initials: MFL. The bottom of the F turned up in a flourish; the L had a curlicue. Slowly he traced the letters with his fingernail. So she was still living at Lamb House with Alex! But of course, he had expected nothing else. And he wondered whether by now any other man had come into her life, and if so, who and how.

He went outside. The night was still. In the west lay a low streak of hazy, lingering pink. No bombers had gone out yet. On most nights at about this time a flight roared overhead from the airbase only ten miles to the north. In early dawn, you heard them again; they never seemed as loud on the homeward flight and you wondered how many had failed to return.

He stood leaning against the cottage wall. The cruelty, the haphazard idiocy of men's lives! The planet was a ship on an uncharted sea cleaving a way through infinite cold space. At least, they said it was infinite. Who really knew what the concept could mean? Perhaps, like a ship heading towards a hidden reef it was even now careening towards its doom in some unimaginable celestial wreck. All we know is that we are whirled through our short days and our transient delights, so quickly over and lost.

Some three weeks later on a Saturday afternoon, Martin stepped out of a train and walked down a standard village High Street. The church, he recalled, was on the left. There one turned into a country lane, and after a short walk, arrived at Lamb House.

No sooner had he arrived there, he wanted to go back. He felt that his presence must announce itself to everyone who saw him, that someone surely must turn to challenge him. He passed a few women carrying market baskets, a Tommy home on furlough and some girls on bicycles. But no one even glanced his way.

The tiny door gardens had been planted in vegetables. Only one scrap of earth, too small for vegetables, bore any reminder of what life had been before the war. It was a patch of mignonette, like late snow, next to a clump of larkspur.

He ought to go back. But he hadn't come here to entangle

anyone; he had only come to see how she was! What could be wrong with that?

The front lawn had been planted with cabbage. He had taken no more than a few steps up the lane when he saw Mary. Her back was towards him but he knew her, nevertheless. She was hoeing the cabbage. And again he felt a powerful urge to go away. Afterwards, he was to ask himself whether he might not truly have done so if she had not happened that moment to see him.

She stood quite still as he approached. She wore a white shirt and a brown skirt. She was sunburned and had a smudge of earth on her cheek.

'I bought your red birds. In the gallery in London,' he said.

She looked at him, not understanding.

'I saw the sketch of Ned, I think it was Ned. Was it? So I came here.' He stopped. 'I'm not making any sense.'

She let the hoe drop. 'What are you doing here?'

'Here? Or in England, do you mean?'

'You've just come to England?'

'No. Since last fall.'

They stood looking at each other for a minute.

'You've not grown any older,' she said.

'Eleven years older.'

The years had told on Mary. There were some lines on her forehead which had not used to be there; also a thinning of the cheeks so that the enormous eyes were deeper.

'Is Alex here?' he asked.

He hadn't planned the question; indeed had had no thought of what he would say when he got here. But the question sounded normal enough.

'With Montgomery in North Africa. He volunteered.'

There seemed then nothing to say.

'You're well?' she asked. 'Your family's well?'

How queer and formal she sounds! he thought. The questions confused him.

'My family?'

'Your wife. Your boy. Aunt Milly writes to me sometimes. That's how I know.'

The word 'wife' flustered him. 'Oh yes, yes, everyone is

well,' he answered awkwardly.

'You've been seeing Claire again.'

'Yes, yes, I have.'

'I was glad to hear it.'

Again he thought: How correct she is!

The sun, glittering in his eyes, gave him an excuse for looking away. He felt that he hardly knew this woman. He felt quite numb inside.

'Will you come inside, Martin? We have five children now and I have to help with the supper for them.'

He was astonished. 'Five?'

For the first time she smiled. Faint lines fanned from the corners of her eyes.

'No, no, mine are away. Ned's in the RAF and the girls are at boarding school. These are evacuees from the bombing.'

'Then you must be busy. I'm keeping you.'

'You're not keeping me.'

He followed her into the house.

'Sit down while I set the table,' she said.

He sat down stiffly with his cap on his knees and watched her laying the places at the carved oak table, an earthenware plate and mug at each place. He remembered her sitting at that table, wearing velvet. He shouldn't have come. How could he tell what feelings she might have towards him now? Embarrassment, no doubt. Perhaps even anger. It was possible. Anything was possible.

'Have you come by car?' she asked abruptly.

'No, I took the train.'

'Then you'll have to stay the night. There're only three trains a day now, and the last one's already left.'

'I'm sorry! I never thought! Perhaps there's a room somewhere in the village.'

'No need. We've plenty of room here, even with the children.'

He tried desperately to think of something to say.

'All these strange children. They're quite an undertaking.

'Not really. I've reared three of my own, after all. These keep me company.'

'Ah, yes.'

'I'm afraid you'll find it bedlam here until they're all fed and sent up to sleep,' she said politely.

'I shan't mind,' he answered as politely.

It seemed to him they were behaving like relatives who, meeting after long silence, had found that they didn't like each other very much any more.

It was impossible that a bloody war was being fought! Or that there could be places like the operating room where Martin bloodied his sleeves every day. A fire was snapping on the hearth. The tough old sycamores creaked in the wind at the owner of the house. Country noises out of a Victorian novel! Nothing in the room had relevance to what was happening in the world outside it, neither the framed ancestor in the plumed hat, nor Alex's copper-and-silver riding trophies on the mantel, nor the needlepoint bell-pull to summon servants who were no longer there.

A door closed above. There were steps on the stairs, and Mary came into the room.

'I'm sorry I took so long. Hermine – she's the youngest – still cries sometimes for her mother. It takes a while to comfort her.'

'I didn't mind. It's peaceful in here.'

'Peaceful and chilly.'

Kneeling, she stretched her hands out to the fire. An enormous sheepdog came in from the hall to flop down near the heat. The tall clock ticked, making a lonely sound in the stillness. At the supper table, the children had created distraction. Now again there was nothing to say.

Mary stared sombrely into the fire. Presently, she looked up.

'Are you happy, Martin?'

The question, following the stiffness of their first hours, startled him. And he evaded it.

'Can anyone be happy in nineteen-forty-three?'

Her eyes said: *That's not what I meant.*

'Forgive me,' he said. 'I know you meant something else . . . I suppose I am.'

'Tell me about your children. First, Claire.'

'Oh,' he answered, relieved at a question he could answer with ease, 'Claire's going to be *somebody*! Whatever she does will be on a large scale. She'll have a great deal of joy or a great deal of pain. Probably both.'

'That's rather like you, isn't it?'

'I don't know. I can't see myself. But she's like her mother, too,' he said thoughtfully.

'Tell me, then, what do you know about Jessie?'

'Only second-hand reports from Claire, and not very many of those. But I can tell that the household is cheerful; that says something.'

'I think of Jessie all the time; I suppose it's just conscience nagging.'

'Eleven years,' Martin said softly, 'and it still nags?'

'Why? Don't you ever feel it?'

Now. Now they were approaching the heart of the matter.

'Yes,' he said, 'I do. But talk about something else. There's nothing to be done about what's past.'

'All right. Tell me about your little boy. What is his name?'

'Enoch, after my father.'

'I remember your father. He was a plain man and very kind.'

'Well. My boy was three when I last saw him, a quiet baby with a kind of sweetness. Very different from Claire.'

Mary rose from her knees to sit near the fire, resting her hands on the arms of the chair. 'You're not wearing the topaz,' Martin said.

'Topaz?'

'That odd, carved ring you always wore on your little finger.'

'Oh, you remember that! I gave it to Isabel. It was my mother's, and Isabel is like her, even though she looks like Alex.'

'So – Alex volunteered, you said?'

'Yes. He had strong convictions about the Nazis long before most people did, and he wanted desperately to go.'

'He's a man of spirit.'

'If he weren't, I don't think I could have stood it all these years.'

Back again now to the heart of the matter. This time he was less afraid.

'Has it been so terribly hard, even so?'

She clasped her hands. He had forgotten that passionate young gesture of hers.

'I don't know. What I mean is, you come to love life more when it's been hard, isn't that true? There are balances. Maybe I wouldn't have been as close to my children if things had been different. Maybe I've learned to care more about other people.'

There was a change in the room. Suddenly he became aware that his heart had begun to race . . . The fire snapped. In its twisting flames flowers burst open, surf tumbled, castles towered and fell. And Martin sat quite still, letting himself be hypnotized.

At last he said, 'You've been very strong, Mary.'

'You do what you have to do,' she said quietly.

'Do you look into the future at all?'

'Not beyond this war. When it's over – whenever that may be – then I'll think about the future.'

She got up and put another log on the fire, making a small thud and a rush of sparks.

'Man is born unto trouble as the sparks fly upwards,' Martin said. And, as Mary looked puzzled, he added, 'I don't usually go around quoting Job. It just came out of my head, stuck there after all those Bible readings in the front parlour when I was growing up. Anyway, it's glorious poetry, even if you can't take it all as literal truth.'

'You think man is born to trouble? Doesn't he make his own?'

'You could argue that till doomsday. Whatever the cause, though, I wish you hadn't had so much of it.'

'My sufferings rank pretty low next to what's happening in the world right now.'

She smiled, and with that unfolding, courageous, lovely smile, time contracted. Eleven years was yesterday. Today was eleven years ago.

'Blue eyes don't belong in such a dark Spanish face. Or is it Greek?' he said.

'There's no Spanish in me, or Greek either, Martin.'

He stood up. She was so close that he could see the pulse in her throat, could see the dark line where the lashes grew out of the fine, white shells of her lids, could even see a glistening of tears.

'I shouldn't have come!' he cried out.

She didn't answer.

'I didn't come here to begin it all again. I swear I didn't.'

'Oh my dear, I know that.'

Enormous happiness flooded. It surged in him. He could have shouted to the skies. He could have sung.

CHAPTER TWENTY-ONE

How could he ever have convinced himself that it was over? He had wanted to believe that those few days on the southern coast of France so long ago had been simply an interlude, one of those delights, mingled with a piquant grief, that life occasionally bestows. Now he knew that those days had been not an end, but a beginning, or more exactly, the end of that beginning which had occurred when he had first walked into a room and found her there, long ago.

They met in London or at Lamb House or at an inn near the hospital. When they were unable to meet they wrote letters.

'Dear My Love,' he wrote. 'All music and all grace are yours. If I could write a poem, it would start like that. I sit at the window of your flat and wait for you. It is night. I can't see you coming down the street, but I know by the sound that it is you. The front door opens softly, not with the crash that other people make who enter here, and you come up the stairs.

'I am never irritable when you are with me, I, a man always in a hurry, who runs instead of walks, who is impatient for people to complete a sentence.

'The little sounds you make are pure pleasure to me. I close my eyes and, half asleep, I listen to you turn a page. Your heels make a delightful click on the floor between the rugs. When you draw the curtains, I hear leaves rustle.

'I open my eyes and watch you pour tea. I am entranced by your hands, by everything you do.

'All this past year that we have been together, all these odd hours, are the reality of my life. The hospital and the war are its dark background.

'What have we not done together? Heard music often, sat in a bomb shelter through eerie hours, lain in an old bed in an old room at Lamb House and tried to believe that there was no time earlier or later than our long, deep lovely night.

'Oh, Mary, it's been a long time coming, this acknowledgement. Did you have the same long sense of loss? Like dreaming of some perfect place, some cool blue place that could be forever home and then waking to find you're not there and never will be?

'But why do I write like this, when I am awake and I am here now?'

The less one has of money or time, the more skilfully one learns to use them. An hour for a supper, one night in the London flat or at an inn near the hospital, rarely a whole day's and night's leave – these were the equal of weeks in an ordinary life. Everything was heightened, sharpened and quickened.

They walked on country lanes and rested under trees. At Canterbury, struck to silence and awe, they stood before the altar where Thomas Becket died, went out afterwards into Kentish fields, smelled the hops harvest, passed the aristocratic pile of Knole and had dinner by candlelight in a room where Dickens had dined. They rode the trains to nowhere and back. In stormy weather they took shelter in museums or stopped to watch Lady Cavendish, Adele Astaire, dancing with GIs. They wandered the streets. One day Mary took him to the place where Alex's mother had been killed in the 1940 blitz. The very earth was mutilated, an open wound filled with a rubble of blasted stone and tumbled brick.

'She was on her way to the Anderson Shelter in the yard. She was hit not six feet from the entrance.'

Half a house stood at the far end of the enormous hole, and over it all had crept the lovely purple willow herb, a veil drawn on a disfigured face.

'It was September seventh,' Mary said. 'A warm day, I remember. The leaves were blown off the trees. It was like green shredded tissue paper, all over the streets. And then there were the fires. Ships on the Thames were burning. It looked as if the river were burning, too. And the streets were full of cats, isn't that queer?'

'Cats?'

'Yes, they were lost, looking for their homes. But their homes weren't there any more.'

'Come,' Martin said. 'Come now.'

Back in the flat they sat down to their plain supper, boiled potatoes and eggs, eaten with wine and by candlelight on the gleaming table which had once held crystal and flowers. Luminous pale fingers touched Mary's forehead and fell across the white lace at her neck.

'The lace comes from an old teacloth that belonged to Alex's mother. I rescued it,' she said.

The homely remark touched him. Her hands, which had once worn polished nails, looked rough. One nail was darkened from a bruise. The naturalness of these things made him feel married to her.

'You look tired,' he said. 'With that house and those children, aren't you doing too much?'

'There are only two left. The others have gone back to their families. Anyway, I could say the same to you about doing too much.'

'I have no choice. Besides, I'm used to it.'

'And I'm not. I've been spoiled all my life.'

'That's not a word I would ever use about you.'

'But it's true, Martin! All that life we had before the war, all the privilege which made things for people like me so charming, that's over, you know. Alex has been saying so for years. He saw the war coming long before any of our friends did, and he was right. So I believe him when he says it will never be the same again. And perhaps it's just as well that people like us won't have so much and others will have a little more.'

Yes, Martin thought, remembering the waiting room in the hospital where that other England brought its ailments, seeing again the wizened clerk-faces, sickly white, with rotting teeth.

'Only I do wish, I hope, we'll be able to hold on to Lamb House,' Mary said.

'I hope so. I know what it means to you.'

'Oh, not for me! For Alex and the children. It's their heritage.'

'Not for you?'

'When the war's over,' she said quietly, 'I'll leave Alex. The girls will be grown by then, and it won't matter any more.'

Something opened up in Martin like a taut spring releasing.

'Leave Alex?'

'I don't say that easily. We've lived under the same roof so long, he and I. My friend: that's how I've come to think of him. My friend. But it's time, or it will be soon.'

He wanted to say, to cry out to her, *Then you and I?* But a packet of unopened letters lay in his pocket, like a warning hand upon his flesh. That morning, a moment before he had left his room, they had arrived from home. Home. So long ago! So far away! Press the eyelids shut and try to imagine oneself back across that ocean, try to hear American voices. Faces dim and fade. They blur and vanish. So long ago! So far away!

From the radio in another room came the BBC's music: the majestic Andante from Schubert's great C Major. It lifted and swelled like a vast, calm, moving ocean.

He shook his head, shook himself free of complex thoughts. Not now. There's time enough to think. She hadn't left Alex yet. The war isn't over. So, not tonight. Just let pure sweetness flow tonight. Drink the wine, a bottle of sunshine taken from a vineyard on the Rhine before the war. There ought to be flowers on the table, but there are none. Imagine them, then. Imagine iris, and roses so darkly red as to be touched with blue. Think of Mary wearing velvet again. Remember night birds, lemons, the sigh and crash of the sea . . .

He dozed. Mary stroked his forehead. He had been on his feet in the O.R. for eighteen hours straight. Her fingers soothed and soothed. He was half aware of the mohair afghan being lightly settled over his shoulders. A pity to waste our little time in sleep, he thought, and struggled to keep awake, but lost.

He dreamed. His mind roved. At the same time, he knew he was dreaming.

A letter had come from Tom; at least it seemed to have come from him. He had had a terrible spinal wound, yet he wrote that he had seen Jessie somewhere in the Pacific. Jessie's back had grown perfectly straight. She was tall and very rich, with a bag of gold coins at her waist. She was married, and her husband's name was Alex. Claire appeared. She had a baby, a boy named Enoch, but Enoch was bigger than Claire. He was already in college. Now he was on a tanker going to Murmansk. The tanker went up in flames, while he, Martin, stood watching, unable to move. *Jump!* he screamed. *Jump! You didn't save him,* Hazel cried. *You knew he was Claire's baby.* Her face was so sad; he had never seen such a terrible sadness. But perhaps it wasn't Hazel's face? Was it hers or his mother's? It was such a sad, old face, but the voice was Hazel's. She still had that rich voice. It was the first thing he had noticed about her. *I'm going to Germany to look for you, Martin,* she said, *because it's so lonely here without you.* The word was drawn out so he could hear the wail in it: *lonely.*

He woke abruptly. One lamp was bright in the room, on the table next to the telephone. Mary was sitting there with her head in her hands. He saw that she had been crying.

'You didn't hear the telephone,' she said.

'No. What is it?'

'They called from home. My friend Nora did. She didn't want me to walk in alone and find the telegram.'

Ned, he thought, the boy. Oh God, no, not her boy.

'It's Alex. He's dead. Oh Martin, Alex is dead!'

Kneeling on the floor, he put his arms about her waist. 'I'm sorry. I'm so sorry. He was gentle, he was kind.'

'It's so rotten cruel! Hard! Cruel!'

'I know. I know it is, my darling.'

'You see death every day. But I – '

For a long time he held her with her head resting on his. At last she spoke.

'How am I going to tell Ned and the girls? I won't be able

to think of any words.'

'You'll think of them.'

'Emmy's been homesick. I've spent hours on the telephone with her. They've been so afraid for their father.'

'You'll know what to say. Tell me, isn't Ned stationed near me?'

'About an hour's drive, I should think. Oh, do you think – could you?'

'I'll switch hours with someone. And there's a fellow in transport who'll get me a car. You remember, he's dropped me off a few times at Lamb House?'

'I remember.' She began to cry again. 'Martin, I've just thought, what if it were you? How could I bear it?'

'People do. And you would. But it isn't likely to be me.'

'I know you feel guilty about not being overseas.'

'I do . . .'

Yet – if he had to go now and leave her, how hard it would be. All, all a welter of conflict, the whole damn business of living! A man's guilts and his desires, pressing and pulling at him.

He caught her to him. In the midst of death, life clamours. Something like that went through his head.

'Unhook the collar of your dress,' he said. 'The lace. I don't want to tear it.'

He picked her up. Almost as tall as he, she was, but so light, so firm and light, so supple and fine. My lovely. Never, never anything in all the world like this! Never. Oh Mary, life clamours.

Winter fog hung in the trees. The car was an open one, and the cold beat about their heads as Martin drove. The boy sat staring straight forward. His first tears had been shed and swallowed. Only a prominent Adam's apple bobbed now and then in his thin neck. They sped through villages, down High Streets, deserted, as afternoon neared evening and people went indoors to shelter. And Martin recalled the day they had buried his father, on just such a still day between Christmas and New Year's, with the dry ground frozen and no wind.

This boy's father, though, would lie in no coffin among

flowers with hands that the undertaker had neatly clasped. This boy's father – and he remembered the smile of the man, the glow of him – was pieces blown somewhere in the desert air, fragments in the desert sand.

'You know he's to get a medal for heroism?' Ned spoke unexpectedly.

'No, I didn't.'

'Mother's friend has a relative in the War Office and he found out. My father saved four lives. Crazy, isn't it?'

'Crazy? I don't understand what you mean.'

'He didn't have to go to fight, that's what I mean. They wouldn't even have taken him if they'd known.'

'Known what?'

The boy turned a clear and earnest face to Martin. 'Why – what you know. He wasn't – he wasn't – ' The Adam's apple bobbed. 'Don't make me say it when you already know about him, please.'

'I see.' Martin was appalled. Was there no innocence left in the world at all?

And he asked, 'Who told you?'

'I heard it around the village when I was still in school. I've known for years.'

'I see,' Martin said again.

'People are rotten about it.'

'I know.'

'Some boy said he couldn't fight his way out of a paper bag. They won't be able to say that now, will they?'

'It would be a rotten thing to say even if it were true.'

They rode on silently until Martin said, 'We're almost there. We'll make it by six, I should think.'

More silence. Then Ned spoke again. 'Isn't there anything you want to ask me?'

'What should I ask you?'

'I thought you might want to know whether – whether I'm like my father. I'm not. I've had plenty of girls already, and they're what I want.'

'What you want isn't any of my business, is it?' Martin responded quietly.

'You're very decent. My father said you were. He said you

were the only person who'd really understood.'

'You spoke of this with him?'

'Yes. After I'd first heard talk, I went and asked him. And he told me. I guess it was one of the hardest things a man might ever have to tell his son. But he did it.'

'And, may I ask, how did you feel?'

'Sick about it. I ran out of the room and cried. I couldn't talk to him or even look at him for days. But then after a while, after I had thought about it, I went back. He was my father, and a better father to me than most of my friends had.'

A boy like this one could make a lot of people ashamed of themselves, Martin thought.

'I felt sorry for Mother, though,' Ned went on. 'She stayed because of us, the girls and me. I knew that. The girls didn't and don't. There couldn't have been much in it for her, could there?'

I love your mother, Martin wanted to say, and imagined the boy replying, I know, my father told me that, too.

But he said only, 'She loved her children. You were worth it to her.'

At Lamb House lights were on, the driveway was full of cars. With his arm around Ned's shoulders, they walked together, Martin with Mary's boy, into the house.

A week or more before the sixth of June in 1944, Martin had gone south on medical affairs and stood where one could look across Southampton Water to the Isle of Wight. From Weymouth Bay across to Portland Bill lay a thousand ships or more, destroyers, landing craft and minesweepers. So in his bones he had known, and was therefore not surprised to be awakened towards morning on the sixth of June by the sweep and drone of hundreds of aeroplanes flying overhead. It had begun.

In the wards expectant faces look up from the beds. 'It's here,' they say, and then, in some primitive ritual of denial, are silent. For if it failed – one dared not think of that.

First announcements, oddly enough, come over the German radio, sounding as if nothing much has happened.

'The allies have attempted a small landing on the coast of France.'

Later in the morning, comes a short statement from the BBC: 'Allied naval forces under the command of General Eisenhower, supported by strong air forces, began landing Allied armies on the coast of France.'

By noon the churches are filled, from Westminster Abbey and St Paul's in London to the smallest village chapel. Under Gothic stone lace, facing the pale tips of lighted candles, old men and women with sons, and young women with husbands, bow their heads to pray.

Martin would give much to be part of that day in France, even as he knows that its first casualties will soon be rolling down the road to his door.

Through summer and autumn, the momentum quickens. The train gathers speed, it tops the hill and goes roaring down the long straight track. Paris is liberated; De Gaulle strides down the Champs-Elysées. The Germans withdraw. The Allies pursue and cross the Moselle River.

In dark December the Germans gather strength for their last stupendous effort in the Ardennes. At first the radio brings bleak reports for the Allies from Bastogne, from Namur and Liège. But in the end, the stupendous effort fails and, late in the winter, the Germans are driven back. The Allies cross the Rhine at Remagen Bridge. The war in Europe is as good as over.

Now orders begin to arrive. Major So-and-so is to proceed to Michigan or New York to receive the wounded from the Pacific theatre. Captain So-and-so is to proceed to California to embark for the Pacific theatre.

One day, Mary speaks what for many weeks has been unspoken between them.

'They'll be sending you home soon,' she says.

It is both a statement and a question. Martin doesn't answer.

He went outside and lay down in the grass. At the top of the rise, he could see the wheelchairs on the terrace where convalescents had been let out to gaze at a spring that some of them had thought never to see again.

At the foot of the modest hill, a stream curved under an arched stone bridge. Gilded catkins hung from the willows, which in summer stood like young girls with streaming, long pale hair. A hawk sailed over Martin's head, paused in the sky and plunged behind the rim of the trees.

He closed his eyes. The air was full of sounds, blending into one long hum of afternoon, of bees, wind and larks. There was a rhythm to lark-song: five beats long, two short. There was rhythm and music in all things. Passionately, he wished he could know more about music.

Someone was playing ragtime on the battered piano in the hall. It was the boy from Chicago, no doubt, the one whose arm he had repaired so well, except for one lost finger. The boy had been worried about the piano; it meant a lot to him, he said, although he was no musician. He was playing pretty nicely in spite of the lost finger! Boom da da-da, boom da da-da.

From the porch came the click and tick of ping-pong balls; there was a cadence in the volleys. All his senses were so sharp today! Most of the time, he thought, we are only half alive, missing things. But perhaps it was better so, better not to feel so sharply.

The dog beside him licked his hand. He had forgotten that the dog was there, he'd grown so used to it. One cold night in the previous winter, he had found it sitting outside the local pub where he had gone for a beer. It was only a shabby mongrel of a type so common as to have become almost a breed in itself, with pointed ears and a setter's tail meant to be carried in pride and gaiety. But some pleading in its face had caught at him, and he had stopped to talk to it. Two villagers had come out and warned him away.

'It'll bite you,' they said. One had picked up a stone. 'Get out of here! Get the hell out of here!'

The dog had moved a few steps and sat down. It had been desperate enough for food to risk the stone.

'People abandon them,' Major Pitman remarked. 'It's a disgrace.'

The man who had picked up the stone rebuked him. 'They

don't have rations enough for themselves. What do you want?'

They had started to walk back to the hospital. At the end of the street, Martin had realized that the dog was padding behind them.

'I'll have to get him something to eat,' he'd said.

'You'll never lose him if you do,' Major Pitman had warned.

'I know.'

At Martin's door, the dog had stood on the step waiting to be asked in.

'Oh, no,' he'd told him, 'I've nothing for you.'

And the wretched creature had licked his hand.

'What am I do with you?' he asked now. 'It's soon going to be over between you and me.'

The dog raised sorrowful brown eyes. *I understand,* they said, and he crept closer. A grasshopper, with green transparent wings like finest paper, lit a few inches from his paw, but the dog took no notice of it.

You will not abandon me, he told Martin; *I believe in you.*

Martin laid his hand on the warm flanks where you could no longer feel the ribs. 'Yes, you know, don't you? You know I can't turn you out.'

The dog's tail thumped the ground.

'Mary will have to take you. I'll leave you behind with Mary.'

And Martin sat up. *Leave you behind?* Was he, then, really to go away? Twice in a lifetime? Haunted, haunted! A fairly intelligent man, supposedly in charge of his own life, he had been obsessed since the very first day.

What was it all about? Why were we here? What was history but a history of turbulent past griefs? Crackle of fires as Troy burned, he thought; splitting timbers as Jerusalem fell and Rome was sacked, weeping of parents when the Black Death emptied Europe, agony and shame of the concentration camps, thundering of bombs on burning London. So little time to flower in the sun and live and take one's love!

Mary, Mary, I can't leave you again. I can't.

The dog crept closer still and licked his hand.

Hazel wrote, 'Lorraine Mays tells me your unit is to be brought home by summer. She was surprised you hadn't let me know, but I understand, darling, that prudent as you are, you didn't want to raise my hopes until you could be absolutely sure.'

There were only three weeks left before departure. In the morning, every morning, while a crowded day still lay ahead, he assured himself that at some point in that day, everything would suddenly be resolved. And always the night came without solution. Well, tomorrow then?

There were two weeks left.

One day in London he passed a toy shop and saw in the window a wooden horse like one that Enoch had played with. Later he had an errand that took him past the Brompton Oratory, where he had pushed the newborn Claire in her perambulator. Here in these old, old places, past baroque stone, through mews and Georgian squares, she had first learned to walk. Always he saw her in that yellow coat and bonnet.

He felt weak, aware of his heartbeat. Turning into a cardiac neurotic, he thought, scornful of himself. But he was trembling when he arrived back at the hospital.

'Don't you feel well, Colonel?' his new lieutenant asked.

'No, I've been fighting a blooming cold all week.'

He sat down at his desk before a sheaf of records which had been left for his signature. The words made no sense.

Was there any possible way he could request postponement? Any way orders could be rearranged, so that perhaps some other man who was in a hurry to go home – as who was not? – could go in his place? He needed time! Time to think! But of course, that was nonsense. This was the army. And shutting the door, he put his head down on the desk.

Write to Hazel? Take courage and put it all on paper? A lot of men in this war were doing, and had done, just that. For one sharp moment, he saw her sitting in the chair at the kidney-shaped desk where she used to read the mail; he saw her eyes crinkling in a smile, her face softening, as she opened his letter. He shivered.

Go home and tell her then. Give her as gently, as kindly, as reasonably as you can, the truth. But what of Enoch? What of Claire? *Carpe diem,* it is said; seize the day, seize life. It speeds away while you watch. And I'm forty-four years old.

He knelt on the floor beside the chair where Mary sat knitting. Narrow blue veins crossed and merged in delicate webbing on her wrists. He took the wool away and kissed her wrists. Had he been asked what he was feeling, he could have said it was not worship, it was not comfort, it was not joy, it was not desire. It was all of these and it was beyond them. It was beyond the furthest reach of longing.

'I can't,' he said.

'Can't go away?'

'No. Can't go away.'

After a few days another letter came. 'Enoch will be in the second grade next fall, imagine! He's so like you, Martin, always reading. People say he looks like you, too. He wanted to have a picture of you in his room, so I had a duplicate made of the one on my night table. It's the last thing I see before turning out the light and the first thing I see in the morning when I open my eyes.

'I think sometimes that if you were to stop loving me, I couldn't bear it. But then I know that couldn't happen any more than I could stop loving you. I don't think there can ever have been two people who understand each other better. I feel that, even though you're three thousand miles away, we're still together. And soon, please God, we really shall be. I'll turn in bed at night and you'll be there, and it will no longer be a dream.'

Martin put the letter down. A dull sadness seeped into the room, like fog. He read on.

'I've saved so much of your allotment, you'll be surprised. Living alone like this, a woman doesn't need to spend much. I hardly ever go to the stores except for Enoch's clothes. And yesterday I bought a necklace for Claire's birthday, seed pearls on a gold chain. She's such an amazing girl. It's hard to believe she's only fifteen . . . Now that you're coming home, though, I shall treat myself to some new clothes.

Would you like to see me in a black lace nightgown?'

She had used to sit up in bed and wait for him when he was called out. She always said she couldn't fall asleep unless he was home. If only there were some meanness in her, some sly and reprehensible selfish streak which could assure her survival while it gave him an excuse! But no, she had wanted only and always to please everyone, even her exasperating relatives. God knew what fears, what chained resentments even, underlay that anxious love of pleasing!

And suddenly Martin heard his father's voice. So often in the crisis of his life, he had recalled that voice, not necessarily its words, rather its tone of earnest conviction. He remembered, too, the expressive movements of the hands, so uncharacteristically Mediterranean for a Scotsman. And he thought of his own little son. What would that boy remember of his father?

He went down to the street. He needed to move. Mary was to come in later from the country, but she had her key. The night was grey and the scudding clouds threatened rain. His footsteps pounded so that he startled himself and made himself walk more softly. He walked across the city and came to the river.

In the middle of the bridge, facing the Victoria Embankment, he lit a cigarette, then threw it down into the iridescent, oily water and watched it blink out. The sky behind the Houses of Parliament blackened as the storm approached. A flash of lightning brightened the long, even facade, the fretwork pinnacles, oriels and turrets of this place where men sat and made rules to keep themselves from consuming each other. He lit another cigarette, threw that one, too, into the water and began to walk home.

Some soldiers passed, their laughter stilling to a startled salute when they saw the American officer. Hearing their muttered, 'Had too many, that one!' as they passed him, he realized that they had heard him groan. Did he look as wretched as he felt? As woebegone? Yes, his head was bent, his hands were knotted behind his back as though he were pacing the floor of his own house. He straightened up.

Mary was asleep on the sofa when he let himself in.

Dismayed, he remembered that he had left Hazel's pages scattered. She had picked them up and placed them neatly on the table next to the lamp.

She opened her eyes. 'I didn't read it,' she said.

'I didn't think you did.'

'It's from home, isn't it?'

'Yes.'

And kneeling down, he put his head on her lap. Then, ashamed of his wet eyes, he couldn't raise his head. The price a man paid for manhood! Valour and steel, the ramrod back, the stiff upper lip!

'You're going home to stay?'

'Yes,' he murmured.

She got up and, going to the window, pressed her cheek against the cold glass. At last she said, 'A commitment. I understand.'

He couldn't answer. What words could he have found? He thought perhaps dying would be easier, going down into oblivion and rest.

'We deserve something better . . .'

'Who knows what anyone deserves?'

'Our timing is always wrong.'

'God knows that's true.'

'Bitterness is ugly, Martin. And I am so damn bitter.'

They lay in bed, talking.

'There was a couple who lived near Alex and me. He was twenty-eight, and he died one Saturday morning after playing tennis. Before the war people of twenty-eight weren't dying. It was a grief so terrible that you turned away from looking at her. And still I couldn't have understood it . . . Tonight I do.'

He took her in his arms. The last time, the last time. He thought he had cried the words aloud; perhaps he had only heard them in his head. A swelling tide of blood crackled and surged as he lost himself in her; never draw apart, he thought; never, never . . . and then he did fall away and lie apart at last, seeing shadows, hearing the sound of rain.

It must have started while they lay in love. Trucks were

passing at the corner, a rumbling convoy of army vehicles, each one guided by a being as filled with his own essentiality as Mary and he. The little room trembled with their thunder. The clock struck three. A few hours more, and it would be over.

When she came out of the bedroom in the morning, he had already collected his things.

'Just your clothes, Martin? Not the Churchill mug or the Rowland prints I gave you or anything?'

'Only your *Three Red Birds*. I don't want anything else.'

They stood in the little hall.

'Do you think we'll ever be in the same place at the same time again?' Mary asked.

'I don't think so.'

'If we ever are, I'll walk quickly away, and you do the same. Will you promise me, Martin?'

'I promise.'

'It's eight, and you'd better hurry,' she said.

But neither of them moved.

'I'll go down the stairs, Martin. I won't look back. Wait two or three minutes until I've driven away.'

'No. I'll see you into your car.'

'Please. I can't just drive off with you standing there. Please. Help me.'

'I want to go down together,' he insisted.

In the instant before he put the light out and shut the door, she began to look like a stranger. She was wearing a skirt he had never seen before. It had grown chilly, and she had put a sweater over her shoulders, a complicated knit of the kind people receive as gifts. Yet, under the skirt and sweater was the flesh he knew so well, more dearly than any he had ever known, or ever would.

And was he absolutely mad to be doing what he was doing, or was it the only way to keep from going mad?

They went downstairs and out to where her car was parked. It seemed to him that they ought to be saying something. He wanted to say: Understand, we are the kind of people who cannot step on other people's faces. He wanted to say: You see, the trouble with you and me is that neither of us has courage enough to preserve ourselves. For, isn't that the first law of nature? Yes, but nature isn't civilized, and we are, you and I. He wanted to say all those things, but he said none of them.

He might have done so – or again, might not have – but just then a man came out of a house and went to his car, which was blocked by Mary's.

'Oh,' the man said. 'You're going? Looks like a fair day! I suppose you will soon be leaving, Colonel, now that the Jerries have given up?'

'I suppose so, yes.'

'It's been a long war. It'll seem strange here when all the Americans have left.'

'I guess it will.' Would he ever go, the fool? Couldn't he see he was in the way? But no, of course, he was waiting for Mary to move the car.

'Well, if I could just back out,' the man said, politely enough.

'Of course.'

The man got into his car and started the motor. Mary got into hers. She placed her hands on the wheel, then looked up at Martin.

'Are you all right?' he asked. 'Can you drive all right?'

She nodded. He wanted to say – God knows what he wanted to say. *Oh, my dear, my love, forgive me, take care of yourself.* And he said nothing.

She put out her hand and touched his quickly. Her little car began to move. Then Martin turned, and rapidly, blindly, walked into the stunning glare of risen light.

BOOK FOUR

VISIONS

CHAPTER TWENTY-TWO

Over the northern shore of Japan's lovely inland sea, in early morning the *Enola Gay* came winging towards Hiroshima. And in one fiery moment of warm summer, the war ended.

In movie theatres across America, people sat with upturned faces, watching the mushroom cloud and the settling ashes of what had been Hiroshima, watching Tojo hand over his sword on the battleship *Missouri* in Tokyo Bay.

When the show ended, they got up and went out into Times Square's electric night, or else on to Main Street's shadowed night to walk home under rustling maples. For the moment, there was only rejoicing. Some years later would come recriminations and defence. Some years later, tourists would visit the museum in Hiroshima and stand in shocked and grieving silence before the pictures of the maimed. But for now, there was the business of living to be resumed.

On laden ships, crowded in passageways, on bunks four tiers deep, the impatient men sailed homewards. Trains were jammed. And the stations which had, four years before, seen so many dreadful partings were witness to a million reunions of sons with parents, of husbands with girl-wives and children who had been babies when their fathers went away.

Of course, there were some who were not being met at the station. These had already been informed, or had informed, that absence had changed things: that she had found another man in the factory or down the street, or that he had found a girl overseas. For such as these, the end of the war was as much of a shock, or possibly more of a shock, than the start of it had been.

But most came back home to the same wife and the same job at the gas station or the bank. And these, the wife and the job, might have been either balm to the heart or else a secret disappointment that the great adventure was over.

Everyone joined the scramble for goods, for everyone needed everything and everything was in short supply. Ration books were torn up and thrown away. Gradually, the shops began to fill again with nylon stockings, sugar, lamb chops, shoes and chocolate bars. OPA was taken off and prices jumped, but since wages did too, no one objected.

Pessimists like Tom Horvath, ever cautious, predicted a bust and a slide back down to the grim grind of the years before the war. It didn't happen. There began instead a long procession of the most plentiful, lavish, dazzling years in all the history of America, indeed in the history of any land or empire on the planet, since histories have been written.

Martin was propelled by events. He needed only to stand still and be swiftly moved as if on a conveyor belt, from that first moment of beholding Hazel's radiance and hearing her glad shaking cry, then of catching the boy up in his arms, the cheerful little boy in whom Hazel's effort had kept alive the memory of Martin.

He got down on the floor with Enoch. Three years before the child had played with blocks. Now he could read *Dick and Jane* and write the note tacked on the bedroom door: Dere Dady. Well come home. Luv, Enoch.

Claire came, quieter now, less impetuous, wearing a feminine blue dress and a hairdo. He sat with her to talk about college. She was barely sixteen, but already the rush was on. Should it be Smith or Wellesley? Where were the better science programmes? She wore glasses now. For some reason, they were becoming to her alert and mobile features, and he thought: She is going to be a rare woman.

The telephone kept ringing welcome. Martin's mother called, her old voice quavering with tears until Alice got on the line. Friends rang the doorbell. One evening the door was opened to Perry, still in Navy uniform, back from the Aleutians; a week later, Tom telephoned from California that he was on his way home.

On the first Sunday they could borrow a car, Hazel and Martin went to visit the Horvaths. Tom had gone quite grey. The men hugged each other, hiding great gulps of emotion, then sat down to eat one of Flo's enormous dinners and studiously didn't talk at all about the war. That would come later.

'You've still got your appetite,' Flo observed.

And Martin answered that, yes, there hadn't been much good eating in England these last years, and the English had never been first-rate cooks, anyway. So he filled himself, while Hazel watched, not able to take her eyes away, and he was grateful that she was still so sweetly pretty, with so much joy in her face, and hadn't grown older and fat as Flo had.

He was grateful, too, for Enoch, who demanded his attention and made, he admitted to himself, a kind of natural barrier or buffer between himself and Hazel's intensity. If she noticed at all that the child was in the way, she did not appear to. So Enoch averted many moments which for Martin would have been sorely strained.

He was in a hurry to be busy again. Work would be his salvation. And his head whirled with the speed of re-entry to the former life.

His old civilian clothes still fitted, but felt foreign, and the first day in the hospital was queer, too, walking in and wondering whether he'd attract too much attention, or perhaps none at all.

On a bronze plaque in the lobby, he found his name on a long list of names, some of which bore stars. The stars gave him a thundering shock, recalling the faces that went with them, faces that would never be seen in this building again, while he could walk in, hale and straight, to be greeted like a hero.

For, indeed, they remembered him. Nurses came crowding up; the old ones, those over sixty, kissed him. Doctors came to shake his hand. Even Eastman was cordial.

'I read your article in the Archives. Extraordinary case! You must have seen more in your three years over there than we see here in ten.'

'More than I ever want to see again. Not that kind, anyway,' Martin told him.

The first thing you had to do was to open an office. Space

was almost impossible to find. One consulted newspapers and agents; one canvassed every possible doctor for news of space to sublet. In desperation at last, he agreed to share a suite with an obstetrician of his acquaintance, also back from the service, who hadn't yet found a place. It would have been an unwieldy arrangement for both of them. At the last minute the other man found something, and to Martin's great relief, he was left with an ample office all to himself on a fine East Side street.

Painters had to be found, at a time when it seemed that everyone in the city must be calling for one. There were furnishings to buy. Hazel wanted to help, but Martin told her mildly that, while the house was hers, the office was his. Here he would spend the larger portion of his days, and he knew what he needed: simple Danish chairs and desks. And on the walls, a series of fine photographs, views of the city done in sepia: a liner coming through the Narrows, an old man feeding pigeons on the Mall, rain on Fifth Avenue in late afternoon with the lights coming on.

He had been prepared to borrow from a bank the considerable money needed to get started again. But when Hazel, with simple pride, showed him the savings book in which his allotment cheques were methodically recorded, and he saw that there was more than enough to pay the bills, he was much moved.

'She looketh well to the ways of her household, and eateth not the bread of idleness.'

Hazel's admiring comment, 'You do know the Bible backwards and forwards, don't you?' embarrassed him. But she was right about it all the same. He was his father's son.

They needed a new apartment. The old one had been cramped to begin with, and now, in the rear, a building was being put up which would have so darkened Enoch's room that he would have had to burn electric light even on the fairest day.

'The new apartment must be sunny,' Martin insisted, which limited their choice even further in the limited market.

Of course there had to be more rooms, for without doubt, they would soon be having another child. Not a day went by without mention of it from Hazel. Martin had no real objection, although surely no desire, either. He had Claire and Enoch; they were enough for him. But Hazel's position was very different.

As with their first home, she had free reign. He had little time anyway to spend in the rose-coloured living-room with its flowered, middle-European embellishments. She liked it, and he was pleased with her liking it. Only his study was to remain as it had always been, a refuge for books and music and plants. For a moment he considered the possibility of hanging Mary's *Three Red Birds* above the bookshelves. But then he realized it would be an affliction to him every day, like a hairshirt, and wrapping it up again in brown paper, he laid it away at the top of a closet behind a row of old medical texts.

He began to fit back into the routines of home: the sounds of a little boy roller-skating down the hall; Claire's dropping in one or two afternoons a week after school; Hazel's resumption of her comfortable life among women, with classes in needlework, PTA and recording for the blind.

'It's almost as if you hadn't been away, isn't it?' she remarked once during the third or fourth month. 'I used to be afraid we'd never make up for our lost time, but it's not been like that at all.'

It seemed to Martin that her thankfulness was an aureole about her head. She glowed with it. And his thoughts would flee to that other woman – his thoughts, like some poor chained dog, that in a sudden rush of glad anticipation, forgetting the chain, jumps forwards at full strength and is jerked fiercely back at the throat.

In the fall Hazel knew she was pregnant. The following spring she gave birth to another boy, whom they named Peter after her grandfather. A placid baby, resembling his brother, he gave promise of being, again like Enoch, a placid little boy.

Martin tried to remember what he had felt on the day Claire was born. He seemed to recall a first aching disappointment that she was a girl, and after that, a surge of absolute exaltation, totally unlike the tender, subdued pleasure he felt now. Again, the circumstances were not at all the same.

They made plans to rent a house in Westchester for the summer, near the beach yet close enough to the city so that Martin could commute by train. On crowded days, he would stay alone in the apartment.

So they were on their way, he in the hospital and the office, Hazel in the busy home, and both of them in a mild bustle of work and children and meals, of coming and going and living. Apparently, out of first confusion, order had quite rapidly been wrung.

He treads the carpet softly, its rough pile prickling his bare soles. The old insomnia which has plagued him intermittently through life has come back. He steps into hazy, pink light: a lamp has been left burning in the hall, so that Enoch will not trip on his way to the bathroom during the night.

He looks in at the boy who sleeps in a tumble of blankets and toy animals. Then he goes into the baby's room. The infant has wedged himself crosswise in the crib, his head pressed up against the sides. Very carefully, the father readjusts his position, concerned for the pulsing fontanel in the tender skull. Although he knows it is foolish of him. The baby is really not that fragile.

Quietly he recrosses the hall to his study. He closes the door and turns on the record player. Perhaps music will help him tonight. It always has.

The Cleveland Orchestra plays 'Ein Heldenleben', doing it better than either the Boston or the Philadelphia, he thinks. He listens carefully to the solo violin, and with pleasure, recognizes the recurrence of the theme from *Don Quixote*.

When the music stops, he starts to reach for *Don Quixote*. It is consistent to stay with one composer, and consistency is part of his compulsive nature. How well he knows himself! But he pulls his hand back and turns the player off. It is no use. For the first time, music has failed him.

He looks at the desk clock. It is past dawn in England. He starts to switch the lamp off, but again halts his arm in mid-air, remembering suddenly a strange thing that had happened in the drugstore that afternoon, where a woman was buying perfume.

'La Fougèraie au Crépuscule,' she had said, mispronouncing the words, and had asked the clerk what it meant.

'Don't know,' the clerk had replied with a shrug.

Martin had answered, not intending to; the words just issued from his mouth, 'Fernery at twilight.'

'Oh,' the woman had said, surprised that he should know.

'It's the only perfume I remember,' he had added awkwardly, most foolishly, as if the woman had asked or would care what he remembered.

It is too cold in the apartment now, and he goes back to bed. He hopes Hazel will not wake up. If she does, he will have to take her in his arms, for although she keeps saying everything is quite normal again, it is plain she still needs reassurance that they are as they always were.

He draws the quilt up over his shaking shoulders. The baby cries out, but it is only a startle, and is not repeated. He is just five months old, and Hazel is pregnant again.

She has brought this pregnancy about, allowed it to happen, without asking Martin. Now she presses and curves against him, like a spoon fitting into another spoon. He understands her needs. She is so good to Claire, he thinks, as he so often does. His thoughts run on, darting and colliding with each other.

Claire is tenacious, spirited and serious. I missed so many of her good years. Jessie has done a superb job. I should like to tell her so. I saw a woman ahead of me on the street who looked like Jessie from the back. When I saw she wasn't Jessie, I don't know whether I was sorry or relieved. I wonder what I would have said if it had been? Why, I should simply have told her she'd done a superb job!

Claire is a merging of Mary's blood with mine. I never thought of that until this minute. A stunning thought! I never had it before; I don't know why. It shocks me.

I've had a dream of Mary on a ship, a sailing ship out of some other century. She was standing on the deck or at the prow. At first I thought she was a figurehead. Things are like that in dreams. The sails were swelling and the wind pulled at her skirt. I was on the dock. We stretched out our hands to each other. The water grew wider between us as the ship moved away. Then the wind whipped the scarf around her face so that I couldn't see it any more, and the ship went faster, straight out like an arrow, to the rim of the world.

It is said that loss grows dimmer with time. But is that true? There was a German-Jewish doctor in my company; Hertz was his name. He was a taciturn, persevering, thoughtful man. He had lost his wife and children. I used to wonder what he carried inside his head. Would it be easier or harder to know that Mary was dead?

It is also said one must force oneself to think of positive things. All right then: my work. I'm grateful for being so busy. I truly am. Think of something beautifully lazy, of swimming to the float and drowsing in the sun. No good. I can't feel it. Think of something gay and funny. That day half-way between her house and London; I was late arriving at the country pub, and someone, some boorish old man, had been trying to flirt with her before I got there. We laughed so to see his face when I walked in. But it isn't gay and funny, remembering it now.

He feels himself beginning to drift finally towards sleep. Cold air seeps through the blankets. It is raw as only an English house can be. The casement bangs, and an air raid warden's shrilling startles him awake. He opens his eyes and stares into the street below, some sort of minor accident. This isn't England. He's home.

Hazel murmurs. She, too, is dreaming. And he feels so gentle towards her, as to a child lying there asleep, and so sorry, just so sorry. Now she stirs.

'What is it?' she asks. 'Is anything wrong?'

'No, no,' Martin says. 'Go back to sleep. It's all right. Everything's all right.'

CHAPTER TWENTY-THREE

At the far end of the apartment's hall, looking on the courtyard, was a dank room used for storage. Even on the brightest afternoon, the bulb, which hung on a single wire from the ceiling, had to be lit. Three storeys below lay the grey cement floor of the court where ash cans stood along a wall. Ten storeys above, by twisting one's neck and pushing one's eyebrows up, one could see a corner of sky.

Inevitably, Enoch was drawn to this room. His mother, who almost never complained about anything and who, Claire thought privately, really did spoil the boy, objected that he messed it up. But since the room was only a jumble, Claire didn't see what additional harm the child could do.

There were cartons of dusty books, thick college texts of Martin's in dark green and brown. There were two old microscopes, one of which had belonged to their grandfather, along with his medical kit that Martin had shown them with its old-fashioned jars and bottles, some still half-full of a desiccated ointment. An American flag, souvenir of a long-forgotten parade, drooped from a stick in a corner next to a dressform which Hazel had used in the days when she still made her own dresses. More busty even than Hazel was, the headless figure would have scared the devil out of you if you had come upon it suddenly in the dark. There was an old easy-chair from whose arms the dried leather rubbed off in ruddy pellets. There were thick black phonograph records of Galli-Curci and Caruso from the days of the wind-up victrola, and a bicycle of Martin's which he had no time any more to use.

Now to all these had been added some possessions of Grandmother Farrell's, sent on after the funeral by Aunt Alice so that Martin would have his fair share of things by which to remember their mother.

Claire sat down on a broken chair. It was raining hard.

Some of the rain fell even in the narrow shaft between the buildings, trickling in the dust on the window.

'Gee,' Enoch said, 'look at these *National Geographics*! There must be a hundred of them. Let's take them all to my room.'

'No, you won't. Your mother'll have a fit if you drag those to your room. You can look at them in here till they come home. I'll look at these old pictures.'

Old photo albums still retained an aura of the forbidden, and she had to think for a while why this should be so, before she remembered the albums at the house in Cyprus when she had been no more than five or six and found in them the pictures of her unknown pariah aunt. A mystery, Claire supposed, that would never be cleared up.

But in these snapshots of her father's people, there were no mysteries, or none that she could see, at any rate. There was only nostalgia and a sort of sadness, which she had thought a person would have to be old to feel. She hadn't expected to feel it when she was just sixteen. Yet she was feeling it. Probably it was because the death of that grandmother last month, a woman she had seen only four times in her life – and the last time when she was dying – had touched her deeply. She had known perfectly well that her mother had not wanted her to go with Hazel and Dad. Jessie would have liked to be able to forbid the trip. But since a death had been involved, she had very likely felt that objection would be shameful. So she had made none, except to indicate by her compressed lips and flat voice that she was not pleased.

Here was the grandmother as a young woman of the Gibson Girl era, her neck collared to the ears in boned net. The anxious, pretty eyes looked out under the brim of a stiff sailor hat. Living is hard, those eyes said.

In old age the eyes had been a faded, opaque grey, as if a curtain had already fallen between them and the living world. She had been sitting up in bed, awakening when they came into the room, and then drowsed off in the middle of a sentence with her mouth dropped open over her even, large teeth. Just gliding gently out of the world, Claire had thought. It was strange to think that if this woman had not lived, *she* would not be living either.

They had buried Jean Farrell in the cemetery in Cyprus, and during the long ride from the place of her death at Aunt Alice's house, her son and daughter had relived their years.

'Remember the hot bricks in bed? Funny, when your feet are warm, the rest of you gets warm enough so you can fall asleep,' Martin had said.

And Alice had said softly. 'The things you remember! Maple taffy! Isn't that a foolish thing to be thinking of today?'

Martin had explained to Claire how maple taffy was made. 'You collect the sap twice a day and boil it over a wood fire,' he had said carefully, as though this were a piece of knowledge so precious it must be preserved. 'Then you fill a soup plate with snow and pour the hot syrup over it. When it cools, it gets hard and sticky like taffy.'

'Your father tells me,' Aunt Alice had said to Claire, 'that you want to be a doctor.' She had spoken formally and politely, more formally to Claire than to Hazel, as though Claire were the stranger and Hazel were of her blood. 'Your father used to keep mice and frogs in formaldehyde, under his bed. Do you remember, Martin, the time you had the dead snake there, and Mama found it when she was cleaning? And how she screeched?'

So it had gone. And at last they had reached Cyprus, drove down its principal street – 'How it's grown!' Alice had cried – and out past the house where Alice and Martin had lived.

Martin had sighed. 'It was all farms here then.'

The town had spread around it. Across the road from the house had been an industrial park. 'Light industry,' the sign had said. Rows of muddy cars had stood in a gigantic parking lot.

'They've taken the porch off, or glassed it in, I see. They must live upstairs.'

Martin had pointed to where, on a frame house with a boxy glass front like a protruding abdomen, 'Guido's Pizzaburgers' was lettered large.

They came to the cemetery. Claire, having never been at a funeral before, had expected something intensely dramatic.

But it had been very simple, just a short prayer before they lowered the coffin. Each of them had thrown in a handful of earth, and then walked away. And that had been all.

'I don't suppose we ever really knew either of them,' Martin had said. He had turned Claire around and told her, 'Take a last look. You may never be here again. Just remember that you come from decent people.' He had stopped a moment, and she had understood that he was thinking old thoughts.

'Look,' Enoch said now, 'I opened it.'

'Opened what?'

'It came off. The hinge broke off.'

'That's Dad's old trunk. Don't go prying in it, Enoch.'

He had already pulled out a uniform.

'Gee, look at the hat!' It came down over his little head, resting on his ears, while the visor grazed his eyebrows. 'Gee, why didn't Dad ever show me this before?'

'I guess he'd just as soon forget about the war.'

'Look at this! Dad used to be an explorer scout. Did you know that, Claire?'

'No. He did do a lot of climbing in the Adirondacks, though.'

'And what's this? "Washington High School, Martin Thomas Farrell"?'

'That's a diploma, what they give when you're all finished. You'll have one some day.'

'Will you?'

'I'd better, if I want to get into Smith and then med school. What have you got there? Don't do that. Those are private letters. You're not supposed to read other people's mail.'

'It's not letters. It's pictures.'

'Here. Put them back in the envelope. You're tearing it, Enoch! Give it to me!'

A packet of snapshots fell to the floor. They had been enlarged so that the faces were clear: her father's and an unknown woman's. They had been taken during the war; her father was in uniform. The woman was slender; her hair was short and curly. In one of the photographs they were holding each other's hands. And one was an attempt at a portrait, for the woman was sitting on a garden bench, wearing a wide straw hat and a full skirt, like a Renoir lady. On the back of this was written: You are everything to me and always will be. The signature read: Mary Fern.

Those clustered words stood out as though they had come to life. Heat rose into Claire's face, up to her forehead. She was shaken. Mother's sister, Mary Fern! This, then, must be the reason one was forbidden to ask about her! Mary Fern and my father! He had intentionally kept these pictures, hidden them away; he so meticulous, precise to a fault, who never left things lying around, who reprimanded anyone else who did! He wouldn't have kept them if they hadn't meant 'everything' to him, too!

'Look at these,' Enoch cried. 'There's a whole bunch of letters here, and look at the snowshoes! Claire! Did you know these were snowshoes? You walk on top of the snow with them. Golly, there's a lot of good stuff in this trunk!'

'Come, come,' she said. 'We're putting everything away.'

She slipped the packet of snapshots into her purse, folded the uniforms into the trunk, replaced the Scout badges and all the memorabilia of boyhood; then led Enoch out into the kitchen to feed him cookies and a glass of milk.

Darkness had come abruptly, giving a forest eeriness to the afternoon. Disturbed, without aim, she wandered through the rooms, turning the lights on as she went. At Hazel's bedroom door she paused. All the cloying sentimentality with which Hazel had furnished her home was concentrated here.

A hanging cabinet was cluttered with china figurines of men in powdered wigs and women in hoop skirts. The carpet had blue roses all over it. A lamp was shaped like a child holding a puppy. And on the desk there was a photograph of Martin, his ascetic face completely out of keeping with the rest of the room.

On a table in the den lay a stack of magazines, professional archives and reports of congresses, along with notes in Martin's crabbed writing.

'. . . approaches to mental disease,' Claire read. '. . . ambivalence of brain and mind.' She stood there, trying to fit what she knew of this part of her father's life – analytical, austere and serious – with the man in the snapshots.

But it was naive, it was absolutely *childish* to suppose a parent was only what one saw on the outside! Certainly one knew better than that. Still, one's father! That there could be such – such taint in one's own family; things not clean, not good!

'You come from decent people,' he had reminded her at his mother's funeral . . .

The door opened, and Hazel came in with Martin. 'We hurried back as fast as we could.' She was out of breath and anxious with haste. 'You're a dear to babysit for us, Claire. Was Enoch a good boy?'

'Oh yes. And the babies are still napping.'

'I'll get them up,' Hazel said, discarding her raincoat.

For a moment Claire stared at her father. It crossed her mind that, in the flash of a few seconds, her concept of him had changed. It was the angle of view that mattered. As the little boy with a Scout badge, as the brother of Alice – that was one way to see him. The woman who had written *You are everything to me* must have seen him differently. Hazel had still another view. And Jessie? Whatever her view might be was well hidden.

Hazel came back with the newest baby, Marjorie, drooped over her shoulder. The mother and the child wore the same expression of innocent, domestic tranquillity.

'You'll stay for supper, Claire?' Martin asked.

His eyes regarded her with affection. In them she read how much pride he had in her and how he would want her to have the same in him. She brushed at her own eyes as though cobwebs hung before them.

'Thank you,' she said coldly, 'I'm going home.'

Only an hour before she would not have believed she could despise him.

They talked till past eleven. Jessie parted the curtains and stood thoughtfully looking out into the night. Over her shoulder Claire could see that the rain had stopped; a ghostly glitter lay on the walls and trees, matching her own fearful mood. The curtains fell back with a taffeta rustle as Jessie turned around.

'You shouldn't have taken the pictures,' she said.

'I had stuck them in my purse and then I didn't know what to do with them.'

They lay spread out now on the coffee table. Claire picked one up, then slapped it down.

'How I would hate her if I were you! Both her and Dad, but her the most!'

'Oh, I've had my fill of hatred, make no mistake about that! But you can't keep it up, year in, year out. It's corrosive. I guess that's why I kept the whole business to myself until now. I didn't want you to be corroded. Also, to be honest, there was a little matter of my own pride.' And Jessie smiled slightly, in the self-mockery that was her habit.

'She spoiled your one chance. She could have had dozens, couldn't she? And she took your only one.'

'Damn it, yes, she did.'

The love seat at the fireplace held small silk pillows, round as jewels: amethyst, topaz, garnet. Jessie fussed with them now, patting and rearranging. Presently she said, 'Yet I always knew I'd been foolish to marry Martin. And after all that – happened – it would have been more foolish to hold him. I could have done it, you know. He wanted to stay. Because of you and a sense of obligation. But I didn't want that. I couldn't bear what I knew he must be feeling towards me, in spite of his merciful denials.'

What could it have been like in bed? Claire wondered. All those books that were passed around among her friends – somehow one always thought of strong and handsome people doing the things that were described in those books. In sudden shame she flushed and could not look at her mother.

Jessie was moving around the room again, at the magazine rack now. She spoke abruptly.

'I heard from Aunt Milly that Fern's husband was killed in the war.'

'How horrible!' And Claire had a quick flash, out of some old war movie, of a sky torn by terrible guns and battering rain, of a man lying in the mud with a leg torn away. 'How horrible!'

'Yes. She's had her share too. But she ought,' Jessie said sombrely, 'she ought to have married Martin in the first place. I knew it the first time I saw them together. Before they knew it.'

'What? Love at first sight?'

'Don't scoff! It happens.'

'Pulp magazine stuff.'

Jessie smiled. The smile enlivened her mouth, but her eyes were still. 'You'll find out.'

'It's just not real.'

'You're sure you know what's real and what isn't? You're sixteen and you already know that?'

'Well, I read, don't I? I see things, don't I?'

'But you haven't lived them.'

Jessie played with the gold chains at her neck. She wore too many and they were too valuable. Why were they so important to her? Claire wondered. The thought was new. And all this business about love – how did Jessie know? Because she had gone through it herself? And this thought too, was new.

'So what you're saying is that they couldn't help it?' Claire asked.

'I suppose I am.'

'That sounds almost noble.'

'Noble! Good God, I? You know better than that, after living with me all your life. No, it's just that I've had to come to terms with things or go crazy. And people like me can't afford to go crazy.'

Jessie picked up the photographs and shuffled through them. 'You can keep these or destroy them,' she said, laying them back on the table. 'Whatever you want. I don't care which.'

'Not return them?'

Jessie shook her head. 'They'd be a time-bomb in that family. They'd wreck it.'

'You care if they do?'

'There are children! How can one wish that on children? It

was enough when you – ' She stopped. 'And besides, that woman – that Hazel – never did anything to me.'

Ah yes, poor Hazel! Why did one think of her as 'poor' when she was, after all, so snug and well off in her home? But there was something – She was so mad about Martin, it was embarrassing sometimes.

Jessie leaned over a photograph. She spoke reflectively, almost to herself. 'Of course, I always knew he was an uncommon man. I always saw how far he'd go if he were given half a chance.'

'He talks about you sometimes. I think he might even like to see you. Why don't you? People who've been divorced can still be civil to each other, can't they?'

'A while ago you never wanted to see your father again. Now you want me to see him.'

The mind is so confused. You are old enough to understand how young you are and how contradictory everything is: other people, one's feelings about oneself, everything. How long will it be before you ever get it all straightened out? Will you, ever?

And, almost angrily, Claire cried, 'I don't *want* anything! I only asked why – '

'All right, I'll tell you why. I'm peaceful the way things are, the way I am. I don't need to complicate my life with him or with my sister or anyone. I've nothing to say to him. I've made my way with no thanks to anyone except myself. Listen. I don't want to hurt anybody, Claire; I only want to be left alone. I'm a realist. I've had to be.'

Jessie's face, in the shaft of lamplight, was coppery gold. It burned. Intelligence was in it, and strength, and pain. Suddenly, through the opacity that separates one human spirit from the other, there came to Claire a flaring white translucence, an opening up, so that for an instant she entered into Jessie, lived as Jessie, was there in that other instant of shudder and shock when the young girl first truly saw herself and knew she had been condemned when she was born.

Jessie got up. 'I'm weary.' She stroked her daughter's hair back from her forehead. 'Come to bed. You've had a hard day. You've done a deal of growing up today.'

Alone in her room Claire stood brushing her hair. The rain had begun again, threatening the window-pane. Suddenly it came to her, so suddenly that she stopped the brush in midstroke, that she pitied, not Jessie only but her father, too. He – in all his competence and strength, he who was able to solve everything – she pitied him! And in this pity there was something new, another kind of love . . . Wasn't that strange?

And now she felt the tightening of things and people. It was a feeling new to her, who had been particularly free in doing and thinking whatever she wanted. Those two, she thought. My father and the woman, Mary Fern – what sort of woman can she be, she with the dreaming eyes beneath a shady summer hat, with the long fingers lying on the silk lap? – Those two have changed so many other lives besides their own! Because of them my mother and I live alone in this house; because of them there are Hazel, little Enoch and the babies –

What may come to me yet, to all of us, bound as we are to one another?

CHAPTER TWENTY-FOUR

The day the office had opened, indeed the day on which the lease was signed, Martin had been terrified lest he had undertaken too much and wouldn't be able to afford it. He was still, and probably always would be, a cautious heir to the Depression. But he need not have worried.

Very quickly the appointment book began to fill. Friends from the old bicycle and handball days had returned from the war and were sending referrals. More referrals came from new contacts in general practice and the specialities; his reputation was wider than he had known. So it became clear that, for the first time in his life, he would not only not be short of money, but would have it to spare, would have that freedom from constraint which comes when all one's bills can be paid without wrinkling the forehead over them.

He came to his desk one afternoon while the office was still empty.

'You're early,' the secretary said. He always thought of her as the 'little' secretary, although she was over forty and had a perfectly good name: Jenny Jennings. 'There's no one booked till one-thirty.'

'I know. I finished early at the hospital.' And he closed his door.

The truth was that he hadn't finished at the hospital in any way he would have wanted to finish. The patient had died. Thrusting aside the sandwich and coffee on the desk, he went over, for the third or fourth time in the last hour, the agony of the morning.

Even before the haemorrhage started, he had known. Disaster had a certain feel and smell. He had known its warning breath often enough, and would know it again. That was in the very nature of the hard and sorrowful work he had chosen. Sometimes you were given an extra bit of last-minute luck to pull you out of a tight place, but not very often, and not today. From the evil growth attached to the carotid artery, the bright blood had just come gushing. Bearing down on the gauze packing, it had taken his whole strength in an attempt to stop the flow, but it had kept coming. And he had wished he were somewhere else, anywhere but there and then.

A circle of heads had surrounded him. He'd been aware of faces watching the open skull, watching him to see what he was going to do. But there had been nothing to do and they had all known it.

'The cardiograph is flat,' Perry had finally said at Martin's shoulder. The words were mournful, final, like the sound of the sea in a shell. 'There's no heartbeat,' he'd said.

'Oxygen,' Martin responded, but it had already been brought. The tube was in the nostrils and someone was pressing on the chest of this young man who had been, so he had told Martin with pride, a varsity basketball player. Now he worked in a bank, and his wife had had twins last winter.

Martin had drawn off his gloves and slapped them furiously to the floor. Leonard Max, who was chief resident now, picked them up without a word. Then they both went to the locker room, where they put on lab coats to hide the tragic blood on their hospital gowns, removed the operating shoes and went down the hall to the waiting room to tell the family that the basketball player, the son, the husband, the father of the twins was dead.

Later he had talked to Perry, protesting. 'It need never have been if I'd got to him a year ago.'

'I know,' Perry said softly. Always he had been a foil when Martin was in trouble, offering some cheerful comment or remark to offset a stillness in Martin, offering as now his listening silence when events exploded.

'Idiots!' Martin cried. 'Treating him for a neurosis when he complained of headache! Pressure of the job, the responsibility of twins, they said. My God, it's shameful . . . Talk of the unity of the neurological specialities!'

He remembered now the young man's courage and confidence, assumed, very likely, for who would not be terrified to know that an evil something was swelling and tightening in his brain? But he had been quietly brave, reassuring his wife, shaking Martin's hand, making a lame joke or two.

Ah, you saw so much death sometimes in this work, you wished you had become a dermatologist, or better yet, a maths teacher, a car salesman, anything but what you were! Some deaths touched you with a knife-edge of anguish, just as some of the war-wounded still stayed visibly in mind, while others had faded, not because any were more worthy than the others, but because – well, they just did. And he remembered now the boy he would always think of as Chicago and how he hadn't been as concerned about dying as he had been about losing that one finger.

Pa, Martin thought. Pa had that terrible concern, so personal sometimes as to be almost unprofessional. He had tried to conceal it, but one always knew by the way he clenched his teeth on the pipe stem, so that his words came out all muffled. His mother would tell the children not to annoy their father that night because a bad thing had happened: a patient had died. And her eyes would be so troubled! Soft people, they had been.

Sometimes he could still feel flashes, for just a second or two, of the grief he'd felt when his father had died. And he was reminded of the day he'd met Leonard Max. It had been the young man's first day on the job. Martin had asked him something or told him to do something, and when Max hadn't responded at once, he had been impatient and spoken sharply. Afterwards someone had told Martin that the boy had just got news that morning of his father's death. He was finishing the morning's work before taking the train home. And Martin, remembering his own father, had been so sorry and ashamed, more sorry than he could say. He had apologized to Max.

'I get impatient too quickly. I'm a damn-fool perfectionist. Forgive me.'

Now the 'little' secretary opened the door. 'Thought you might want a second cup of coffee, but you haven't touched a thing,' she said reproachfully.

'I know. I've been thinking.'

'You've only got another fifteen minutes.'

Obediently, he unwrapped the sandwich now and leaned back in his chair. This room was where he really lived. It was the core and centre of his life, when you came down to it. Here he sat to hear one anxious recital after the other, the tales of symptoms that would end either in success and health or in disaster. Each began here on the other side of this desk. Each was a new and terrifying adventure.

What did these people see when they first walked in here with the damp palms and the dry mouth of fear? They saw a neatly furnished room with cheerful pictures and many books. They saw a man with a calm, professional manner, a stranger on whose reputation their hopes were fixed. They could know nothing of *his* fears, his private guilt, empty longings and high ambition.

Jenny Jennings had put a sizable stack of mail before him to be answered. On top lay a still-unanswered letter from Mr Braidburn. Martin hadn't heard from him in years, hadn't even gone to see him during the war. Why? Probably, to his shame, because he hadn't wanted to be asked about Jessie or Claire.

Anyway, here was his letter, asking whether Martin had any suggestions for a most excellent young man who wanted to go to America. He had been doing some fine research in neuro-pathology and would like to combine that with further surgical training. Could Martin find a place for him in his laboratory?

Research! A kind of angry shame crept over Martin. What had he to offer such a man? Very little, except, as the practice kept growing, what Eastman had offered him: a chance to do important surgery and make money. There was nothing wrong in that. But it wasn't what he had had in mind at the beginning, was it?

And suddenly he thought of Albeniz, who had wanted his own institute, who had deserved it and who would have done a greater service to the sick if he could have had it. Then it occurred to him that he had been so hurried lately that he hadn't thought of Albeniz in months. So he picked up the telephone, and reaching the number, was told that the doctor was dead. He had died of a heart ailment almost a year ago. Martin must have missed the notice in the paper and so, apparently, had other people. *Sic transit gloria.* You are here, you make your little mark and you are forgotten.

Miss Jennings knocked at the door. 'There's a man outside,' she said, 'without an appointment. He says you operated on his son-in-law this morning. The one who died.' She looked worried. 'He seems all right, but do you want me to stay?' *People have been known to be distraught and threatening*, she meant.

'No,' he said, 'it's all right. Let him come in.'

Martin stood up and put out his hand. 'I'm so sorry,' he began, 'I can't even begin to tell you, Mr – '

'Ambrose. I was at the hospital this morning.' The man was slight, tired and apologetic. 'I just took my daughter home.'

'Oh,' Martin said again, 'I'm so sorry! He was a fine young man.'

'We know you are, Doctor. But you did the best you could.'

'It wasn't good enough.'

'It was too late. I knew that. The poor boy didn't; at least, I don't think he did. Maybe he had thoughts and didn't want to worry us. Who knows?'

The voice trailed away and Martin felt the heavy weight of sorrow in the room, the old familiar sorrow of his work, so acquainted with grief. 'Acquainted with grief,' that poignant phrase from the *Messiah,* he thought, and then was aware that the man had said, 'I knew.' He came quickly to himself.

'You knew? How could you have known?'

'No reason.' The man held his grey fedora on his knees and kept smoothing the crown with the palm of his hand, round and round. 'It was just a feeling. So we talked about it, my daughter and I. We thought, if Michael dies, we want to know why.'

Because, Martin answered silently, the diagnosis was delayed. It wasn't malpractice, it was just bad judgement, all too common. And there's not enough co-operation between the fields.

'We want to help so that it won't happen again. We're not

rich, but I have a few dollars put away, and I want to make a donation. I read in the papers about all this research in brain diseases, so I've written you a cheque, and we want you to use it wherever you think best. Put it where it will work so they can learn more about these things.'

The shining innocence, the goodness, the courage!

And gruffly, because those damned humiliating tears of his were rising, Martin said, 'It's five hundred dollars. I don't want to take it. There are children, the twins – '

Mr Ambrose stood up. 'It's all right, Doctor Farrell. We've decided. It's the way she – we want it. And he would have wanted it, too.'

So they stood there looking at each other with the presence of the dead boy between them. Then Mr Ambrose shook Martin's hand. 'Thanks, Doctor,' he said again, and Martin watched him go out.

Damn it to hell and back! Maybe that boy wouldn't have died if – But maybe he would. Don't play God, Martin. Yes, but maybe he wouldn't.

He got up and walked around the room, picked up a book, put it back, went to the window, looked out and saw nothing but a dazzle on the street. Then he sat down at the desk again and vaguely saw the snapshots, old and new, under the glass: his children with Hazel; himself with Claire in front of an old wall on a proud visiting day at Smith; his father wearing a duster, standing on the running board of his first car.

'You will see things I haven't even dreamed of,' Pa had used to say, and Martin swore again.

Braidburn's letter still lay on his desk. Oh, if he had a place to take in that young man, he knew exactly what it would be like! He'd planned it, outlined it on many a sleepless night.

Once he'd begun a study of pituitary tumours and abandoned it in the middle when he left old Llewellyn, years before. The whole problem of circulation in the brain – there was so much he wanted to find out! And it would have to be, need to be, combined with surgery. Then, of course, the psychiatrists would be welcome too; they'd be needed in problem-solving –

He thrust a fist into his palm. There'd be room then for

Braidburn's protégé, and many more. Perry, of course, to head anaesthesiology; good, dependable Perry at one's side. And Leonard Max. Now there was a fellow in whom intelligence and devotion were written tall!

Jenny Jennings opened the door. 'Seven waiting outside already,' she said accusingly.

Martin sighed. 'All right. Send the first one in.'

He walked slowly home. On a Madison Avenue corner, a discreet display in a window caught his eye. Behind a very fine antique desk, French, eighteenth-century, stood a lacquered Oriental screen; an old engraving hung above it; the whole was most quietly elegant, made vivid with a splash of violet fabric. He stopped a moment to admire. The sign read: 'Jessie Meig, Interiors.' He stood there gazing at the sign and remembered that Claire had said Jessie was expanding into new quarters.

Baffling and extraordinary, this life! So strange the ways in which we act on one another! There was Albeniz, now dead, who had lit the spark in him. There was this woman, Jessie, who had fanned the spark and given him Claire besides, the pearl, the treasure of his life. Then Hazel, the warm and tender. And always, always that other, hidden, and beloved – What am I doing in return for these? Martin thought, and, standing momentarily outside himself, saw himself in all the complexity and contradictions of his nagging, Calvinist conscience, his zeal and his zest.

As soon as he got into the house he went to his study, picked up the telephone and quickly, before his nerve should fail, called Robert Moser.

'Hello, Bob? This is Martin, Martin Farrell.'

'Everything all right with you?'

The voice held surprise. Martin had never called Moser at his home or anywhere else. Such contact as the families had was made by the women, by Moser's wife calling Hazel, to be exact.

'Yes, all right, but I want to see you about something.'

'No trouble, I hope.'

'Not really. Or rather yes, in a way. I need money,' Martin

said bluntly, and correcting the clumsiness, explained, 'not for myself. You may remember years ago I mentioned my – well, sort of pipe dream, I used to call it, of a neurological institute here at the hospital?'

'I remember.'

And Martin detected impatience, masked by courtesy.

'Well, something happened this morning. No need to go into details. But I've been galvanized into action. I've been thinking, when you want to do something, do it.'

'Can't quarrel with that.' Amusement now, and a trace of sceptical suspicion.

'And since you're a trustee, the only one I know, it seemed logical to begin with you.'

'Money's not plentiful, Martin. We're operating at a deficit. You know that.'

'Hospitals always do, don't they? And somehow they always find what they need.'

'Yes, but you're talking millions. Prices have soared since the war.'

'I know all that. But there are always the foundations. Maybe even government funds. Matching funds, if only we could get started and have something to show.'

'Why do you want this, Martin? Have you any idea what you're letting yourself in for?'

'The answer to the second question is yes, I think I know. As to why I want it, that goes way back. Let's just say I'm convinced we need it. The profession needs it. The patients need it.'

'There's no lack of neurological centres, as far as I can see.'

'True. Although they're not exactly what I have in mind. But aside from that, don't you think our hospital, one of the finest in the city, or the whole country for that matter, deserves this honour, this crown on its head?'

Moser smiled. Martin could hear the smile in his voice. 'You put it well. You'd like to run the whole shebang, naturally.'

'I'd like, Bob, to teach and do the research I've been missing. That's what I'd like.'

'You'd have to give up a lot of time from your practice, wouldn't you?'

You're doing very well, you can make a pile for yourself. Why don't you let well enough alone? That's what Moser was saying in effect, exactly as Eastman used to say it.

'Bob, I want this,' Martin said.

'You want the moon, too?'

'Call it impossible, call it what you will. I want it because it's right.'

'I'd never get the trustees to go along. The world's full of naysayers.'

'Once the building's up, ten, twenty years from now, no matter how long, and the patients start coming and the work is being done, they'll be the first to applaud, I promise you.'

'Maybe so.'

'Bob, I'm going to do it, even if you won't help me.'

'Talk sense, Martin. You don't know the first thing about finance. How in hell are you going to do it?'

'I don't know. I'm going to begin. You built up Phoenix Tool and Dye. You didn't sit around, afraid to take a chance, did you? You began with nothing, didn't you?'

'Well, you might say I did, yes.'

'Okay. Enthusiasm I've got. And I'll get others behind me. I know I will. I'll go to meetings, I'll talk. We'll get contributions from the public, too, you know.'

'I doubt that.'

'I already got my first cheque this afternoon. And I know we can get more.'

'How much?'

'Five hundred dollars.'

There was silence.

'Five hundred dollars from a grateful patient who had no reason to be grateful.'

'You're not serious, Martin?'

'About what? The patient? Of course I am.'

'I meant the money. Just what the hell do you think you can do with five hundred dollars?'

'The Chinese have a saying, "Every journey begins with the first step".'

'Well, all right, but – '

'We need a campaign. We need to organize. You have contacts in industry. I'll tackle the foundations; maybe you can. too.'

'You've absolutely no idea how hard it will be. The foundations are inundated with appeals.'

'Bob, I know it can be done.' And suddenly inspired, Martin cried, 'If there hadn't been this kind of drive and confidence all through the history of medicine, if they hadn't found the means to build hospitals and fund research and train people, your daughter wouldn't be playing tennis now.'

Again there was a silence, much longer this time. Martin, holding the phone, heard traffic noises, noises from the kitchen and Moser's silence. At last there came a tired sigh.

'Okay, Martin, you've got me. We'll need to do a lot of talking, though. You'll need to get some tentative figures together, very rough, so at least I'll have some idea of what we're talking about.'

'I'll do that.'

'Better get advice on those figures before you bring them to me. I have no confidence in you at all as a businessman, I must tell you that.'

'I couldn't agree with you more. But I can get the facts you want. Give me three weeks. I'll call you.'

'Fine, Martin. You do that.' And Moser hung up.

A sense of unreality was left in the room. Martin's head went light, as if he were going to be sick. He looked at his hands as if they belonged to someone else. What had he done? And he sat there thinking: Perhaps it will be too big for me after all.

Then, after a long while, reality flowed back. A bag full of apples or potatoes rolled over the kitchen floor and a child shouted. Trucks stopped on the street below, the workman cursing cheerfully at each other. Life was proceeding in all its noisy, brave confusion.

Can do, he resolved. Anyway, I need to be overworked. It's the way I am. Otherwise I think too much. It's always better to be doing and trying, even if I fail.

He got up from the chair. Every journey begins with the first step.

CHAPTER TWENTY-FIVE

Arrivals and departures made a modest bustle in the lobby of the Connaught. Fern, waiting for Simon, could identify by clothing and accent the varied travellers: Americans, West Germans and British county people spending a few days in town. He hadn't wanted her to go upstairs with him to meet the customers, who assuredly would have been flattered to meet her. The man was a haggler, he said, and he'd be able to get a better price for her work if she wasn't present.

The money would be very welcome, she reflected with an unconscious sigh. Alex had told her often enough that there wasn't sufficient inherited wealth to live on, and there certainly wasn't.

Yet she would be sorry to part with the picture, a quiet, cloudy seascape which she had done while on a visit to Isabel and her husband in Scotland. It had been one of those rare, remembered days when everything had seemed to fit, and she had thought, observing the happiness of her newly-wed daughter, that life would probably go well with Isabel, that unlike her mother, she would see it through into hearty middle-age with little conflict.

They had been very close that afternoon, and the memory was all there on canvas: the gauzy, cloud-striped sky, the enormous loneliness of the dun beach and the kindness of three who were friends.

Paintings, she thought, and not only her own, were like children being shunted between foster homes. To sell them was to demean them. One felt such tenderness for them, as one peered close to marvel, especially at a Turner or other masterwork, to study the way in which the brush had been applied, the way in which colour could be used to hold the life of light! It pained you when all that love – yes, it was love that went into it – fell into the hands of people who didn't understand it, who perhaps didn't even like it very much but knew it would be talked about because it was expensive. Or worse still, knew it would rise in value so that in a few years it could be got rid of, traded up!

She opened the newspaper to the critic's column which had so delighted Simon that he had telephoned her an hour before breakfast that morning to read it aloud.

'Not to be missed,' she read again, 'is the retrospective exhibit by M. F. Lamb at the Simon Durant Gallery. Once past the collection of her earlier works, sensitive foreground figures, all seemingly in mourning in a grey-black world, and influenced, it is rumoured, by depression after the loss of her husband in the war, one can allow oneself to be enchanted by a lyricism which recalls the young Matisse. Her landscapes and interiors alike display a balanced organization and taut harmony. Empty space has indispensable meaning for this painter. It must be said that, unlike Matisse, the somewhat tender colours produce a dreaming, feminine effect which is fortunately never sentimental.

'Of particular charm is the *Girl with Flute*, the muted reds giving a fragile – ' And so on.

Well, it was all very fine, very wonderful. It would never have happened if she hadn't met Simon at a quite casual supper in the country a few summers before. He'd given her a tremendous push, had brought her forth at a time when she had relinquished the possibility of being anything more than a Sunday painter. And in bringing her forth, she saw clearly, he had forced her to grow. Recognition was tonic. She *was* doing better work. And for the first time in years, she could feel the stirring of new possibilities.

The elevator opened and a young couple came out. Their glossy leather bags were already waiting for them at the front entrance. These must be the people. Bolivians, Simon had said, honeymooning on a mining fortune. Yes, they were speaking in Spanish. The girl was very young and shy. He was handsome and tough. An arranged match, perhaps? They still did that among important upper-class families in South America.

So that is where my Scottish afternoon is going, Fern thought. I don't think it will bring him any joy!

The elevator opened again, and here was Simon. By his smile she knew that negotiations had gone well. It had probably been trying, since the richest people could drive the hardest bargains.

'Sorry to keep you so long,' he said.

'I haven't minded. I've been watching the crowd. So it went all right?'

'Splendidly. We got our price. It's a good thing you didn't come up, though. He even sent his bride out of the room. Apparently money is a dirty subject to discuss in front of women. Shall we have lunch?'

'But I've got the car in town, and I wanted to drive home this afternoon.'

'Can't we at least have a quick salad or a sandwich some place?'

It touched her whenever his cheerful animation subsided into disappointment. His generosity merited generosity in return.

'All right,' she said, 'a quick salad.'

'I never get to see you.'

'You do. We had dinner only last Sunday.'

'Well, but this is Friday, isn't it?'

She took his arm and they went out on to the street.

'Goodness, there must be a million foreigners in the city this summer, don't you think?' she said gaily. She was fending him off, leading away from the personal. And a little chill of guilt went through her, as it does when one has ignored a child or been sharp to someone who doesn't deserve it.

They sat down at a table in a bay window. Fern busied herself mixing oil and vinegar for the salad. Simon gazed out to the street, his lively face gone still, the heavy eyelids dropped like hoods so that he could only have been seeing the bottom half of the passers-by.

Ordinarily, he had so much to say. He talked better than anyone she knew, with a great deal of sophistication and yet very little scepticism – an unusual combination of traits. It was not easy to be an optimist without being also something of a simpleton.

He was an attentive listener, too. But sometimes he would look at her with such close attention, as if he were seeing far inside, as if she could hide nothing from him, that she would feel her thoughts coming to a fumbling halt.

She stole a troubled look across the table. A few grey strands had come into his sandy hair; she had never noticed them. He would stay young for a long time, being of the thin, supple type that at eighty or thereabouts has thick white hair and wears good tweeds and remembers how to dance.

So they sat for a little while until presently Simon found something to say.

'Everyone all right at home?'

'Oh yes, thank goodness.' Fern grasped at conversation. 'I heard from Emmy yesterday. She still adores Paris. I don't suppose she'll ever come back.'

'You never know.'

'No, you don't, do you?' she agreed.

'She may marry some sturdy British businessman, and you'll have her back here again.'

'Maybe so.'

Silence. Why was it especially awkward today?

'Strange how different my daughters are from one another. And they look so alike,' she remarked, feeling instantly embarrassed at her own banality. As if Simon could care about the personalities of her daughters, whom he had seen perhaps half a dozen times! But she went on, 'Emmy knows four languages, so she's perfect in the European business world. I can't see her satisfied living Isabel's life, having one baby after the other.'

'I didn't know Isabel was – '

'No, not yet, but I'm sure she will be. They both want lots of children.'

'The way it looks,' Simon said, 'you'll be rattling around alone in Lamb House, won't you?'

'Well, I don't know about rattling around. It was left to Ned, naturally, although I have the right to live there as long as I want. Maybe some time Ned will marry and come back. Then, of course, I'll move out. Although, I don't know really.' Now her thoughts ran seriously, for the subject was of genuine concern. 'He doesn't show any signs of settling down. He's due back from Egypt soon, does well in every job he's had, but right now someone's put a bee in his bonnet about America. So many of the young men want to go where the "action" is. That's their expression.'

'Where the money is,' Simon said. 'I daresay you can't blame them.'

'I wouldn't say that was true of Ned. He's creative and imaginative. I really think it's just change that he wants, something new. He ought to do splendidly in advertising.'

'Of course, New York's the base for that.'

'So very likely he'll be flying off again. I miss him,' she said simply.

'From what I see, children are ungrateful wretches. You put everything you've got into them, and all they do is forget you.'

'They have to live their own lives, Simon.'

'I suppose so. Still, I've never regretted having none. Margaret did. It must be a much deeper need in a woman, after all. Almost the last thing she said to me before she died was that she was sorry she wasn't leaving me with a daughter or a son to remember her by.'

'But you remember her anyway,' Fern said softly.

'Shall I tell you something? It's been ten years, and by now I really don't remember very much. Yes, I recall how loving and good she was, and that we lived well together. But I don't really remember her. I can't quite see her face any more. Do you understand?'

Fern didn't answer. Alex's face? It came back to her only in some swift movement of Emmy's mouth or when Isabel threw her head back to laugh too loudly. She had never seen Alex in Ned. He might have been of different stock, so different was he, with those musing eyes and that odd half-smile, reminding her, improbable as it was, reminding her of Martin.

And suddenly she was aware that her fork was half-raised to her lips. She laid it down.

'I've upset you,' Simon said kindly. 'I didn't mean to, Mary. I'm sorry.'

'You just called me Mary,' she said. 'No one ever does.'

'You told me once you liked it better. I try to remember that. I try to remember everything you like.'

'You're so good,' she said. 'Just good. There's no other word.'

'Am I?' He shrugged. He took a cigarette from the pack, choosing it carefully, tapping it, lighting it, pursing his lips and blowing the curled smoke towards the ceiling. Then he ground it roughly out, twisting it in the ashtray, and reached across the table for her free hand. His own was trembling.

'Marry me,' he said. 'I've been on the verge of asking you so often and you know it, don't you, Mary? I've all but said it a dozen times.'

'I know.' And lowering her eyes away from his gaze which was so intense, so strong that it frightened her, she thought: I am not ready for this.

'With a little push, even a glance, a bit of something in your voice to encourage me, I would have said it long ago. Well, now I'm saying it. Marry me.'

It was too bad, too bad, that tears should spring into her eyes.

'I know I'd always take second place.'

'You shouldn't be satisfied with second place.'

'But if I'm content, Mary, isn't it for me to choose? Besides, it's not like a recipe, is it? Loving, I mean? You can't measure it: a cup of this, a spoonful of that. Loving is different every time.'

She murmured pointlessly, 'I don't know.'

'So even though I understand how you loved Alex, this would be different.'

She didn't answer.

'Besides, Alex is dead.'

The waitress came to take the plates away. Simon released her hand and she put it in her lap, not wanting to be held, not wanting to be fastened.

'I'm not ready yet,' she said, looking down at her hands.

'You're not a girl any more. There's not all that much time.'

'That's true.'

'When will you be ready, then?'

'I don't know,' she said again.

'I would be good for you. I've been good for your work already, you've told me so.'

'Yes. Yes, you have. You would be.' She looked up. He was so grave, so fine and grave. 'Oh, I wish I could,' she cried, and now it was she who stretched both hands across the table and took his. 'Oh, Simon, whatever you say about not caring, not minding, you deserve so much better!' Her tears rolled over and slid.

'Don't cry here,' he said gently. 'We'll go now. I'll take you to the car.'

The top was down and the rushing wind, the sound and touch of it, calmed her grieving spirit. That Simon's proposal should have been so painful! Dear, trusted friend! Considerate, tender, and demanding, too, as one wanted a man to be! What was wrong?

In the late afternoon when she kissed him good-bye on leaving the gallery, his cheeks were rough, for his beard grew quickly. He was clean, so very clean. She knew so much about him. She knew what he liked to eat and to read, the kind of friends he chose. What was wrong?

That ache. That other. Still she saw him as on that last morning when, through the rear-view mirror of the car, she had watched him walking down the street in his American uniform, walking out of her life again, going away. She had not been on that street since, had taken care to avoid it. The flat where they had said good-bye had been given up, the excuse being, and it was the truth, that it was too expensive to keep.

Her thoughts ran in tangents. Even Lamb House could only be maintained by opening it to the public two days a week. American tourists came crowding to see how an English county family lived, or had lived. But she had an obligation to keep the place for Alex's children. The girls wouldn't want it, but perhaps Ned might one day. He had understood his father's feeling for it. My feeling, too, Fern thought. The house speaks to me. Martin saw that. 'You love each tree,' he told her once. He had understood. It always came back to Martin. Everything always came back to him. Everything joined in a circle: Alex's house and Martin and Alex's son. Her son. Where did it all end?

Circles don't have an end, she thought. And life is linear, with a beginning and an end, somehow, some time. I'm very tired.

At the toll booth, an elderly man with an automatic smile took her change. For some reason he made her think of an animal at the zoo, imprisoned without having committed any crime. To think of spending your life in a little cage, taking coins! Nothing that lived, animal or human, ought to be confined. She hated zoos and belonged to a committee for their abolition. Alex had always laughed, in a nice way, with mild amusement, and so had Martin, because she had joined so many causes: against the slaughter of whales and seals; for the preservation of the forests; against drug abuse; for foster homes and battered wives. Well, as long as you lived in the world, you owed it something, didn't you?

And she felt a piercing compassion for everything that lived, the sort of feeling that flashed through you now and then with such dear intensity, that you couldn't possibly feel like that all the time, or even most of the time. It would sicken your soul. But shall I ever clear my own way, she thought?

The little car moved off the highway and slowed around the curve of the road. It was a lane, really. She still had enough memory of America and its roads to call this a lane. The car crept up the drive at Lamb House into the garage.

In the burning afternoon the house lay shadowed among hovering beeches. It opened its arms. When she had stepped inside, it would close them around her again, walling the world away.

And she stopped a moment to listen to the infinite buzz and hum of a thousand little creatures busy in the grass. A butterfly, Parnassius, pale crystal grey, lit on her arm, its frail folded wings trembling there before it fluttered off into the light. And a leaf fell, a very small leaf, oval and yellow, spiralling slowly through the quiet air.

Oh, lovely, blooming world! Birth into life, life into death, the leaf and the bird in me. I am the leaf and the bird, unending round of radiance and darkness. But shall I ever clear my own way? she thought again.

The maid, Elvira, one of the last remaining village girls who hadn't preferred the factory, had seen her from the window and come running.

'There's a young lady in the hall. She asked for you. She's been waiting. An American, I think.'

Now, in the summer before their final year at Columbia College of Physicians and Surgeons – known informally as P and S – five young women were travelling through Europe. They followed the route troden by generations of students since the days of the eighteenth-century's Grand Tour: through Italy's museums, cathedrals and ruins and up over the Alps, westward and northward to the chateau country in splendid summer leafage, and at last across the Channel to London. Together and on foot they went down the guidebooks' lists from the Tower and the palaces to Samuel Johnson's house.

Alone, Claire made her personal and private explorations. With some reluctance, Jessie had given the address of the house where they had lived when Claire was born: an austere white house of expensive flats in what had once been an aristocrat's town mansion. The street was quiet under its linden trees. Having no exotic attractions for tourists, it seemed yet as foreign as a hill town in Tuscany.

Claire felt a mingling of excitement and nostalgia. She stood there for a while and then, following the city map, walked over to Kensington Gardens to see the statue of Peter Pan. She had perhaps not realized how intense had been her need to see these things, for under the neat and capable exterior of this young woman – neat, now that she had learned the requirements of simple grooming – lay a core of sentiment. A sentiment, she thought humorously, a sentiment almost Victorian.

The group was to spend a week in Scotland before going home. On the morning of the day they were to depart from

London, Claire made a decision. Then, having prepared herself in advance with a railroad timetable, for she had been playing delicately with the idea ever since they had left New York, she proceeded to the station and took a train into the country.

These little villages straight out of Thomas Hardy followed a design: two rows of cramped, quaint cottages flanking a broad street which ended in a country road. Then, that branched off into three or four lanes, each leading to a fine, great manor at the back of a field on which one was not at all surprised to see a flock of sheep cropping the grass. So it was easy enough to find the place.

She stood in the high, square hall of a very old house. A young maid had admitted her, then left her alone among dark portraits, a vista of long rooms and smells of flowers overlaid with a pungent whiff of brass polish.

Now that she was actually here, Claire felt her first sinking apprehension. How could she have dared to come? It was an imprudent intrusion upon a past that didn't belong to her, an invasion of privacy. One would have every right to order her away –

Someone asked, 'You wanted to see me?'

A thin, dark woman stood in the doorway. An instantaneous impression flashed in Claire's mind, as when a picture snaps on to a screen: lady of refinement. She wore the delicate, plain dress that such ladies wear to the city in hot summer. She could have been a young woman ageing too soon, or an older one who had stayed young.

'You don't know who I am,' Claire said, trembling a little. 'But – '

'But I can guess. You're Jessie's daughter. You look like her.'

'I've startled you most awfully, haven't I?'

'You've startled me, yes. Why have you come?'

'No reason except curiosity. My own. No one else knows I'm here.'

'Well, curiosity's a good enough reason, I suppose.'

The eyes, Claire thought; those strange, light, startling

eyes, at once dreamlike and perceptive, they – they struck you!

And she said softly, 'A family feud! All that secrecy and for all those years! Do you never think how strange and sad it's been?'

The fantastic eyes swept Claire from head to foot. 'Oh yes, oh yes, I think!'

The eyes looked away for a moment and then returned. 'It's rather awkward just standing like this. As long as you're here, you might as well have a cup of tea with me, don't you think?'

Claire followed into the kitchen. The little maid had disappeared. Fern poured water from a copper kettle into the teapot. A huge white cat slept on a chair beside the table where a tray of violets flourished. She moved the cat and the violets.

'Sit down,' she said.

Her tan, long hands were clasped tightly, and nervously, in her lap. Then she loosened them and put them on the table, as if commanding herself.

'I used to wear my hair like that when I was your age.'

'I've seen pictures of you. They didn't do you justice. You're beautiful.'

'Thank you.'

'What shall I call you? Aunt Milly and my mother call you Fern; once, a long time ago when I asked him about this house, my father spoke of you as Mary.'

'I didn't know I was spoken of at all.' And this was said with a slight, rueful, humorous turn of the lips.

'Well, you aren't very often. But you still haven't told me what I should call you.'

'Whatever you choose. I don't mind.'

'Well, Mary then. Aunt Mary. It suits you. It's an ordinary name, but not on you.'

'You may even drop the "Aunt", you know.'

'All right, then, Mary. Although it doesn't make much difference, does it, what I call you for one afternoon, since I shall probably never see you again?'

Mary poured more tea. The cat slept on, and the old clock

chattered on the wall. A stranger entering the kitchen would have thought that these two women were carrying out a daily ritual.

Mary said abruptly, 'I wish sometimes I could see Jessie again.' Her hand moved round and round the cup, stirring the tea. 'I wrote to her. I wanted to explain, if I could. But she never answered.'

'What could she have said?' Claire defended. 'After all, you couldn't have expected her to answer, "It's all right, forget it, I understand." She couldn't have done that, could she?'

'That's true.' And the two plain syllables, spoken in minor key, touched Claire with a sense of finality.

'I hear,' Mary said, 'I hear from Aunt Milly that Jessie has made a great name for herself.'

'She has. It's amazing what she's done.'

'I'm glad. If you care to tell her you've seen me, say that I'm glad.'

'I'll do that. Is there anyone else you want to know about? Anything you want to ask me?'

'No,' Mary said.

There was a little silence until Claire spoke again.

'My mother has no ill will towards you any more. That's past. I thought you might want to know.'

'Is that really so?'

'Quite so. Not that she would want to see you . . . just that she has no anger.'

'And you?'

'I? Well, I would hope to have some understanding of people. It would be a pity if I hadn't, wouldn't it, since I'm a doctor, or will be by this time next year?'

'Yes, I know you are.'

'Aunt Milly, I suppose?'

'Of course. The town crier. That was what we called her when we were children. How is she, by the way?'

'Failing, since Uncle Drew died. She's long past eighty, anyhow.'

Silence again. What should she say next? When ought she to leave? And frowning a little, Claire squeezed more lemon into the cup, fussing to occupy her hands.

'Elvira thought you were an American tourist come on the wrong day.'

'An American tourist? The house is open to tourists?'

'Yes, it's the only way one can afford to keep a place like this.'

'It's an enchanting house,' Claire said.

'You haven't seen it. If you've finished your tea, I'll take you around.'

They walked down three steps into what must once have been a banquet hall, Mary explaining, 'It hasn't been used in years, it's so enormous.'

'But I remember it!' Claire cried.

'Yes, you were here a few times. Can you remember Emmy and Isabel, too? And Ned?'

'Only vaguely.'

'Come, I'll show you their pictures. This one's Isabel in her wedding dress.'

Claire observed that the girls looked like Valkyries.

'Yes, don't they? Ned's quite different. Would you like to see the grounds? At the gates there, those are temporary kennels for the visitors' dogs. The English always take their dogs when they go tripping, you know. And over here, back of the orchard, is the byre. We only keep four cows now, and of course, I hardly need all that milk. But people want to see the place as it was in its best years.'

It was that time of late afternoon when in northern countries the sun slants at so acute an angle that the grass is gilded, and trees in the middle distance are washed in silver light. On the path ahead of Claire, Mary's silhouette was dark against this ecstatic flair of light.

Fey, Claire thought suddenly, recalling the word her mother had once used to describe Mary Fern. She belonged in this place. No proper reserve of dress or manner could belie the different and secret thing that was hidden in her. And she remembered the destroyed and long-forgotten photographs of the woman on the garden bench, the shadowed face under the straw brim –

'Here's where I work,' Mary said.

She opened the door of a small brick structure in back of the main house. At the far end of the single room, a glass wall faced the northern sky. The other three walls were covered with paintings. Even at first look, one saw that they were of important quality. Claire was stunned.

'Surely not all yours?'

'All mine.'

On an easel stood an oil of a very old man in front of a stone shed. The man was as strong and winter-grey as the stone; the whole was without a single superfluous line or stroke of brush. For a few minutes Claire studied it.

'Lonely,' she said.

'Yes, that's Jasper. He's almost ninety, and he comes to milk the cows.'

'The end of an ancient way of life. That's what you're saying, aren't you?'

'Of course. You can't blame the young people for wanting to go to the towns. And yet the old country people seem so cheerful. I don't know. But then, there seems to be more all the time that I don't know.'

Claire walked slowly around the room, past the fair head of a genial girl, Isabel or Emmy perhaps; past a spray of reddening oak leaves in a copper bowl; a slum street, semi-abstract, with animated crowds under lines of hanging washing; a mourning woman with her head on her arms.

'My God,' she said. 'You did all this? Nobody ever told me.'

'They didn't know. And if they had known, why should they have told you?'

'But you're no – no talented amateur! You must be a name.'

'They tell me so,' Mary answered quietly.

And standing there in the sudden stillness that fell between them, something went all soft in Claire. This woman had lived through passions of which she, Claire, still knew almost nothing. She had endured and had come through to create all this. As Jessie had come through also, in her way. And Claire thought: *Women survive.*

There came then an acute, abrupt awareness of blood tie.

There had been so few in her small separated family, and she had always suffered from their lack. She had a swift recollection of the house in Cyprus, a mental picture of every dim, high room. She fancied, although no one had told her which bedroom had been Mary's, that the one at the top of the stairs must have belonged to her in childhood. From its windows one would have looked down on the side lawn and the table to which, on sultry afternoons, the lemonade was brought . . .

'What are you thinking?' Mary asked.

'I feel sad here,' and Claire touched her heart.

'Yes,' Mary held out her arms. 'Oh yes! We could have loved each other, you and I.'

Afterwards it became clear that if Mary had known her son was to arrive from Egypt, she would not have invited Claire to stay overnight. But Ned had not been expected until the end of the month.

Shortly after breakfast, an athletic young man in a sober business suit came striding up the driveway carrying in each hand an enormous travel-worn suitcase. Five huge dogs clamoured all over him in exuberant and loving welcome. When the greetings were past and the clamour had died, Mary made the introductions.

'So you're the American cousin. I remember you,' he said.

'You couldn't possibly. I was only three years old.'

'And I was eight. You cried because of my dogs. I had to put them outside, and I was mad as hell.'

'I don't blame you. You must have hated me.'

'I did,' he said.

The top half of his face was earnest. He wore tortoise-rimmed glasses like Claire's. The bottom half contained a well-marked, cheerful mouth, strong teeth and a square chin made gentle by a touching cleft. He was a boy come home to shelter and food ('Hotels for six weeks! I'm starving!'). He was also a man come back from conquest.

This combination of positive competence with lively eagerness was extraordinarily attractive. It was a perfect reflection of Claire herself. She saw that instantly. Perhaps this is one of the meanings of 'love at first sight', although no doubt there are more meanings than one . . .

By the end of the first hour they had learned everything that was important about one another.

'There's nothing else I ever wanted to be except a doctor. It's my life,' Claire had told him, along with the facts that she loved animals, music, travel and art, although she knew very little about either music or art; she was a night-person, very sloppy and forgetful and hated to cook.

He told her that he loved dogs, music – about which he knew rather a good deal – cooking, history and old houses. Business, its competition and expansion, fascinated him. He despised 'social' people and 'class'. He thought he would be at home in America because there was so much less of that sort of thing there.

'I've seen half the world, anyway. Now I want to see the States.'

'It's so funny to hear people say "the States".'

'Why? What do you say?'

'America. The United States.'

'I like your accent.'

'You do? Most Englishmen don't. I like yours because it's so neat, which sounds funny coming from me.'

'You're free and easy. I always think Americans are like that. But I've never known any very well.'

'Your mother is American.'

'Not really. She's been here so long, she even speaks like an Englishwoman.'

After a moment, Claire said thoughtfully, 'I shouldn't have come here.'

'Why shouldn't you have?'

'Because the air's thick with things we mustn't mention. Chiefly, my father. Do you know what I'm talking about?'

'I know.'

'If I did the right thing, I would leave here now.'

'Do you want to leave?'

'No.'

'I don't want you to either . . .'

They bought a Wedgwood plate for Jessie in the village, bicycled to a country pub for lunch, climbed the belfry, read on stained glass windows the distinguished names of military heroes and, in the churchyard, deciphered the eroded names of the humble unknown. And they talked.

'My father doesn't know I found those photos or that I know anything,' Claire told Ned, 'not even why he and my mother were divorced. I'm supposed to think it had something to do with money – or just generally not getting along, I guess,' she reflected. 'Mary thought he would stay on after the war.'

'I don't know. I remember hoping for her sake that he would.'

'But there was Hazel! He couldn't have stayed.'

'Some men would have, even so.'

'Not my father. He's steadfast.'

'Mine was too, in his own way. Are you shocked over what I told you about him, Claire?'

'Not *shocked*. But, tell me, has it made any difference to you?'

'What do you mean?'

'That you might feel you have to prove you're not like him?'

'I should wish to be like him in every other way. He had a fabulous mind and was one of the kindest men I ever knew.'

'Well, then, as for the other, it's no crime, Ned, or shouldn't be.'

'A lot of people wouldn't agree with you.'

'I'm a scientist. We look at things without judgement, without cobwebs. My father taught me that, I think.'

'You're very proud of your father, aren't you?'

'He's a great doctor. They send patients to him from all over the country. It's so strange that I can't mention him here! Or do I only imagine I can't?'

'You don't imagine it. There's a locked room in the house. It's in my mother's head, and you mustn't ask for the key.'

'Dad's got a locked room, too, now that you put it that way.'

It seemed to Claire that she had never spoken as easily to anyone in all her life.

Of those few, swift weeks, only disjointed scraps remained, frames in a moving picture running backwards and too fast, as on returning from a journey, we forget the lecture in the museum of antiquities, recalling instead a shabby restaurant where a girl sang 'Chagrin d'Amour' in a heartbreaking voice; remembering a family grouped on a railroad platform with a basket of tomatoes and a feeble yellow dog.

In Ned's small car they toured the south of England. She was to remember wet ponies in a downpour on Dartmoor; a flat tyre on the road to Stonehenge; a dinner by firelight in a room with a seven-foot ceiling. She was to remember – later they would laugh about it – hearing footsteps outside of her door one night at an inn and hoping it was Ned. It had been.

'I had my hand on the doorknob,' he said, 'but then at the last minute I lost my nerve.'

For a long time Claire had been concerned about herself. Many of her friends were married, some were living with a man and a few 'slept around', which last would have been repugnant. She had had proposals enough, both for living arrangements and for marriage. In each case the man had been personable, intelligent and kind. Yet none had reached her and she needed deeply to be reached. She was a romantic in spite of herself and she knew it.

So, when the day came, she was ready.

It was a day on Devon Hill, an afternoon of bee-hum and heather, with great cumuli boiling in the sky. Flat slabs of glacial rock thrust out of the earth, making wide, warm beds on which young lovers must have lain together for unrecorded centuries.

Claire spoke through the wind-rush and the hum. 'I'll remember this place. Sometimes I do that, promise myself to remember a place or a time, and I always do.'

Ned didn't answer. He was playing with a blade of grass, twisting it around his finger. Then he looked up. There was something in his eyes, something radiant, eager and at the same time reverent, which she had never seen in anyone before. So how could she have known what it was? Yet she recognized it.

'Have you ever?' he asked softly. 'Claire, have you ever?'

'No.'

Imperceptibly he drew away, but she put her arms out and pulled him down. 'I shouldn't have told you that. I want to, Ned. I want to very much.'

'And you never have before?'

'I never wanted anyone before.'

'You never loved anyone before?'

'Never.'

He stroked her hair. He took her face between his hands and kissed her eyelids, kissed her mouth . . . Everything was at the zenith: the season, the day and the years of their youth. That was the beginning.

'You'll marry me, Claire,' he said when he brought her back to London.

'Is that a statement or a question?'

'A statement, of course.'

The blood ran high in her veins. She felt light, triumphant, flirtatious. 'How do you know I'll say yes?'

'The same way you knew I was going to ask you,' he said, laughing.

There was so much laughter in him! He took such pleasure in small events: a game of Scrabble, a walk in the rain, an amusing conversation with a barber. He was astonishingly observant. Once after a ride on a bus he remarked on a couple who had sat across from them.

'She hates him, didn't you see?'

'Why, how can you know that?'

'All the time he was rattling the newspaper she never took her cold eyes off him.'

'Really? Why do you suppose she does?'

'Oh, I've no crystal ball! Still, he was an earthy man, with that full red face; likes his ale, I should think, while she was beaten, so drab and shrunken. An implausible pair,' he said compassionately.

'Ned, you're amazing!'

'No, I just like to observe. Now over there, that house, the one with the smashed Georgian portico and the peeling paint – there's a story behind that. Divorce or some family scandal or bankruptcy.'

'How on earth can you tell?'

'Because. This is a wealthy row and it's the only house on the street that's run down. There has to be a reason.'

'Ned, you ought to write! Really write a novel or a biography or something. You describe things so vividly, you've a gift.'

'It's not that easy. But some day, maybe.'

Life with Ned would be sunny, filled with the vigour of the unexpected. Whatever came, he would manage it and make some good come out of it. In this most curious way he reminded Claire of Jessie and she told him so, assuring him that he would like her mother. It never occurred to her to ask herself whether Jessie would like him.

'I remember your father,' he told her. 'I saw him once or twice. It was a long time ago and I was very young, but I remember liking him.'

'He's a wonderful man,' Claire said soberly.

'And you are your father's girl, aren't you?'

'I suppose so. He's a wonderful man,' she repeated.

It never occurred to her to ask herself what her father would think about this whole affair, either.

They parted in London with Ned's promise to be in New York in the fall. So closely had they grown together that the parting was a tearing. It crossed Claire's mind, although she did not say so, that it had probably been the same for her father and his mother. For a moment she thought how strange and sad that was; then immediately, as befits the normal, healthy selfishness of youth, she forgot it.

In the tropics there are certain plants which grow half the height of a man during a single night. They reach for the sun. So can a man and a woman reach for one another. Those whom this incandescence touches are not necessarily unusual people; it is only the heat of their yearning which is unusual.

CHAPTER TWENTY-SIX

Pink dots like the crowd faces in a photo, Martin thought, observing the audience while he waited on the platform foı his turn. The first speaker had addressed this Pan-American conference in Spanish, the translation coming over ear-phones. The second was speaking now in accented, fluent English. A blackboard hung behind him, and when he stepped back to chalk a diagram, Martin, craning to look, could see through a part in the draperies the slanting rooftops along the San Francisco street, as it pitched sharply downhill.

He looked back over the audience, wishing that Claire were there to hear him. But she was still in England, or had possibly just got home. Hazel was sitting with some other wives about six rows back. Catching his eyes, she smiled slightly and shyly.

He had expected to be nervous as his turn approached. Because he was himself intolerant of error, including his own, he needed to be sure that what he said was beyond challenge. He hoped – he thought – he had here today a gleam, albeit a small one, of something new, an original fragment to add to what was known about the convoluted mystery of the brain.

Now his name was spoken. He was being introduced. He stood to meet a few seconds of applause, and waiting for it to cease, felt a merciful calming of his heart and a flow of confidence. His mind cleared of blur. He looked out at all the faces tilted upwards like plants turned towards the light.

'I shall make three points,' he said clearly, 'beginning with the nutrient arteries to the midbrain. It is generally understood that – '

In plain, crisp words he made his three points, observing with a fraction of awareness that one listener's forehead was knotted in thought, another looked dubious and a pair were nodding towards each other as if to say: Yes, he's got something there; do you agree?

So he came to the end, and feeling a warm internal glow, sat down to long applause. He had done well.

Later in the lobby, a little crowd gathered with compliments and handshakes.

'You speak the way you write,' one man told him. 'You don't waste words. I like that.'

Another said, 'You had something of your own to tell. It was no mere rehash, no cut-and-paste job.'

And Hazel cried, 'I'm just so proud of you, Martin! So proud! Even though I didn't understand a word.' She added generously, 'I wish Claire could have heard you.'

They walked out into full sunlight. Hazel observing that it was their first day in the city without fog. The fair light, the excitement of the morning and the alluring, unfamiliar streets filled Martin with euphoria.

Everything, everything had come together! He thought of his work bearing fruit. He thought of climbing a long hill to stand now at the top and be crowned.

'Too bad we can't start for Carmel now,' Hazel remarked.

'I can't get the car till tomorrow morning. But you can have a swim in the hotel pool this afternoon, you know.'

She had been a counsellor at the Y during girlhood and was a strong swimmer, unlike himself who had learned by splashing around in a swimming hole. It was a pleasure to watch her in the water; he always admired professional skill, whether at chess or piano or anything else.

'You don't mind one or two stops on the way? Marjorie wants a Japanese doll, and I saw one in a window. I can't for the life of me think of anything for Peter, though.'

'A chess set,' Martin said promptly, the image of chess having just passed through his mind.

'Oh, do you think?' Hazel was dubious. 'He's only eight.'

'I'll teach him. It will exercise his brain.'

For Peter, who was tender-hearted, jolly and surely not unintelligent, had as yet not much ability to concentrate. Neither does Enoch, Martin thought, with a dimming of euphoria. He writes poetry, he dreams. Does well enough in school, but not the way Claire did. Oh, not fair to set her up as a measure!

'Here's the place,' Hazel said. 'I won't be long.'

He stood at the entrance and watched her. After great effort, she had lost ten pounds, and this loss revealed angles in her face which had been hidden by that roundness of youth which had so touched him when he first knew her. Yet perhaps he liked this more; it gave strength to her face.

She wore a becoming dark-blue linen dress. It occurred to him that her clothes had been different lately. She had become acquainted the previous winter with the Roman wife of an American doctor. The woman belonged in one of Hazel's glossy fashion magazines, in some photograph of a beak-nosed, thin aristocrat from a papal family, sitting in her marble palazzo wearing a plain expensive dress with one splendid jewel at the throat. She was certainly not a beauiful woman; yet she was arresting. Possibly Hazel had been learning something from her.

But still she smiled too eagerly, too timidly. Now she was thanking the saleswoman for the fourth time. He kept telling her not to apologize her way through life. Of course, she denied that she did it, and his telling her so only made her defensive.

Ah, Hazel, dear and loving Hazel, of what are you afraid? Do you sense something that lies too deep for you to understand? There is such sweetness in you, and yet beneath, there must be so much anger, too! How can you not be angry at a world that has somehow forced you to be so good, so thoughtful and mild? Was it your people who made you like this, or were you simply born that way? You pretend. Often, simply to please me, you even pretend to have pleasure in sex when you aren't feeling any. I never tell you I know because it would humiliate you.

And, with a kind of shock it crossed his mind that, for the second time, he had married a woman who, although for a different reason, was unsure of her own worth. Might it have been because of some insecurity in himself? There was so much one would never comprehend, even about oneself.

What if he had been living all this time with Mary? Then he

asked himself why, for God s sake, he should have thought of Mary at just this minute, while standing in this store in San Francisco between the doll counter and a shelf of toy cars? He never *really* thought about her any more! He didn't permit himself to! (She was just always there, as his past was there, his room in Cyprus with the slanted ceiling; his mother's voice; the dark hills and all else that had made him what he was.)

Hazel handed him the packages. 'We ought to get something for your sister, don't you think so?'

'What did you have in mind?'

'I saw a little bracelet in a window near here. Alice never really gets anything, does she?'

'Fine,' he said, and suddenly saw his mother coming in at the kitchen door with her 'good' hat on, its sorrowful feathers ravelled and drooped; saw her, then, and Alice, now, as though they were one figure. 'Get something for Alice's girls, too,' he said quickly.

'Yes, of course.'

'And don't you want anything for yourself?'

'I have everything,' she answered simply. This simplicity of hers was always poignant.

'Last night in the hotel arcade, you were looking at a tablecloth.'

'The Venetian lace? It was awfully expensive, Martin.'

'You loved it. I could tell.'

'Well, but, can we afford it?'

'Yes,' he said, 'I think we can,' and was pleased at the smile that came and went on her mouth.

From the terrace outside their room, he could hear her singing cheerfully while changing into a swimsuit. He had been concerned that she would regret having come on this trip, that her mind would be at home with the children. They were her centre, as they were not for him. (Yet, hadn't he always seen himself at the head of the table surrounded by the wealth of family?)

To tell the truth, at fifty-plus he was over-age to father such young children as the last two were. When he came home at night, he was tired, and quite naturally, they were noisy. He was sometimes impatient with them. Hazel never was. She was so patient with Claire, too! Once, not long ago, she had even spoken up when he had scolded Claire for something.

'I'm surprised,' she had said. 'You so seldom criticize Claire, even when she needs it. This time she didn't need it.'

Suddenly, now, he remembered that. And he wondered whether Hazel ever thought he might favour Claire over the others? Because in his heart he did, and he knew he shouldn't. He had such hopes for Claire! And up to this minute, every one of his hopes had been fulfilled.

She had done brilliantly, had even written a paper on genetics which might possibly see publication. For such a girl one was justified in having extravagant hopes. She qualified for the finest training, the best internship. After that a neurosurgical residency, or perhaps her interests might lie more deeply in neurological research. Whichever she might choose, there would be a place for her on his team, father and daughter; she would –

'Sure you won't change your mind about a swim?' Hazel inquired.

Through the open robe he could see her full breasts, her strong thighs in the swimsuit, a figure no longer young, but firm still and sturdy. She looked like health itself.

'No, you go. At the moment I feel too lazy.'

'Good. It's what you need, to feel lazy.' She smoothed his hair. 'I do worry about you, Martin. You never have any private time. Between patients and teaching, working three nights in the lab, and now this institute business – ' She reminded him more and more of the way his mother had used to worry over Pa.

'And writing another textbook on top of it all!' she added.

'Not writing,' he corrected. 'I'm only contributing a chapter this time. The rest is a symposium.'

'Well, whatever it is. I don't know how you do it all.'

'Go along with you,' he said, 'and work up an appetite for dinner. We're going to Trader Vic's'

He lay back in the lounge chair. The good warmth of the sun went through his bones. How he loved it, and how he hated the cold! It shrivelled his spirit and always had, even when he had been a child in Cyprus.

The beach, that was what he loved. Tomorrow they'd go down to Carmel, and for a whole week he'd get up early every morning, he promised himself. While everyone still slept, he'd go down to the beach and stand there looking out at the endless blue, the sea blue and the diamond dazzle. At dawn there would be no footprints on the sand except the ones he would put there. All others would have been washed away during the night. In a cleansed and pristine world there would remain only the pure curve of sea and the parallel curve of sky.

I could have been a beach-bum, he thought, and was amused at himself, knowing that that was one thing which he, the precise, the exacting, the apprehensive and conscience-laden, could never, never be.

Even here, even now in this hour of solitary peace, while the wind hummed in his ears and his eyes were bemused by two sail-boats on the bay heading outwards under the Golden Gate Bridge, his thoughts were travelling back east. They'd made tremendous, incredible progress! After almost six years of arduous effort they'd reached the Dobbs Foundation at last, and now finally were moving in high gear.

In part the crucial contact had been brought about through efforts of Bob Moser's, but the decision to make the grant had come because of Martin.

'I've gone as far as I can go,' Moser had told him. 'The ball's in your court, now. You'll have to put the idea across.'

And he had done so. In one fateful evening on the Mosers' terrace after dinner, Martin had been able to convince Bruce Rhinehart, then the acting president of the foundation. Rhinehart had been a careful listener. There had been something southern about him, with his long, narrow face and pince-nez, his way of inclining the head in courteous deference. Bob Moser was obviously in awe of him. The control of millions, even though they are not your own, commands respect, Martin thought. The power of money. Human nature.

First he had produced an estimate of the cost. Then, restraining the tremble of his hand, he'd shown the rough sketch, dog-eared by now, which he always carried in his pocket.

'You're familiar with our old two-storey wing on the side street, Mr Rhinehart? Our thought is we'd tear that down and build ten floors up, with entrance into the main building, of course. We'd have laboratories and auditoriums for teaching on the first two floors, with patient floors above.' He'd kept his voice even, not too boldly confident, but not pleading, either. 'I've got a lot of thoughts about the operating rooms. There've been so many improvements since ours were built. We'll need facilities for photography of the brain, somewhere near the Department of Encephalography. See? Over here on this end.'

Rhinehart had inquired when and how Martin had first got his idea. He recalled now that he had answered, 'It's been a dream of my whole life, my life as a doctor, that is,' and hoped that hadn't sounded grandiose, becase it was the simple truth.

'We're an old, honoured hospital,' he'd explained. 'I've felt deep loyalty to it ever since I first came to work here under Dr Eastman. I believe we need and deserve this institute.'

They had talked until midnight, Rhinehart listening all the time with that attentive courtesy.

'It's gratifying to see how much we've been able to raise from private contributions, Mr Rhinehart. Three hundred thousand dollars.'

At that moment Bob Moser had injected humour.

'That includes fifty from a friend of mine, a plastic manufacturer looking for a tax deduction,' he'd said with a grin. More soberly he had added, 'We've a long, long way to go, Mr Rhinehart, and I hope you'll see the road ahead as clearly as we do. We – I – that is, Martin here, Dr Farrell, is in my opinion, for what it's worth, one of the outstanding –

And Rhinehart, perhaps observing Martin's embarrassment, had put in quietly, 'Indeed I know of Dr Farrell. His text on neuropathology is the current standard. We do so much medical philanthropy, we have to keep abreast of these things.' And he had turned to Martin. 'I assume, of course, you will expect to head the institute.'

Martin had made a small gesture of assent.

'It would be a question, then, of our gambling on you.'

'To an extent, yes. Although I would hope the project would encompass a broader span than any one personality, and last a good deal longer.'

He had asked Martin in what ways this institute would differ from existing ones.

'Naturally, every man has his individual methods,' Martin had told him. 'This has been part of me for so long, this conviction that I have about encompassing mind and brain in one study – Yes, it's done elsewhere, of course. But I have worked out my own ideas about modes of research and patient care.'

'Well,' Rhinehart had said, and there had been something so decisive in the syllable that Martin had stopped with a tug of fear that he had perhaps overreached himself.

'Well, Dr Farrell, I'd like you to come before my committee next week and tell them everything you have been telling me.'

And so they'd be laying the cornerstone, if all went well, some time next spring!

Hazel wanted the date to coincide with his birthday. She loved grand celebration. Half drowsing now, he lay back in the chair, reflecting on birthdays. What a great fuss Hazel always made! They, like holidays, were an excuse for having a crowd, from friends like Perry and Tom to distant cousins whom one never saw during all the rest of the year. She would cook Martin's favourites: roast beef, corn pudding and apple pie. The bought and fancy decorated birthday cake was for the children's benefit, so each one could have an icing-flower. He could see them now: Enoch, so cautious and agreeable, that you wondered what he might truly be thinking; the little ones, Peter and Marjorie, who had more of Hazel than of himself, although Marjorie looked like him. And Claire. She seemed to bring air into the house with her.

She'd fling her coat to a hall chair, and Hazel would hang the coat up in the closet, for Hazel was neat like Martin. Where did Claire get her careless ways? Why, from Pa, of course!

And he thought, with smiling rueful remembrance, of Pa's desk and his mother's sighs over things forever mislaid or lost. Yes, of course, from Pa. Genes were a funny business.

A liner was coming in at the Golden Gate; coming from Japan, perhaps? He'd like to see Japan some time.

What had he been thinking? Oh, yes, that genes were a funny business. Families were a funny business. You'd never think Hazel belonged in hers! When they got talking, the whole lot of them, it sounded like the rattle of machine-guns. It made you aware that English is a guttural language. Tess, her sister, had the drone and sibilance of a nonstop talker.

But he had been, and would go on being, good to them. One of them was always in some need or other, either because of illness, or simply because of having more children than he could afford. He never minded helping them, even rather liked it, in an odd way. Because their need made him feel superior to them? Yes, because after all these years, he still smarted over having needed the help of Donald Meig. He could still feel half-naked shame at the memory of standing in that room.

'If it weren't for me, you'd be peddling aspirin tablets.' That was what Meig had said, and the worst part of it was that it was true.

So it was good for the ego, it was salve and balm, to be a kindly tactful giver when one could just as easily say to one's brother-in-law, 'You're a fool and you're lazy; you shouldn't have had seven children when you can't even support two.'

No Meig, he! And Martin wondered what Meig would think if he were still alive and could know about the institute.

Hazel came out on to the terrace. 'Oh, did I wake you? We've a letter, or rather you have. You won't believe it – it says Jessie Meig on the envelope.'

He sat up instantly and opened the letter which had been forwarded from his office.

'Dear Martin,' he read, 'No doubt you will be astonished to receive this. I thought it better to write because, frankly, it's less of an embarrassment for both of us than the telephone would be.

'I'll be brief. Claire has returned from Europe with shocking news. While in England she took it upon herself to visit Lamb House. There she met young Ned Lamb. They spent three weeks touring together and have now decided to be married. He is to come to New York in the fall – has a job in the offing. The wedding will take place next summer after Claire's graduation.

'You have influence over Claire, maybe more than you realize. You need not answer this. I shall simply assume you will do what you can to prevent this folly. Sincerely, Jessie Meig.'

'Whatever's the matter?' Hazel cried.

Martin crumpled the letter. Did anything ever go smoothly? Was there ever a time when you could sit back and say to yourself: 'Come now, rest a little. You've earned it'? Only a moment ago he had been feeling fairly satisfied; perhaps he had been *self*-satisfied and this was to be his rude punishment?

'Talk to me, Martin!'

He came to. 'It's all right. I mean, it's Claire. She wants to get married.'

'I thought someone had died, you looked so stricken!'

'She met him in England. Went to visit Lamb House. God-damned crazy thing to do! It's Ned, her aunt's son.'

'Oh? But then, he's a cousin, isn't he? How can they marry?'

He realized he had never given her any more than a few barest facts at their first meeting, so long ago.

'They're not. His mother died when he was born. She – Mary – brought him up.'

'I see. Well?' Hazel touched his arm. 'Martin, you look dreadful. Does it really matter so?'

He turned on her. 'Of all the stupid questions! It's an insane folly, and you can ask me – '

His vehemence appalled her.

'I'm sorry,' he said. 'You didn't mean anything. But oh, damn it, one's children can wreck things!'

'You're thinking of Jessie, aren't you? Yes, I can see why. It would be awful for her, wouldn't it?'

He pressed his lips together and leaned against the wall. He felt like a traveller in a depot in a strange city, uncertain where to go.

What the hell had she been doing, going to that house? She shouldn't have gone abroad this summer! But how in blazes could he have guessed, when he made her a present of the trip, that she'd do a crazy thing like that? And then he remembered how the child Claire had come to him. Independent as hell, did what she wanted and the devil take the hindmost! Well, the devil had taken it now, that was sure.

How in God's name to bear with this, when he already had so much to crowd his brain: the institute, the daily round, the family? For so long he had stifled memory, by sheer force he had crowded it down. Would 'anguish' be too strong a word for what he was feeling at this minute? He thought not. There would be grandchildren. They would belong to him and to Mary. Also to Jessie. It was – it was unthinkable! He groaned.

'Oh,' Hazel cried, 'I've never seen you like this!' She mourned over him. 'But surely if there's nothing wrong with the young man, it can be worked out somehow. I mean, you don't even know him, do you?'

'He's her son. That's awkward enough.'

'Yes, of course, but much more so for Jessie than for you. After all, you only had a few days' – affair – and never saw her again. My goodness, it's ancient history! Anyway, there's nothing you can do to stop it, is there? I mean, Claire's a woman. You can't very well order her around, can you?' She gave a small, nervous laugh. 'Especially not Claire.'

He knew what she wanted to say: 'Claire's headstrong and obstinate. She always has been and you ought to be used to it by now.'

Jessie must be in a fury! Or would she have swallowed her wrath and grown silent instead? As though it were yesterday, he remembered that Jessie could do just that.

He tried to recall the boy: sensitive, decent, thoughtful and pitifully young in the RAF uniform. Yes, but that was ten years past! And anyway, what difference did all that make? What difference could anything make beside the fact that he was *her* son?

Suddenly Hazel's hovering presence annoyed him. He wished she would go inside and leave him alone.

'What are you staring at, Martin?'

Controlling himself, he answered evenly, 'There's a gull on that balcony. It's been there all afternoon.'

'Perhaps it's got a nest.' She kept standing there, troubled and hesitant. 'I hope you're not going to grieve too much over this business with Claire.'

'Let's fly home in the morning,' he said abruptly.

'But we were going down to Carmel and Big Sur!'

'I don't feel like taking another week. I've got a hundred things to do at home, anyway.'

'You mean you've got to see Claire.'

'Well, what if I do?'

Her lips trembled. Then he thought: She asks for so little . . . And he felt torn, pulled this way and that.

'Let's compromise,' he offered. 'Four days at Carmel. We'll go to Big Sur another time. I really want to get back a little sooner, Hazel.'

Her eyes softened. 'Fair enough. I understand.' She put her arms around him. 'Let's dress for dinner, shall we? And try to take your mind off things a little? I've heard so much about Trader Vic.'

They were eating chicken in coconut sauce when a couple came to sit at an adjoining table.The man hailed Martin.

'Colonel! Colonel Farrell! It is you, isn't it?'

'Why yes,' Martin said, hesitating.

'Dickson. Floyd Dickson. Don't tell me you don't remember?'

'Of course I do. For the moment I couldn't think.'

'Yeah, I've put on thirty pounds since then. Meet my wife, Dot.'

'And my wife, Hazel. Dr Dickson and I were stationed together in England.'

'I was a crummy lieutenant. Used to hang around and

watch the colonel stitch the boys together.'

Martin sighed inwardly. He was especially in need of a quiet dinner on this night! And of all people now, he'd had to encounter this loud, restless individual whom the years seemed to have made louder than ever.

But he inquired politely, 'Living in San Francisco?'

'No. LA. We come from Minneapolis, you know, but I got sick and tired of shovelling snow. I've got a paediatrics practice in LA. Dot likes 'Frisco, so we run up now and then. You been to Carmel?'

'We're going in the morning for a few days.'

'Where you going after that?'

'Home. I'm due back in New York.'

'What you should do is, you should hop on a ship or a plane and go off to Hawaii, as long as you're this far. After that, the Orient. Say, waiter, how about pushing these two tables together so we don't have to shout? That is, if you don't mind?'

'Well, no,' Martin said.

Scraping and shoving, the Dicksons settled down.

'I hear you're making a name for yourself,' Dickson remarked. 'I always thought you would.'

'Thank you.'

'I met a fellow in the hotel lobby this noon who'd just come from your speech. He was telling me something about you heading a new institute in New York. Neurological research, he said.'

'Yes,' Martin said quietly. 'It's under way.'

'Well, they all say you're the man back east! But seriously now,' Dickson addressed Hazel. 'You ought to make him have a little fun, too.'

She smiled. 'I try.'

'Sure. Take a couple of months off. You're a long time dead.'

Dot Dickson asked whether they had children.

'Three,' Hazel answered. 'Two of them are only seven and eight. We can't leave them yet for any length of time.'

'We went to Greece last year. Left the kids with my mother-in-law. Took the cruise around the islands.

Beautiful, beautiful,' Dickson said.

'I'd like to do that sometime,' Martin admitted. 'Greece is the place I've most wanted to see. All my life.'

Mrs Dickson assured him he would love it. 'And the shopping's incredible,' she told Hazel. 'You can get gold jewellery for practically nothing. Oh, I adore travelling! Two years ago we took a fjord cruise out of Copenhagen. I almost bought a silver service. They're hand-made you know. But then I thought it probably wouldn't go with our dining-room – it's French provincial. What do you think?'

'I really don't know,' Hazel said. 'I'm afraid I'm not very good at things like that.' She fell silent.

And Martin thought how much he appreciated a quiet woman. Even a woman like Flo Horvath, who was otherwise dear to him, he couldn't have tolerated for a week. All that chatter and twitter!

Then Hazel, apparently feeling a need to be more sociable, remarked, 'I've always wanted to see England, but Martin doesn't want to.'

'Oh, really? I just love England,' Mrs Dickson said enthusiastically.

'I guess the men saw enough of it during the war,' Hazel responded.

'I feel that way,' Martin agreed.

Two years ago, flying to a conference in Geneva, they had come down through clouds; England had lain on the left, with the sun just setting over it, and he hadn't wanted to look. He had turned away and got a magazine.

'I wouldn't mind going back,' Dickson declared. 'In fact, that may be our next trip. Dot here is wild about antiques, old houses and all that. Of course, we don't have much of that here in California. Say, Martin, speaking of old houses, you remember that place you used to visit out past Oxford?'

'No,' Martin said, startled. 'I saw a lot of places and it's a long time since.'

'Sure you must! I drove you there a couple of times and picked you up in the ambulance on the way back. Talk of old! That house must have been three hundred years old if it was a day.'

Martin asked Hazel, 'Would you like a salad? I forgot to order one. Waiter, may we have two green salads, please?'

Dickson turned to his wife. 'You would have flipped over that place, Dot. Martin said somebody said Oliver Cromwell slept there once. I never got to go inside, though.'

There was no malice in the man. Martin himself had covered so skilfully, had made his visits appear so innocent, that Dickson could have had no idea what he was doing.

'What did they call it again? Lion House? Cock-eyed names, all their places have names. No, what am I saying? Lamb House. That was it. Lamb. Wasn't it Lamb, Martin, where you used to go?'

Martin raised his eyes. The anguish in them must have communicated itself to Dickson, bringing a sudden, terrible comprehension.

'Maybe I'm thinking of somebody else,' he said quickly. 'I rode around with so many guys, you get mixed up, your memory goes back on you.'

A flush like a scald rose in an even horizontal line from the man's throat to the hairline. It looked like water rising in a glass. And strangely enough, Martin felt sorry for him.

A queer silence fell over the table. Martin looked back at his plate, moving the rice around with his fork.

Presently, in a flat voice, Hazel spoke.

'Ask for the cheque now, Martin, please.'

'No dessert?' Mrs Dickson remonstrated. 'You don't know what you're missing! They have the most fabulous desserts! The pineapple – '

But Hazel had already risen. 'I don't want any,' she said steadily. She walked to the door. Martin excused himself and followed her. They got into a taxi-cab.

'Hazel,' he began.

'I don't want to talk,' she said.

In the hotel elevator, she faced forward. He tried to place himself where she would have to look at him, so that by some expression, perhaps, he might convey to her what words could not. But she did not let him meet her eyes.

In their room she took off her coat and hung it in the closet. Then she went into the bathroom. Martin walked to the window. Lights festooned the great bridge. Lights quivered on the bay, where little boats moved festively and people were all free of care. He turned back into the room, the quiet, pearl-grey room that spoke of money and the serenity that can go with it. His lips were dry with dread.

Hazel came out of the bathroom. She stood leaning against a table. It shook, and her purse fell to the floor. She didn't pick it up.

'So you did see her when you were in England,' she said at last.

'Yes.'

'Why did you lie to me?'

'I didn't lie. We just never talked about it.' And immediately he was ashamed of the cheap evasion.

'You made love to her.'

He had a sense of standing at a crossroads. With one syllable, 'yes', he would take a turning from which there could be no retreat. Also, he had a feeling of déjà vu, as if he had always known that this might happen, although really that made no sense. The chances of its happening must have been one out of a thousand, at least. Yet here he was.

'You made love to her,' Hazel repeated.

'Yes,' he said.

'It wasn't just one time. You stayed together.'

'Yes.'

She clapped her hands to her face and dropped them.

'I wouldn't have minded other women, prostitutes least of all! Believe me! I understand that a man can't be away for two or three years without – But her! Why did it have to be her?'

She began to weep without changing expression. Her face was smooth and uncontorted, a fixed face, with streaming tears. And this strange control dismayed him more than a frenzy would have done.

'Why?' she cried.

He trembled. What could he say? He thought of something.

'I came back, didn't I? Doesn't that tell you anything?'

'Yes. It tells me that you loved your children. Especially Claire.'

'No, no. It was more than that.'

'Your career, then, your precious career.'

'I thought of you,' he said.

'Oh, I believe that one! I surely do believe that one!'

'But it's true.'

Hazel began to speak rapidly, with mounting pitch and force. 'You were my whole life, do you know that, Martin? You were what I lived for. And to think that all the time, every loving word you ever spoke to me was a lie! That everything, everything was an act and a rotten lie! Oh my God, I understand what that poor cripple went through! What is this woman anyway? What sort of a whore is she, that she couldn't leave you alone? Not once, but twice?' She sobbed now, she pulled at her hair. Her mouth was twisted in the mask and grimace of grief. 'A whore, that's what, a whore!'

'Ah, don't, Martin said. 'Ah, don't.'

'First her sister. But it wasn't enough to ruin one marriage, was it? Oh, I could tear her eyes out! If it weren't for my children I would kill her. Oh my God, I hope she dies in agony with cancer! Cancer!'

'I want,' he began, 'I want to tell you – ' and stopped.

What did he want to tell? Had it been anyone other than Mary, some WAC or nurse or English village girl, he might have said: *I couldn't stand being alone any more,* and might have expected to be half understood. But Mary was different, and more's the pity, Hazel knew it.

Yet he tried again. 'I can only beg you to understand my conflict. My weakness, if you like. Weigh this against our years. I've been a good husband to you, you know I have – '

'Claire's marriage,' she interrupted. 'I see it now. No wonder you can't bear the thought of it! No wonder!' She flung herself on the bed. 'Get out. I want you to get out.'

'Be reasonable, Hazel. Please. I'll get you some medicine, a pill, to help you get through this night.'

'I don't want a pill. Do you know something, Martin? I hate you. I wouldn't have believed a human being could change as I have in just five minutes. Whatever I felt for you all these years is gone. It left me at the table in that restaurant. Just left me.'

'You're frantic and I don't blame you. But can you try to put everything aside till the morning? We'll talk it over more calmly, we'll straighten it out, I know we will.'

'I don't want to talk. In the morning I'm going home to my children.'

'All right, we'll go home, then. Will you lie there quietly while I go out for medicine?'

'I'm not taking any.'

'You have to pull yourself together. Never mind how you feel about me. You've got three children to think of.'

The crowded street was almost as bright as day. It was easy going down the hill. One almost had to hold back to keep from hurtling forward. Two prostitutes with crayon pink cheeks approached him. Except for their hard bright eyes, they looked like children. They couldn't have been older than sixteen. Their scornful laughter followed him.

In a shop window he saw the bronze Dwan Yin which Hazel and he had looked at on their walk that afternoon. It seemed now to have been a month ago. It seemed to have been a month ago that he had read the letter about Claire. And he stopped again to study the merciful goddess, perhaps to find in her benign expression some comfort for his raging pain.

Ah, he would give anything, anything, even his precious hands, not to have done this to Hazel!

Mary, Mary, he thought then.

'That one's had a bit too much,' the soldier had said when Martin passed that night in London, all those thousands of miles away and so long ago.

Too much.

When he had got the medicine, he walked back up the hill. Cable cars were still running, but he forced himself to climb. It took the last of his breath.

She was undressed, lying in bed, neither reading nor sleeping, just lying there. Her eyes were swollen. She looked ugly, and this moved him terribly, the fact that she looked ugly because of him. He came over to the bed and stood looking down at her.

'Is there anything I can do? Anything that can be undone?'

'I don't see what.' She spoke quietly now. 'You never got over her.'

'But I love you,' he said, not denying the other. 'Can't I make you believe me?'

'No, Martin, you never did.'

'You're wrong. I did and I do.' He knelt down at the side of the bed so that his face was level with hers. 'Please, Hazel. Please.'

'Please what?'

'You know. Understand. I never *wanted* it to happen.'

'You couldn't help it, you mean?'

'No.'

'That makes it worse, doesn't it?'

He didn't know what to answer.

'You spent two years with her. Two years out of your life while you were married to me.'

How to explain? How to say that there are different kinds of love? That there are circumstances, timing, fate, enchantments – ah God, call it what you will. He stroked her hand. He wished he could feel the way she wanted him to. Indeed, he did feel something very deep, but it was not what she wanted and he knew it.

In the morning they packed their belongings and flew home. On the way to the airport, the cab-driver was chatty, which would ordinarily have been an annoyance. But this time, Martin found relief from awful silence in the flow of talk.

They boarded the plane. Their seats were three abreast, Martin at the window, because Hazel never liked to look out, and on her other side, a man, a lawyer or accountant, very likely, who was deep in documents. Martin had a newspaper and a paperback, but couldn't concentrate on either.

As clouds parted, one saw the speeding shadow on the plain in ink-blue wash. Ahead, clouds curved like the drooping petals of enormous peonies. A river ran in a red-rock canyon where ocean fossils lay five thousand feet below the surface of the ancient earth.

What matter any of our transient sorrows in the face of these?

Hazel was crying again. He didn't dare to look in her direction. He heard the click of her purse as she got a handkerchief out, and hoped for her sake that the man on the other side wouldn't notice. The embarrassment would crush her.

Long hours later, somewhere over Pennsylvania, the sky grew dark. The plane lurched and the 'Fasten Seatbelt' sign came on. Then began the long descent towards the million lights of eastern cosmopolis. Thunder crashed around the rocking plane as they came down into the storm, and a woman in the seat behind cried out in fright.

'Don't be afraid,' Martin said to Hazel. 'We aren't going to crash.'

She turned to him. He saw that she was dry-eyed. 'Do you suppose I care if we do?'

He thought of the ride out to California, of yesterday's euphoria and elation. And now this.

Oh God, help our fevered struggles.

BOOK FIVE

LOSSES

CHAPTER TWENTY-SEVEN

For two months gloom like a heavy shroud had lain on the house. On an evening in mid-September, Martin sat alone on the screened porch. It was hot, but not with the sweet heat of summer. This oppressive heat was lasting past its season into the time of fleeing birds and silence. He wished they were back in the city. With no particular logic, he thought it might be better there. At least he would be able to walk over to the office at night and do some paperwork. Anything to get out of the house! But school would not open for another week, and Hazel had wanted to stay here as long as possible, obviously because she could hide more easily in this place where they were merely summer transients and very few people knew them.

He could hear her moving about in the kitchen. Every evening now after the maid had gone upstairs, she found occupation in the kitchen cooking and baking. He got up to stand in the doorway. Ginger and sugar scented the warm air. The complicated paraphernalia which Hazel had brought from home – pots, moulds, terrines and cookbooks in glossy jackets – shone in a yellow light. And still it seemed to Martin that rot lay over everything.

She took a pie out of the oven. It had a high meringue, coloured delicately brown, like toast. He wished she would stop filling the children with stuff like that! Marjorie was big and rawboned like Hazel's mother and had already gained ten pounds over the summer.

Hazel set the pie on the counter. 'Can I make you a cup of tea?' She spoke politely as one does when a neighbour has unexpectedly dropped in.

'No, thank you.'

Her eyes with their round, pure whites had always in their mild innocence been appealing. Tonight they were dull. Stubborn, he thought, and was ashamed of the thought.

Suddenly he saw that she had grown very thin. She must have been losing weight for weeks.

'You've lost weight,' he said.

She wiped the sink and hung the dish towel on the rack. 'What difference does it make?'

'A great deal. If you lose any more, we'll have to check into it.'

'Why? You think it's cancer? I'd be out of the way, then, wouldn't I?'

'Don't be a fool! This sort of talk won't work, Hazel. There's a limit to sympathy, as with anything else.'

'You want to know something? I really don't care whether I have your sympathy or not.'

'What do you care about then?'

'I should think anyone could see what.'

'The house, you mean? The chidlren? Yes, you're doing everything according to the book and better. But there are other things.'

'Yes, there are other things, and it's a little late for them.' She pushed the loose hair back from her forehead. 'I'm going up,' she said wearily.

He understood that the subject had been switched off again. 'I'll stay and let Enoch in. And Claire. You remember she has two days off this week?'

'The room's ready for her. And you needn't wait for Enoch, he's staying overnight with his friend Freddy.'

The ceiling light made hollows and shadows on her cheeks. For a moment she stood there as if she were looking for something and had forgotten what, and Martin felt a mixture of pity and exasperation.

'Well, I'll be going up,' she said again. 'Good-night.'

'Good-night.' He went back to the portable television on the porch. A heated drama was taking place on the screen, a drama about doctors. He recognized the hero and could have written the plot, in which the intern, pure in his astounding brilliance, solved with no trouble at all the problem that had been baffling the most renowned specialists in the world. Idiocy! He switched it off and wandered into the living-room, picked up the newspaper, and finding it filled again with a repetitious litany of murders and burglaries, of bankrupt cities, defence budgets and election speeches, put it down. He sighed and wondered whether the returning owners would feel any emanations of his frustrated spirit in their house. He thought he could feel theirs, from the faded cretonne with its stiff maroon chrysanthemums, to the Victorian desk in the corner with its rosewood fretwork, solid as a cathedral and inherited from either his or her great-grandmother.

He reconstructed the family. It was a game, a pastime for him. Their silver would be inherited with their politics – Republican, naturally. On their inherited Lenox china they would eat their formal meals of thin roast beef, clear watery soup and mint-green gelatine dessert. He hadn't liked this house when they rented it because it had the spirit of bleak, repressed emotions. The man in the yellowed photograph wore a nineteen-twenties' straw boater at a jaunty angle, but the face was no Scott Fitzgerald face of celebration: the lips were pressed too thin. Furthermore, the house had smelled of wet bathing suits and tar-stained sneakers on the day they had walked in. Still, it was on the water, and after all, that was what they had sought for the summer. One good thing, though: the master bedroom had twin beds. He wondered how they would have managed during these past weeks if Hazel and he had had to share a bed. Next week back home they would have to.

He had been trying to straighten things out. God how he had been trying, since that ghastly night at the restaurant in San Francisco. She would sigh. 'Why are you sighing?' he would ask, and she would answer, 'Was I? I didn't realize it.' Maybe she didn't. Often a sigh was only unconscious relief of tension. Her tears brimmed unexpectedly. They'd gone to the movies a few times, and there in the darkness he'd heard that snap of the pocketbook opening and shutting as she got out a handkerchief. In the reflection from the screen he could see the wet glisten of tears and had known they couldn't possibly have been caused by the banal and silly story on the screen. Sighs and tears. Two or three times he had gone over to her bed and put his arms around her. She hadn't pushed him out, only lain there like an unresponsive lump as if to say: 'Take it or leave it; it means nothing to me.' He had grown quite empty of whatever complex feelings had brought him to her in the first place: need for sexual release, tenderness, sorrow, a wish to heal. All had simply drained away and he had lain stiffly beside her thinking of what he might say to break through, and then finding no way, for he had many times used up all the words he could summon, had gone back to his own bed.

He wondered now how long a family could hold together like this. Enoch, at least, must sense something. This summer he'd been counsellor at a day camp for retarded children. He related to the rejected and the weak. He wasn't – fortunately – one of them; still, he would never make an Ivy League college or be on Law Review. He wasn't the type to lift his head high above the crowd. He'd be a good teacher of the young, especially the troubled young. He wouldn't sympathize with me if he were to know the truth, Martin thought. Youth can be awesomely puritanical. It takes seriously what we teach, till it discovers what we really are.

But surely Enoch must know something? he asked himself again. There'd been one quarrel when they'd first come back from California, during which Hazel's voice had been loud enough to be heard across the road. She had been in a rage, pounding her fists on the wall. He hadn't known she was capable of such passion, of whatever sort. Afterwards she had been contrite and trembling, as if ashamed of having given such offence. And this docility had sickened him as much as the rage, which was, after all, not abnormal in the circumstances. For he had pulled the rug out from under her emotional security.

They had sat down at the dinner table and Hazel, smiling, had served the salad and sliced the cake. But her eyes had shown pink swollen lids under the heavy powder. He wondered why Enoch had never asked about that and then thought maybe the boy didn't want to know. He had an instant's flash-view of supper tables, millions of supper tables all over the country, of families sitting with a man and a woman and the children in between. How thin the fabric which held them together! My God, you know nothing from an outward view! And he remembered that doctor across the hall in his building, a distinguished obstetrician, an amiable grandfather with a refined and pretty wife. One afternoon he had suddenly closed the office door for good and gone to Arizona with his secretary. Was anything, was anyone, ever simple, direct and clear?

He got up and, from the drawer of the desk which he had appropriated for the summer, took out a folder. 'The Institute', he had scrawled on the cover. This at least was direct and clear. Every detail had its purpose, whether scientific, technical or artistic. Across the entrance, below the pediment, he wanted a single sentence to be carved in the stone. Searching, he'd gone back again, as he had always done, to the Greeks. No other culture before or since had been able to express either in words or stone, probably in music also if one could only know, such fundamental truths with such comely grace.

He thought now he had reached a decision. *'For he who loves man loves the art.' = Aesculapius*. These few words above the door would say it all, he thought again. He would submit it to the trustees at the next meeting, although most certainly they would be willing to leave it to his choice. Men like Moser, and most of them were like Moser, wouldn't know very much about the Greeks and would care less.

Also, there was the question of a mural for the lobby. Martin wasn't at all certain that one was indicated – you didn't want the place to look like a post office or a courthouse. Yet there were those who pressed for it. And the idea might not be a bad one if the right artist were found to do it. He'd been collecting photographs of samples. Thoughtfully now, he held them to the light, visualizing the proportions, the way they might appear to visitors turning left down the corridor, as they would do. The figures mustn't loom too large, or they would be lost in detail . . .

He had begun to enjoy himself, his tension loosening, when he heard Claire's brakes screeching on the gravel drive. She drove too fast! No matter what you said, people of her type never learned. Impetuous, slam-bang, charming! Capable of stunning surprises, too. He was still not, maybe never would be, over the shock of learning that she had known about Mary and himself since she'd been sixteen and discovered those photographs.

In the beginning, he knew, he'd had Jessie to thank for their daughter's discretion, and perhaps for her compassion. Now he had Claire herself to thank.

He opened the door for her.

'Hi, Dad, how's everything?'

'Fine. I've just been going over designs for a mural in the lobby. Want to see? Or want coffee first? There's some kept hot in the percolator.'

'Coffee first, please.' She followed him into the kitchen. 'Have some, Dad?'

'No. It keeps me awake. I'll just watch you.'

She studied him. 'You're a bit charged up, aren't you? Well, I don't blame you. They've really been racing along with that foundation. I watched the cement mixers and all the rest of the stuff today, and I got sort of charged up myself. Or choked up, thinking that it's really happening at last, and you did it.'

'I and a few hundred others.'

'Oh, don't be modest!'

Martin reflected, 'Jessie always used to tell me that.'

'Anyway, it becomes you. You may be sleepless with excitement,' Claire said cheerfully, 'but it becomes you.'

Blind, blind. She's so happy herself that she sees nothing else. Happy over that fellow! He'll be arriving soon, Martin thought with a sinking in his chest, and I'll have to see him. Funny how things change their proportions. Since this trouble of my own, I haven't had time to think about that affair. I'll have to, though.

'I did a delivery today,' Claire was saying. 'It's the happiest part of the hospital, isn't it? Dr Castle was there, but I did it all myself. The kid was dark blue and I was scared, but I put the tracheal tube in and the kid turned a nice pink and let out a good loud howl. I felt great.'

'Not sorry about turning down the Chicago internship?'

'Well, I did want it, but that was before I knew Ned. He'll be here next month, you know.' As if Martin didn't know! 'He's landed a terrific job: White, Davis and Fisher. They're one of the three biggest in the business.' Claire got up and went to the cake box. 'What a baker Hazel is! It's a wonder you're not fat.'

'I think I'll have a cup after all,' Martin said. He poured the coffee and took a few swallows. Then, forcing cheerfulness, he inquired, 'So, you're growing sure of yourself, are you?'

'Yup. No butterflies in the stomach. There's something about even a little clinical experience that gives you confidence.'

'For a woman who ranked number five in her class last June, I should think you'd have plenty of confidence.'

'This business of measuring people against each other is a mean thing when you think about it,' Claire reflected. Then she smiled. 'Still I must admit it's kind of exhilarating when you happen to be at the top of the list.'

She wore contact lenses now and Martin wasn't yet used to her face without glasses. It seemed less earnest. Could 'genuine' be the right word for her, with the still-boyish curls and the charming tilted nose and the long neck? She has the world before her, he thought, including, damn it, Ned Lamb. I wish to heaven –

And suddenly she turned sombre. 'Dad, I wish people wouldn't make everything so hard for Ned and me. Mother simply will not open her mind.'

Small wonder, Martin thought grimly.

'It seems to me one ought to be able to come to terms with the past. Why should a new generation be tied to a past it had nothing to do with?'

Nothing to do with? Where did these young think they had come from? Risen out of the sea or sprung from the head of Zeus? He managed to murmur, 'It's not so simple. You've revived old pains. It's not only the young who feel.' And he thought: I wish I could talk to her about Hazel . . . But some parental dignity and pride was shocked at the possibility.

'Oh,' she said quickly, 'oh, Dad, I know.' He could see the

frank compassion in her eyes. 'You'd be surprised if you could know how well I understand many, many things.'

Martin smiled dubiously. 'You think you do?'

'You and Mother both think you're being asked to give up the peace you've made. Mary thinks so, too. Ned wrote me.'

'Well, wouldn't we?'

'Yes, but – Oh, I grant it would be easier to start clean with a new family and no skeletons in the closet. It's not ideal that nobody speaks to anybody else.'

'Can't you see what this means? Shall I give you all the old clichés about how marriage is hard enough without starting in with problems? How they come along fast enough through the ordinary business of living? I can give you those clichés, but you know them already. What you don't know is that they're all true.'

'I suppose they are, but they've never deterred anybody yet, have they?'

A cricket set up frantic, repetitious chirping in the kitchen. Like human chirping, Martin thought. We repeat and repeat, but we don't change each other's minds.

'How about some sleep?' he said kindly. 'We'll solve nothing tonight.'

Claire yawned. 'I've been looking forward to these two days. I plan to spend every minute on the beach tomorrow. The last of the year.'

He watched her go up the stairs. Superb product to have come out of so strange a marriage! And with an ache of understanding, he fancied he knew how Jessie must feel about this daughter of her flesh. Then he turned out the lights all over the first floor and stood a while in the dark hall before going up to bed. Over the creaking in the old walls and the swish of passing cars on the quiet road, he seemed to hear voices filling a vast room. All the voices in a foreign, low cacophony were saying urgent, serious things to one another, yet, heard all together, they made only a contradictory buzz and murmur so that you could make no sense of anything. You knew only that many things had gone wrong.

'I'm tired of thinking,' he said, as he went up.

He woke with the uncomfortable sensation of being looked at. Hazel was sitting on the other bed in her nightgown, staring at him.

'How long has this been going on?' he demanded.

'Why? Can't I look at you?'

He got up out of bed without answering. From the closet he took a suit and from the dresser drawer, a shirt. Then, returning to the closet, he selected a tie, took his shoes and went into the bathroom to dress. He was trembling. Another day. When he came out of the bathroom, she was still sitting there.

In the dining-room Esther, the new maid, had put his orange juice, coffee and toast on the table. She was from the South, a young, brown girl who actually looked pretty in a pink cotton uniform.

'Eggs or cereal this morning, Doctor?'

'Eggs, please,' he began. Then, the thought of eggs suddenly sticking in his throat, he changed his mind. 'Neither. I'm not hungry.'

When he had swallowed the coffee, he remembered that he hadn't shaved. He ran his hand over his chin to feel the bristles and went back upstairs. Hazel was still sitting on the edge of the bed.

In the bathroom he scraped once over, a sloppy job, but he was already late and it would have to do. He had left the bathroom door open so that the bedroom was reflected in the mirror: the unmade beds, the clutter on the dressing-table, and then Marjorie coming in to have her braids done. She had thick mouse-coloured hair, the kind that she would probably want to bleach when she was sixteen.

'Hi,' he said through the mirror. 'What are you doing today?'

'Jane's mother's taking us to her grandmother's. They've got a pool.'

'That ought to be great.' He spoke heartily. The heartiness was a form of condescension to the child, not like his usual manner, but he was conscious of trying to brighten the atmosphere. He wondered whether the child saw anything odd in the way her mother had been sitting on the edge of the bed, still in her nightgown.

The little girl stood patiently with head bowed to the brush and comb. There was such pathos in the nape with the centre part ending in those babyish wisps! He watched as Hazel worked the braids. How many hundreds of mornings would she have worked these braids before Marjorie had grown up or cut them off? Now Hazel fastened the ends with rubber bands and a narrow black ribbon tie on each. For an instant she put her face down between the girl's frail shoulder blades which, in spite of the baby fat, were outlined beneath the thin cotton of her summer dress. It looked to Martin as though she had placed a kiss there. Then, turning the child about, she kissed her again on the cheek.

'Have a good time, darling,' she said.

'Have a good time,' Martin called and they heard Marjorie clattering down the stairs.

When he came out of the bathroom, Hazel stood up. She seemed to have lost more weight during the night, her eyes were so large.

'Hazel, how long will this go on?' he asked.

'I don't know.'

'It's been weeks. What do you want of me? I've said a hundred times how sorry I am. What else can I do? How can I make it up to you? I've asked and I've asked. Tell me what you want of me,' he said desperately, 'and I'll do it.'

'What I want you can't give.'

'What is it?'

'I want it not to have happened,' she whispered.

Martin threw up his hands.

'Oh God!' she cried. 'What does a woman have to do to be like – like Flo Horvath, or the woman next door, or practically anybody up or down this road, with nothing to think about except what to have for dinner or what dress to wear next Saturday? Should it be the blue with white dots or the yellow with brown stripes?'

'Listen,' he said, 'you've got to stop feeling sorry for yourself. You try my patience, Hazel.'

'I can't.'

'How can you know what any other woman has to think about? You think you're the only one who's had any trouble? People don't – don't – ' he stumbled, 'dine on champagne and strawberries every day. That's not life.'

She clasped her hands. 'Champagne! It would be good to have a taste of that. Oh, I know one needs bread and meat and you've given me that, and I've always been grateful – '

'Bread and meat? What are you talking about?'

'I mean, you've given me a home and you're a good father: you've been kind, very kind. At God knows what cost and effort! Oh, how my heart goes out to Claire's mother!' This must be the fiftieth time she'd said that in these last two months, Martin thought. 'I always felt so terribly sorry for Jessie. It was such a sad story. So many errors that ended in sadness. Why, I even felt sorry for – for Fern, Mary, whatever you call her. Isn't that a joke? Sorry for her?'

Martin stood with a hand on the doorknob and that queer weakness draining through him again. It would follow him all day. Sitting in the train he would be unable to read the newspaper. At the office and in the hospital he would dread the homecoming, and yet at the same time look forward to it with the hope that this day, maybe at last, something might have changed while he was gone. 'I remember the first time you talked to me, the night you operated on the Moser girl. I remember every word. "I have a little girl," you said. "I haven't seen her since she was three." And then you went on and talked about how it happened. You were so honest that my heart hurt for you. "I was overwhelmed," you said. Those were your words. "I was overwhelmed." But it was all over, you said. And I understood. Those things happen. An infatuation comes and it goes, like a storm that passes. How was I to know that every word was a lie?' Her voice went up an octave, harshly, resounding as if she were calling through a tunnel. He was certain it could be heard through the closed doors and the walls.

'The children,' he warned. 'This is our business, not theirs.'

'No, we certainly don't want the children to know, do we,

that their heroic father spent the war years with the woman he loves while his wife was three thousand miles away, unable to defend herself? I wouldn't have cared, I say again, if it had been some casual affair, I would have understood. I've told you.'

'Yes, you have, six dozen times.' And Martin thought: Strange, that's exactly what Meig said to me. He asked heavily, 'What do you want me to do?'

'What do you want to do? Claire says she isn't married. Maybe you want to go back to her. Yes, maybe that's just what you want to do, go back.' She had affected a taunting posture, hand on hip, with a sly expression. It drove him to sudden fury.

'Ah, you're obsessed! There's no talking sense to you, God damn it!'

'I should never have married you! My sister always says – I never told you – you think you're too good for our family, anyway.'

Blab-mouthed pest with the bell-clapper tongue! After he'd been so decent, so generous, to them all! Surprising though, that the woman could have sensed, in spite of all his careful tact, what he thought of her. Coldly, he said, 'You're in pretty bad shape if you have to take your opinions from your sister.'

'I know what you think of her! Maybe I shouldn't have married anyone at all, or just picked out a man from the phone book to have children with and to share the expenses. We'd have no pretence of loving each other. It's a worthless trick of nature, the whole business, anyway.'

'You don't believe a word you're saying, Hazel.'

'I believe it now. Then, then I was so in love with you I wasn't thinking clearly. Maybe I wasn't even altogether sane.'

He thought for an instant: Then why can't you understand how I – And in the next instant thought: But you do understand, that's the whole trouble.

'I believed in you, Martin. How can I ever believe anyone, how can I ever trust anyone again?'

It was true. How could she? But he said, 'You can believe

in me. It's just that you ask too much. I don't say you had no right to ask it. You had every right. I simply wasn't able to give it, that's all. And I'll be sorry till the day I die.'

She put her face in her hands for a moment, then flung her head back. She looked, he thought, like a woman coming out of shock after an accident. 'So where are we?' she asked.

He wet his lips. 'We are – we are here, a family, together. We've a whole future,' he said, speaking deliberately, 'years and years, I hope. Even though the past hasn't been exactly what you wanted, can't you put it behind, since it can't be altered? I do love you, Hazel.'

'Fine words. I wonder. Nights when you stay in the city, do you bring your women to my bed in the apartment, or do you go to theirs?'

Outrageous accusation! He'd always felt a certain fastidious scorn for an habitual chaser. It had only been one he'd ever wanted, one other.

'You know that's crazy,' he said.

She sighed. 'Yes, I suppose it is. I'm sorry.'

'All right then, we're back where we started. What can I do to end this?' He caught her hand, but she pulled it away. 'Tell me. I'm deadly serious, Hazel.'

'It's all ruined. I'm a second choice. What can you expect me to feel for you?'

'You're not a second choice. I came back to you.'

'We've gone over this again and again. You came because of your children.'

True. Yet if there had been no children, might he not have come back to her anyway? Son of his parents and child of his times that he was, would conscience have driven him? After all, Hazel hadn't *asked* to marry him. There was no answer.

'I can't work and come home to this, spend the rest of my life with someone who is so miserable, Hazel.'

'Then leave! Go on, leave!'

'Damn you, I'm not going to leave and you know damn well I'm not, so cut it out!'

'I don't care,' she said very low, 'whether I live or die.'

'Ah, you've gone crazy!'

'Damn you! Do you hear? I don't care whether I live or die!'

He stood at the top of the stairs. 'You're crazy!' he shouted again. 'And I'm sick of it!'

She slammed the bedroom door. The vibration shook the walls. Below in the hall, the chandelier swayed, the prisms tinkling.

'Hazel, open that door! I want to tell you something. I have to go to work. I can't leave like this, and I have to catch the train.'

No answer.

He looked at his watch. Seven minutes to get to the station. The hell! He fled down the stairs and out the door.

Claire woke early. The curtains were swaying in the damp wind off the Sound. Once the first haze had burned off, the day would be bright. That was her first thought. Her second was of Ned. She had always believed that sex was talked to death, everywhere from learned texts to movies. Now she was certain of it. How or why pull apart, dissect and analyse that loveliness, for which there could really be no words any more than you could describe music or – One thing, though, you could say: sex feeds on its own appetite. She had been dreaming of it every night since she had left Ned behind. There was such an emptiness, such an ache! A sweetness now which she could not have imagined before that first day on the warm rocks there on the Devon hill! And it seemed to her that October was a measureless, unbearable age away.

If only Jessie would accept with generosity! 'I don't want to be reminded of home,' she complained. Strange that she should still think of Cyprus as home, even at this remove. And Claire remembered the weedy canals, thick with the green murk of algae, the bleak snow banked head-high along the streets.

'I've become a new person with another identity. This marriage will draw me back into the old.' Jessie had spoken like a petulant child or a wheedling woman, neither of which roles befitted her or was at all familiar to her daughter. 'When you marry him it will all come back,' she cried. The incredible selfishness of such words, as if you could ask someone not to marry because it would bring unpleasant memories to someone else.

'He's not even her son,' Claire had protested.

'He grew up in her house, so he is her son. He has her touch all over him. He has her ways.'

Ways. What ways? It was all ephemeral, like trying to grasp a cloud.

'It'll pass over,' Jessie said, reassuring herself. 'You hardly know him.'

But it will not pass over, Claire thought now, angrily.

'How was I to know that every word was a lie?'

Hazel's voice pierced through the wall. She was crying, and Claire sat up. Martin's voice came now, an angry rumble. The voices rose, becoming more distinct.

'What do you want me to do?'

'I should never have married you!'

Embarrassed and alarmed, Claire got out of bed and moved noisily around the room. She ran the water in the shower. This was not her affair and she had no right to hear it. A door slammed. It made a vicious noise. She thought of a finger being caught and winced as sympathetic pain shot through her own finger. Then she heard her father thudding heavily down the stairs, heard the front door close sharply and a few moments later the car backed down the drive with an impatient spurt of gravel.

She went down to the dining-room. Esther opened the swinging door from the kitchen.

'Will you have eggs or cereal, Miss Claire?'

'Cereal, please. Has Mrs Farrell had breakfast yet?'

'No, ma'am.'

Oh, why this artificial, stupid, servant-employer relationship? Claire spoke forthrightly.

'That was pretty awful this morning. Does it happen often?' And as the girl hesitated, 'It's all right, Esther. They're my family, after all, and I love them. I've just never heard anything like that before. I thought maybe you could tell me something that might help.'

'No, ma'am, I only been here three weeks and they seem

like real nice quiet people. I never heard nothing.'

'Well,' Claire remarked tritely, since some answer was required, 'these things happen, as they say, in the best of families.'

'Oh yes, married folks is bound to have their troubles. I was married once and it ain't easy. These muffins are nice and hot.'

Hazel came in from the porch. 'I thought I heard you. I'm sorry I wasn't up to greet you last night. I wasn't feeling very well.'

'All right now?'

'Oh yes. It was nothing after all.' Her eyelids were red and her lipstick hastily smudged. She wore a terry robe. 'I've got a suit on under this. I thought I'd go for an early swim,' she explained. She sat down decorously, clearing her throat like a nervous old lady making an afternoon visit.

Claire thought: Good heavens, Hazel, you needn't put on an act for me! Why don't you just cry or swear or get up and leave the room if you feel like it?

Hazel asked, 'Have you got everything you want?'

'More than I should have, thanks. These muffins! I'd be fat as a house if I lived with you!'

Hazel contradicted her. 'You'll never be fat. You'll be like your Aunt Mary.' And as Claire looked astonished, she added, 'Of course, I've never seen her. Of course, I've never seen your mother either.'

'No,' Claire said.

'Do you think you look like your mother?' Hazel persisted.

'I don't really know whom I look like.' Very odd, these remarks! And what could be their purpose?

'Life's been hard for your mother, I imagine.'

In all the years they had known each other, Hazel had observed the strictest tact concerning Jessie. The nearest she had ever come to acknowledging that Claire had a mother was to inquire, 'Everybody well at home?'

'She's managed quite comfortably,' Claire said, sounding cool without having intended to.

'I saw one of her model rooms at the Antique Show last

winter. I went with a friend of mine one afternoon. I don't know much about those things, but I thought it was the best room there. A red-and-white library, it was. She's very talented.'

'Yes. Are Marjorie and the boys gone for the day? The house is so quiet.'

'They've all gone off. Their last freedom before school starts next week.'

'You've got marvellous children, Hazel. I hope I'll be as lucky as you.'

'You've got time for children, haven't you? I suppose you'll want to wait until you finish your residency with your father.'

'Your father' came out with an edge of sharpness. But why not, after the morning's events?

'Well, Ned and I will have to work that out,' Claire replied cheerfully, the words 'Ned and I' making a fine warmth in her chest. 'You know, sometimes I feel so young, I think I have all the time in the world. Then some days it seems as if I ought to hurry up and do right away whatever I'm going to do, like having children, for instance.'

'You're twenty-six, and I'm forty-six,' Hazel said.

'You don't look it.' That was mostly true, although not this morning.

'I feel seventy-seven,' Hazel said.

She got up and went to the sideboard, picked up a saucer, examined and replaced it, then walked to the porch door and stood looking out.

Martin's not easy to live with, Claire thought suddenly. No, that's not fair! I never lived with him, so how would I know? He's compassionate, kind and perceptive; but he's difficult, too. And he's driven. That's it, he's driven. He's obsessed with this institute business. He wants perfection and he's tireless in seeking it. Yet he could shut his eyes for hours, all alone, listening to music. She'd seen him sitting there with that half-smile on his face, just letting the music pour over him, and she had wondered what he might be thinking. Complex.

Hazel's drooping posture and bleak words made gloom in

the room. Claire sought to enliven it, but found only hackneyed words.

'Everybody feels old sometimes. We all have our days.'

Hazel turned to her as though she had said something profound. 'Oh, do you think so? Do you think people are fundamentally alike? I ask you because you're a doctor, you must have had so much experience.'

'Well, the differences can be amazing sometimes. I've been on paediatrics up to this last week. I've seen mothers frantic over a minor cut, and then last week I saw a woman come with not one, but two mongoloid children. She was so courageous and accepting! I thought: I don't know how you bear it.'

'If I could have had more education,' Hazel said, 'I think I would have liked to be a doctor. As it is, nursing was as far as I got and I loved it. Except,' she reflected, 'except sometimes I'm afraid I got too personal. Some patients just touch your heart. Cancer patients, especially. I never did know which was right: to tell them they're going to die or let them think they're going to get better. What do you think?'

'Most of the psychiatrists and the chaplains say to tell the truth. They guess it anyway. And you can always tell them that many people are cured, which happens to be so.'

'Sometimes I'd turn the light out after the night's last medication and I'd think, as I left the room, how frightened they must be, lying there in the dark and wondering how much longer they had to live. But other times I think it may not be hard at all to die. After all, there's mercy in nature, too, isn't there? Maybe when people have to leave, they're ready to leave. Don't you think so?'

'So far in my experience I've actually seen just one person die. He'd had a heart attack and I can tell you he wasn't ready. He was damn scared.'

'Well, I don't know,' Hazel said vaguely, turning back to the door.

Over her shoulder and through the trees Claire saw the white sheen of water. A feathery wind moved the leaves. It was hard to think of a morning when you wouldn't be here to feel all this or hear Beethoven or lie in bed with a man's arms around you.

'Why think about things like that?' she cried impatiently, almost angrily. 'Your time won't be here for years! Do you often have thoughts like these?'

'No, no, of course not. I'm sorry. It is a stupid conversation, especially for a young woman in love.'

Claire stood up. 'I think I'll go put my suit on. I've a great book and I'm going down to the beach. You coming too?'

'I'll meet you there,' Hazel answered.

They swam the length of the beach and back, Hazel slowing for Claire's benefit.

'You could be a pro,' Claire told her as she spread a towel and propped herself against the seawall.

She had brought binoculars. It amused her to watch boats crossing the Sound. 'There's a yacht to end all yachts. Must belong to a Greek shipping tycoon. Here, look, Hazel.'

Hazel took the binoculars. 'Could you cross the ocean in that?'

'I'm sure you could. Which reminds me, I've been thinking, Dad and you really ought to have a vacation from the children. Why don't you go to Europe this fall? All those old, old places! They do something to your heart.'

'I'm sure they do.'

'Of course, I know it's hard to get the time.'

'Oh, I don't think that's the problem. Certainly it isn't for me. I don't do anything.'

Something in her tone, something oblique, touched Claire. 'What do you mean, you don't do anything?'

'What do I do? I'm just Dr Farrell's wife. I go to meetings of the Wives' Auxiliary. I'm on a committee to raise money for this or that and I'm treated with respect because I'm his wife. Otherwise I'm nobody.'

There was some truth in what she said. This was the status of women and had been so for centuries. Yet it was not altogether true. Hazel might see herself that way; yet there were plenty of women in her position who didn't see themselves that way at all. Hazel had simply lost her *persona*.

'That's not so,' Claire said emphatically. 'You *are* a

person in your own right. Your job is bringing up children, and they're fine children, too. What's more important? You've sunk into routine, Hazel, that's what's the matter with you. You have got to get away.'

Hazel stood up. Her hair streamed out in the wind. 'I'll get away. Feel how strong the wind is? I'm going in again.' She put on her cap, tucking the hair back. 'Coming?'

'Not now. I feel like reading.'

Hazel walked into the water and turned over to float.

No life except through her husband, Claire thought. Poor thing. It's all right if you're satisfied. Apparently she isn't. Thank goodness Ned will never expect that of me. We're a different generation, she thought.

The beach was empty, summer renters had returned to the city and year-round residents didn't feel such eager need to use the beach, especially in September. Claire read a few pages before growing drowsy. The sun burned through the clouds and she turned over to let it bake her back. Last sun of the year until next summer

Hazel's dog was barking. 'Oh do stop, you fool!' Claire cried crossly, having been jolted awake. Fritz, a black dachshund with a shattering voice was standing at the water's edge. Esther must have let him out of the house to follow Hazel.

Claire sat up. Hazel had been swimming parallel to the shore, up and down the length of the beach. Now, though, she was swimming away from it. What was she doing? Claire took up the binoculars. The red cap rose to the top of a swell, sank out of sight and rose again. She could clearly see the raised arm of Hazel's strong, determined crawl. No doubt of it, she was swimming out! Swimming away! Claire looked up and down the beach. There was no one in sight. She stood up and ran to the shore.

'Hazel!' she called, cupping her hands. 'Hazel! Come back!' and knew as she called that she couldn't possibly be heard. Good God, what was the woman doing? Claire stood there. She looked down at the dog as if he might know. He had stopped barking. He looked back at her with pathetic, questioning eyes. She frowned, squinting through the binoculars. The cap and the arm were growing smaller, moving with astonishing, deliberate speed away and away. What could the woman be thinking of?

And suddenly Claire knew what she was thinking of.

She thought of plunging into the water and following. But she wasn't a good enough swimmer, and wouldn't have been able to catch up with her anyway. She began to run towards the house, her shocked heart thudding, but there was no one at home except Esther, and what could she do? She looked up and down the beach. The club was a quarter of a mile away. There was no time, no time! Then she remembered the Mayfields, two houses down. They had a speedboat, moored at a little dock.

Sinking into the sand with every step, she ran. A boy of fifteen or so was pumping a bicycle tyre in the driveway.

'Please!' she cried. 'You've got a boat! The lady! Mrs Farrell! I think she's drowning! Please get the boat!'

The boy dropped the pump and stared.

'Hurry! Please, for God's sake, hurry!'

'Miss, I'm not sure I can run the boat. I only learned just now, and my dad said never to take it out without him.'

'Is your dad home? Who's home?'

'Nobody, just my grandmother. You can use the telephone.'

'There's no time, please! Try, please!'

The boy climbed into the boat and tried the engine. It sputtered and died. Claire got in. The boy bent over and tried again. It sputtered, coughed and died.

'I only learned,' he apologized.

Two minutes. Three. Claire scanned the open water. The sun had come out again and there was only a vast grey dazzle, a sheet of steel.

'There, I've got it!'

Triumph. The engine had set up a regular putt-putt-putt. Claire pointed the direction. Hazel's dog marked the place, shrilly barking again at the water's edge.

'There! Out there in a straight line from where I was sitting! Exactly straight. Hurry!'

Clouds rolled back over the sun. The air grew chill. The

summer sweetness had gone out of it and the water had roughened. The prow pointed to the sky, then fell as the little boat rose and sank through great swelling hills and troughs. Claire shaded her eyes, straining and peering.

'Sure we're going right?' the boy asked.

'Yes. Yes, I'm sure.' Claire gripped the seat. 'You look to the right, I'll look to the left. She had a red bathing cap.'

'But what would she have been – ' he began, and fell silent.

The water came alive as if some huge creature far below were rolling and turning. How could anything as frail as a human being contest its power? Claire hadn't known the Sound could turn so evil so quickly. Nor had she ever known such terror, such absolute sheer terror.

The boy, holding fast to the tiller, looked around at her, asking doubtfully, 'Could she have swum this far, do you think?'

Claire looked back at the shore, where a line of houses stood white and no larger now than scattered boulders.

'Or this fast?' the boy said. 'Even though we started later we'd have passed her anyway.'

Claire's teeth were clenched. Panic, as well as the rocking of the boat, had churned her stomach. But she commanded, 'Let's go a little further.'

The boat pitched like a roller coaster. 'We've gone a mile and a half,' the boy said.

'Yes.'

'We'd best turn back.'

'Yes.'

They stared at each other, the boy's face scared and wondering. Claire began to cry.

'Was she – is she your mother?'

'My stepmother. Oh God!'

The boy became practical and manly. 'We've got to call the police, I think. And the Coast Guard. That's what you're supposed to do.'

The boat tore back towards the shore, slapping the water, Claire still scanning the surface from side to side. Nothing. Nothing. Far out, heading north, a cruiser took its leisurely way. People in vacation mood were sitting on the deck, very likely, eating and drinking, maybe even singing in their gaiety, while, only a mile or two from them, another soul had cared so little about life that she had thrown it away. How was that possible?

I didn't see, Claire thought. All the time she was talking to me, this crazy, desperate resolve was inside her, and I didn't see. Oh Hazel, poor foolish, suffering Hazel, why did you? What made you? Out here, beyond the surf and at the bottom, they say this turbulence grows quiet. Anything which falls to the bottom lies there quietly. Or do the currents carry it away? Claire closed her eyes. The nausea mounted. At some spot, perhaps here where they were now, the exhausted, driven body had made its last effort, the arms made their last curving stroke, the legs given their final flutter-kick. The heart and the lungs had strained. How had she gone down? Struggling and crying, perhaps, having changed her mind, screaming for help?

The water was dark green, opaque, like sculptured glass. She would have cleaved it narrowly going down and then it would simply have closed over to resume its rhythm – moon rhythm, wind rhythm – as before. All this morning I was irritated with her. Yes, she bothered me with her queer remarks and her mournful, ghastly air. I wanted to get away from her. I got away from her, politely, with my book. Not that it would have made any difference if I hadn't. Or would it have? Could it have?

Objects on the beach were growing larger. Some children had come out to play with an enormous ball. The dog was still there, running up and down with a lopsided bounce. Claire and the boy went up to the house. She heard the boy taking charge, heard him at the telephone and in the kitchen, talking to Esther. She sat down on the stairs. She felt empty. The little dog came in and lay down on the bare floor where it was cool. Meat was roasting in the oven. The house looked normal, as it did every day, as it had looked only thirty, maybe forty-five minutes ago, before everything changed.

Esther began to cry, a high, terrified wail, keening on one note. From nowhere out of a quiet morning, the empty street filled. People came to stand on the lawn and murmur. Cars drew into the driveway. Men came to question Claire. Someone led her to the sofa and brought a cold drink. She looked at the clock. It was noon. Dad would be leaving the hospital for the office just about now. On his desk he kept an oval photo of herself in gown and mortarboard at the Smith commencement. Next to it stood a large colour picture of Hazel and the children, wearing Sunday clothes and nice smiles. The telephone was placed to the left of these in front of a comical wooden figurine of a singer which someone had given Dad years ago. He would pick up the telephone.

'Claire,' he'd say.

'Yes, it's Claire,' she would answer, and then what?

Oh, how could Hazel have done this thing and why did none of us know? If I'm a doctor, I ought to understand, oughtn't I? Then perhaps no one can know what lies inside another and to say you can is a pretentious lie. In the most ordinary people, and some claim that Hazel was such, for she had no particular distinction, in each of them lie secrets. Such secrets! Old childish hurts that make us what we are, powers that are never exercised, visions of what life ought to give.

The answer is, of course, there are no ordinary people.

CHAPTER TWENTY-EIGHT

The odd thing was that Martin knew so clearly what was happening to him. He understood his own progression from first numbness to most awful pity and self-accusation – (If I had gone back upstairs to talk to her that morning instead of going to work) – through sleeplessness and then sleeping-to-escape, through all of these in a long slide to the sombre place where at last depression closed around him darkly, like a curtain.

He had thoughts of falling, of crashing down the cellar stairs or worse, of opening a door and stepping into an elevator shaft. He could hear his own screams borne away in the wind of the fall. He had nightmares of interminable stairs – stairs again! – only this time going up and coming out at the top to stand on a beam ten inches wide. He was alone, ninety floors above the beams: thin as wires, they were. He awoke in a sweat of terror.

He dreamed he was addressing a meeting in some great city in some enormous, echoing hall. He mounted the rostrum. Hundreds of dark suits and white faces waited respectfully. There were coughs, chairs scraped and programmes rustled. He opened his mouth. No sound came out of it. He struggled, he strained. Still nothing came. People were staring at him. Oh panic and shame! From the back of the room came the first embarrassed, nervous laughter. It spread, that tittering laughter, that high and hooting laughter, it ran all up and down the hall. Oh God! He woke with a pounding heart.

His children turned to him at table, searching his face. Their eyes asked: Why?

'Eat your vegetables,' he would answer kindly, 'if you want to grow tall like Enoch and me.'

It wasn't fair to link Enoch with himself in the rank of adults. He was only sixteen, and seemed younger. Martin tried to remember what he had been at sixteen, but was unable to. There are times when the past closes over like waves, is hidden and drowned.

Oh, drowned.

'You spoiled my doll's hair!' Marjorie wailed at Peter, 'and I'm going to tell Mommy!'

Shocked, Enoch looked towards Martin. But Peter spoke first, scornfully.

'Mommy isn't here any more. Mommy's dead, don't you even know that?'

'Well, when she comes back, I mean.'

'She isn't going to come back. Don't you know what "dead" is?'

Enoch choked on his food, put the napkin to his mouth and left the room. Martin heard him go clattering up the stairs. Should he go to the boy with comfort of some sort? Words were needed, many words, and there were none. To die in bed of pneumonia, even to die in a crashing car or plane was acceptable. But to will to die! How to explain to his son that his mother had wanted to die?

Nevertheless, he got up from the table and went upstairs. Enoch lay on the bed, his face twisted by weeping denied. Martin laid a hand on his shoulder.

'Don't hold it back,' he said. 'It's always better just to let it out.'

But Enoch struggled. Like my mother, Martin thought. Like me. Everything held in to the bitter end – disappointments, grief, desires – all held in. So history repeats itself.

'Why did she do it, Dad?' Enoch whispered.

'Let's not talk about that, shall we? She simply swam too far out and probably didn't realize.'

'Don't treat me like a child, Dad, will you? Everybody knows it was on purpose. Please don't treat me like a child.'

'You're right. I won't then,' Martin said softly.

'Then tell me why. Don't you know?'

'Son, I don't. I wish I did.' Well, it was half a lie, but only half. Truly, he didn't understand. How could that business have mattered so much, weighed against this boy and those two down stairs? How could anything have mattered that much? Yet it had. 'Son, I don't know,' he repeated.

From the yard came the long dry rattle of a locust. The evening sun, dark and sickly yellow, glared at the window. Martin wiped his forehead. Fall would be welcome. A chill grey misty morning might be more cheerful. Any change might be more cheerful.

'Let's go down and finish dinner,' he said. 'We have to eat. We can't afford to get sick.'

Yes, the dinner hour was the worst. Esther had thoughtfully removed Hazel's chair. It stood now between the windows, facing Martin. And he knew that his puckering mouth and racing heart were symptoms of a panic state. He sat quite still, knowing that in a minute or two it would pass and ease. He studied his plate. Surrounding the mound of string beans, potatoes and meat ran a key design in gold. There were sixteen repetitions around the rim and, in the centre of the plate when the food was pushed away, there was another design, some sort of geometric enclosed within a circle. A mandala. Buddhist. O jewel in the heart of the lotus. Something like that. He shut his eyes.

The weight of everything! These poor three! And Claire, too, adult as she was and on her way, but still a responsibility of his. That young man, Mary's boy, would be arriving soon, and then that would need coping with, God only knew how. All these lives, all such a weight upon him, as if he had to lift them, pushing them up a steep enormous hill.

Things bothered him that never had before. Esther hummed in the kitchen, with a tuneless maddening drone. He wanted to scream; Quiet! You're driving me out of my mind! In the early mornings, gardeners arrived to mow the lawns all up and down the road. Lately they had introduced a wicked new device, a leaf blower with a sustained humming howl. Then came the garbage truck and its infernal grinder. Wherever you went in this frantic world you heard metal grating and power droning; cars, planes, radios, lawn mowers, attacked the ears, the head, the very soul of a man. He could have gone out and smashed them all. And he longed for an empty place, anywhere at all, with no one or nothing in sight, just wind and trees.

Hazel's dog came whining. It was always sniffing at her closet, although Claire had removed the clothes. Claire had been so tirelessly strong and sensible during those first terrible days, caring for the children, the house and telephone and all the letters to be answered. He had made her take Hazel's new fur coat, scarcely worn, and a pearl necklace. The rest of the jewellery was in a safe deposit box to be kept for Marjorie. Not that there had been all that much! He worried that he had not been generous enough with Hazel. She had so rarely asked for anything. He ought to have insisted. She'd been such a simple woman. Simple! Oh, my God. So his thoughts ran like a fox pursued, darting, hiding, running to cover and dashing to escape.

But he must pull himself together. He must. If only he had someone to talk to, someone to hear everything from the beginning! There was no one. He certainly couldn't talk to Claire, not to his daughter. He thought of Alice, his sister, so much like himself, or so she had been when they were young. Flesh of his flesh; she would, if she were here now, put her hand on him in mercy and love, without judgement. Yet had she really been all that much like himself? So long ago it had been; still he could recall in her a strain of Puritan abstinence. He thought of Jessie. Curious that he should think of her now! And yet, in those long days when they had first known each other, there had been no mind more responsive to his own.

Tom ought to have been the one. Damon and Pythias, David and Jonathan: yes, up to a point, they were. Trust and loyalty lay between them. Kindly Tom would claim to understand, but he wouldn't understand. For he had never wanted very much. Smallness contented him in all things. But he, Martin, had wanted everything – an exquisite love, exalted knowledge, the warmth of a family, all the colour and music of the earth. He had been born wanting them.

His hands bore down on the arms of the chair where he sat through that first dreadful week; the pressure was wearing the cloth away. There came a spell of rain. It sluiced through the gutters and splattered on the roof. It dropped in gusts from the trees and churned the Sound. And he sat on, listening to the many sounds of rain. Was there a motif of water in his life? Storm and flood had torn him too early from his mother's womb and killed those other children, whose faces in old hazy snapshots were so real to him. How had his parents survived their loss? He thought, too, of the story of the scalded child, which, of all his father's tales, he had never forgotten.

How Hazel had loved water! Sometimes they'd gone in the winter to walk on the beach; he, hating the cold, had done so for her sake only. But she would tie a babushka under her round chin and laugh at herself. 'I look like my own great-grandmother on the farm in Hungary.'

'I hate this house,' Martin said aloud, 'and all this water. We'll never go near water again.'

Friends came to help. How many friends they had! People brought food and offered to take the children. It was astonishing how good people were. And still there was no one to talk to. The words they spoke were mechanical, as were his answers. None of them came near the heart of things.

Back in the city, he thought: Everything is loose, life has come loose. I must tighten it up again. I must. Do things with my children. I'll take them to the zoo, he resolved, buy books and read together. So his mind ran.

He could sit at his desk across from a tense and frightened patient, listening and replying, but all the while, at the bottom of his mind, were his children: I robbed them of their mother. He was offered reassurance: children forget. But that was certainly not true. Anyway, Enoch was no child. He suffered, Martin suspected, daily, hidden lacerations. His mother's son. Mine too, Martin thought.

In the elevator, on the street waiting for the light to change, his teeth were clenched and his jaws ached with the tension. Would he be able to manage everything? The office, the looming responsibility of the institute, the house, the children? Yes, of course he would. He would have to. Yet an evening came when, from his chair in the den, he heard them quarrelling fiercely over a bag of doughnuts, which their mother would not have allowed them to eat before dinner. He knew he ought to rise and go in to stop the uproar, but he only stirred in the chair and didn't go. Let Esther handle it as best she could! It was suddenly too much for him to cope with.

The telephone rang. 'Just to remind you,' Leonard Max said, 'we've got the Devita woman at seven-thirty in the morning.'

Martin had been going regularly to the office and the hospital, working automatically and well. But perhaps he hadn't really been working all that well? And all at once he knew he wasn't prepared to operate in the morning. He heard himself saying, 'I don't think I can make it. You'd better get someone to help you.'

'I can get O'Neill, I'm pretty sure,' Leonard said quickly. Too quickly? 'Martin, maybe you should take a rest. People have been saying maybe you should.'

'They have?'

'After what you've been through, a few weeks abroad would do a lot for you.'

'I couldn't leave my family to go abroad, you know that.'

'Well, then, how about a rest at home? Sleep late, relax, spend some time with the kids. You could say you'd gone away on vacation and nobody would bother you.'

Falling, falling.

'Yes, I could do that,' Martin said.

Leonard Max was hearty. 'You'll be back better than ever.'

'Thanks, Len,' Martin said, hanging up.

He's thinking that I'll never be back, I can tell by his voice, so comforting, so cheerful. I'm finished, everything's ebbed out.

He got up and locked the door, then put a stack of records on the turntable, three hours' worth of Beethoven, Schubert and Brahms. He pulled the curtains shut, so that the room grew soft and dark. Like the inside of the womb, he thought scathingly, and lay down.

It was surprisingly easy to hide. For a week he feigned the flu.

Claire kept telephoning, but he warned her away from his contagion.

At the beginning of the second week, on a raw November afternoon, he got up on sudden impulse from the chair, where he had listlessly been reading the news – all discouraging, nothing but strife – put on his coat and went out. He had walked three blocks down the avenue when a wind came up and it began to sleet, so he turned around and went home. It was not the weather that had driven him, though. It was rather a peculiar sensation that had overwhelmed him. The world was too large with too many people in a hurry. There was too much empty air. He knew that these feelings were bizarre, and he was frightened.

Now he had an excuse to stay inside for another few days! He had foolishly gone out too soon and was running a fever again. Claire scolded him by telephone with threats of pneumonia. He ought to be ashamed of himself, she said. He promised meekly not to do it again.

But he couldn't maintain this pretence, couldn't stay in hiding. He would have to force himself, find something pleasant to do. Yes, that was it, find something happy. Surely there was something colourful and happy left in the world? Christmas shopping, perhaps, before the season got too late and crowded? It was a long time since he had bought anything or even been in a store.

So,with a careful list, he set forth. He would walk downtown. Exercise, that was the thing; the healthy body, the fast walk. Make the heart work and breathe deeply.

A truck, swinging around a corner, almost ran him down so that he jumped back in terror. 'Why the hell don't you look where you're going?' the driver swore.

A fat man got out of a taxi, fumbling in the pocket of his bulky overcoat, while traffic behind the taxi blared furious horns. And these sounded like swearing too. Everyone was so irritable, so angry!

He thought he would buy a sweater for Claire, but he wasn't sure of the size, and wasn't sure whether she would like a plain one or a cardigan with an embroidered collar. He stood a long time looking at the sweaters, knowing he was taking too long and unable to make up his mind. The saleswoman, a dry creature of outrageous hauteur, left him for another customer. 'Well, when you've decided,' she said, 'I really can't – '

Oh go to hell, he shouted at her silently, full of hatred. It seemed to him that the arrogance of these expensive goods, which she merely handled and would never own, had been transferred to her person. Strange. Very strange. And he left without buying anything.

On the sidewalk in front of the store, he stood and watched the women going in and out. They were like animals on the prowl for meat with their slouching walk and their darting, avaricious eyes. Parasites and predators, he thought contemptuously, spending the hours away while their husbands laboured, and half of them not even grateful, he'd guess. Hazel had never been like that.

He was terribly tired. His overcoat weighed him down. Turning towards home, he walked a few blocks north and then east. Everyone seemed to be hastening in the opposite direction, so that he was constantly bumping shoulders and grazing people who were annoyed with him for having done so. He felt out of breath.

A little crowd stood before a pet shop window looking at a display of parakeets in ornate cages that were too cramped. Poor marvellous creatures! Turquoise and jade and topaz, brilliant as any jeweller's art! A masterwork, each one, with its powerful, tiny heart and net of tiny veins; an imprisoned marvel, meant to ride the bright air. And as so often, tears came. A man leaving the shop looked at him with alarm, but being well-bred, looked immediately away.

He must go home. At the corner he tried to hail a taxi, but they were all occupied, and he began to walk. Faces wavered as he passed. He tried to focus on them, growing queasy with the effort. He began to walk faster. Something was at his back; he was being pursued. Now he was almost running. The thing was coming closer, reaching to grasp the small of his back. And at the same time he knew that there was nothing there, that he was having what they layman might call a nervous breakdown, or at least, the harbinger of one.

When he arrived at the apartment house, he was panting. He thought the doorman, young Donnelly, pink-faced and fresh out of Ireland with the class deference still in him, looked at him strangely. But all he said was, 'Good evening, Dr Farrell.' The upholstered elevator cage took him to his floor. He was safe, then, in his own apartment, in his own room.

But his heart kept pounding. Perhaps there were symptoms he didn't recognize? After all, he was not a cardiologist. Heart attack. Taste of salt, of blood under the tongue. The chest squeezed in an iron fist. Swirls of red and yellow lights before the eyes like a Jackson Pollock picture: Daubs they were, in spite of fashionable opinions! What if he were dying? He would vomit on the carpet, Hazel's good rug. Or struggle to the bathroom and fall on cold tile, clutching the smooth porcelain sides of the tub. Pa had died clutching the dining-room table.

He lay down on the bed without taking off his overcoat and thought: I'm dying.

'You can't go on like this,' Claire said.

Martin opened his eyes. 'I fell asleep. What are you doing here?'

'Enoch called me. He looked in and saw you. He was scared.'

'No need to be. I'm weak from the flu and I fell asleep, that's all.'

'Dad, you're not fooling anyone, so don't waste your breath. Sit up,' she ordered. 'Let's get your coat off. Now lean back.' She moved briskly. 'You're shivering. I'll get you a brandy.'

He felt, in the face of her authority, like a child. 'Claire, Claire, I'm falling apart,' he said suddenly and for the first time was not ashamed.

She took him in her arms. 'Dad. Dear, dear. No, we're not going to let you.'

'There are things you don't understand.'

'Do you want to tell me about them?'

'I don't think I can.'

'Don't then, if you think you'll be sorry afterwards. But,' she said steadily, 'you really ought to talk to somebody and get it off your mind.'

Off your mind! As if you were excising a tumour! That would be easier. A tumour can at least be seen, not like this amorphous, secret pressure in the head where, so they say, almost any unsuspected thing can lurk: desires to rob a bank, rape a neighbour's wife or assassinate the president, God only knows what.

He began, 'You don't know why Hazel – '

Something in his daughter's expression – oh, he had from the beginning been so sensitive to the slightest nuance of her expression – something said to him that she might know.

'I've a pretty good idea. She found out about you and Mary.'

Martin sighed. He put his hands on his knees, turned them over to regard the heartline on the palm and the whorls on the fingertips, then back to the cuticle. No pair of hands in the world like any other pair, no life like any other life.

'It was in California. We met a man I'd known during the war.'

Claire said softly, 'If I were a man I would fall in love with Mary, too, I think. Maybe you should just have stayed there after the war. Ned thinks you should have.'

'Ned does? He's very young.'

The room was still. No sound came from the apartment. It was as though the household had suspended its life in wait for Martin. And suddenly anxiety came fluttering back like bird wings in the air, like those poor, caged creatures he had been looking at that afternoon.

'Ah, Hazel!' he cried. 'I destroyed her anyway! Didn't I?'

'No,' Claire said. 'She did it herself. You are the only one who can destroy yourself. Other people can't, unless you let them.'

'You believe that?'

'I do.'

'I hear your mother talking.'

'Well, she's got a lot of strength. And Hazel didn't, no fault of hers, God help her.'

Years ago when he was an intern and that nurse – Nora, was it? – had killed herself, he remembered thinking how he'd hate to be in that man's shoes.

'You make it all sound very simple,' he said.

'I don't mean to. Listen to me. Listen. You've been stumbling along with a load of guilt enough to break your back. But you were good to Hazel! You gave her good years! She was totally content till the very end.'

'If I could undo it,' Martin began.

'Well, you can't. You know what your trouble is? You think you ought to be a saint and you're only a man.'

'You think so?'

'I know so. Everything in your life has to be perfect, and it can't be.'

Martin laughed. It flashed through his mind that he hadn't laughed in months. 'You've analysed me pretty cleverly, I think. I hope you'll do as well with Ned.'

'Does that mean you've decided to approve?'

'No, it just means I've decided not to fight it.'

'Because you know you'd lose.'

'Not only that. I want you to be happy, Claire. As long as you're bent on doing it, I don't want you to start off with bad feelings, that's all.'

She gave him a look of purest gratitude. 'Thanks, Dad. I'll bring him here, then.'

'Have you brought him to your mother's?'

'For a short visit. Naturally, Mother was correct but cold as ice.'

'The pain's too deep, too old. And Claire, on my part I want to say –'

'You want to say you don't want to see Ned's mother. You won't have to, I promise.'

They sat for a while without speaking.

'I wish it could be different – joyous and warm,' Martin murmured.

'It's all right, Dad. For me things don't always have to be perfect.'

He felt something soft and calming in his chest: strength, pouring in some occult way from this child of his back intc him. It was a fine tingling, a rising of hope, anticipation Whatever it was, it was a benison. And just as he had known when he had been falling into sickness, now just as surely he recognized the first faint start of healing.

The door opened and three heads appeared around its edge.

'Come in,' Claire called. 'Don't be afraid. Dad's feeling much better. He's going to be all right.'

CHAPTER TWENTY-NINE

The new apartment was complete a month or more before the wedding and Ned had officially moved in. Most of the time, Claire stayed there with him, too. She was perfectly aware that Jessie knew. They simply didn't talk about it.

With a certain amount of reverse snobbism, or perhaps only to be different from her mother, Claire had always liked to say that she cared not a whit for things. Yet now, because these particular things were really her own, she liked to walk around touching them or just to look at them in the light that poured from the afternoon sky when the curtains were drawn back. Many of these new possessions were actually old: her grandfather's leather sets of Thackeray and Trollope, brought from Europe long before the century had turned and handed over with appropriate ceremony by her father; the blue-and-white quilt made by Grandmother Farrell that Aunt Alice had generously parted with for Claire; a lacquered Chinese chest that Jessie had been saving for a client, but had given to her when she saw that of all the objects in the shop, it was the single one that Claire really wanted.

Then of course there was a bed, the centre, the heart of the new home. They had bought it together after days of searching: an outsized Victorian relic, large enough to make babies in blissful comfort and later to nurse them and play with them on winter Sunday mornings. They liked to fantasize.

'We used to think our parents' bed was a ship or a castle,' Ned had told her. 'Those shadowy halls could be a forest or an ocean full of scary things, and we'd run through them as fast as we could and pounce on that safe bed in the lamplight.'

Except for the children, Claire thought, there hadn't been

much joy in that bed. Not much joy anywhere for Mary Fern.

Ned's key turned in the lock, and he came in looking, now that he had given up the umbrella and the bowler, like any prosperous, young American coming home from work. He hadn't expected her so early, and she was pleased to surprise him.

She laughed, 'You're the only person whose face wreathes in smiles. I always thought that such a silly description, but you know, your face does wear a smile like a wreath. A conquering hero's wreath.'

'Idiot,' he said, kissing her.

'I've brought stuff to eat, sandwiches from that great deli down the block. And Mother's cook made a cake. I snitched it because Mother's up in Vermont and there's nobody at home to eat it.'

'When you said "stuff to eat", I thought you meant you'd cooked a dinner.'

'God, no! I can't cook, Ned. That's one thing I never fooled you about. But I will learn. As soon as I've more time, I'll really learn.'

She had set the table in the kitchenette, and now she put out the food. 'Here's potato salad, here's coleslaw, a French bread and a beautiful melon.'

'Leave that a minute and sit down. I want to tell you something,' Ned commanded. He sounded so serious that she turned at once from the refrigerator, but his eyes were smiling with excitement.

'There's another silly expression that fits you. "His eyes danced." Isn't that ridiculous? Have you ever seen eyes dance? I never have except for yours. They're dancing right now.'

He grasped her hand and pulled her down. 'Listen. Listen. Anderson called me in today and said we were going to the president's office. For a minute, I got cold. Jergen never sees anybody. I didn't think he even knew me except maybe from seeing me in the elevator or the men's room. No, not even the men's room – he has his own. But as we were walking down the hall, Anderson told me what it was about. They're reorganizing the offices in Hong Kong. The operation there has been falling way behind and the top man is due for retirement anyway. So Jergen asked Anderson to make a recommendation, and – and, Claire, I'm the one!'

Claire put her sandwich back on the plate. 'I don't understand,' she said.

'Me! Us! I'm to be head of the office! We're going to live in Hong Kong! They know we're being married and they were very nice about a honeymoon and all that, so we won't have to be there until September first. Also, of course, they'll pay for moving our stuff. What do you think of that?' And he sat back with his face wreathed in smiles and his eyes dancing.

She was perfectly sane and she had heard it all correctly. Still, the thing was totally unreal.

'I know it's a shock. Here we were settled with a fine view of the East River, and instead we'll be on the other side of the world with a view of the junks in Hong Kong Harbour.'

Claire wet her lips. Then she took a swallow of water. 'But aren't you forgetting something? I've got one of the most desirable internships in the world here at Fisk and a Fisk neurological residency next year. So this can't make any sense to me, Ned.'

'Darling, I know it must be awfully upsetting to you. Anything as totally unexpected and sudden as this – I know.' He put his arms around her, his safe arms. She laid her head on his shoulder. Then she remembered something.

'You talked about writing. You used to dream about being an investigating journalist, probing in hidden places, exposing wrongs, you said.'

'Yes, I know, that was all very fine, but I've come up against hard facts and the hard facts are that you have to seize your opportunities. And this is my opportunity. A bird in the hand, as the saying goes. Darling, I'm sorry. So sorry to be confusing things like this for you when you've been so efficient, working so hard and still managing to get this apartment together and . . . and just doing the work of two people. I'm just damned sorry to do this to you.'

'Well then, do you have to?'

'A man wants to get ahead, Claire.' Ned spoke softly. 'A

man needs to. I want you to depend on me. That's what being a man is all about.'

She drew away. Depend on him? Yes surely, in a way, but –

'Can't we just rearrange our thinking and look at this as a great adventure?'

'"Our" thinking? I'm the one who is being asked to give up –'

Now Ned interrupted, 'I'm not asking you to give anything up, Claire. We won't be there forever, because I most certainly don't intend to live in the Orient for the rest of my life, and anyway, that's not what they plan. I'm sure we'll be transferred. In fact, Anderson said, speaking unofficially, of course, it wouldn't be more than four or five years.'

'Four or five years!'

'Yes. And you'd still be young enough to begin a residency then. Your father would get one for you. We'd have a lot of money saved up, too,' he said enthusiastically. 'There's extra pay for working overseas, you know.'

He didn't see that she was devastated. There'd been a photo in the paper that morning of a woman who had come home to find her house burned down. All day that anguished face had kept rising in front of Claire's eyes. And now her own face must be looking like that . . . But Ned was sitting there, looking fresh as he always managed to look after a day's work, not perceiving her at all.

He reached out to unwrap a sandwich.

'You must be crazy,' she said.

'Crazy?' he repeated mildly. It took a good deal, she knew, to ruffle him, and this steadiness, this calmness in storm, was a quality she had cherished in him. 'Crazy?' he said, and this time he sounded hurt. 'I thought you'd be thrilled for me. I don't think you know how unusual this is. I'm the youngest man ever to head a foreign office for the firm, and I'm new on the job to boot.'

'Oh,' she cried, 'oh, Ned, of course I know! I'm terribly proud of you.' Actually she hadn't thought about it until just now. 'I do see what a fabulous honour it is, I really do!'

'It's more than an honour. I'll be earning thirty-five

thousand a year, plus all the extras!'

'It's wonderful, of course it is! But what about me? I can't just table my work, can I? I can't just put it aside for a while and pick it up again some time later when it's more convenient, can I?'

'You could.' He spoke gently. 'I know it's not the ideal way, but it's not impossible, especially in these circumstances.'

Dumbfounded, she made no answer. And he went on, 'After all, you're not a man. You don't have to get through with it as fast as possible to earn a living.'

'Earn a living!' she cried now. 'That's not what it's all about for me! I thought you understood me better than that! Medicine is all I ever wanted, Ned! It's my – my life!'

'I do understand you. You know I do. And yet I thought I was your life. Your love and your life.'

Claire got up from the chair and leaned against the refrigerator. The hard, slick metal cooled her burning shoulders and back. 'Oh God!' she said, closing her eyes. When she opened them, he was staring at her. He looked frightened. She tried to speak very quietly now, with seemly control. 'What I mean is, we can't, we mustn't lose contact with each other over this. You see – oh, I don't want to sound conceited, but perhaps you don't know how hard it is, don't understand that this residency is an – an achievement. And it wasn't my father's name that did it. It was my own record. Dr Macy's daughter was turned down, and – and others were, and it's not something I can possibly walk away from and begin over in five years.' She went suddenly weak. 'Five years, Ned! Five years out of my life! I would never go back, and in your heart, you must know it.'

'You could if you wanted to.'

She couldn't answer. It occurred to her that the little supper, the fruit, the iced tea and the sandwiches looked pathetic, lying untouched on the table, waiting and wasted as she would wait and waste.

'If I don't accept, I'll stay an underling in the firm. Once you refuse a thing like this, they never offer you anything worthwhile again, don't you understand?'

She did understand; that was the hard part of it. She knew it meant a harsh, continual struggle to survive out there in the world.

'My father left no great legacy, Claire. I've got to make it on my own.'

'I know you do.'

'I have a feel for this work. At any rate, it's what I've got my start in and I can't very well become a – a lawyer or a civil engineer, for heaven's sake, can I?'

'No.'

'And I like the work. Naturally, people like what they do well. But it's really incredible to be paid so much for doing what you like – putting together words that can change people's minds.'

'I see.'

'You get a feeling of power. Strength and power in a world-wide enterprise.'

'I see.'

There was silence. Lowering her eyes to the floor, she studied their feet: Ned's still in his good English shoes, russet with a fine gloss; hers in the summer sandals she had put on when she came home. They were careless, happy shoes made for running on grass or sitting beside a pool with a drink in hand. Her thoughts ran at this odd tangent. Then she raised her eyes.

'What shall we do?'

He stood up and strode into the living-room as if the kitchenette were too confined for his feelings. Two or three times he walked the length of the room. She understood by the pounding of his feet that frustration was turning into anger. Then he turned upon her. It came to her that she had never before seen his anger.

'How can you ask what we shall do! I've been trying my best to explain! How can there be any question? We'll go where I can carve out a future for ourselves. It's the man who supports the family, after all.'

'Not always, Ned.'

'Well, it's still the usual pattern. The primary income is the man's.'

'That will change. It's changing now. Why am I not entitled to use my energy and brain as much as you are? Tell me, why?'

'Listen, Claire, I don't want to get into an abstract argument. Sometimes though I wonder whether your mother really gave you the best example.'

'I'll say she did!'

'Not if this is the result.'

At ten-thirty they agreed to stop wrangling and went to bed. Exhausted, Claire fell immediately asleep, but in the middle of the night woke up. The wind was blowing the shade. It was snapping, as if it were angry, which was absurd; but still it seemed as if the world were threatening at the window. She got up to close it and went back to bed and lay there thinking. She thought about all the hundreds of millions of men who had been born and died and will be born and die, so many transient little lives, each lifting its tiny head above the mass of the rest, each seeking out one other tiny body to cling to. With such fierce, tiny strength, they were drawn to one another as the magnet pulls towards the north. Why just this man, this woman and no other?

I want a fabric to be woven between us, a strong, unbroken tissue, unblemished from beginning to end, not like Martin or Jessie or Alex or Mary.

Ned moved, making a sound like a mutter or a sigh. His dream was troubling him. What was his dream? She reached out her hand to wake him, to say, 'Oh Ned, my dear and darling, what shall we do? Don't leave me!' But, thinking then it would be cruel to wake him from merciful sleep, she drew her hand away.

'What does he think?' Martin cried. 'That medical training is something you put down and take up like a piece of knitting, as simply as that?' And she knew he was thinking: My girl, my brilliant girl, after your grades, your record, your potential, and you're to give it all up so he can go off to an advertising job? An advertising job, compared with medicine?

'He could get a job elsewhere, after all,' Martin said more

calmly. 'Inconvenient, perhaps, but not impossible.'

'That's exactly what Ned said about me.'

'Well, it's entirely different, and I'm astonished that he doesn't see it.'

'Dad, don't turn your anger against Ned. Help us. Advise us. We've spent three days talking, and I don't know how to solve it.' She wiped her eyes roughly. 'I don't want to cry. You know I hate crying.'

'Yes. Yes, you're between a rock and a hard place, as my father used to say.' Martin sighed. 'Sometimes I think we doctors ought to be like priests: don't marry and don't have children. When there's no one you love and have to care about, then you can do what you want. Nothing can hurt you.'

'Well, we're not priests, are we?' And she thought as she pressed him, of all the secret things written inside us, as on a scroll, unrolling back and back.

'Ah, you know in what direction my hopes lie! You're my own and I want so much for you. How can I think clearly, fairly? For you I want "the world and all that's in it".'

'Then you don't know how to solve this either,' she murmured.

'You will have regrets either way – how I wish I could spare you!' he said gently. 'Only remember that you're not alone. I'm here, for what I'm worth.'

She thought: All of a sudden he looks the way he will look twenty years from now. He raised his eyes to hers. She thought she had never seen eyes of such soft, penetrating sadness.

The argument had gone into the second hour of the fourth day. 'Machismo, Ned,' Claire cried. 'That's what it is! You have to play the dominant male to show you're not like your father.'

'That's a Goddamned rotten thing to say!' Ned cried.

She was instantly contrite. 'I know it. I apologize. I didn't mean it that way. But you are being a heavy male, you really are.'

'When you break free of your father and his ambitions for

you, maybe you'll grow up and be a woman,' he said coldly.

She was furious. 'Maybe one day you'll learn there's more to being a woman than just taking care of a man.'

'Don't dodge the issue. Ever since I came to New York I've seen and thought – I haven't spoken out but I'm going to now – you're letting your father plan your life! How do you even know you want to be a neurosurgeon? *He* decided it for you when you were some sort of a child prodigy and now you – '

'You're crazy! Nobody ever said I was a prodigy. Don't make a fool out of me! Putting words in my mouth, or my father's!'

The air quivered between them with the intensity of summer storm.

'I'm going for a walk,' Ned said. 'I need to get out. Maybe it will clear our thoughts, being quiet for a while.'

She heard the elevator door clash open, followed by the whirr of its descent. 'Whither thou goest,' and so forth. Ought she not go to the ends of the earth with him? Had she not come from a long line of women who had done just that, following their men across oceans, bravely leaving home and parents, all the dear, familiar places? 'Whither thou goest . . .' Yes, but women were different then, and I am different; certainly not better, only different. I am a doctor first. Secondarily, I happen to have female organs. Why should I be controlled by a uterus and a pair of ovaries? Why should these make all the difference?

Maybe, maybe, he will come back from the walk with another point of view. Maybe he will come to an understanding of what I mean. You love a man, and suddenly you're fighting. He turns into a stranger.

She got up and put a record on the player. This need for music, this, too, was a legacy from her father. Laying her head back, she willed herself into another place and time, while Respighi's 'Birds' rustled in Rome's cypresses. Thousands of birds fluttered and wheeled against a background of triumphant Sunday bells. The birds filled her head. Most living of all living things, so free, whirling and beating through the windy sky! So free!

The door opened and Ned came back. He turned the record off.

'We've talked it all out,' he said, not looking at her. 'We've gone as far, I think, as words can take us. So for the last time I ask you. Have you changed your mind? Will you come with me?'

She took a deep breath. 'No, Ned. I can't.'

His face was closed up tight, like faces at funerals. Who knows what regrets and terrors lie behind the faces you see at funerals?

'You see,' she said, 'I have to do what I have to do.'

He looked at her. 'Well, that's it, then, isn't it? I suppose it has to be. I'll take my things in the morning when you're out. It will be easier that way.'

'Yes,' she said.

Once she had been standing on a sidewalk where a dreadful accident had happened in the street. Someone had been run over. She'd had the same sense of unreality then, queer and remote as voices heard across water or snow.

'Well,' he said and stopped. He opened his mouth again to speak and closed it without another word and went out. Again she heard the clash of the door and the whirr of the elevator as he went down. But this time was the last. And silence fell.

The apartment looked abandoned, although two months after Ned's departure, Claire was still living there. The cleaning woman had been in, leaving fresh towels in the bathroom and the morning paper on the coffee table. It was cold in the room, even though on the street below heat blasted yellow-hot as if from an untended furnace. She turned down the air conditioner and sat huddled, shivering and swaying. I must look old, she thought. Bitter, old, and as desolate as I feel.

For almost a month now, she had known she was pregnant. And she sat with her secret knowledge, looking around the room as though in some corner of a cabinet or shelf lay an answer to her questions.

A closet door had been left ajar, and on the top shelf she saw a forgotten hat, that crushable Irish country hat which he had worn in England and brought with him when he came here. He had come here to be with her. That hat looked sad. In Hong Kong now he would be wearing a panama hat, wouldn't he? Or maybe one of those tropical topees? Or did they only wear those in India? He would be wearing a white suit and drinking a gin sling in a garden, or else in some cool room where a ceiling fan turned slowly. No, that was Somerset Maugham in Singapore, half a century ago. In Hong Kong he would be in an air-conditioned room like this one, fourteen floors above the street. Would he be working late and thinking now and then of Claire?

My nerves, she thought. Good God, my nerves! I'm a moth beating and bumping on a windowpane, trying to get out. Get out where?

Feeling ice-cold, she ran a tubful of hot water. But her shoulders and knees, protruding from the water, were still cold. And she wondered whether the creature inside her, the tiny, fishlike thing, could feel the cold. Some said it wasn't really alive yet, but of course it was. There might even be a way in which it could sense the misery in its mother. Who really knew? It sleeps. It rocks in the warm pool and already contains within itself all that it will ever be: a cherub with curled lashes and a cleft chin, like its father's; a fleet running boy; a timid, good girl with large feet. To destroy these possibilities? Yet, to be a child without a father?

She got out of the tub and dressed herself, then began to cry. A tabloid writer would describe 'heart-rending cries', she thought disgustedly. I'm sick of tears. But the truth was that they were heart-rending. My heart is rent. I hope they can't hear in the apartment below because I can't stop. She slid to the floor and knelt with her face on the seat of the chair. I'm crying for everything. Why have I spoiled everything? Why has he spoiled everything. Damn him! Still, there's nothing else I could have done. And now, this baby –

Think! Don't let tears and fears carry you downhill! Fear rides a toboggan over the ice; once it slips past the brim of the hill, it can't stop. So hold on, Claire, hold on.

Across the park in the heart of the city there waits a man with an expert knife, a skilled and sterile knife that can solve the problem, that can destroy or save, whichever way you care to regard it. *Sub rosa* he works, but he is well recommended. Doctors send their wives and their mistresses to him. Medical students send their friends.

Nevertheless, fear followed at her back. It pursued her into a waiting room which was no different from a dentist's, with an etching of the Cologne Cathedral and a neglected sansevieria in a green pot. It reminded her of those places where you take a crucial examination, where a pencil sharpener grinds, a proctor assembles a pile of blue books, and then a crisp rustle tells you it is too late to run away and claim to be sick. Too late.

'Mrs Blake,' the nurse called. For a moment she forgot that was the name she had given, so that the nurse had to repeat it. All heads in the room turned towards Claire as she rose. They were all scared. And they all knew that was not her name.

It was done with extraordinary speed.

'Well, that wasn't too bad, now, was it?' the doctor said.

He was three-quarters of the way out of the door. He hadn't spoken a word up till then.

'No, it wasn't,' Claire said, unclenching her teeth. Actually, the pain had been quite bearable. She remembered the sound of scraping and willed herself not to think of it.

'You can go home now,' the nurse told her.

'Can I do anything?'

'Well, I wouldn't suggest a ten-mile hike. Rest today and take it easy for the next few days, that's all.'

Heads went up again when she came out into the waiting room. She felt so sorry for them all. She wanted to say: Don't be afraid, it's not so bad. A young girl sat there, a child no more than fourteen. A couple sat there; they were no longer young. He was shabby in a crumpled summer suit. Probably they already had more children than they could afford. She felt sorry for them all.

Out on the sidewalk she stood hesitating. Suddenly she didn't want to go back to her apartment alone, which surprised her, for she had imagined herself, when this was over, going back to her own place and quietly resting, pulling ierself together, not so much in body as in mind.

Mother was still in Vermont. She decided to go to her 'ather's. Having overcome his dread of water, he had rented ı summer house again near a beach. She hailed a taxi and lrove to Grand Central.

There was no one but Esther in her father's house when ;he arrived. Claire sat down in the kitchen.

'You want something to eat, Miss Claire?'

'No thanks.' I only want not to be alone. 'You just came ›ack from visiting your folks in Florida, my father says.'

'Yes. Tarpon Springs. My kids live there with my mother.'

'It's beautiful there, isn't it?'

'Yes, but you can't earn enough to support the kids.'

'How many do you have, Esther?'

'Me? I only have two. But my sister, she's got eight here in Vew York. Six born since her man left her.'

'How do they live?'

'Oh, she on the Welfare. Gotta be.'

'Tell me, Esther. Why does a girl have all those children? I nean, because she's all alone and – '

Esther raised her eyes. The lashes rolled slowly, scorn-'ully up from her cheekbones as if she were reluctant to eveal a deep, old enmity. 'That's just the reason. A girl gets onely.'

Lonely, Claire thought, wondering. I'll need to learn so nuch about people that I don't know at all.

She got up and walked to the kitchen door, looking out at he lawn where stood the picnic table, the string hammock ınd the barbecue, the apparatus of American suburbia. At he bird-feeder a cardinal feasted on sunflower seeds, while ıis partner picked up the overflow on the grass. Suddenly nto the silence came a running flash and a flurry of desperate hrills.

'Oh, Esther, come!' Claire screamed. 'The cat's got the ;ardinal! Come! Run!'

Esther ran outside and came back. 'It's too late. Don't ook,' she said with surprising gentleness. 'There's nothing 'ou can do.' And she turned Claire away from the pathetic ıeap of scarlet feathers. 'Don't you feel well, Miss Claire?

My, you feel very hot. I'll make you a cold drink.'

With curiosity and disbelief, the girl looked into the face o this strange woman who could cry so over the death of bird.

Towards dawn, Claire woke. A shaft of light fell into he eyes, making her head ache. Then she became aware o another ache, deep in some pit between her spine and he stomach. Something was knotted, tight and hard and sor She felt her forehead. It was hot. Then she remembere yesterday, and alarm struck. Could there be anythin wrong? No, no, surely there was nothing. It was only th natural effect of an unnatural procedure. It would certainl take a few days to feel normal again.

She drifted back into sleep, turning her head away fro the irritating light. When she woke again, the soreness insic had turned to pain. She was shivering and her head was ho it felt hollow. No, this surely wasn't right.

She sat up in bed just as Marjorie came through the doo The girl's long hair fell like a curtain over her shoulders.

'You said you'd do my braids for me.'

'Of course. Sit on the bed.' Claire raised her arms. The were weighted at the shoulders. She raised herself in the be forcing her strength, forcing cheerfulness. 'Got plans fo today?'

'Lisa's mother's taking Peter and me to the beach.'

'Oh fine!'

People were thoughtful of these two who had no mothe Children without mothers. Mothers without childre Would hers have been a sturdy peaceable child like this on An affable boy like Peter? No. These were predominant Hazel's children. Hers would have been someone differen But who? Her arms fell.

'I seem to be tired this morning,' she said. 'Maybe you' better ask Esther to finish.'

She lay back and dozed again. When she woke, the hou was quiet and she had a sense of morning lateness. And sh stumbled out of bed, calling, 'Dad! Dad!'

Esther appeared at the foot of the stairs. 'It's ten o'cloc

Your father left on the seven-forty-five,' she said in some surprise.

'And the children? Where's everyone?'

'Enoch's gone to his job and Miz Baily took the kids to the beach.'

'Oh yes. Marjorie told me.'

'You're sick,' Esther said accusingly.

'I know. I'm sick.'

'I told you yesterday I thought you was.'

'I know. I need to see a doctor. I'll get dressed.'

'You came all the way to Jersey in a taxi?' Tom Horvath repeated.

'Yes.' A surge of pain shook Claire, cold sweat dampened her hands. 'First I thought of Dad. Then I thought better of it. Maybe we needn't upset him with this.'

Tom Horvath looked at her seriously. 'He will have to know,' he said.

'I'm very sick, aren't I, Uncle Tom?'

'I'm afraid you are, Claire.' There was no reassurance in his homely face. 'I'll have to take you to the hospital.'

'Oh, can't I go home? Tell me what medicine to take and – '

'Come, you know better than that. You've an infection, dear girl. You've got a hundred and four fever.'

'Peritonitis?' Her voice trembled and chirped. Suddenly the room went dizzy with stripes and blocks of brilliant colour. The chairs bent in the legs. The floors tilted, and Uncle Tom swam slowly towards her, curving his way through heavy water.

'Yes, Claire. Peritonitis.'

'Who did this, Claire?'

'I can't tell you.'

Her body twisted in the bed. Her stomach twisted. Was something holding her head in a vice? Was she vomiting or only feeling the need to?

Dad's face came close. The eyes pinched up and there were knobs on the forehead. Then the face vanished. Hands did things. Nurses' hands, delicate and chilly. Voices and echoes sounded at the end of a long corridor or somewhere in an empty auditorium. The ceiling spun like a top slowly wobbling before it falls.

She ripped, she tore and split. Trees cracked open and animals shrieked. I can't stand all the noise in this place, all this noise and all these bright lights in my eyes, she said. Ah bloody froth and bubble of pain, rising and cresting! Hold on, hold on until it passes. Will it pass? Slide now as it ebbs down and down, into a dark, burning trough. So hot, the glowing fire! Now rise again, splinter and crack. Rise up and up. Ah! Hold on! Hold on and twist. Oh God! How much How long?

She opened her eyes in a later time. An hour? A year?

Lightly, quietly, she lay on clouds, on seafoam, in a white bed in a vast landscape where there was no sound: land of the dead?

Her father's face leaned over her again. Blinking, she looked and looked again to make sure it was he.

'What day is it?' she whispered then.

'Tuesday.'

'Tell me what happened.'

'It's the fourth day and the drugs have taken hold. Your fever's down.'

'I'm going to be all right?'

'Yes, thank God, you are.'

'I almost died, didn't I?'

'Yes, Claire.'

'I've made so much trouble for you,' she said as reality rolled back.

'You surely did. Oh my darling, why did you do this to yourself?'

She sighed. He would want a lot of words, so many words and in the end, they would say nothing. For how could she begin to explain it all?

'Tell us at least who did it.'

'No.'

'Claire, it's your obligation to tell. The man's outside the law.'

'I was, too, for going to him.'

'That's true, but he's a butcher. He's got to be stopped.'

'No. He's very skilled, I'm sure, but there's always a risk. You know that. There's a risk when you operate, too.'

'I operate to save life, not to take it.'

'Don't be proud, Dad. And don't make me feel more guilty than I already am.'

'I don't want to. But talk to me! Don't make me feel as if I'm facing some sort of conspiracy between you and this – this nameless person.'

'But it is a conspiracy. It has to be. It's a conspiracy of trust,' she murmured. 'I trusted him to help me and he trusted me not to talk.'

In anguish, Martin cried, 'He didn't help you!'

He took her hand. She felt the pressure of his hands on hers, although she had no strength to return it. Cool sunlight flickered peacefully over the walls and it pleased her to watch it.

'It's so good not to have things hurt inside,' she murmured.

'Nothing hurts, Claire?'

They could understand each other's most elliptical remarks. She answered. 'Something always will, I guess.'

'You didn't want to let him know, to call him back?'

'No.' She spoke with pride. 'He made his choice once, didn't he?'

'So did you,' Martin said quietly. He released her hand, got up and changed chairs. 'I liked him in spite of myself. You know that.'

'Yes.'

'But I hated the marriage. I couldn't help hating the thought of it. So in a way I'm relieved it's not going to be. And also, because you loved him, I'm guilty as hell over being relieved. It's so damned complicated! I can't unravel anything.'

'Don't try. It doesn't matter any more.'

'We seem to do everything the hard way, you and I, with the best of intentions.'

'I know.' She felt the smart of starting tears and turned her head away.

'Dad? Let me sleep, please. Let me sleep now.'

Jessie stood by the side of the bed. Her lipstick was smeared
She must have been in an awful rush to go out like that.

'Well, Mama,' Claire said and remembered that sh
hadn't said 'Mama' since she had entered first grade.

'So, Claire. You've messed things up a little, I see.'

'I thought you were in Vermont.'

'I was. Your father telephoned me there. He got th
number from my office.'

'He called you?'

'Yes. I've been here every day.'

'You've seen Dad, then?'

'No. There isn't any reason to see him, so I take care no
to.'

Like a child of separated parents, Claire had for just a
instant a fleeting picture of Martin and Jessie standin
together again; an unfounded, useless, silly hope, it was, th
result, no doubt, of her own exhaustion.

'Well, what do you think of me?' she demanded. 'I'n
waiting for your opinion.'

Jessie regarded her. 'What do you want me to tell you
That you've been wicked, or that you've been a fool? O
neither? Or both?'

'Tell me whatever you're thinking.'

'I'm not thinking anything. I'm just glad you're alive
Other than that, I feel numb.'

The nurse came in with a drink and a right-angled straw
'Lemonade for you. Drink it all, you need plenty of fluids
Can you manage?'

'I'll help her,' Jessie said.

Claire made the introduction. 'This is my mother, Mis
McGrath.'

'Oh, Mrs Farrell, pleased to meet you,' the nurse said
careful not to look at Jessie.

Jessie braced Claire's head. There was surprising strengt
in her arms. It seemed to flow right down into Claire's spine

'Finish it,' she commanded.

When she had done so, Claire leaned back on the pillow

'Have they told you,' she asked, 'that I may never be able to have a child after this?'

Jessie closed her eyes. When she opened them, her face had sunk into sadness. 'They've told me.'

The room was still. The crash of a tray in the hall reverberated like an explosion.

'What else could I have done?'

'You could have had the baby,' Jessie said. It was more a question than a declaration.

'Without a father? I had my own experience of that.'

'You could have gone with Ned.'

'I'm to be a doctor. I have a life as a doctor. I'm Martin Farrell's daughter.'

'I understand. Also you have your pride. I understand that, too.'

Claire smiled faintly. 'Yes, you would.'

'I'm not sorry you didn't marry him. I don't have to tell you that. It would have been a miserable all-around situation – and not just for me.'

'I've told you, that old business had nothing to do with us.'

'So you say. But there's no need to argue it any more, is there? I'm only sorry it ended in the way it did for you.'

'It's crazy,' Claire said, very low, 'that I've been trained to save lives, yet I took a life away.' And after a minute, she repeated, 'What else could I have done?'

'I can't tell you. There're just so many things I don't understand. There're just too many things I can't solve, and this is one of them, and I never shall.'

'Do you know how I feel this minute?'

'Tell me.'

'As if nothing I may do after this can ever matter very much, as if the world were empty.'

'Empty? No, no.' Jessie shook her head so that the long gold ear-rings swayed like tassels. 'It's too full, Claire. Full of opposites and contradictions. There's charity and hatred, there's art and vandalism. There's loving and not being loved. Oh my God, it's so crowded with wanting things and fighting for them! And sometimes it's sheer hell.' She sighed.

Her eyes went vague. She seemed to be dreaming into the space above Claire's bed, beyond the window and far out. Then abruptly she jerked her head back, crying cheerfully, 'Empty, Claire? Never. Soon you'll walk back into the world again and you'll find out.'

CHAPTER THIRTY

Judy was eight years old, and the first thing Martin had noticed about her was her curly hair, his favourite kind that springs between the fingers. She was not a pretty child, but more poignant than any prettiness was her bright humour. Or perhaps she only touched him so for the simple reason she was just eight and she was going to die.

He had been keeping her alive – he and the hand of God –for eleven months. Sharply, distinctly, he could recall his grief when on the day of the first operation he and Leonard Max had opened her skull and discovered the gluey, spreading glioma multiforme. She had asked him whether he would fix her up so she could skate again. She was a very good skater, she said, and he could come and watch her some Saturday morning at the Rockefeller Center rink. Her parents had promised figure-skating lessons, but her left leg had been too weak this past winter. He had given her an evasive answer which could be interpreted as comfort and hope, but not too much of either.

It was very hard to look into a child's face and to parry her questions when you knew what was going on inside her head. Of course, she had not been on skates again: walking was difficult enough. The entire left side was going. He had left an opening in her skull, covered only by scalp, so that the growing tumour might have room to move outwards instead of further in upon the brain. Like seed in fertile earth, the tumour grew, bulging into a lump like a potato surrounded by a new growth of curls. In a few weeks at most, they would have to operate again. And then one Sunday afternoon Leonard Max telephoned.

'Martin? I'm at the hospital with Judy Wister. They called me from home for morphine, and of course I told them to bring her right in. The intracranial pressure's shot up. We can't wait till Monday.'

'I'll be right over. Get the O.R. ready and call Perry, will you?'

'What if I can't get him? It's Sunday. He may not be home.'

'Then get anyone you want but I always feel better with Perry for anaesthesia.'

'Of course.'

Martin hated this operation. When he came into the operating room, he knew everyone would see how much he hated having to do it to this child. He knew that he was not like most surgeons, who managed to keep a cool, professional dispassion. But it was not the way he was, never had been, and it was too late to change now.

The child lay on the table under the lights; so small under a short skirt of yellow or red. He could see beyond her to her home, an apartment in the more respectable reaches of the Bronx, where you pressed the buzzer to get in at the front door and then went through corridors that smelled of onions to the bedrooms where five children slept and where you would look past the courtyard into other people's bedrooms.

The parents were waiting now at the foot of the hall. They knew she was going to die long before skating time next winter. He hadn't told them so, but they could understand what he had not told them. And he thought of them going back to that apartment without her, of how they would remember her flashing on her skates; he saw the father plodding back to the telephone company where he laboured for the rent and the food and the shoes and the dentist. All this went through Martin's head while he took the few steps from the door to the table where she waited for him.

Leonard Max was ready. Martin wondered whether it had been a disappointment to Max that he had returned, able and well from a dark depression. Otherwise Max could have got the practice and hired an associate to be junior to *him*. Yet he might be doing Max a terrible injustice in thinking so. You never knew about people. Never again would he presume to understand the workings of the human mind including his own; so delicate, subtle, secret and precious it was.

Perry came in and took his place. It seemed to Martin that he was panting, as though he had been fetched in a hurry. But it was so good to have him there, he and Leonard and the familiar, competent, swift nurses.

So he picked up the scalpel and began. He cut through the fine silk sutures that he himself had sewn in the scalp. Blood, as was to be expected, came spurting into the automatic sucker. He cauterized the surface vessels. Now further further, knowing all the time that the thing was too deep for hope. How it had grown in these few months! Like weeds in a week-long spell of rain it had flourished, spreading roots and arms, branches and tentacles, and from each of these the finest, toughest fibres. Hopeless. Hopeless. Still he worked on, cutting away at the yellow, bulging brain and tumour, so interwoven now that they had become a single entity.

Doggedly he cut. *But why are you doing this?* The answer is the same as the mountain climber's famous reply: Because it is there. Until the last breath has left the body, you do whatever you know. Everything you have ever learned or practised, you do. Given another few months of life, so the theory goes, who can say that some miraculous therapy may not suddenly be discovered, so that at the very last second, this child might be pulled back from the grave? So you work, even when you know it is too late for any theory or therapy to be applicable here.

The room was unusually quiet. Everyone remembered that this little girl had been here before All knew that the most Martin could do this time was to remove as much more of the tumour as possible to relieve the pressure on the brain. Then he would close up the scalp and wait for the bulge to form again. Maybe once, or at most twice more, this would all be done again, and after that would come the end.

At Martin's elbow Perry's eyes and freckled forehead turned copper under the lights. Like some priest of an ancient rite, Martin thought – queer thoughts he was having today – Perry stood beside the silvery metal cylinders of anaesthetizing gas and oxygen, listening to the stethoscope, monitoring the pulse, announcing, at regular intervals, the blood pressure. Occupied with his own exploration, Martin was still always alert to everything else around the table, from the nurses handing instruments and gauze to the gas bags expanding and contracting with the child's indrawn and outgoing breath. Suddenly it seemed too long since Perry had last spoken.

'Blood pressure,' Martin called.

From the corner of his eye, he looked up. Perry was standing there with a kind of absent-minded, dreaming look. For an instant Martin followed his gaze to the window and the sky, where evening crept.

'Blood pressure, Perry!' he called sharply now. And at almost the same moment, he saw that the oozing blood from the wound he had been excavating was turning dark, turning blue.

'For Christ's sake,' he cried. 'Oxygen! For Christ's sake!'

Perry leaped. His arm appeared to leap through the air, turning one cylinder up, the other one down. Oxygen purred with a soft, liquid rush: whish, whish. He looked up at Martin. Such a strange, helpless look! It crossed Martin's mind: something's the matter with him; his eyes are swimming.

Then Perry said, 'Erratic pulse.'

'Adrenalin,' Martin commanded.

'I don't think I can get the pulse,' Perry said.

'Oxygen,' Martin commanded.

'I definitely can't get the pulse,' Perry said. It sounded in Martin's ears like pleading.

'Cardiac arrest!'

There was a swift, disciplined scurrying in the room. Someone jumped on the table and began to thump the child's chest.

'Two amps bicarb!'

'Let's get the paddles.'

'Open up the fluids!'

'Open the intravenous line!'

These low commands went back and forth; arms and hands reached back and forth. The needle of adrenalin pierced the heart; it seemed like hours and was, actually, minutes.

'The EKG is flat,' Perry said, and then, finally, 'It's finished.'

Someone was still working, working desperately on the chest.

'No,' Leonard Max said, 'it's no use.' And he repeated, 'It's finished.'

There was a tired silence until Max broke it again. 'Perhaps it's a mercy,' he said gently. 'She hadn't very long.'

Martin didn't answer. He had gone through it before and would go through it again; each time was a separate agony. And in a familiar gesture, he drew his gloves off and threw them on the floor.

They went out into the hall to the waiting room where the second act was to be played, the act of notification. The three paced down the corridor abreast, Martin and Leonard and Perry. Martin wanted to ask, 'What happened, Perry?' But then he wasn't sure he ought to because there was a fuzz of confusion in his mind right now, and anyway, there was this to be got through, and he was exhausted.

The mother went mad. She had been standing with her hand over her mouth as the three men approached. Possibly, he thought afterwards, the news had been written in their eyes or their walk. And he knew he would always see her face out of a long line of such faces going back years and years. It was wide across the top like a cat's, with a delicate pointed chin and round pale eyes. Her scream was the most terrible sound one could ever hear, worse than the cry of an animal being slaughtered or a woman in labour. Her husband and some other young man, a brother or brother-in-law, took her to a room. Nurses came running. Someone gave her a hypodermic. It was over.

And Martin went home to have supper with his children, who had, as far as he knew, no alien things growing in their heads, and he was thankful for that.

Later, in bed, he tried to reorder his thoughts. Had the child become cyanotic because of the surgical shock or had Perry in some way failed? He recalled that in the flurry he had sensed something strange about Perry. But then, perhaps it was only his imagining as a result of the flurry.

Everything had happened too fast to remember the sequence of events. He often thought he'd make a bad witness to an accident. It had been proven that three people could witness the same event and give three completely different reports of it. So his mind went spinning and rotating towards sleep.

In the morning at the office Leonard said, 'That was some rotten Sunday afternoon yesterday.'

Martin, going over mail at his desk, had a sense of Leonard's hovering half-way to the door, as if he were waiting to say something more.

'Did you see Perry afterwards?' Leonard asked.

'Afterwards?'

'Yesterday, before you left.'

Martin looked up. 'No, I went straight home. Why?'

'Well, there was something odd about him.'

Martin waited.

Leonard sat down. 'I think – Jesus, I hate to say this – but I could swear he'd had a couple of drinks.'

'You know what you're saying, Leonard?'

'I sure as hell do! I'm not saying it to anybody else, Martin, for God's sake. I'm only telling you. He was talking to one of the kid's relatives, the uncle I think. The young guy with the parents. I saw him in the hall after I got dressed and he just – well, he was talking too loud and too much and – Well, you know that faint something you can detect, not drunk exactly, but – '

Martin interrupted. 'Did you notice anything in the O.R.?'

'I only thought – well, I thought he wasn't paying attention. The kid should have got more oxygen. He wasn't monitoring.'

For a long minute neither of them spoke. Martin tapped a pencil on the desk. Certain things came back to him more clearly now: Perry looking out of the window; the sky streaked rust and claret. He felt the slow thud of heart.

'Yesterday was his anniversary, they were having a party at his house.'

Perry was not a drinker, but at an anniversary party surely he would have had a few? 'I just don't know,' Martin said again.

'Well, of course, little Judy's days were few and cruel. When you consider, it's just as well. Merciful, in fact.'

'True. Undoubtedly true. But not the issue exactly.'

'I wonder,' Leonard began.

'Wonder what?'

'Whether we should – I mean you or both of us, or whether we should – '

'Say anything to Perry?'

'Yeah. What do you think?'

'Or wait. Maybe he'll say something. Maybe something will – '

Leonard stood up. 'Right. Nothing hasty. It's all vague. See whether he says anything.'

Perry said, 'Tough about the little girl, Martin. But I guess you knew before you started how it was going to end, so it was no surprise to you.'

'It was a considerable surprise,' Martin said distinctly.

Perry's expressive eyebrows rose to his freckled forehead. 'I don't understand. You honestly expected her to survive the operation?'

'I certainly did, and maybe one like it a few months down the road.'

They were in an empty corridor, waiting for the elevator. Nevertheless, Martin lowered his voice.

'Perry, were you feeling all right yesterday?'

'What the devil makes you ask that?'

'Because. Level with me. You weren't monitoring.'

'The hell I wasn't!'

'I don't think you were. She went cyanotic.'

'So? That's never happened before?' A bright flush of anger inundated the freckled forehead.

'Yes, but this time I – '

'Just what the hell are you trying to prove, Martin?'

'I'm not trying to prove anything. I'm only asking. Don't get excited.'

'Don't get excited! When you're practically accusing me of negligence, you expect me to – '

'I'm not accusing you of anything. I repeat, I'm only

asking whether you can clear up something in my mind. If friends can't talk frankly with each other – '

The elevator came. It was crowded. The two men stood abreast, not touching, Martin aware of Perry's fast angry breathing. He regretted having spoken. The whole thing might be a dreadful error on his part. If so, Perry had every reason to be hurt and furious. Yet –

On the third day Leonard came into Martin's office. 'You know Perry's car, that imported job he bought last month?'

'What about it?'

'The front fender's crumpled up like a handkerchief. I saw it in the parking lot this morning. So I told him, I said, "That's some fender-bender. How did you manage to do that?" And he said it happened Sunday afternoon, backing out of the lot, after the surgery.'

'That doesn't prove anything,' Martin said.

'No, but it adds up.'

Martin didn't answer. He felt like a cheap detective, one of those matrimonial snoopers. Then he thought of something and rang for Jenny Jennings.

'Did I remember to have you send flowers to the funeral home for Judy?'

'You did. I sent a spray of roses from you and Dr Max.'

'Good. Good. Thanks.'

So she's at peace. No more vomiting, dizziness and pain. No more shaved head, medicines and bandages. At peace. But I'm not. Still, can't play detective, prosecutor and judge. Too difficult. Drop it. What's done is done.

The nursing supervisor met him one morning in the lobby and drew him aside. 'I've had a call from a lawyer, a Mr Rice. He wants to see the record on Judy Wister. It looks like trouble.'

So it's come! was Martin's first reaction. All these years he'd gone without a suit for malpractice. It was bound to come once in a lifetime anyway, he thought grimly. Still, he had done his best for the child. He would have said, naively no doubt, that the Wisters of all people would never do this to him. They had seemed to worship him, to be so grateful

And he felt a small, sad hurt.

'Well,' he said, not wishing to let the hurt show, 'I guess my turn's just come. I've got plenty of company, that's sure.'

So he was quite prepared when a few days later Jenny Jennings informed him that a Mr Rice had called on behalf of his clients, Louis and Martha Wister, and would be in to see him at three that afternoon.

Mr Rice was a garish individual with oiled hair and a rasping voice. Two strikes against him anyway, Martin thought, feeling some amusement at his own surprising calm.

'Well, Mr Rice, what is it you want to know about me?' he began.

'Nothing about you at all.'

'You're not here to serve papers, to sue me?'

'No, no. Mr and Mrs Wister specifically exclude you from any culpability in the death of their child. The matter concerns the anaesthesiologist alone. We want your testimony to the effect that he was negligent as a result of being under the influence of alcohol.'

'Oh, no,' Martin said. 'I've known Perry Gault for years, and he's the best man in his field that any surgeon could want. As a matter of fact, I don't like to operate without him. He's completely reliable.' He heard himself babbling.

'That may all be true, but the fact is that on this particular day, he had been drinking. Mrs Wister's brother, Arthur Wagnalls, had conversation with Dr Gault and smelled alcohol on his breath. Furthermore, the doctor had an accident in the parking lot on the way out, and the man whose car he hit believed either that he had been drinking or wasn't feeling well, he wasn't sure which. Also – '

Martin raised his hand. Something in him was frightened for Perry and wanted to defend him. 'Wait. This is all unsubstantiated. The child's uncle is not an impartial person, after all. And anyone can say anything about anyone, can't he? You could go out of this office right now and say I'm drunk, couldn't you? And it would only be your opinion.'

Mr Rice smiled. It was an all-knowing smile. It said, 'I am a step ahead of you and no matter how fast you run, I shall always remain a step ahead.'

'We have an impartial person, as you say. One of the nurses, Delia Whitman, has already given a statement to the effect that Dr Gault had been drinking.'

'Delia Whitman? There was no such person in the operating room, and I'm well acquainted with them all.'

Mr Rice said patiently, 'She's a student nurse. You probably wouldn't know her. She was attending Mrs Wister and was present when Dr Gault and Mr Wagnalls were talking. Afterwards Mr Wagnalls remarked on Dr Gault's condition, and she answered, she told him, yes, it was clear to her, too.'

Martin, stunned, resorted to pencil-tapping.

'Furthermore, the record of the operation says a great deal. The girl became cyanotic. Anaesthesia was hurriedly lowered and oxygen increased after you, the surgeon, ordered it. Dr Gault had not been monitoring the flow.'

Ugly, ugly! The only other brush with law that Martin had had in all his life had been his divorce and he had come away from that with no love for lawyers. Word-mongers, sophists and procrastinators, they were; their aim was to trip you up, to trick you into saying what you didn't mean.

'I'm not a lawyer,' he said somewhat brusquely, 'so will you come to the point? What do you want of me?'

'I want you to be a witness for the Wisters in a suit for malpractice against Dr Gault.'

'No, no,' Martin cried. 'I want to be left out of this. I don't have time, I'm a busy man. There's a roomful of patients out there. I'm concerned about them and only about them.'

'Exactly. And you want them protected against this sort of thing, don't you? Isn't it your duty to protect them, since you're so concerned?'

Mr Rice stood up. 'I won't take any more of your time now, Doc. Think it over. When you do, you'll do the right thing, I'm sure.' He backed towards the door. 'I'll be calling you again.'

I'm sure you will, Martin thought with enormous distaste.

Perry looked large and clumsy in Martin's little den.

'I'm sorry to come busting in on you like this,' he said, 'but I was sitting around after dinner tonight and I thought "Well, why don't I go see Martin and talk it all out?" We've been avoiding each other. I was hasty that day in the hall, very upset, but as you see, it turns out I have reason to be upset. I'm so damn sorry, Martin,' he finished.

'Yes. Well – '

'You know, of course, you've heard they've served me with a suit?'

'I heard.' He estimated that the entire hospital had heard within an hour.

Perry leaned forward. 'Martin, I'm going to level with you. I did have a couple of drinks. You know I don't drink much. A little goes a long way with me. Too long.'

Oh Jesus, Martin thought.

'I shouldn't have gone to the hospital at all. I know I ought to have told you to get somebody else, but the thing is, when you're a little bit dazed, under that thin edge of sleepiness, you don't know you are. Martin, you're not going to testify against me? She was going to die anyway.' There were tears in the friendly, copper eyes and Martin couldn't bear to look at them. 'You don't know how I feel. That kid – If I could bring her back! But nobody could. How long did she have? Three months? Six at the most? So when you come down to it, what great difference did it make?'

Martin was silent.

And Perry continued, 'It should never have happened and you can bet everything that's holy, it never will again. Never. Martin, what are you going to do?'

Martin spoke very gently. 'I don't want to do anything to hurt you. Do I have to tell you that?'

Perry stood up and began walking the length of the little room: twelve paces to the bookshelf at the far end and twelve paces return. 'Martin, for myself – Oh, I won't say anything grandiose and tell you it wouldn't matter, because of course it would. But the truth is, there's more than myself. The truth is I've got the two boys in college and Leonore's having a mastectomy. A radical, I'm afraid.'

'I didn't know.'

'Well, we just found out last week. Now I've got to put this on her, too. You see, what I'm saying is, I'll need all the support I can get from my friends. Martin, I'm scared as hell.'

'Take it easy, Perry, take it easy. Things have a way of working out. We all want to help you get through this, stand by you.'

What was he saying? Words, cheap, smooth, easy words. meaning nothing. How was he going to 'help out'? Just what, exactly, was he going to do? His head whirled with it.

A week after that the lawyer came from the company that insured Perry, that insured them all. This one was a gentleman. He wore a nice dark suit and had a nice quiet manner. He was from Harvard Law. You would like your son to grow up and be like him.

'What is it you want of me?' Martin asked for the second time in as many weeks.

'To testify on behalf of Dr Gault. The child died of natural causes. There is no convincing proof of anything to the contrary.'

'Convincing,' Martin thought. Semantics. All law is word twisting. Convincing to whom? He passed his hand over his forehead.

'I'm not cut out to be a lawyer,' he said apologetically. 'I'll confess my head's beginning to whirl.'

'Of course. Let me get in touch with you in another few days, to go over specifics. I'm sure we can work things out with satisfaction, and despatch this nasty business as quickly as possible.' And with a pleasant smile and handshake, he, too, departed.

The case seemed to fill Martin's life. He wished it would go away, wished he'd never seen Judy Wister or Perry or anyone. It was becoming uglier, with a creeping element of vengefulness. The Wisters telephoned him at his home – he ought to get an unlisted number, damn it! – to plead. The mother wept. Well, he couldn't blame her! Perry's wife came to his office late one afternoon and walked five blocks with him towards his home, red-eyed and begging all the way. Couldn't blame her, either.

One afternoon the hospital superintendent called him in. 'There's talk that you don't want to work with Perry's lawyers,' Mr Knolls said.

Martin answered slowly, 'It's not that I don't want to work with them. I don't want to work with anybody. I want to be left out.'

'You can't be. You won't be.'

'Why?' Martin burst out. 'Why can't I mind my own business and be left alone!' The instant he had said it, he knew the lament was puerile.

Mr Knolls didn't even deign to answer it. He said instead, 'Of course, I can't tell you what to do, and I'm not trying to tell you. I've known you a long time, though, and I feel free to point out a few things you may have overlooked.'

'Such as?'

'Perry's had twenty-two years here at Fisk. A distinguished record.'

'I certainly know that.'

'Unblemished. The publicity of this affair, the strain, the emotional damage can wreck a man after all those good years.'

'I know that, too.'

'Now he needs all the help he can get. Don't condemn him. It won't bring the child back, anyway.'

Martin looked at him.

'He's suffered enough from this already. His wife's undergoing – '

'He told me.'

'Well, then, I'll say no more.'

Martin nodded. 'I understand.'

Martin began hearing unpleasant things about himself. 'You're acting like a boy scout,' he was told. 'The guy had one extra drink. We all agree he shouldn't have come into the O.R. But he's never slipped before, and he'll never slip again. So what's to be gained by crucifying him? What?'

Purpose. Abstractions. A man's whole professional lif
versus a dead child who was going to die anyway.

'You'll be a great hero to no one but yourself, Martin
Perry's going to win the case. He's got prestigious people t
testify for him. And the O.R. nurse is sweet on him: yo
know the chubby blonde. What's-her-name? And tha
resident Maudley is scared shitless. He'll say what he'
expected to say. So where does that leave you if you go to th
other side?'

He spoke to Tom. 'Awful, awful,' Tom said, sighing an
shaking his great leonine head. Then he said cautiously, 'I
puts you in a bad position. Tough on you.'

Martin waited.

'Yes. Tough. It's always hard to testify against anothe
doctor, I guess because you never know when it could b
you. There but for the grace of God – that business.' H
mused. 'Any one of us could make one slip in a lifetime
couldn't we?'

True. And Braidburn long ago had warned not to be to
quick to judge: you never knew when it might be you who'
make a fatal mistake. One mistake out of a lifetime of goo
service . . .

At night he lay awake conducting internal dialogues whil
shadows flickered over the ceiling.

Tomorrow the lawyers will be calling again. I've tol
Jenny Jennings to stall them off, but that can't go o
indefinitely.

Cold, stony looks in the hospital now. I used to think it'
simple. One side or the other. Angel of truth versus monste
of corruption. Not like that at all! Generals on the battlefiel
lose thousands of men through miscalculation, errors o
judgement, quirks of behaviour. Nothing happens to them.

You're comparing canaries with alligators.

Not so. Death is death, whether of one or thousands.

She was going to die anyway, remember that.

But if it hadn't been that child, that case; if it had been
benign encapsulated tumour, a meningioma, somethin
relatively easy and Perry had not monitored, what then
Then there would truly have been disaster.

Yes, but it wasn't an easy case. It was death-writ-large.

They won't recover, the Wisters won't, whether you're for them or against them or if you take a boat to China and disappear. The biggest names in the county medical society are going to testify for Perry. So you'll be a boy scout! You'll lose a friend and make more enemies.

You could retrieve a lot of goodwill by agreeing to testify for him. You could. You have tremendous prestige, which is respected. Don't underestimate it.

So the long nights passed.

After dinner the doorbell rang. Enoch came into the den where Martin was at his desk. 'There's a lady wants to see you, Dad.'

He hoped it wasn't Perry's wife coming again, but probably it was. And, suddenly very tired, he made a decision. He would just simply say 'yes' at last. Throw in the sponge and say, 'Okay, how do you want me to help?' Get it over with. It made sense, really.

Instead a young girl walked in and sat down. He didn't recognize her.

'Delia Whitman,' she said. 'I know you but you don't know me. I'm a fourth-year student nurse.' She swallowed hard. 'I'm the girl in Dr Gault's case.'

Oh, not more of that! 'Why have you come to me?'

'Because – I don't know. I wanted to talk to somebody, some doctor. And I thought – the things they say about you, the nurses, I mean, a person gets a reputation – ' Her voice trailed off in tears and she took out a handkerchief.

'Don't cry,' Martin said, forcing patience. 'Just tell me what's on your mind.'

'Well, it's – this is what happened. After the operation when the little girl died – the mother went to a room. She was crying and Miss Hannigan called me to come and help. Stay with her, you know?'

Martin nodded.

'So, then I had to go out in the hall for medicine, and this man, the uncle, was talking to Dr Gault, and he called me over and asked me how his sister was, and I said we were getting her some medicine, and I'm awfully sorry about the little girl. And Dr Gault started to talk. And, Doctor, he was acting awfully funny. He was talking loud, not very loud, but the thing is he was just – funny. And afterwards, when they were taking the mother home, the man saw me and he stopped me and said, "That guy, that doctor, he'd been drinking, hadn't he?"

'And I said, "I guess so." And he said, "You smelled liquor on him, didn't you?" and I said yes, I had, because it was the truth. I did smell it. And now, now the lawyer for Dr Gault – he's an awfully nice young man, but he keeps coming around and they want me to say I had only been joking, that the man had put the words in my mouth, that I had thought he was kidding.' The girl wiped her eyes and blew her nose.

Jesus, Martin thought, will this business never end?

'The thing is, I just don't know what to do, Dr Farrell. And I haven't got anybody to ask. Some of the girls say one thing and some say the other. And it seems to me what they say is all according to whether they like Dr Gault, and it seems most of them do. Or else what they tell me depends sort of on my looking out for myself and not getting the doctors offended with me. And it seems the doctors are mostly sticking up for Dr Gault. So I've come to ask you what I should do.' She finished, balling the wet handkerchief in her palm.

It surprised him that out of this confused narration, a single thread could emerge so quickly and clearly. He had no hesitation at all in replying to this troubled, honest, childish girl.

'Why,' he said softly, 'you must just tell the truth, mustn't you?'

'Just like that?'

'Just like that,' he repeated.

Explanations and justifications would only confuse her some more. What she had come for was plain direction, as when a child, needing to obey, asks to be told what to do. When she had thanked him, too apologetically and too effusively, she went out. Strange how easy it had been to tell *her* what she must do and so difficult to tell himself what *he* must do!

He opened the window. The night air washed over him, bathing his hot face. Then he turned on the record player where a record had been left, the *Reformation* Symphony. For long minutes he stood listening, while his unfocused eyes rested on the sky over the river. The music was a shaft of light. It was a great plea and answer. And in some absolutely crazy way it seemed his father's voice was mixed up in it.

Suddenly everything was very simple.

He went to the telephone book. A pleasant young man from Harvard Law School would live somewhere in Manhattan, on the East Side. Yes, here it was. Might as well do it now, get it over with before the morning and be able to sleep tonight. I'm very tired, he thought again. I haven't slept well in so long. And he picked up the telephone.

'This is Dr Farrell,' he said. 'I'm sorry to disturb you at home, but I'll be brief. I've made my decision. It's a painful one. I want you to know that it is, and I should hope perhaps you might find a way to tell Dr Gault it is. But I cannot, I simply cannot, help you. I couldn't do it and rest.'

CHAPTER THIRTY-ONE

Martin, having changed from operating clothes to street clothes, looked in for a moment at the door of the doctors' lounge. It reminded him of the passing glimpses he'd had of London clubs where old men napped on brown leather chairs. The walls held Piranesi etchings of broken classic columns with vines trailing over the stumps. Why did dentists and doctors always seem to go in for broken classic columns?

Young Simpson, he of the good cheer, called out, 'Going back to the office so late, Martin?'

'No, waiting for my daughter. We've a party on the Island.'

'Enjoy yourself,' young Simpson said.

Going down in the elevator Martin felt the smile still on his mouth. It was remarkable how even the most casual proof of being liked and accepted could freshen and support a man. As for enemies, you could hardly get through life, he supposed, without garnering some. And he thought regretfully of Perry, who having won his case without Martin's help now ignored him whenever they chanced to pass and of others, too, whose greetings, if any, were noticeably cool.

In the lobby he waited for Claire. The rotunda was solemn, like an edifice of ancient Rome. A new bronze plaque, glossier than the rest, displayed the names of the most recent benefactors. He was standing there reading the names almost mechanically when his daughter appeared. He watched her before she saw him. Her face was set in gravity; as soon as she saw him it bloomed into a smile. Real or assumed? he wondered.

'Reads like Dun and Bradstreet, doesn't it, Dad?'

'I don't like this lobby,' he said. 'It's pompous. The institute will have quite a different feel.'

She patted his shoulder as if to say: I know it will be the

zenith of your life. They went into a benign spring afternoon and walked towards the parking lot.

'Up to the second storey already,' Claire observed as they passed the new construction at the end of the block.

'Right on schedule. Yes, we ought to be functioning a year from this month.'

For the sake of some obscure and foolish dignity, Martin tried to keep the jubilation from his voice. Two months ago they had laid the cornerstone, a great chunk of mauve brown marble set in a row of granite. There had been a committee to select the artifacts which in some distant, unimaginable century would be uncovered; the city might be rubble and ruin by then. And as always, Martin thought of the schoolboy poem: 'My name is Ozymandias, king of kings. Look on my works, ye mighty, and despair.'

Anyway, Braidburn's text had gone in, he'd seen to that. Now almost fifty years old and much outmoded, it was still worthy of honour as the great pioneer. Outmoded! Every five years a text became outdated, so fantastic was the explosion of medical knowledge, a proliferation like leafage in a rain forest!

Thinking aloud, which he often did when in Claire's company – it pleased him that she found nothing odd in his doing so – he said, 'It's the most challenging intellectual field of all, medicine. More than any science, as far as I'm concerned, including space exploration. What's more important than humanity? Each step, each advance whets your curiosity so you have to go on to the next. I sometimes imagine a composer must feel like that when a symphony unfolds in his head.'

And for some reason Judy Wister popped into his own head, the skinny, trustful little thing who had lain down beneath his hands. He recalled the lawyer, that well-dressed, affable young man who had told him, 'You're a man of probity, Doctor, after all.' Probity!

The suffering, he thought, you could never rid the world of it! Even on this brief walk, in these few blocks, you saw its symbols: a dirty old woman mumbling to herself; a lost, bony mongrel foraging in a trash can; a drained young man, sallow-cheeked, climbing up out of the subway.

How we are driven! We prate of free will and of course it is a fact, but what of accident, chance meeting, timing, health, the very luck of the genetic draw? On another day, for instance, Hazel, even given what she was – and I don't suppose either she or I really knew what she was – might not have done what she did. It was just that moment, that particular day. He could think of it now, could even talk about it, although he seldom did, without that terrible choking inside.

They got into the car and Martin took the wheel. Claire sighed. 'I can't say I'm looking forward to the Mosers' little shindig.'

'You're doing me a big favour. I like to show you off, you know. Besides, it doesn't hurt you to become known. The world doesn't beat a path to anyone's doorstep.'

'The people you meet at their place – they're all such wastrels.'

'The Mosers are decent people,' Martin protested.

'They may be, but the crowd you meet there just isn't real. You get the feeling, at least I do, that everybody's out for something.'

'We're all "out for something". We all want recognition, to stand out from the crowd.'

'Don't mind me,' Claire said. 'The fact is I'm starved and I get cranky when I'm starved.'

Martin said, 'The crankiest of all was your grandfather. He had an appetite like a bear.'

'Well, that's another way I'm like him then. You always say I'm like him.'

Martin looked over at her. 'Yes, you are, rather. You don't give a darn how you're dressed. You'd better catch that button, it's hanging by a thread.'

'Oh damn!' she said. She pulled off the button and stuffed it in her pocket. 'You know, I think I would have liked the way he lived: simple, no pretences.'

'You don't know what you're talking about. It was a life so hard you couldn't begin to imagine it.'

They drove along in silence for a minute or two, during

which with swift recall Martin saw again the snowfields and poor dark houses, felt the brutal cold, heard the voice of the kind ascetic, so devoted to his work, and of the wife who paid her full share for that devotion.

Claire asked, 'Did the orthodontist send you the report on Marjorie's teeth?'

'Yes. She needs the work. They'll start next month. You've been so awfully good to the kids, Claire, with all you have to do. Do I thank you often enough?'

'You don't have to. They're good kids. Peter's sweet and so serious and Marjorie's a housewife, already.' Claire sounded amused. 'I swear she knows more about keeping a house in order than I ever will.'

'She's like – ' Martin began, and stopped. For an instant he had forgotten that Hazel was dead. He thought of something. 'I forgot to tell you. You know that man from Salt Lake City I operated on last winter? The one who owns half a copper mine? Well, I got a letter from him today. I'd been talking to him about the institute, and he hadn't said a word, but now in a letter he wants to know how much we'd need to pay for an operating room. An entire operating room! Imagine!'

'A true GP,' Claire said.

'A what?'

'Grateful Patient. And you've certainly had loads of them, if anyone has.'

They were riding now along a maze of highways, past clusters of apartment houses twenty storeys high; and these clusters were like islands in a sea of cars. This crowding gave Martin a vague melancholy. Then glancing over at Claire, he realized that the melancholy was because of her . . .

There was something remote about her these days. Oh, she was talkative as always, enthusiastic about her future with him, and so appreciative! But there was – something. No use asking her to talk about it, because she would refuse. Just as I, he thought, am unable to talk about Mary. Especially now, after Hazel – Sometimes a thought leaps, a thought of seeing Mary again, and my mind clamps down, just shuts down sharply. So it must be for my daughter, with Mary's son!

Apartments gave way to grids of tiny houses, row on row and all alike among flat fields, with no trees. Baby carriages and tricycles were scattered on their tiny lawns. Each house must hold at least two tiny children; and in each house a woman was living a life so different from Claire's – He wondered whether she would indeed ever have a child, and if not, how the lack would affect her. He would have liked to talk to her about that too, but he dared not.

The suburbs became the exurbs. There was restful space between the houses. Behind brick walls and wrought iron gates the over-arching trees were budding so that the land was veiled in pale green lace. When Martin's car rolled up the Mosers' driveway it came to a stop among Mercedes and Rolls-Royces. Chauffeurs stood about talking. From the water side of the house a choir of peepers piped and trilled. And Martin, moved by some old nostalgia, stopped to listen.

'Another spring,' he said. 'Every year I'm glad I've lived to see it again.'

Hundreds of daffodils were scattered over the lawn. 'Naturalized,' Claire observed, and Martin thought: Where did I see this before? In some place far off – and suddenly remembered the lawn in Cyprus and Pa saying, 'They don't just grow like that. Somebody put them there.'

It was warm. The press of people, the fires under the great carved mantels and the good scotch produced this hearty warmth. The chatter might be a silly waste of energy, as Claire had remarked, but it was good, nevertheless, to be here. Martin stood with his little plate of canapés and his drink, listening to tag ends of three conversations at once.

'He gave two floors to the new wing in Tulsa. Oil people, of course,' someone said.

'My wife's cousin is on the board of directors, and that helped. Frankly, his grades weren't all that good.'

'There wasn't time for a wash-and-set between lunch and my tennis lesson.'

Claire had found a young couple whom she knew. They were at the far end of the room. Martin was relieved that she had found people her own age to talk to. Most of the people ıere were too old for her, as he had known they would be. He vatched her in her quiet dress standing among all the bright ilk plumage. Distinguished. The authentic article, he hought, wanting so much for her. Academic honours, yes, hose she had; and he was so proud, thinking of that. But she ıeeded someone, he thought again; she oughtn't to be alone. Men ran after her, he knew they did; yet she didn't seem to :are about any of them –

Bob Moser came up with a drink in hand. 'Having a good ime?'

'Very. It's a spectacular party, as always.'

'I'd like to talk to you for a minute if you don't mind. Let's ;o in the library, it's quiet there.'

They sat down. Moser's head was framed by a row of golf rophies, and above them a shelf of smooth leather-bound ets. He seemed to be studying Martin. There was an odd ›ause which Martin found necessary to fill.

'This house was meant for parties,' he observed ›leasantly.

'Yes,' Moser said. He took off his glasses, revealing tired yes. 'I suppose this isn't the right place for what I have to tell 'ou. I had thought of ringing you on the phone, but one can't alk properly on the phone. And then I thought we might go ut to lunch together, except that you're so busy.'

Martin waited attentively.

'We've been friends for a long time, Martin.'

Martin nodded.

'Christ! I don't know how to start.' Moser's mouth made a ıueer twist as though he were about to cry. 'I feel, I feel the vay you must feel when you have to tell a family the patient ıas died.' The familiar open face closed up and Moser shut ıis eyes.

Alarmed, Martin asked, 'Is anyone ill? What is it, Bob?'

'I wanted to be the one to tell you. I didn't want you to get coldly at a meeting or by letter or however they planned to o it.'

And suddenly Martin knew. He thought: It's crazy, but I now what he's going to say. He set his glass down and vaited.

'You know Dr Francis? Stanley Francis?'

'From San Diego. I've met him at meetings.'

'I understand he's a good man, done some fine work.'

'Yes, he's head of the department out there. Does a lot of teaching.'

'Like you. Kind of a duplicate of yourself, if I may say so, only younger.'

'About five or six years, that's all.'

'Yes. Well.' Moser got up from the chair. A large globe stood in a corner. He placed his hand over the top, the splayed fingers covering the Bering Sea and the North Cape. He twirled the globe.

'Christ, Martin! I haven't slept these two nights. It was decided – this is still confidential, of course, but the trustees had a meeting the day before yesterday and it was decided – the fact is – oh hell! They've offered the directorship of the neurological institute to Stanley Francis, and he's accepted. That's it in a nutshell.' And giving the globe a violent twirl so that it rattled as it spun, he walked away and stood with his back to Martin.

Martin trembled. The room had a feeling of unreality. The ripple of voices in the next room was suddenly remote, like fading voices heard when one's hands are held over one's ears.

'I see,' he said. 'I see . . .'

Moser turned back to him. 'New blood,' he said dully. 'That's the reason they gave to make it sound convincing. You can make anything sound convincing, can't you? But it was yours by right.'
His fist slapped into his palm. 'You're the one who dreamed of it and worked for it; your patients gave funds for it; you set up the teaching programme, attracted the young men to train and be trained. It was yours.'

'Yes,' Martin said, feeling faint. 'Yes, it was.'

'I'm sick!' Moser cried. 'Sick over it! Jesus Christ, I tried! I tried! I was two hours in there fighting for you, Martin! And I want you to know the vote was very, very close. I don't feel free to tell you who voted how, naturally, but – '

'You don't have to,' Martin said breathing deeply. 'I

pretty much know.'

'I suppose you do. Well, you made enemies, Martin. What can I tell you? You made enemies. You threw it away.' Moser spoke angrily. 'I don't want to say it again, I don't want to rub salt in the wound, but I can't help it. You were a fool, a Goddamned fool!'

'You think so?'

'I know so! My whole life experience tells me so. Look out for number one, it says.'

'Maybe you're right. At this point I don't know. I don't know anything.'

'Yes. But I'd still go to hell and back for you. What are you going to do?'

'First, get my balance. My head's spinning.'

'Want another drink? Brandy?'

'No, that's just what I don't want, thanks.'

'Want to lie down?'

'No, no, I'm all right, Bob. I'll be all right.'

'Want me to send Claire in?'

'No, no, I'm okay, Bob. Really.'

Moser looked doubtful. 'Positive?'

'Positive. Just leave me. Please. Please.'

'Then I'll go back in. And, Martin?'

'Yes?'

'Maybe you can spare an hour for lunch with me one day, especially – '

Especially now that I won't be working my head off for the institute, you mean? And Martin answered, 'Sure, Bob, sure I will.'

French windows led to a terrace. They were ajar. After long minutes he got up from the chair and went outside. Light from the house stretched long gilded fingers among Moser's cherished, nurtured trees. Beyond this small enclave of light and safety lay unknowable darkness, the menacing water gurgling on the rocks below the bluffs. And over all was the vast cold sky.

A world of danger. You get on a plane and it crashes in flames the way that one did last month, a plane full of vacationers with their cameras and new bathing suits. You go to swim in warm water and under that warm, bright indigo lurks a shark. You walk to the post office and the shoe repair shop doing your friendly, simple errands, while all the time a cancer grows secretly within you, corruption and death waiting quietly for their hour. It is a world of danger. You can depend on nothing except yourself, and sometimes not even on that.

He walked to the edge of the terrace and leaned on the balustrade, looking downwards on Italianate descending terraces, an imitation of the Villa d'Este outside of Rome. And this ostentation to which he had grown moderately accustomed, chilled him now as it had when he was young.

Beyond the terraces lay rough marsh grass, out of which the peepers were still trilling. They would still be there a thousand springs from now, long after the terraces had been worn away and the balustrades crumbled. 'Look on my works, ye mighty, and despair.' He thought: I ought to be full of hatred, but I'm not. And isn't that strange?

It began to rain and he heard the chauffeurs behind the shrubbery scurrying to the cars. From the deep shelter of the doorway, Martin stood in a trance of exhaustion, watching the branches dripping in the squall, watching the steady rain. It was almost tropical, the way it fell, so fast that it seemed not to be moving at all, as if it were a solid, luminiscent curtain hanging between himself and the outer world. He thought again: I ought to be full of hatred. Why am I not?

'I've been looking for you everywhere,' Claire said. 'What have you been doing out here in the rain?'

'It's letting up. I've been smelling spring in the air.'

'I thought you'd be where the food is. They've got great lobster mousse that's like nothing Esther feeds you at home. Why, what's the matter?'

'Will you not get excited if I tell you?'

'You look white. Are you sick?'

He told her. She leaned against the wall as if she had been struck.

'No! I don't believe it! I simply don't believe it!'

'You can believe it. It's true.'

'The bastards! The lousy bastards! It's because of that

ase, isn't it? You betrayed the club, the good old boys, the
ld school tie!' She began to cry.

'Ah, don't, Claire! It's not worth it.'

'Yes it is! It is worth it! Oh, I could murder, I could kill
hem all! It's immoral, it's obscene. And I'm so helpless.'

'Don't, Claire. Don't take it so hard.'

'But, Dad, you earned it! You earned it.'

I did, he thought. By God, it hurts. Like a knife, it hurts.
unishment, because I did what I know, *and they know*, was
ecent. Yet it doesn't seem as much of a punishment as I
ould have said an hour or two ago it would be.

And he reflected, 'Do you know, I'm not as crushed as
ou'd expect?'

'That'll come later.'

'I don't think so.'

'Why? All your life, as long as I've known you, I've heard
bout the neurological institute.'

'So it's come to pass, hasn't it? It'll flourish and I'll work in
, without the status and the name, that's all.'

'That's all? Well, I'm crushed, if you're not! Why don't
ou get out and fight? Why doesn't Mr Moser get out and
ght for you?'

'It wouldn't do any good. He did fight. And one has to
arn how to lose with a little dignity.'

'That's Eastern fatalism. Resignation. That's why they
ever accomplish anything in those countries. They're
signed to misery and loss.'

'I shan't be miserable, my dear. Anyway, I didn't speak of
signation. I spoke of acceptance, and there is a difference.'

'Yes? What?'

'You accept what you can't change. A good thing to learn,
laire.'

'You mean *I* need to learn it?'

He thought – or perhaps he only imagined? – a certain
tterness. And he answered gently.

'I only mean, it's a good philosophy. Use it as you see fit.'

Claire rested her head against the stone. With eyes closed,
er face was classic. It was eloquent. How blessed he was for
aving this daughter! He mustn't let himself be too proud of

her, or too careful of her if he could help it. For there wa
nothing that couldn't be taken away. He should have learne
that by now. He thought then, maybe, after all, I'll hav
more time now. Forgo the glory, but forgo the endles
committees and the dreary wasteful paperwork, too. Mor
time to teach – to teach Claire. More time for the quiet lab
the way it was all those years ago in London, down in th
basement with old Llewellyn.

And he stood wistfully looking out at the trees, drippin
slowly now that the rain had stopped, and at the sequine
lights along the shore.

Claire murmured, 'You know who's going to be furiou
about this? Mother.'

'You think so?'

'Yes. You know she always says you were born grea
Anointed, you'd think, the way she talks.'

'She still talks about me?'

'Not about you the man, but about you the doctor.'

'How is she?' Martin asked. 'I don't inquire often enough

'She's fine. Making money hand over fist. Busy all day an
half the night.'

Fro somewhere in the room beyond came a bright gust c
laughter. Curious, Martin thought, but I'm never part of th
laughter. I'm on the outside rim of the circle looking in, an
always have been.

'What are you going to do?' Claire asked, just as Mose
had.

What did they think he was going to do? 'Go home, fc
one thing,' he answered.

'All right then, let's get out of here.'

'Shouldn't we go in and say good-night and thank you?'

'Ah, the hell with them,' Claire said. 'In that crowd w
won't even be missed.' She took his hand, and they wei
together across the grass.

BOOK SIX

TIME AND TIDE

CHAPTER THIRTY-TWO

All that winter Jessie had been admonishing, 'You're overworked. You don't even rest on your days off, what with running around on errands for those children of your father's.'

Quite truly, Claire, like every other intern, was overworked. It was not uncommon to go twenty-four hours without sleep and, when sleep came, it was like being drugged. Once she had been so exhausted, she'd started to laugh at nothing and hadn't been able to stop. Yet all that was to be expected. No one ever complained with any seriousness.

But as for the children, well, Jessie was simply jealous of them! Ever since Hazel's death, Claire had felt poignantly their need for patient hours of childish things: museums and walks and ice-cream treats. A life of Martin's kind was inevitably paid for by the family. He tried to care for his children but it was very hard: he had so little time and, never having been with them all that much, his beginning attempt was bound to be awkward.

Now, too, since her own -- loss, should one call it euphemistically? – she had felt more sharply not only the children's needs, but also some new need within herself. The wholesomeness of children, still so removed from the ugly agonies of adulthood, gave basic comfort. It was like warm food, like milk and bread after sore sickness.

All this crossed her mind one free morning while she stood in the operating room watching Martin at work. He had suggested that she ought to witness as much neurosurgery as possible, so as to get a head start on next year. So she stood now among a group of residents, interns and even some fourth-year students who liked to wander into the operating rooms where big names were at work. Her eyes went from one face to the other: all wore the absorbed expression of total interest and respect. Her eyes went to Leonard Max and rested kindly on him. He had been so devastated by Martin's defeat that he had sworn he would refuse to work under the new man from California. Fortunately, for the sake of Max's fairly young career, Martin had been able to dissuade him from such beautiful, impractical, fierce loyalty.

And Claire felt a thrill of pride: strip a man of title – as they had – but it made no alteration in his true value, and even the enemies, those who had stripped him, knew it and had to acknowledge it.

Now she watched the small vertical line between Martin's brows as he worked with the loupe. With utmost delicacy, with excruciating concentration, he laboured among the most minute nerves of a leg that had been mangled in an accident. The process was exhausting to watch. She could barely imagine what it would be like to do it. Not until the procedure was finished was she aware how her hands had been clenched, how painfully the muscles of her neck had tensed.

She waited in the corridor for Martin. The nurse at the charge desk looked up with a pleasant remark.

'Pretty soon we'll be seeing you up here every day.'

'Next year.'

'What a privilege to learn from your father! Nobody needs to tell you that, I'm sure. I've known him since I was capped. Downtown at Fairview it was, that's where I started and he was an intern. Yes,' she reflected, 'he used to come up and watch Dr Albeniz, just the way young people come to watch him now. He was one of the greats, Albeniz was.' And taking her sheaf of charts, she went down the corridor.

A privilege, Claire thought. Not a day passed without someone, some nurse or intern or clerk in the clinic or even her mother, reminding her of the privilege. She had begun to be tired of hearing it.

They sat at lunch in the doctors' dining-room. The paper napkin, on which for her benefit and instruction Martin had diagrammed the morning's procedure, lay alongside Claire's plate.

'Well,' he said, 'enough of that for today. Got any plans

or the week-end?'

'Thought maybe I'd join you and the kids and go skating on Sunday afternoon.'

'Sure, fine. But I meant – social life is what I meant.' His mile was anxious.

'Oh, I'm going out Saturday night. Maybe Friday, too if I t'll feel like it when the time comes.' She knew he wanted to sk, but wouldn't ask, with whom she was going and how she iked him, and was she doing anything foolish again? – he oped not! He wanted, of course – parents always wanted – o be told that their child was safe, was happy. And feeling udden compassion for his anxiety, she added gently, 'Don't vorry about me, Dad, I'm really, really fine.'

She was rewarded by the relaxing and brightening of his ace. 'That's all I ever want to hear,' he said.

'And I'm not doing anything foolish.'

'I know you're not.'

Actually, the opportunity for doing anything 'foolish' had carcely presented itself, certainly not as frequently as Martin might be thinking. There had been relationships ince Ned, of course there had been. One didn't live in a onvent! Yet there was no life in any of them. She had elapsed into the years before Ned, to that era of intelligent, greeable men, most of them inevitably doctors, who didn't *each* her. The current companion, Patrick Moore, had onsiderable charm with his Irish sparkle and cheer, but even t was petering out and they both knew it. She supposed she vas waiting again for the feeling she had first had on that hill n Devon.

Martin shoved his chair back. 'Well, I'm off.'

'Back to the office?'

'No, it's Tuesday. The neuropathology conference.'

'Oh, of course, I have the GYN clinic.' Finishing her offee, she watched him go down the room, saw nods and a ew greetings exchanged on his way. Perry Gault, among thers, did not look up as Martin passed. That anger would emain, no doubt of it. And she wondered how deep, ctually, the wound must lie in Martin, how deep the multiple wounds, the whole affair of the institute. It was

plain that he gave himself now completely to teaching and t
his own long solitary hours in the laboratory. These thing
that he loved he would talk about with eagerness. About th
wounds he would not speak, and one had to respect hi
privacy.

The clinic and emergency rooms were already filled. In th
corridors waited babies, the sick, the old and the healthy wh
had brought them here. A small Puerto Rican stood up an
smiled.

'Hello, Mr Filipe,' Claire said.

'This time I brought my daughter Angela, Doctor.'

'Good. I'll tell Dr Milano. She'll see her in a few minutes.

Dr Milano was a handsome woman in her forties, wh
seemed able to manage with great calm a large practice a
well as a household of two teenagers and a husband. Fron
her Claire was gradually absorbing a manner and feel for th
ill.

'Mr Filipe's outside. He's brought his daughter, can yo
believe it?' Claire said as she went in.

Dr Milano smiled. 'I can believe it. It's happened before.'

Mr Filipe had made a memorable scene only a few month
ago when his wife had died. She had been a patient of D
Milano's. The man's grief had been one thing, but his fury a
Dr Milano had been another, a fury based on the fact tha
women had no business practising medicine and that if D
Milano hadn't been a woman, Mr Filipe's wife wouldn'
have died. A woman should stay home and raise kids
Everybody knew that. A doctor should be a man.

It had taken a good deal of effort and some hours befor
he had been quieted. But something, time or goodness knev
what, had done an effective job, because here he was actuall
back again, bringing his teenage daughter for treatment.

'You're the one who won him over. You know that, don'
you, Claire?' Dr Milano said.

'Oh really,' Claire began.

'Yes, yes you did. You have a way with people that's ver
warm, my dear. Well, let's begin, shall we? I have to quit a
three. I'm going up to do an abortion. Want to see it?'

Oh no, Claire thought. Oh no! 'I don't think so. I've neve

seen one,' she said.

'Well, then, it's time you did. All right, start calling them in.'

So they came filing in, the old known faces and the new ones who would in all probability become familar too. Most of these women's troubles were not of the kind that could be solved overnight. One came to know them and their pains quite intimately before one was through.

There was the diabetic girl whom they had warned against becoming pregnant. But her husband wanted children, so she had gone ahead anyway, only to produce a monster who, luckily for itself and its parents, had been born dead.

Now came an unmarried, pregnant addict, accompanied by one of her four children; this was a twelve-year-old boy, also plainly addicted. Outside the door he waited for his mother, as if afraid to let her out of his sight. He had sly, sliding monkey's eyes. Like a monkey's, too, were the dark sadness and the wordless questioning.

And there was the girl who had been impregnated by her brother.

And there was the girl whose infant was born with sore eyes from gonococcus.

Was there no end to the ignorance, the helplessness, the need? Poor women, Claire thought. Poor women!

All these foreigners, she thought, too. Sometimes it almost seems as if I'm not in America at all. The fact is, I really resented them at first. The language difficulty makes such a tiring struggle. And they're so confused, so scared. And they mostly smell of garlic. But I should be ashamed! After all, they came here driven by the same needs that brought my grandfather out of his poor village. Oh, it's a disgrace the way some people treat them! Clerks, lower middle class themselves, feeling superior because these people can't speak English and have nothing, not even pride any more, what they had of it having been knocked out of them. I spoke sharply to a clerk who was being nasty to some poor woman yesterday. Now she'll have it in for me if she ever gets a chance. If I dared, and of course I don't dare, I would say something to Dr Norris, too, one of the few obstetrical residents who have no compassion for these women. He's so arrogant, you'd think he was a vet handling a cow!

In a curtained cubicle, Dr Milano was examining a woman. On a straight chair near the desk where Claire was filling out a form, sat the woman's friend, who had come with her. They both looked up at the sound of soft weeping.

'Then she must be pregnant,' the woman said. 'That's why she's crying.'

Claire could have predicted the comments that followed.

'She's my sister-in-law. Her husband's a devil. They have five kids already, and he don't make enough to buy their shoes. Sometimes I help out, even though I can't afford it, but the kids have to have shoes, don't they? And she's all nerves, Doctor. She's forty-two, and the boys are wild sometimes. I keep the two big ones at my house for a couple of days. She can't manage, she gets so nervous, she cries. Doctor,' the woman pleaded, unconsciously clasping her hands, 'she can't have another baby! It will kill her or she will go crazy, either one.'

Victims. Victims. Women and their children.

'I understand,' Claire said. 'Some day it will be possible to take care of things like this.'

'But not now?'

Claire shook her head gently. 'Not now.' Except for the rich, and even they take a chance. And she thought, looking at the clock, at three I have to go upstairs and watch. God, I don't want to. But I have to.

The woman is covered with a sheet that has a hole where it lies on her abdomen. Why is she here? What ailment, pretended or true, permits the doing of this thing today?

Dr Milano has been overly rushed and that is Claire's excuse for not asking her to explain. The truth is, Claire doesn't want to ask.

She is required to look. The area where the doctor is to work has been rendered antiseptic and has been anaesthetized. The doctor takes a needle. Claire has read what is to come, yet she trembles. The doctor plunges the needle into the abdomen, into the uterus where the baby lies growing in the warmth, in the dark. His head is bent; he rests so comfortably. Each day, each hour he expands into a complexity of fingernails, eyelashes, delicate, convoluted shells of ears . . . The doctor takes a syringe and injects the stuff which will, a few hours from now, contract the womb and force him out of his warm home to die.

Claire's fist is clenched on her mouth. My baby, too, she thinks.

Dr Milano looks up. Her eyes tell Claire she understands her questions. How can a woman, herself a mother, do this thing? Or how, when she has seen so many of the hungry, unwanted and abused, can she not do it?

Oh God, make everything more simple, so that I can know, finally, and for all time, what is right.

The smell of snow was in the air when she reached Madison Avenue. She began to walk a fast mile towards her mother's house. They had drifted into the habit of a weekly dinner together, on any day convenient for Claire. The sky was smudged in sombre grey, but at street level was spread the glitter of approaching holiday: Santa Claus and wreaths, gilded angels, velvet robes and brocade evening bags. Wafts of perfumed air came through revolving doors along with segments of canned carols: 'It Came Upon a Midnight Clear'.

With heads bent against the looming wind, people brushed into each other. Some were too tired and hurried to look up and apologize. Others, having just come from office parties, were too crocked to look up or care about any tidings of comfort and joy.

Claire had visions, sentimental visions, of people carolling around fireplaces or on doorsteps in places where people all knew one another. In such places the carols would really mean something. This world was so hurried, so enormous and indifferent, that one could almost feel afraid in it. 'Lonely world,' she said aloud, and was surprised at the sound of the words and the feel of her own warm breath caught in her coat collar. 'Lonely world.' (That baby will never see it, lonely or not.)

And passing a flower shop, she stopped impulsively to buy

a dozen dark-red roses. Mother had a greedy need for flowers and she, Claire, had sudden need to make a tender gesture. Waiting there while the roses were being wrapped in green tissue, she felt this tenderness at the vision of herself mounting the steps of her mother's house with a gift in hand.

And then, above the exuberance of trailing fernery and roses – colour of blood, colour of life – among all that moist, triumphant burgeoning, she unexpectedly caught sight of her own mirrored face. For an instant, she did not recognize it. So white! So old! But that was absurd. She was only twenty-eight . . .

Outside again in the cold, the lonely mood came flooding back. She had been sleeping poorly, waking in the middle of the night with oppressive thoughts. Tonight, surely, she would wake up to think of a baby. Just whose? That woman's today or her own?

There are no answers to most things, Claire. You're gradually learning that, aren't you? Answers, that is, which are always right or always wrong.

How strange to think that she and Jessie, both at work in the same city, only a mile or two apart, could exist in such different worlds! Jessie's ladies concerned themselves with silks and marble. But those poor women who came to the hospital, the ones who scrubbed the city's floors while others slept, what of them? How did they bear the injustice of their lives? (Yet who is to keep the floors clean? Answer that!)

You belong with Dr Milano's women, Claire, not with the silk-and-marble ladies, decent and good though many of them may be. You were made to belong with those others.

In Jessie's house the lights were lit. Grateful light, grateful warmth, she thought as she went in. Above the hall table where she laid her hat and gloves hung a portrait of somebody's eighteenth-century ancestress, not Jessie's, although she had hung there so long that possibly Jessie had by now convinced herself that she was. The woman had a handsome, critical face in which there was no sympathy for Claire's modern malaise.

'Well,' Jessie said, holding out her cheek to be kissed, 'how e you? You look worn out again.'

'I am, a little. You're not, I see.'

'I don't allow it. Nobody thanks you for it. Sherry?'

'Yes, please.'

'What are you looking at? The jewellery? It's new, if that's hat you're wondering.'

'It's magnificent.'

Jessie's taste in jewels was exotic and conspicuous. onight she wore jade in ornate gold filigree. The chain owed on her dark dress, and the ear-rings swung half-way her shoulders.

'I know I attract attention. I will anyway, so I might as ell make a bold job of it.' With a twist and jab, Jessie uffed out a cigarette. 'By my possessions I can show I have complished something. Vulgar, I suppose,' she said, garding Claire's blouse and skirt and ringless hands.

'No, I understand it,' Claire answered quietly.

Twirling the sherry glass slowly between her hands, she ared into the fire. When you have been reclusive all through rlhood, tolerated, pitied and excluded, you were entitled to joy your release, especially when you had achieved that lease by your own strength and efforts. She could imagine e sort of perverse thrill that must come to Jessie when a w client, one who had not been forewarned, crossed the rpet to face her at her desk. She could even imagine her other's silent amusement: Yes, this little person is the Jessie eig you've heard about. Yet in spite of this bravado, Jessie ever went out on social occasions unless a client was along. was true that she was too busy to build a social circle of her wn, but actually she wanted the company of important ients because at parties they gave her the shelter of their ysical presence and prestige.

'You saw the article in the magazine section last week?' ssie inquired now.

'Yes. I was going to mention it. Only there've been so any, that I'm quite used to seeing your name.'

'I had so much publicity on the Arizona place that they've ked me to do a small Bermuda inn for the same people. I all enjoy that. I'll get away from the tropical, I think, and do it in pure eighteenth-century English with a lot of colour. She mused. 'I'm seeing it in my mind's eye already.'

'It's getting so I should think one almost needs a introduction from a friend to persuade you to do a house.'

'Not quite, but almost,' Jessie smiled. 'Let's go in t dinner. Tell me what you did today.'

'Very different things from what you did I watched a abortion.'

Jessie raised an eyebrow.

'Sometimes I feel so sorry for women! Their poor bodies all their conflicts! I saw a young woman who had a botche abortion. She'll never have a baby, short of a miracle, tha is.'

Jessie was silent.

'I don't believe much in miracles,' Claire said sombrely Suddenly the food was hard to swallow and she put the for down.

'You're not hungry.'

'I was when I came in, but now I'm not.'

'Ah, Claire, Claire, you have more in your heart tha you'll admit!'

Claire felt the threat of tears. Lowering her eyes from he mother's gaze, she stared at the flowers on the centre of th table: anemones, each as rare and languid as an Edwardia beauty. Their pale stems curved in the water, which tremble slightly in the shallow bowl. The stem was the beauty's neck and the spreading petals were her head, top-heavy with pile glossy hair.

'Ned would have loved a child,' she said softly. 'How h would love a proudly pregnant little woman waiting at hom for him every evening after his exciting day!'

'Most men would, you know.'

'I know most men would. There's nothing wrong with . . . So, he'll find somebody, if he hasn't already, who'll b glad to give it to him, I'm sure.'

'I hope you're not too bitter, Claire?'

'You've been bitter often enough, haven't you?'

'Yes, but that doesn't mean I want to see bitterness in yo Anyway, mine was different, it couldn't have been helpe

The circumstances I mean.'

'And mine could. I made my own. You don't have to tell me.'

'I won't tell you anything. It wouldn't do any good anyway. But I will say, come stretch out on the sofa. Take the pillows away and stretch out.'

The fire had settled down and purred softly now, like a cat. 'Smells good, doesn't it?' Jessie remarked. 'Cedar logs.'

'I was rummaging today,' Claire began, after a minute, 'and found my Brearley yearbook. God, how fresh-faced and hopeful everybody looked! With all the sentimental sayings under the pictures. And when you think of what's actually happened – '

'What has?'

'Well, Lynn's a model, living in Beverly Hills with a squat, rich old man. June's already had two divorces. Paula broke her neck diving into a pool that had no water in it.'

Jessie shuddered. 'Do tell me something cheerful, will you? You're not yourself at all tonight.'

'You don't think so?'

'As a matter of fact, though, maybe you are yourself. The self you've been for quite a while now. I don't know exactly when you became what you are, but I suspect when.'

Claire didn't answer. Her head ached with the held-back tears, with weariness and the weight of things. The room was weighty, heavy with the accretions of a way of life that was going, she suspected, if not gone. Jessie's independence was no first choice, but had been forced to birth out of courage and desperate need. Jessie would have rejoiced to be cherished and guarded by a man.

'I want to go away,' she said suddenly. 'To India or Brazil, some place. Any place.'

'What? Why? You don't want to train with your father?'

She began to cry. 'No! But I don't dare let him see it.'

'I don't understand! Such a fabulous opportunity, Claire!'

'Yes, only I don't want it.'

'Good Lord, why ever not?'

'"We are such stuff as dreams are made on." Our parents' dreams for us.'

'Never mind the quotation. Tell me why you don't want it.'

'Because I hate it. It's awful. The whole atmosphere is awful.' Claire shuddered. 'The shaved heads and the people who can't talk afterwards. All the physical therapy and phony – no, not phony – the contrived cheer because somebody can take one step. And you know he'll go home and maybe take six steps after a while. To say nothing of the ones who die under surgery. It's just too depressing, and I can't see myself spending my life with it.'

'Well!' Jessie cried, throwing up her hands. 'I just don't know at all! When did you start to feel this way?'

'I don't remember. It just grew. I don't think I ever really *thought* about it at all until I began to get into it, don't you see? And found out what it was like?'

'You wanted to please your father. You always have,' Jessie said, accusingly.

'No, I don't think I even thought that much! Not consciously. It just seemed to be the thing I was naturally going to do. After all, if one is a doctor and one's father happens to be Martin Farrell, one is sort of expected to – I mean, you expect yourself to – it's not as if he were any ordinary man, just anybody – ' And to her own dismay, Claire began to sob. Everything just surged up and burst. 'I hate Dad's work! I'd be no good at it! Everybody says, "Oh, you're so unbelievably lucky!" And I know I am. I'm so proud of Dad and so guilty, and – I know you're shocked.'

'Claire, I'm not shocked. Surprised, but not shocked.'

'He's been so wonderful to me. And I've been so depressed because apparently I don't appreciate it enough.'

'All the same,' Jessie said quietly, 'I think you ought to tell him.'

'I can't! Oh my God, I can't do that! Don't you see? He's counted on it for years! He's already had so many failures! How can I give him one more?'

'How? You're not obliged to compensate for his disappointments! Or for anyone's.'

'You say that because you – '

'I say that because it's the truth and not for any – any

:rsonal reason you're thinking of.'
'I'm so ashamed!' Claire gasped. 'I don't know why I'm
ying like this.'
'You're entitled to cry! You don't have to be so damned
'ave! Shall I leave the room? Would you feel better if I did?'
'No, no. Stay.'
Presently Jessie laid her hand on Claire's forehead. 'Move
ver. I'll massage your neck. You're all knots. Does that feel
ood?'
'Yes.'
'Tell me what you want to do in India.'
'Oh – go somewhere with one of those agencies that sends
edical help to people who haven't got any. I don't want to
: a medical great. I'm not cut out for it. I'd like to bring
imary care, simple care and hope to people, especially to
omen, because they're the most trod upon. They're at the
ottom of the heap. Wherever you go, women are at the
ottom of the heap.' And to her own horror, she began to cry
gain. 'But there's no use talking about it, I can't do it. I'll
ay here and – and petrify.'
'You were speaking of Ned a while ago,' Jessie said softly.
'What about him?'
'You still think about him.'
'He treated me badly. *Badly!*'
'Why don't you just forget him, then?'
'Oh!' Claire cried. 'A good question! Why don't I? I don't
now . . . I don't sleep. I wake up every night and I'm scared.
don't understand why I'm scared. Maybe of being so alone?
ut I do understand how it was for Dad when Hazel died . . .'
Jessie's fingers soothed and soothed. 'It's not the same,
arling. No one's died.'
'Our baby died. I made it die.'
'That's not the same.'
Claire sat up. 'What else could I have done? Should I have
one after him?'
'Certainly not,' Jessie said stoutly, 'not then and not now.
ne doesn't run after a man!'
They both sat looking into the fire. At last Claire's tears
opped, and the fire flickered out.

'I guess I'll go home,' she said.

'No, stay here for the night. Take a sleeping pill and get good night's rest.'

'I never take pills, Mother.'

'Well, Doctor, take one tonight. Just one mild pill.'

'No pill. But I will stay. That I'll do.' It would be good t avoid the apartment tonight, and the bed where she had slep with Ned, and the sight of his Irish woollen hat, which he ha left on the shelf.

Like a little girl, she followed Jessie up the stairs and int her old room, where a doll from her tenth year still stoo next to a first year Latin text and a souvenir birchbark cano those innocent relics of easy years before real life had begu

A great square desk covered with papers, medical periodica and sundries stood between Jessie and Martin. How many c life's salient encounters take place among three, two peop and a desk?

'He still looks like a doctor,' she thought, 'and that's od because what does a doctor look like? Yet he does.'

For the last half hour and for two weeks before that sh had been resisting a confusion of emotions: stubbornne and pride, worry and embarrassment and cowardice, alon with anger at the circumstances that were forcing her into supplicant's position. Still, she reminded herself, she wa doing this for Claire: for Claire she would take sword again monsters if need be. Happily, Martin was no monster, sh thought with a certain grim humour; he was Claire's fathe and as concerned this minute as she was herself.

'It's cost you a good deal to come here, Jessie, and on serious need could have brought you. I want you to know understand that.'

'Quite so.'

Once more the doctor had spoken: comprehending kind and firm. Through Jessie's head went scraps of flittir thought: *It seems a century (another age of man) since w walked in Kensington Gardens while Claire in her yellow co rode the tricycle. It seems yesterday since Cyprus.* A bit poetry went flitting, something about 'time in its flight'. *Th nmer he bought painful new white shoes. The little car nced over the back-country roads and the doctor's bag lay the seat between us: Fern wore blue linen and our mother's arls.*

There was a queer turmoil in her chest. Weakened, she sat , straightened and spoke decisively. 'Claire mustn't know e been here, or ever know I've told you how she dreads ur kind of work. This must come from you as if it were ur own idea. That is, if you agree.'

She really hates the work all that much?' Martin repeated h disbelief.

Apparently so. It's tearing her down.' And I'm tearing u down by telling you, but I can't help it.'

When – when did she first know this about herself?'

How can anyone say exactly "when" anything happens ide one's head?' Like falling in love or out of it: does ybody know exactly 'when'? Answer that if you can, artin. 'It's tied up somehow with Ned, that I know. Maybe at's when it started. I don't know. At any rate, it's been owing more and more – the conviction that she doesn't nt your kind of work. She's absolutely devastated at the ought of a lifetime of it.'

Why hasn't she ever told me? For God's sake, why?'

She knew it would be a terrible wound.'

Martin was looking at his hands, which gripped the edge the desk. She understood that it was difficult for him to ok at her. Her eyes, too, avoided him, as they circled the om. On a shelf near the desk stood the photograph of a man with a quiet face, a trifle too round, and timid, pretty es. Claire's description of Hazel had been remarkably curate. Yes, Jessie thought, he's had trouble enough for e lifetime, whether of his own doing or not, doesn't atter.

'Such a waste of her skilled mind!' Martin cried abruptly. he'd be doing the most rudimentary medicine. Useful, odness knows, but rudimentary. Does she know that?'

'Of course she knows it. It's what she wants.'

'She'll deliver babies, but if there should be complications, e'll fail because of not knowing enough. She'll set a broken

bone. but if it's a compound fracture of the shoulder, sh
be unable to cope with it. She'll do a lot of things passab
but nothing expertly.'

Jessie replied with patience, 'She understands all that.'

'I had been counting on her more than I know. Looki
forward to something so special! Father and daughter. Sl
in a way, beginning where I, in not too many more years, w
leave off.' He tapped a pencil. With a small shiver
recognition, Jessie remembered the habit. 'There's so mu
new. Every day it comes piling in. One would need fi
lifetimes to learn it all.' His face sank into a tired sadness.

Again she looked away and was silent. A typewri
clacked in the outer office. A fire engine screeched past t
windows. The stillness when these sounds ceased was ble
and lonely.

At last Jessie spoke. 'I'm remembering something,' s
said softly, 'that you may have forgotten. I'm thinking
you and your father.' It was the only personal remark th
had passed between them.

And now Martin gave her a long look. 'I haven't forgott
. . . What you're reminding me is that every human bei
must develop in his own way. And that I ought to be the fi
to see it.'

'True, isn't it?'

'Yes. Yes. You always did like to get at the heart of thi
in a hurry, didn't you? Well, you're right, of course. And
tell her. You can depend on it. I'll tell her that I've be
thinking it would be better for us both if she were to go h
own way. I'll find words to make it convincing.'

'I thought you would. Otherwise I wouldn't have come.

'What about that – other affair? She never talks to
about him.'

'Nor to me, until that night. It shocked me so! Cla
almost never cries, you know she doesn't.'

'Everything's bottled up inside.'

'That's what worries me! Not that there's anything to
done about him, to be sure.'

'He was a fine young man. I tried hard not to like him, b
– Martin threw out his hands – 'it didn't work.'

'A fine young man? It was an impossible situation! mpossible!'

'I grant that. But then – human situations often are.' Martin hesitated. 'I suppose there's no way of finding out where he is? That old aunt of yours?' He broke off and Jessie understood he meant that Aunt Milly could write to Fern and find out.

'Aunt Milly died last year. Anyway,' she said, suddenly ndignant, 'I wouldn't dream of asking! Claire would never orgive it and I wouldn't blame her. Pride is the last thing a woman wants to lose.' Martin would be thinking, no doubt: *Well, you ought to know.* And well I ought, Jessie said to erself. Aloud, she went on, 'With a little effort I could hate he fellow for the mess he's made of her life.'

Surprisingly, Martin replied, 'It was Claire's fault, too.'

'You don't mean you would welcome him back, for eaven's sake?'

'He's not my first choice. But if she wants him?'

'This is all academic, and may I add, I'm glad of it?' She tood up. 'But I might as well bring you something pleasant long with all the bad before I leave. You remember a patient amed Jeremy from Tucson?'

'Yes. I operated on him a few months ago.'

'His sister-in-law is a customer of mine. She's been singing our praises everywhere.'

'That's nice to know.' The quick smile was youthful, as hough praise were an embarrassment.

'She was telling everyone he'd been given up. Something bout the tumour being in both lobes and six other doctors aid it was impossible, but you said you could do it?'

'Well, yes.'

'She said his doctor came from Arizona to watch you. He'd been convinced it couldn't be done.'

'Yes.'

'So those people all think you're something of a hero.'

'Hero? I know my work and I love it, that's about all.'

'That's enough, isn't it? Well, call me if there's anything I hould know about Claire. Otherwise, of course, I won't xpect to hear from you.'

'Of course,' Martin said courteously.

He came from behind the desk and opened the door. It wa like taking leave of one's lawyer or banker, and she wa grateful for his calm tact which had so eased the difficul meeting for them both.

She put out her hand. 'So, having told you what I came t tell you, I'll be going.'

'I'm thankful you came. I had no idea, none at all. But I' set her free – for India or wherever she wants to go. Withou guilt or any looking back.'

'India,' Jessie murmured, going through the door. 'Of a places.'

For long minutes Martin sat looking at the wall, th bookshelves and the windows all blurring in the wintry ligh He was vaguely aware when the typewriter fell silent an when Jenny Jennings poked her head in at the door to sa good-night. The sight of him sitting here in a fog c abstraction aroused no concern in her, for his people wer used to seeing him puzzle over his problems.

But his problem hurt so much! He turned it over in hi mind, examining it as though it were an X-ray. Jessie woul never have come to him, after all these proud years, unless i were really serious and she were really alarmed. It took good deal to alarm Jessie, too. Well, he would break the ti that was all! How could he have known it had become s painful? Never by one word had Claire revealed herself. Poc little soul! May this be the right thing for her! May she neve regret it! May I get over my loss with good grace.

Then he thought of that other pain of hers, the mar woman thing. What it could do to a human soul! So sh wanted him still, that boy! There was no sense in it, when th world was full of young men who would gladly have he Claire, with all that life in her, that bright life! And her eye with their grave gaze, and their soft lashes, flashed throug his memory. No sense in it at all!

She wanted Ned Lamb. He could see them still: handsom couple! They had looked as though they belonged togethe There had been something between them which, although one might not wish to admit it, one recognized. Little Claire, so proud, so foolish! And remembering how close she had come to dying, he trembled. Her longing – if it was anything like what he had suffered over that boy's mother – was dreadful. He tried to remember how it had felt and could only recall that he had felt it, been sick with it, almost overcome by it and that every day had been a struggle against it. And remembering, he actually began to feel it again. A soft ache, creeping, settled like a lump in his throat . . .

It had grown quite dark. Suddenly he sat upright and turned on the desk lamp. He looked in his telephone book for a number, and dialled it.

'I want to leave a message for Mr Fordyce,' he said. 'He always books my trips. Can he get me a flight to London towards the end of the week? Yes, Thursday or Friday would be fine.'

CHAPTER THIRTY-THREE

From the hotel window Martin looked out on a dull sky, out of which beat a steady rain. An English winter: he had forgotten. He had ordered breakfast in his room. The rented car would be delivered shortly so he could make an early start. The route was clear in his mind. That he had not forgotten.

Night had just faded away. A car with headlights on moved slowly in the street below, the light picking out the remains of a discarded Christmas tree that had been tossed in the gutter. It was a mournful sight so late in the winter, those broken branches with tinsel scraps still clinging. A cat came prowling, foraging for food perhaps, and finding nothing, set up a bitter wail. Hunger? Or hunger of another kind, a tomcat crying for a female shut up somewhere in a house?

Thoughtfully he drank his coffee, still not sure he ought to be where he was. On the plane above the Atlantic, he'd had his moments of thinking he'd made a mistake, that he would just turn right round at the airport and take the next plane back. He'd had moments at home, too, in which he'd tried to extricate himself from his own undertaking. Calling the New York office of Ned's firm to ask whether he was still in Hong Kong, all he'd found out was that Ned wasn't even with them any more. Only the remembrance of Jessie had spurred him to persevere. Sheer guts it had taken for her to have come to him! But she had done it for their daughter, and he could do no less than try, at least, to straighten things out for Claire, if it was not too late, and if he could.

And thinking with some pity of his daughter, he recalled something Mr Meredith had said on the day she was born, something about the Achilles' heel: 'Whatever happens to that child will happen to you,' he'd said. Yes, yes. If Jessie were correct in her report, and there was no reason to think she wasn't, how Claire must suffer! Fantasies of reunion:

imagining what you would say if you should meet by chance. Imagining yourself walking haughtily away, wanting to hurt, leaving him or her staring helplessly after you. Or imagining outstretched arms and healing tears.

Fantasies! Had he not had more than a few himself? He had meant to do right; yet had he not wronged all the women he had known? He should never have gone back to Mary during the war. In his heart he must have known what was bound to happen. He had only made it hard for her to find someone else. His fault.

He looked at his watch. Too early. Now that he had made up his mind, time was going too slowly. And he sat on, brooding and mulling over, denying and reconsidering, a thing he had never dared to examine in the light of day. It began to take shape. It grew so rapidly that he knew instinctively it must have been lying there, stifled inside him, for longer than he could know.

They called from the desk to say that the car had been delivered. He went downstairs and took the wheel. A sudden enormous excitement possessed him, an astounding surge of energy. The tension made him hot and he lowered the window, not minding the rain.

The last he had heard, she was still living at Lamb House alone. What if, as long as he was going there to speak for Claire, what if he were to speak for himself as well? Why not? Was it absolute madness? Why not?

The rain ceased. Fog lay in shreds and tatters, snagged on the lower branches of the trees. A pure light touched the tops of the worn old hills. The wind rushed in his ears like ringing silence. He was almost there. And he had a curious sensation, an expectation of reward as at the theatre in the moment before the curtain rises.

The maid said, 'There's only Mr Ned at home. He's in the studio. Shall I fetch him?'

'Thanks. I know where it is.'

For a moment Martin stood in the doorway, watching Ned who, in shirt-sleeves and work clothes, was removing a painting from a crate. At the sight of this stranger, who could possess such power over his daughter as to bring her father here to beg for her, strong feelings of resentment, shame and grief churned up in Martin. With them was mixed the memory of Claire lying ill and drained, of Claire so hurt, so still. Strange! It was only after Jessie had pointed it out to him that he remarked how the stillness had lasted. She had always been so vigorous; why, then, had he not noticed the change? And all these feelings were so strong in Martin now that they pounded in his head; he felt almost ill with the pressure of them as he stood there.

Ned saw him. Astonishment spread over his face. He didn't, or more likely couldn't, speak.

'No,' Martin said, 'you're not imagining things. I'm sorry to have startled you.'

'Well – well I – '

'I've come looking for you. I didn't expect to find you so easily. I rather thought you'd be in Singapore or somewhere.'

'No, I've been home a while.'

They stared at each other. In their looks were anxiety and wariness, puzzlement, embarrassment and a certain hostility.

'Come in. Sit down.'

Martin took an uncomfortable straight-backed chair. Ned sat on a packing case. It seemed to Martin that he looked tired and older than one ought to look at his age.

He began resolutely. 'I'll come to the point. I want to talk about Claire.'

Ned's expression was unreadable.

'It's not, as you suppose, the easiest thing I've ever had to do. But first I have to ask you something: Is there another woman in your life? If there is, I'll go about my business and you can forget you saw me.'

'There's no one.'

'Then that's one hurdle past. The next is: No matter what, if anything, should come of this conversation, I want your word that my daughter will never know I've been here. She's proud; I don't have to tell you that. Perhaps too proud, though I'm sometimes not quite sure what that means. Anyway, I want your word.'

'You have it.'

'Because if she were ever to find out, I'd have your head.'

'I said you have my word.' Ned waited.

'Now the hard part. The fact is, she's still in love with you. She's miserable. She's never told me, but her mother knows. She's made herself miserable ever since – ' And idiotically, he felt tears skimming over his eyes. He swallowed. 'Ever since she lost the baby.'

'The baby!'

'Yes. You left her pregnant.'

'Oh my God!' Ned cried. 'A baby! But when? It died?'

'Yes,' Martin said. 'Or, I mean – Oh damn the language! It didn't *die*, she had an abortion and *she* nearly died of it. There's the whole thing in one sentence.' And taking out a handkerchief, he wiped his eyes unashamedly.

Ned let out a long sigh. 'I would have come back. She knew where I was. I would have come back.'

'Yes. Yes. Well, it would take a Solomon to figure out what went on in your two heads. Nowadays they call it a breakdown in communications or some such stuff.'

Ned put his head in his hands. The room was very still while he sat there, not looking up.

'I wish I knew what happened,' he said at last. 'I've asked myself and asked. I wanted to go to her, but she sent me away. Somehow I couldn't get over that.'

Martin felt a flare of anger. 'You could have written.'

'Yes, it was small-minded. We hurt each other so.' Now he looked up at Martin. 'I thought about her . . . I'd take a girl out, and driving away, I'd see Claire's face. It's been like that ever since. I'd get to thinking perhaps it would always be like that, and I'd always see her face. You know how it is?'

Martin said steadily, 'I know how it is.'

Ned flushed. 'Where is she? What is she doing?' he asked.

'She wants to go to India or Brazil or some far place like that. Probably India.'

'Not going to work with you?'

'No. She has very different ideas which I wasn't aware of. Another failure of communication. Life seems to be full of them. I don't understand why they happen. Is it pride or stubbornness, or both?'

'Claire and I, we're both proud and stubborn. Both of us, I mean.'

Somehow, the rueful half smile was appealing, Martin thought. And Ned added, 'Machismo. Do you suppose I overdid it?'

'Ah well, she's a feminist! Was one before she was old enough to know what the word meant. Still, you asked an awful lot of her, you know. And times are changing. You can't treat a woman like a child any more.'

Martin thought again: What am I doing here, pleading for this reunion which will only complicate my life, unless – unless what I thought of this morning were possible? And the thought came leaping back. Mary and I. How improbably tidy! How neat, how perfect! And yet, why not? Why not?

Into his thoughts, swirling like flares in a dark place, came Ned's plaintive question. 'What can we do now, do you think?'

'That's rather up to you, isn't it?'

'India,' Ned repeated.

'Yes. She wants experience working with the poor, women in particular. Women and children.' He added sharply, 'I think you ought to know, she may not ever have a child.'

'I understand.'

'You'd have some mending of her spirit to do if she can't, I should suppose.'

'I understand.'

'This India business – you might well guess it's not my idea for her. But then that's hardly relevant, is it?' And Martin hoped he didn't betray the remnant of bitterness. 'How could you manage that if – if you should straighten things out with her? She's determined to go, you know.'

'Oh, I'm a free agent now. I quit the work in Hong Kong. I was miserable there, thinking of her – ' Ned cleared his throat and stopped.

Martin thought: *I really have hit him where it hurts,* and was keenly sorry.

'I found that I didn't really *like* advertising anyhow. It seemed suddenly much ado about very little, persuading

eople to buy things they often don't need and can't afford.'
'Rather a sudden revelation, wasn't it?'
'Not really so sudden, when I piece it all together. I'd lways wanted to write. To write truly, I mean, without ·icks. To use words honestly and well. Claire knew. She ever told you?'
'She mentioned something. But then you were so nthusiastic about the job – '
'Yes, well you see, doing the kind of journalism I had in ıind, reporting on things I cared about and felt people ught to know about – conditions in slum schools or saving ıe whales or revolt in Iraq or whatever – you don't just reak into that whenever you feel like it. So I'd got a bit iscouraged and then sidetracked into advertising, making a ›t of money – a lot for me, at any rate – getting this great romotion, very flattering to the ego – ' Ned threw up his ands.
I like this man, I really do, Martin thought. He said aloud, A man's ego. That always figures.'
'Perhaps it figured too much with me.' Ned looked away. Claire told me at the end – we were wounded and angry with ne another – she said I was trying to compensate, to be the ıan my father wasn't. Yet I had always, or so I'd thought, een very proud of my father, while overlooking that other usiness. So I couldn't forgive her for saying that.' Now he ›oked directly at Martin. 'But perhaps she was right. erhaps I did want to feel big and powerful and manly, limbing up in the corporate world, running around to nportant meetings with my briefcase.'
Martin asked gently, 'So you've quit that world?'
'Yes, I've taken a chance and it seems to be working out. I o abroad on contract and report on things for newspapers nd magazines. I've an article on changes in Spain coming ut in the States next month.'
'Congratulations, then!'
'Thank you.' Ned added abruptly, 'I don't need a great eal of money to live. I never did, even when I was earning it.'
'Come to think of it, Claire doesn't either. She buys a pair f shoes when the old ones have worn out.' Martin smiled,

remembering worn shoes and missing buttons.

'I could go wherever she went.' Ned spoke thoughtfully 'We could work our schedules on an equal basis.'

'You're really ready to accept that "equal basis" business I'm not sure I could. But then, I keep forgetting, you're a nev generation.'

'Yes, sir, I have to remind myself of that sometimes, too and I'm not all that old.'

No, you're not. You're very young. You've a long way t go. Pray it will be easier for you than it has been for me Martin thought, with surprising tenderness. Then h thought of something else.

'You know, I don't even know whether she'd have yo after all that's happened. Her mother says she would, eve though her mother's not enthusiastic about it herself! On th strength of that, I came here. It may have been a wild-goos chase, Ned, I must warn you.'

'I'll chance it. I'll go and find out . . . But I haven't aske you about yourself, sir. I suppose the institute is open by nov and running under your hands?'

'It's open and running well,' Martin said, addin unemotionally, 'but not under my hands.'

Ned's eyebrows went up.

'That's another story. Now's not the time to go into it. And wanting to turn away from the subject, he looke around. 'These pictures, they're all – '

'All Mother's. They've been sent back from an exhibit We're rehanging them.'

Martin got up and walked around the room. Claire ha said something once, quite briefly, about Mary's achieve ment, but he had not imagined anything like this. A embarrassment of riches, he thought, given as he was t remembering phrases. Beautiful, beautiful! Grace and lov shone in these trees and human figures, these faces, this frui and running water, that ragged child, this tired old woman those clouds like flowers in the sky. And he remembered al those years ago when she had told him with such youn wistfulness, 'I don't know yet who I am.'

Ned touched his arm. 'This I would call a masterpiece. D

ou agree? It's called *Music of the Sphere*.'

On a tall vertical canvas, she had drawn the earth as one ight behold it from another planet. Glowing, golden-green ad silver-blue, it hung or seemed, rather, to be spinning in a entle rhythm through vast darkness. A jewel it was, a living eart, sending a radiance into the frozen universe. Around it a aureole of tender light was shot with sparkle of tropical in and of petals that might have been musical notes or usical notes that might have been petals. A work of most mptuous and subtle imagery, it could only have been onceived by someone who was in love with the world.

Profoundly moved, Martin could find just commonplace ords. 'Magnificent. Magnificent.'

'The critics thought so. People have been calling to buy it. ut this is one she won't sell, which, of course, I can nderstand.'

Martin's heart hammered. He looked straight into Ned's es. 'How is she?' he asked.

'Happy in her work, as you can see. Happier all around an she's been in a long time, I should guess.'

'I wouldn't want to shock her by walking in without arning.' And yet if she were to walk in suddenly upon him, would be a shock to rejoice the soul, he thought with a nall rise of joyous laughter. 'Claire's told me that you new, of course, about Mary and me. Not that we've talked uch about it. We're all too reticent, I sometimes think. But well, I thought, coming here, that maybe after all this time, e and I – ' Something in Ned's expression stopped him.

'I'm not sure I understand your meaning, but if it's – '

'I think you do understand,' Martin said.

'Oh, then . . . Oh then, I'm sorry! You didn't know . . . other's been married almost a year.'

'Married!'

'Yes. Simon and she have known each other a long, long ne. He owns a gallery; he's done wonders for her in every ay. I'm very fond of him.'

Married! It crossed Martin's mind that he must look astly, for with extreme kindness, Ned added, 'Things can a muddle sometimes, can't they, sir?'

'Muddle?' Chaos and storm, more likely!

Devious and strange is the heart of man. Certainly his ow was. And feeling dreadfully weak, Martin sat down again c an upended packing case, thinking of that bright thread th had been woven through all the twisted, turning patterns c the loom of his life.

Married.

She, she, from the first day, with the eyes and the drean and the dark, lovely face –

'Fey,' Jessie said. 'Fern is fey.'

Married.

'I thought you would have heard through that old aun Milly.'

'No, Milly's dead.'

'I'm sorry.' Ned looked considerately away.

Sorry about the old woman's death? Or about – Marti pulled himself together. 'I'll have to be going. I've done wh I came to do. The rest is up to you.'

'Can I give you a lift to the station?'

'Thanks. I have a car.'

He was going out when the door opened and a ma entered. He was a tall man, of middle age, wearing count clothes and a pleasant outdoor face.

'Simon,' Ned made the introduction, 'we've a visitor fro America. This is Dr Farrell, Claire's father.'

Simon shook Martin's hand. 'I'm glad to know you. B you're not leaving?'

'I'm afraid so.' Martin felt weakness and dizziness agai 'I only came for a word or two with Ned. I have to get back

Ned explained. 'Dr Farrell came about Claire. I may going to New York next week, Simon. I'm going to see he

Simon looked from one to the other. 'So that's it, is Why, I'm delighted, Doctor! I've been suspecting it w Claire all along, if you want to know the truth of it.' H pleasure was genuine. 'You see, I understand what it is know what you want and not get it. Have you ever met n wife, Doctor? But of course, you must. How clumsy of m Her sister. Forgive me, I forgot for the moment.'

'Quite all right. It was a long time ago,' Martin murmure

'This is all her work. Perhaps you've heard of her
eputation? She's not well known in America yet, but we may
now some of her work there some time.'

'Ned's been showing me. It's very, very beautiful.'

'Has Ned shown you this? It's her portrait. I had it done by
uan Domingo. He's a Mexican, a very fine artist. He's
aught her to perfection, I think.' Happiness exuded from
e man. He guided Martin to the far end of the room. 'Here
is. She must have been a young girl when you saw her last.
Vould you recognize her from this?'

There she was, full length, next to a table on which stood a
owl of flowers, some large, white flowers, hydrangeas or
yacinths. His eyes swam so he couldn't tell what they were.
ne hand rested on a pile of books. Her dress was a subtle
lash of ruby and flame, but all he really saw were the great,
ondering eyes looking out at something far away.

'Would you recognize her?' Simon persisted.

'Yes,' Martin said. 'I would recognize her.'

'I had this done ten years ago, but she hasn't changed
uch since then.'

'You've known her ten years,' Martin repeated, for no
eason at all.

'Yes. It took me that long to persuade her to marry me.
ut I'm a persistent man.' And Simon laughed with the
ontentment of a man who can afford to laugh.

Martin looked up and saw the pity in Ned's eyes. 'An
xcellent likeness,' he said, it being necessary to say
omething more. He moved again towards the door. He was
n interloper here, a trespasser and a thief who ought to run
efore he should be discovered.

'Mary will be here soon. She only went out on a few
rrands,' Simon said. 'Can't you possibly stay to tea?'

'Thank you. You're very kind, but I have an appointment
t my hotel and I really can't.'

They shook hands. Martin nodded to Ned: 'Perhaps I
hall be seeing you in New York.' And he went out.

At the top of the rise where the road curved, he stopped
e car and looked back. Through bare trees one could see
e roof and one wing of Lamb House. There it lay, as it had

lain for centuries. To the passer-by it was a fine and hones
house with nothing extraordinary about it, surely not th
shimmer and glamour of the forbidden. Well, he had com
for Claire, hadn't he? And he had done his best. Wha
happened next would not be of his making. As for the rest
the other business, he didn't know. He couldn't say. H
could hardly feel. He was numb.

Mary came into the studio where Simon and Ned were stil
arranging pictures.

'We had a visitor, darling,' Simon said. 'If you took a
hundred guesses, you couldn't guess who.'

He looked so happy, Mary thought, it's like coming hom
to a warm fire just to see his face when I walk in. 'Well, then
you might as well tell me.'

'It was your former brother-in-law. From America. Th
doctor. Isn't that strange? I invited him to tea, but h
couldn't stay.'

'Martin!' And she repeated softly, 'Martin was here?' Sh
looked at Ned.

He nodded. 'He came to talk about Claire.' Ned spok
steadily and she understood that this tone was meant t
steady her. 'I think, Mother, I'll go back and see her.'

Mary sat down. Her mouth trembled. She hoped no on
would see it. And she said almost apologetically, 'I'm just
stunned. I – seem to be shaking.'

'Well, of course!' Simon cried. 'Oh, you've worried you
mother, Ned. She may not have let us see it, but I've known i
all along.'

'She oughtn't to worry about me at my age.'

Mary said, 'Of course I wasn't happy about it at th
beginning . . . Jessie and I . . . But, oh I do think Claire'
exceptional, and if you can work things out, why . . .' He
voice left her.

'Her mother didn't like me at all.'

'Not you yourself, I'm sure,' Simon interposed. 'Wh
would anyone not like you? I'm sure it was only because o
that miserable feud. How a family can split itself apart ove
money! I've seen it time and again – it's always a pity. An

ne longer you let a thing like that continue, the more npossible it is to mend it.'

Mary managed to collect herself. 'Well, if it's my sister ho stands in the way, if that's all, she'll come around, Ned, o matter how she feels about me. She'd do anything for laire, as I would for you.'

'And the father likes you, I could see that,' Simon bserved. 'An awfully nice chap, Mary! He took a great iterest in your paintings, too.'

Ned spoke lightly. 'Well, naturally, anyone who admires our work ranks on top with Simon.'

'So you'll be leaving us! It'll be restful here without you,' imon joked back.

'Go to Claire,' Mary said. 'If she's what you want. Even iough being a doctor comes first with her, Ned, go to her. hat's what you first admired and why you were drawn to er, after all. Perhaps you've never thought about it like iat.'

Ned bent down and kissed his mother. 'I understand,' he iid. 'Thank you.' For a moment they looked into each ther's eyes before Mary turned away.

'I'm going up to the house,' she said. 'That is, if you don't eed me here, Simon?'

'No, no. We're almost finished. Go ahead.'

She went slowly up the path. Suddenly, not wanting to go side, she sat down on a bench near the wall where in immer perennials would bloom. The beds were covered ow with a mulch of dark wet leaves. She laid her head on the ick of the bench.

Suppose he had come last year before I married Simon? hat then? Oh, Simon is everything that's steady and good id male. There's such peace and ease now in my heart. But he had come last year?

So many, many ifs! When we were young and that doctor ith the Spanish name invited him to go on for three more ears: if I hadn't been willing to wait and he had chosen me stead, would he have come to hate me for it afterwards? If. . And if we had spent our lives together, would I still feel iis softness going through me at the thought of him? I wonder. Could there possibly be any joy now between u after so much grief: after Jessie and then that poor dea woman Ned told me about? Could there?

Always, always, what we could have done or should hav done, and what we blame ourselves for having done or no having done. Do we truly have choice? Or is it all writte beforehand in the stars or the genes? God knows.

Two small hot tears gathered in the corners of her eyes an she wiped them away with her knuckles. At least she coul hope: maybe it will turn out well for Ned. She's a extraordinary girl, that Claire. You have to admit that, eve though the union of those two will be a burden for the rest o us. But they must do what's right for them. They'll onl know whether it was right long years after they've done it.

And I? Simon and I will stay here, in this house that I lov so much. After we're gone, some movie star will probabl buy it. But until then, we'll be here. Alex would be glad t know that. Perhaps, where he is, he does know it. I used t think that was nonsense, but now that I'm older, I'm not s sure. I'm not sure of anything any more.

'I thought you'd gone inside,' Simon said.

'I was going to, but it's so warm and lovely here. One ca almost imagine it's summer.'

He bent and kissed her. 'Mary. Mary Fern. Are yo pleased about Ned?'

'Whichever way he wants it, if it works out well for him, will be.'

'You're a good mother, the kind of mother everyon should have and the kind of wife. Do I tell you ofte enough?'

'You do, my dear, yes you do.'

'I've been thinking, would you like to go to America?'

'I don't know. I haven't been there since I came here t marry Alex. They say it's so changed.'

'What doesn't change, my darling?'

'Highways and tract houses – all built up, I read. And sti the fall must be the same, and those hot Augusts when th grass burns brown and the locusts drill all afternoon.'

'We'll go to California, take some of your work to sho

nd have a bit of vacation at the same time. And stay in New ʼ ɔrk for a while.'

'Not New York,' she said quickly. 'Let's just pass through :. I never liked New York.'

'Whatever you say, as long as we're together.' And he sat ..ɩwn on the bench beside her. In the windless afternoon not twig stirred. A mild sun broke through the clouds, and ƅove iron-grey winter hills, pale fire striped the sky.

CHAPTER THIRTY-FOUR

Ned and Claire were to be married very quietly on a Saturday evening at Jessie's house. Two of Claire's friend from Smith, along with the husband of one of them and a London friend of Ned's who was on business in New York made the sum of the guests. Because of the smallness of thi group and the resultant intimacy of the occasion, there ha been tacit agreement that Martin would not be present Instead, he was to give a little dinner for the bridal couple a his apartment on the night before. To this, and for the sam reason, Jessie had not been invited.

'It will be much more *comfortable* for everyone that way, she had said sensibly, and Claire had agreed.

'That's just what Dad said, too.'

The mantel in the library had been cleared of it ornaments. On the afternoon of the wedding Jessie covered i with a flowery spray of white: stephanotis, roses an carnations, twined together with narrow white silk bows Claire had insisted on wearing a very simple suit, but Jessi had managed to persuade her that it ought at least to b white and silk and adorned with one of Jessie's ow handsome necklaces.

Jessie hummed. She would not have believed, som months ago, that she could actually feel happy at Claire' wedding to this particular young man; but her terribl concern over her daughter had outweighed everything els and the sight of that daughter's face during these last week had brought enough joy and ease to cancel out whateve doubts or regrets still lurked.

'The rest,' she said now, half aloud, 'is in the lap of th gods. So far so good, anyway – ' and she fastened the la bow.

The house was quiet. The cook was busy in the kitche Claire was out having her hair done and Jessie was placin the flowers on the dining-room table when the doorbell rang.

'I'll answer, Nora!' she called.

She opened the door. Her hand was still on the knob and that steadied her in the instant of recognition.

The woman on the doorstep smiled uncertainly. 'Jessie, may I come in?' asked Mary Fern.

Jessie was curled in the wing chair. She must be lost in a room without a wing chair, Fern thought.

'I didn't come for the wedding,' she said. 'I didn't even know this was the day. Ned's letter mentioned some time this month but in the circumstances, naturally, we didn't expect to be asked.'

'You have a right to come to your son's wedding if you want to. No one told me you might want to.'

Of course. Jessie would be correct in all things. They had, after all, both been brought up to be. But what were the real thoughts in that elegant, small head and behind that cool face? Suddenly Fern was sorry she had given way to her unreasoned impulse.

'Perhaps I shouldn't have come. If I'm not welcome, Jessie, just say so and I'll go.'

'Have I said you were unwelcome?' Jessie asked brusquely.

'No, but – well, you see, we're only passing through the city . . . We're flying to California Monday morning . . . And I was sitting at lunch just now . . . I had such an overpowering sense of your presence . . . You were not a mile away . . . I got up and walked out of there thinking I must see you, even for a minute, even if you were to slam the door in my face . . .' She stopped. Tears stung her eyes.

'Well, I didn't slam the door in your face.'

A basket of needlepoint stood on the floor next to Jessie's chair. She picked up the unfinished work. 'I have to do something with my hands, I don't ever seem able to sit still and do nothing.'

'Then you haven't changed.'

'None of us ever do, do we?'

One could take that remark in many ways. Fern made no

answer, and silently the two women sat, Fern stiffly and uneasily, while Jessie poked the needle in and out.

Presently Jessie spoke. 'I'm told you've made a great success with your paintings.'

'Yes,' Fern replied simply.

'So Father was wrong! A pity he didn't live to see himself proven wrong for once.' She looked up at Fern. 'You think I'm vindictive? Maybe so, but the truth is the truth, all the same.'

'He would have been proven wrong about you, too,' Fern said gently. 'Ned's told me about you.'

'Has he?'

'Yes. And this house is lovely. Mellow, like Lamb House.'

'Hardly like Lamb House! So you're still living there?'

'Still there. For me, after all, it's home. And Simon loves it too.'

'You're happy with Simon?'

'He's very good to me. He's strong and kind.'

'That's not answering my question, is it?'

Fern threw her hands out. 'Oh Jessie,' she said.

Jessie thrust the needlework away. 'I'm sorry, I shouldn't have said that. I'm upset. You've upset me.'

Fern started to rise. 'I know. It wasn't a good idea. I'd better go.'

'No! Stay there! I wouldn't forgive myself if you were to leave like this. Now that you've come we must finish what you've started.'

'Finish? How?'

'Clear it up. Freshen the air. Whatever you want to call it. What I want to say is, I'm not angry any more. I don't hate you, Fern. And I haven't for a long, long time.'

Fern got up and walked to the end of the room. On a round table in a corner stood a group of photographs, mostly of Claire from babyhood to the present; among them was one of Fern's and Jessie's mother, her pensive face surmounted by a World War One feathered hat. For a long time Fern stayed looking at the remembered face. At last she turned back to her sister. Her voice quivered.

'I don't know whether you'll understand – but you've

relieved a pain that has been so sharp – so sharp, Jessie. You can't know.'

'Maybe I can.' Jessie stood and put her hand on Fern's arm. 'Maybe I can.'

Fern's arms went out and Jessie's head, which reached no higher than Fern's shoulder, came to rest on it. Fern's hand moved over the curly head; her other hand lay on the misshapen little back. So they stood, holding one another, while something miraculously, slowly, eased in the heart of each.

'It's so simple after all, isn't it?' Fern murmured. 'Why didn't we do it before?'

'I don't know. Damn fools both, I suppose.' Jessie wiped her eyes. 'Sit down and talk to me. I want to hear about your daughters. I want to know more about the man who's going to marry my daughter. In one hour give me the story of the last twnty-five years. Can you do it?'

She can still charm, Fern thought as they talked. The wit was there as it had been years ago in Cyprus; the eagerness was there along with the laughter.

'Remember when Aunt Milly came to visit and we put the kittens in her bed?' Jessie cried.

'I wonder what Cyprus is like today?'

'I passed near it last summer on my way to a client on Buffalo but I didn't drive through. I want to remember it as it was for us, with the tower and the iron deer and lemonade on the lawn.'

So they talked, while the hour passed. They spoke of everything and everyone except the man whose name would best remain unspoken.

Then Jessie said, 'You'll need to go back and dress for the wedding. You and Simon be here at seven, will you?'

'It's been – it's been beautiful, Jessie.'

'Beautiful. Bitter and sweet.'

Yes, sweet to be together after so long, and bitter that it had taken so long to happen. Old wrongs and ancient grievances! Like climbing weeds they cling, twisting, twining and thickening until the day that somebody gathers the strength to pull out all the roots – or almost all of them.

CHAPTER THIRTY-FIVE

Their plane was leaving for India tonight. Martin had already bid good-bye to Ned and Claire, but it came to his mind that he would like to see them just once more. They were, after all, going to the other side of the world.

It was a fine spring Sunday with a flush of pink in the light. He walked south towards the Waldorf where Ned and Claire were staying. Strollers pushed British perambulators and led dogs of exotic breeds like puli and Briard. Expensive children and expensive animals, he reflected. A group of hearty boys, not expensive, zoomed past on roller skates: iron ground on stone. A Hindu couple passed, she with a gold-edged sari and red caste mark. The variety and vigour of this most marvellous of cities! He passed the Institute for Neurological Research. On the shady side of the street it stood in modest elegance, like some quiet scholar in resplendent cap and gown. Unnameable sensations flowed through Martin.

'A lot of water under the dam,' he said aloud, surprising himself.

Yes, a lot of water. And he thought there ought to be a better way than that tired cliché to express what he felt about the changes and crises of a single life, not just his own, but any life, every life.

With Claire gone it would all be very different for him now. At least he had tried not to let her know. He was sure he had kept things festive for her.

The little dinner he'd given had been gay. Enoch had come in from Brown; the Horvaths and a few friends of Ned's and Claire's had been invited. He had even brought his sister and her family to New York. (Dear Alice! His gift of an annual trip to the city was the high point on her calendar.) Esther had prepared a fine meal and Marjorie had arranged the table. Already she had developed her mother's domestic ifts. and Martin actually had been able to smile a little at the ight of Hazel's fine ruby glass, so long unused. But the lace loth, bought that day in San Francisco, had brought a winge of sadness.

He'd been alone with Ned for a few minutes during the vening, and Ned had offered assurance. 'I want you to now, sir – ' his English courtesy – 'I want you to know that verything will be all right this time. You can depend upon .'

And Martin had replied cheerfully, 'I know I can. I'd be aising hell otherwise.'

Her boy! Out of all the young men on the planet, it had had o be *her* son who, having grown up in her house, with her ouch on him and the sound of her voice in his ears, would ring so much of herself into Claire's life, and so, inevitably, nto Martin's own. But he was a decent young man. And Martin remembered that long ride through the winter fternoon after the boy's father had died. A decent young nan: he had compassion, that was one good thing.

Yet only time would really tell how it would work out. erhaps even a couple of generations before one would really now. The modern woman! Mary and I, Hazel and I, we ame from the old times. You made a compact, you gave our word, and you stayed with it at whatever cost. This was ll new, this uncertainty, this flux. Jobs, marriages – you ried them on for size; if they didn't fit perfectly, you simply hanged them.

'Take care of her. Love her,' he had told Ned, hoping he asn't sounding too old fashioned, too protective. Well, the evil if he did!

Love. From all he read and saw on the screen and heard eople say, it didn't seem to have the passion and intensity it ad when sex was hedged about with rules and mysteries. he concern then was for the other, the object. It was a kind f – yes, it was – adoration. Today the concern seemed to be ith self, with the act of sex as if it were a game. Is my partner iving a full, fair share? Am I performing well? Obtaining the atisfaction that the experts say I should? Pleasure-measure, hat's what.

'How do I love thee? Let me count the ways. I love thee to the depth and breadth and height my soul can reach.'

And yet, in his living-room, he'd seen his daughter and the man she loved holding each other's hands with such a look in their eyes. They've been through the fire, Martin thought, and come out safely on the other side. God bless.

In the hotel lobby there was the usual genteel flurry of arrival and departure. Luggage and messages and florists' boxes moved back and forth. A little man at a counter was raising a storm about theatre tickets. The seats were way over on the side, he said, and he'd be damned if he was going to pay those prices.

'Well, but ' replied the harassed young fellow on the other side of the counter. 'You wanted them for the same night, and those were the only ones left.'

Why did people contend so savagely over trivia? Maybe one needed to have gone through fire, as he had been thinking a moment ago of Ned and Claire, to weigh the true worth of things.

Dr Farrell and Mr Lamb were still upstairs. Their bags were to be taken down at half past five, the clerk said. In the elevator Martin shook his head with rueful amusement. 'Mr Lamb and Dr Farrell', indeed!

At the fourth floor, he got out and stood wondering in which of three directions to find the room. Across the corridor a man and woman were also hesitating, with their backs to Martin. The woman was tall, almost as tall as the man. She wore a suit of thin wool the colour of wheat. Her hand, in a light glove, rested in the curve of the man's elbow. Her hair, worn in a curly cap, was lightly touched with grey. And he knew her at once, even before he heard the unmistakable voice which he would have recognized anywhere on earth.

'It's number eleven, I think,' she said.

Turning just then, she caught Martin's look. Her own glance swept down the corridor beyond him, swept lightly back and paused. Eyes recognized each other in that fraction of an instant and spoke: spoke what? Such messages as may circle through space and touch and vanish. He thought he ps moved, but perhaps it was only the quivering of his own sion.

'It's this way, Mary,' her husband said, 'lcft.'

The elevator came again, and Martin got in. There was a)aring in his head. He needed to sit for a moment in the bby, but there were no vacant chairs. Then he thought he eeded to get away, but there was a scramble for taxis at the otel entrance; he hadn't the patience or the nerve to wait. c began to walk, almost to run. He fclt as if he had been ruck.

'If we ever see each other again,' she had said, 'walk away, o you promise?'

'Yes, I promise,' he'd told her.

And he thought that possibly the best proof he loved her as his wish that she might be happy now. He was not noble, knew he was far from that; yet he could wish it for her. A ood man and kind, was Simon. He'd seen that at once: a anly man who would know how to make a woman happy.

Mary Fern. Mary Fern. A distant glimmer, fading and ightening, fading and brightening. For how long? For ways? Until the end of his days?

He had walked two blocks when a car drew up just ahead f him. It was a foreign limousine, driven by a chauffeur in a aroon uniform. A little woman, wearing a loose cream-loured coat, got out and dismissed the car.

'Jessie!' he cried.

'Martin?' She hesitated, then put out her hand. 'How are ou, Martin?'

'I'm fine, thanks. You're going in here?' he asked, dicating the apartment house before which they stood.

'No, walking home. I need the exercise, so I sent the car ck to the garage.'

It seemed necessary to say something further, so he marked politely that the car was handsome.

Jessie smiled. 'What you really think is that it's too lavish. known your Spartan tastes.'

'No, no.'

'You don't fool me, Martin. But I love that car. It means a t to me.'

'Well, it's certainly handsome. And I like your coat Jessie.'

'Rats! It's the same outfit I wear year after year. The same cape to cover the hump. The only things that change are the colour and the fabric.'

Little Jessie! Tart, plucky little Jessie! And something touched Martin sharply near the heart, some old memory and a sense of déjà vu. Oh, but his heart was vulnerable today!

'Do you mind if I keep you company?' he asked her. 'We seem to be walking in the same direction.'

'Come along, of course.'

They had gone a block before either of them spoke. Jessie said, 'You've been to see Claire, haven't you?'

'I went to the Waldorf. But then I didn't go upstairs.'

'Because you saw Fern instead.'

'Now, how did you know that?'

'You have a faraway look. Didn't I always know when something was on your mind?'

'That's true. You always did.'

'No, you never fooled me, Martin.'

He didn't answer. He was remembering something he'd seen only a few weeks ago, a painting in a Chicago museum Albright's *That Which I Should Have Done I Did Not Do.* It was a simple picture of a funeral wreath hung on a wooden door, and it had touched him profoundly, reaching into dark places far within.

'I did you a very great injustice,' he said now. 'Not that it helps you any for me to tell you so. But I've carried the guilt of it with me every day of my life.'

'I'm sorry to hear that! Very sorry, Martin. In the last analysis you did me an enormous favour, you know. I've got Claire because of you, haven't I? And you know as well as I there was no Prince Charming waiting in the wings to carry me off and "get me with child" as they say in the fairy tales.'

He looked down at her. Her hair was smartly cut. Her face, which had sometimes seemed older than her age when she was young, now seemed younger than her age. It was alert and keen as ever.

'Did you know Fern was in New York?' she asked.

'No,' he replied and couldn't resist asking, 'Did you?'

'I didn't know she was coming. Nobody did. She arrived in time for the wedding.'

'She was at the wedding?'

'Yes. She came to my house that afternoon. I'm glad she came. I would never have asked her to, not in a hundred years. But I'm so glad she did. We had a good, long talk.'

Martin was so astonished that he could think of nothing to say.

'The wonderful thing is that seeing her didn't hurt me as much as I would have expected it to! I suppose it's because I've made something out of my own life. I don't have to feel like – like *nothing* any more! Oh, it went back so far! To when I was still in a high chair, probably, and she was running around with a beautiful, straight back . . . You understand?'

'I think I always have, Jessie.'

'I don't say it still doesn't hurt. And always will, a little Sometimes I think how queer and sad it is that I never loved anyone enough. Not even you, for if I had loved you enough I wouldn't have had so much pride, would I? And if I had loved Fern enough I could have forgiven her for being herself.' And she reflected, 'I don't count Claire, because that's just biological.'

Martin said painfully, 'You're a very loving woman, Jessie. Make no mistake.'

She ignored the little protest. 'It's natural to think it's on account of the hump that I was inhibited from loving. But what if it had nothing to do with that? What if I was just put together without the capacity to love?'

'No, no. I can't believe that. Can't buy it, as they say.'

'Well, buy it or not, that's how it is.'

Martin was silent. They walked on, their steps brisk on the pavement.

And suddenly Jessie said, 'I'm sorry about what happened with your institute. Claire's told me how they cheated you.'

'One gets used to things.'

Jessie smiled wryly. 'Not to everything.'

No, one would never accept a hump on one's back. never, he thought, relinquish the longing to be graceful and beloved.

'We shall miss Claire terribly, shan't we?' she said.

'Yes.'

'You, at least, have three others.'

'True. But she – ' He stopped. It sounded theatrical to say, although no doubt Jessie would believe it. 'But she is my special child, my heart.'

'You have awfully nice children, Claire says.'

'Gentle. Like their mother,' he said soberly.

'Like you, too.'

Wishing to return the honest compliment with equal honesty, he said, 'You did a fantastic job, bringing Claire up. I've always wanted to tell you.'

'You had something to do with that yourself, you know. You were her hero from the start. How I suffered when she went to claim you!' And Jessie raised her eyes to Martin with a look of pure and simple honesty. 'I had so wanted to keep her all for myself!'

'You've kept her, Jessie. She loves you, and has such admiration for you! Believe me, I know.'

'Yes. But now this marriage! It seems like another loss. We won't be seeing her much at all any more.'

'It's lucky we're both busy.'

'I didn't cling to her when she was with me, that's one good thing. I hadn't the time, and I wouldn't have done that to her anyway.' Jessie sighed. 'Oh drat! I never could stand mournful people and that goes for myself. Here's my place. I won't ask you in because we really have nothing more to say to one another today, have we? But it's been nice, all the same.' She held out her hand. 'Luck, Martin.'

'And to you, Claire's mother.'

Street lamps flared on and the sky above the craggy rooftops turned dark green. He walked home more slowly now, through a clement, deepening dusk. His thoughts roved loosely. Strange day! A day in which the past had rushed forward to tie up with the future. In some ways, he thought, Jessie always understood me the best. Yes it's true, she did

:om the very beginning. A sound like a chuckle of
musement rose in his throat. Barely five feet high, and the
rength of her! But then, Mary is strong, too. And Claire.
1y Claire. Enormous strength in all these women! Poor
lazel didn't have it. No blame to her: You're made the way
ou're made. For that matter, I don't even know how much
rength I have myself. Pity one can't ever see oneself.

. light shone through the crack of Peter's door long after
ipper. When Martin opened the door Peter was sitting at
is desk.

'Math again?'

'Algebra. I hate the stuff.' The boy's troubled mouth
uckered like a child's, yet on his upper lip there was the faint
:ginning of down.

'Just do the best you can. Try to relax over it,' Martin
ounselled sympathetically.

'I've got to do better on the next test.'

'There's no "got to". No one person is expected to excel at
erything, Peter.'

'Claire always does. I wish I was smart like her, Dad.'

'You are smart in your own way.'

'Not like her,' Peter said stubbornly.

'We're all different.'

A fine boy, Peter was, a serious, responsible child. But it
as true, he'd never have the intellectual fire of Claire. Too
d! And he thought: A boy needs it so much more. Then he
ought: Claire would be furious if she could hear me say
at.

He put his hand on the child's shoulder. And something of
e tenderness that was in him must have been conducted
.e a current through his touch, because Peter looked up
xiously.

'Are you unhappy, Dad?'

'No, no, of course not. Why should I be?'

'Well, I thought – Enoch says you'll miss Claire so much.
ill you?'

How many more times would he be required to answer
at question?

'Yes, we all will, won't we?'

'But you will especially.'

The boy's eyes, trusting and shy, rested on his father' face. And for the first time, Martin did not turn away fron the reminder of Hazel, that quiet gaze.

He cleared his throat. 'Gosh, you're growing. Is that th only sweater you've got to wear?'

'What's wrong with it?'

'The cuffs are half-way to your elbow.'

'I grew three inches since last year. Haven't you noticed?

No, he hadn't noticed, he'd been so absorbed with othe things.

'We'll go shopping next Saturday morning. I guess you' need practically everything, won't you?'

'Marjorie's been wanting things ever so long. Her dresse are too short, and last year's spring coat doesn't fit at all.'

'"Ever so long"? Why didn't she ask me?'

'I guess she thought you were too busy.'

'She could have gone shopping with Claire again.'

'But Claire's been getting ready to go away.'

'Gosh,' Martin said doubtfully, 'I don't know anythin about what little girls should wear.'

'You could just get what the other girls in her class hav couldn't you?'

'You're right,' Martin said.

The boy's kindness struck to his heart. Ever since thei mother's death, it seemed these children had been graduall drawing together. And he thought of the adult fears the must have, these good children of his. They had still so muc to go through: teeth to be straightened, homesickness a camp, sex education with its wonders and dangers. (How t convey to them some rudimentary knowledge, when yo knew so very little yourself?) Then college boards, and afte that, the earning of a livelihood. How to do that withou being trampled in the crush, and still refrain from doing an trampling, still keep some of that first, clean, Sunday-schoo decency?

Claire sees the world the way my father saw it, Marti thought suddenly. She thinks she's sophisticated, and i me ways, superficially, she is. But fundamentally, she is e my father.

He looked at the clock. They would have taken off by now, aded eastwards towards an old, poor, dangerous land. No, couldn't allow himself to grow old even if he wanted to. still had too many people to think about.

He smiled at Peter. 'Well, we'll take care of everything. ow I suggest you go to sleep. It's late and tomorrow's onday.'

He went into his den. All the little objects in the room, the nps and bookends, the ashtrays and the clock, glowed like vels in the light of the naked white walls. Suddenly and for first time, he understood why he had surrounded himself th whiteness. That first room of hers – And he opened the set, where on the top shelf, still in its English wrapping per, gone dusty and brittle with years, stood the *Three Red rds*, summertime version. Taking it down, he propped it ainst a shelf, then stood a moment, studying the rhythm of birds and the background of that living green which she loved.

Among trees,' she used to say, 'one hears the world athe.'

So tomorrow he would hang it up at last and face reality. d it, though, been all real? Sometimes it seemed unreal, an chantment that couldn't possibly have been as he nembered it. And if they had lived together, sharing a of, childhood diseases, plumbing bills and fatigue, how uld it have been then? How endured?

That, my friend, you will never know.

t was time for sleep, if he was to do his best in the rning. Tomorrow's surgery was going to be tough. The ient was a student, a young physicist, already possessed awesome knowledge beyond Martin's comprehension. d something was growing in his head, something which rtin would reach in to find, probing deeper and deeper, t knowing until the very last whether his most educated njecture had been correct. How could a man ever get used such a venture? Each time was like the first time. And on slipper chair in his bedroom he sat down to go over the steps and possibilities for tomorrow.

When he had reviewed his mental diagrams to h satisfaction, he allowed his mind to wander and ate an appl Hazel had always provided a piece of fruit for him bedtime. Now Marjorie continued the custom. He sat ba to enjoy the comfort of it: a fine tart apple, a Northern Sp he'd guess. There had been a tree outside his room. Oh, t life in that tree! Midsummer rustlings and rapping all nig at the house wall when polar winds drove. The apples boyhood: Russets, Greenings, Gravensteins. Wasps sweet, rotting piles of apples on the grass. Baskets on t porch when Pa sickened and died.

When I die, my patients will bring neither apples nor tea to my house. Some of them will not even remember n name. 'Some big doctor did the operation,' they will say. B my father – how they loved him! And he loved them! Th never knew – how could they? – how little he knew. And h even he didn't know how little he knew. Not his fault, course. He wouldn't believe it if he could come back and s what I am going to do to that young man tomorro morning.

So one pays for everything. We know more, we can more: but we are not the fathers to the sick that my fath was, and they do not love us.

He walked to the window to pull the curtains shut. Und a white sky glow, the city throbbed. Even from this heig Martin could hear its murmur. Only yesterday he'd stood a window looking down at the crowd pouring in for l medical school commencement. The cap and gown, so reg and austere, had hung ready in the closet. Alice had s between his parents in the second row. The parents h looked small and grey. He could remember thinking th some of the parents had been young. He could rememb Tom being solemn and Perry, lost now, choking on laught Dr Perrault gave a long speech about medical advanc great changes coming. Names were called. He'd had awful feeling he'd stumble up or down the step getting t diploma. Then majestic music, marching out. Pa shook h hand. Had those been tears or only blinking into the ligh

:o the sun? 'Dr Farrell', Pa had said, the first to call him ıt.

Thirty five years, he thought now. There's still so much I ven't done. And as always came that sense of rushing time, e the wind in a boy's ears as he runs downhill.

He pulled the curtains and picked up the telephone. 'Who this? Miss Kerrigan? My patient Bateman in Room 1002, he still restless?' (Restless, yes, why not, poor boy, on this ng, long night, this speeding night, not long enough for m?) 'Have Dr Cotter come in to look at him, will you? Yes, ınk you.'

He was worried about young Bateman, so bright, so eager, terrified. When a man didn't expect to recover, Martin d found out, he often didn't. There really was such a thing the will to live. Once he had thought it an old wives' tale d had said so with some scorn when his father had told of

'There are some things we'll never know,' Pa had said, and was true. Body and mind are interwoven. Or call it soul, if ıt is the name which satisfies you.

Sighing, Martin drew off his shoes. You could relax a little ıen you had a resident like Fred Cotter watching over ngs. It didn't happen often. Once in a blue moon, among waves of perfectly competent, willing young people, me one who had that special feel, a sort of inner birthlight, bright, so flaming, that nothing would ever put it out, not e, nor money, nor prestige, nor even love. A man like that a partner in the universe, you might say. Albeniz would ve approved of Cotter.

He had got his old diary out to show to Claire before she nt away. It lay now on the table, opened at the frontispiece ıere he had written that quotation from Aesculapius ıich, forgetting that he had known it long before, he had osen again for the pediment of the institute: And he saw nself on the bed under the sloping roof of his room in prus – sweet scent of warm wood shingles in July – writing th the book propped on his knees.

That Greek physician, alive in a time and place so different om this as scarcely to be imagined any more, he perceived the truth. The lustrous sky of Attica, Martin thought; he ha always fancied it as having been particularly blue. Oh, would go there yet, take his children some day and see 'Yes, yes,' he murmured, turning out the light. Then clear loving the sound of the old words, he spoke them aloud in the darkness.

'For where there is love of man, there is love of the art.'